Also by Erica James

Erica JAMES

THE *SUNDAY TIMES* BESTSELLING AUTHOR

MOTHERS *and* DAUGHTERS

ONE PLACE. MANY STORIES

HQ
An imprint of HarperCollins*Publishers* Ltd
1 London Bridge Street
London SE1 9GF

www.harpercollins.co.uk

HarperCollins*Publishers*
1st Floor, Watermarque Building, Ringsend Road
Dublin 4, Ireland

This paperback edition 2022

2
First published in Great Britain by
HQ, an imprint of HarperCollins*Publishers* Ltd 2022

Copyright © Erica James 2022

Erica James asserts the moral right to be
identified as the author of this work.
A catalogue record for this book is
available from the British Library.

ISBN: 9780008413736

This book is set in 10/15,5 pt. Meridien by Type-it AS, Norway

Printed and Bound in the UK using 100% Renewable Electricity at
CPI Group (UK) Ltd, Croydon, CR0 4YY

For Samuel, and Edward and Ally, and the mighty Mr T and the mightier still Beanster!

Chapter One

Martha made sure the bathroom door was firmly shut. Which was stupid. The door was either shut, or it wasn't. Just as there were no degrees of being pregnant. You either were, or you weren't. And that was something she knew all about. The not being pregnant part, that was. She was all too familiar with that state of affairs.

Opening the package which she had bought on the way home, she followed the instructions to the letter. Not that she needed to read the leaflet contained within the small box; she knew what she had to do.

Afterwards, and while counting the seconds away in her head, she flushed the loo, then washed and dried her hands. When she had reached a hundred and twenty, she added on an extra thirty seconds in the hope they would make all the difference.

They didn't.

As before, the appearance of the minus sign told her that once again she and Tom had failed in their attempt to create a baby. This time she had really thought it might happen, that she was pregnant. She had convinced herself that this month she felt different, that her body was already nurturing a tiny speck of miraculous life. But it was just a cruel false alarm. Or no more than a case of wishful thinking.

Cross with herself for putting too much store in being eight days late, for allowing her hopes to be raised, she stared at her face in the mirror above the basin. Too soon to panic, she told herself; she was only thirty-five, there was plenty of time yet for her to become a mother.

The important thing was to remain relaxed about it.

Anxiety, she reminded herself, would only make things worse. Besides, she wasn't the worrying kind.

She was Martha Adams.

Cool-headed and practical Martha.

Efficient Martha.

Reliable Martha.

As Dad used to say of her, if you needed a steady pair of hands, then Martha was your girl.

Pep talk over, the disappointment in her face now replaced with a determined smile, she put the pregnancy kit back inside the chemist's bag, screwed it up, and put it in the bin under the basin in the marble-topped vanity unit. She then scraped her shoulder-length dark hair back into an obedient ponytail. Mum had described her hair that way when she'd been a child.

'You're lucky to have such obedient hair, Martha,' she would say while brushing it ready for a day at school, 'it's so perfectly thick and straight, it will always do what you want it to do.'

In contrast her sister, Willow, had baby-fine blonde hair that had a careless way about it. As a girl, Willow's plaits had nearly always worn themselves loose by the time the lunchtime bell rang.

2

Downstairs in the kitchen, Tom was chopping onions with an ostentatious dexterity he had learned while on a cookery course Martha had given him for his fortieth birthday earlier that year. An avid fan of *Masterchef*, he never missed an episode, he loved to cook. He read cookery books the way most people read novels, devouring them page by page, word by word.

'There's a bottle of wine open in the fridge,' he said, tipping the onions into a large ceramic frying pan.

When she'd poured out two glasses of Cloudy Bay, Martha asked him how his day had gone.

'Oh, you know, same old same old for a Monday,' he said, deftly crushing a garlic clove beneath the blade of a knife by banging it with his fist. 'How about you?'

She tried to think back to her day in the office, before she came home with the pregnancy test kit and the day was ruined. Before that small seed of hope that had taken root in the last few days was ripped from her. Before she felt . . . well, never mind all that. 'A bit like yours,' she said with a shrug. 'Same old same old.'

He smiled and added the garlic to the frying pan. 'Pass me those mushrooms, will you?'

She did as he said, then sipped her wine. Her friends and family said she was lucky to have married a man like Tom, a man who was the perfect embodiment of patience and so handy in the kitchen. They were right; she *was* lucky. A previous boyfriend had dumped her with the damning criticism that she was too organised and sensible. She didn't think she'd ever felt more insulted, but had then rallied with the acknowledgement that she was who she was, and that was that.

Amazingly Tom loved her for just that reason.

'If I wanted an impractical and empty-headed girlfriend,

I wouldn't now be sitting here with you,' he'd said when she'd warned him what she was like on their third date. She hadn't seen any point in things progressing between them if he was hoping to discover that hiding beneath the tough exterior there was actually a hopelessly incapable girl longing to have her life organised by a strong man. There really wasn't.

As for how she felt about Tom; she loved him with her head as much as her heart. She loved that he regarded the two of them the way she did, as an equal partnership, a strong team that together could face any challenge thrown at them.

Their life goals were probably the same as most people's – the desire for a fulfilling work life, combined with having children and a nice home. Two of those things they had accomplished with relative ease, it was just the small matter of conception they had yet to achieve.

'What are you making?' she asked.

'Mushroom risotto topped with a sprinkling of toasted walnuts and a drizzle of walnut oil. That okay with you?'

'More than okay.'

'Do you want a salad to go with it? Or what about some kale?'

Feeding her with good wholesome food was Tom's way of preparing her body for creating and carrying a new human life. He regularly scoured the internet for the latest super-foods that would aid their ability to have a child. Cutting out alcohol should have been on the list of dos and don'ts, but they had both agreed a glass or two on alternate evenings would help them relax. Of course, the moment Martha became pregnant, she wouldn't dream of touching alcohol. Or caffeine. Or soft cheese and whatever else was deemed harmful.

If there was one thing she was good at, it was abiding by

4

rules. She was a stickler for rules. She was pretty good at making them too.

'Thou shalt not break my ten commandments, so says Martha Miller.'

That was what her sister used to say when they were children and when Martha would invent a game for them to play. It would start simply enough, like pretending they were shipwrecked on a deserted island and had to make a camp before it was dark. It was all imaginary play; the island was the Turkish rug in the hall and the tent was an old sheet pegged over Mum's clothes airer. But at some point, Willow would lose interest because Martha would keep devising things they could or could not do, like why Willow's oversized cuddly polar bear couldn't join them on the island.

'We're not on an island in the Antarctic,' Martha would point out – helpfully in her opinion – 'we're marooned on a tropical island. Polar bears would find it too hot and they don't eat coconuts, do they?'

'They might if they were given the chance,' Willow would say.

They had finished eating supper and were loading the dishwasher when Martha was seized with a depressingly familiar cramping sensation in her stomach. It was confirmation, as if she needed it, of what she already knew. It drew a defeated sigh from her, which she immediately tried to cover up by pretending to cough.

'You all right?' asked Tom.

'A tickle in my throat,' she said.

She rarely lied to Tom, and when she did it was usually a white lie to keep a surprise from him, like the time she had organised a secret weekend away in Venice for their first wedding anniversary. Just as she did with everything, she had planned it down to the last detail, other than factoring in that Tom had planned a surprise of his own.

'That puts paid to the dinner reservation I'd made for us,' he'd said with a laugh when she'd presented him with a card and their flight reservations.

But now she found that trying for a baby – what a ghastly phrase that was! – had turned her into a wife who regularly sneaked around behind her husband's back.

They were only small indiscretions that she committed, like not telling Tom about the pregnancy test kits she bought, or about the baby clothes she had smuggled into the house and kept hidden in the wardrobe in the guest bedroom.

She couldn't bring herself to share any of this with Tom for fear of him thinking she was becoming obsessed with having a baby. Because if he suspected that was the case, he might also start to think that was all she cared about, to the exclusion of him.

It happened all the time; couples torn apart through not being able to conceive. She didn't want that to happen to them. They were stronger than that. *She* was stronger than that. Through sheer force of stubborn tenacity she would make life bend to her will. She was not her father's daughter for nothing.

But she was getting far too ahead of herself. They had only been trying to get pregnant for ten months. It was no time at all. It was just that she was so used to getting things done, methodically ticking items off her list of things to do. As an inveterate list maker, she liked to start her day with a list of tasks she had to achieve, both at work and at home. It gave her a sense of purpose and achievement. She never actually wrote down the words 'make a baby', but it was there in invisible ink right at the top of every list.

Thinking of today's To Do list, she had one other outstanding job to tick off and that was to speak to her sister. She would need Willow's support if there were to be any chance of convincing their mother that it was time now to consider the future and do the sensible thing.

Not that Willow knew the first thing about being sensible, and really Mum wasn't much better either. During the Coronavirus pandemic Martha had nagged her mother constantly to be careful and not risk leaving the house, but Mum had been adamant that she should do her bit to help in her local community. Along with a team of others, she had shopped for the elderly and vulnerable and made sure they were coping with the fear and loneliness of lockdown. Martha had been convinced that her mother would catch the virus, just as Tom's poor mother had.

Having lost Dad only months before anything was known about the Coronavirus, the thought of losing Mum as well would have just been too much to bear. It was the aftermath of that worry that was behind Martha's determination now to make Mum accept that it would be better if she sold Anchor House and moved from West Sussex to be conveniently nearer to her daughters.

Especially if there was a grandchild for her to help out with.

With Willow onside there might be a greater chance of convincing Mum that it would be the sensible thing to do.

Chapter Two

Willow was fast asleep when her mobile rang.

It had been a deliciously deep sleep, the sort that didn't respond well to being disturbed, but in fumbling for her mobile on the bedside table she woke with a jolt, realising two things.

Firstly, she wasn't in bed, she was in the bath.

And secondly, by flinging out her hand for her phone, she had knocked over whatever had been on the wooden stool next to the bath.

She had found the sweet little stool in a junk shop and carried it home triumphantly, filled with plans to do it up with some pretty chalk paint and then sell it on eBay. She had thought it might be the start of something new and creative for her to do, a bit like Mum's old gardenalia business. She had imagined gathering enough stock together to open a small shop called Willow's Emporium. Full of enthusiasm for the idea, she had bought the necessary tins of paint, brushes and whatever else was required, but had somehow never got around to painting the stool.

If ever she needed a symbol to capture the complete lack of achievement in her life, that stool was it.

'Willow, are you there?'

At the sound of her sister's voice in her ear, she shook herself fully awake, then she shivered at the coldness of the water. Leaning forward to turn on the hot tap, she said, 'Yes, I'm here.'

'Are you in the bath?' asked Martha above the noise of the gushing water. She said it as though Willow had been caught doing something indecent.

'I am,' she said.

'So what do you think?'

'What do I think about what?'

'What I've just been telling you.'

Oh Lord, thought Willow, she must have been so busy thinking of that wooden stool, she hadn't heard a word of what Martha had said. Attention span of a goldfish, that's what Dad used to say about her. In one ear and out the other.

'Sorry,' she improvised, 'it's a bad line, I didn't hear you.'

There was a frustrated sigh in her ear.

'Try turning the taps off and you might hear a lot better.'

Willow did as her sister said, and Martha went on.

'My idea is for us to go down to Mum's at the weekend and take her out for lunch and then put forward our plan.'

'What plan?'

Another sigh. 'The one about encouraging Mum to sell Anchor House.'

Willow frowned. She had hoped Martha had forgotten about that. Her sister had first mentioned it a few months ago, but Willow hadn't taken it seriously, or given it any more thought. She just couldn't imagine Mum wanting to leave Anchor House and all her friends down there in Tilsham. And apart from anything else, it was home.

Not just any old home, but *their* home. It was where Willow and Martha had grown up and where Willow's every happy childhood memory revolved around Anchor House and the pretty harbour village that was squeezed in between Bosham and Chichester.

Her memories were full of days spent playing on the beach, of crabbing in the rock pools, of squelching around the mudflats in her wellingtons, of lying in the sand dunes, and of hours spent walking through wheat fields and along narrow flint-walled lanes lined with pretty cottages. If she closed her eyes, she could hear the cry of seagulls and smell the salty sea air.

How could her sister ever think that Mum would leave all that to live near Martha and Tom on the outskirts of Cobham? There was nothing wrong with Surrey, of course there wasn't, but it wasn't Tilsham. It wasn't what Mum was used to and where she was happy.

'So are you free at the weekend to spend the day with Mum?' asked Martha.

'Nothing planned as far as I . . .' Her words trailed off. 'Can you smell burning?' she asked her sister.

'What do you mean can I smell burning? Of course I can't!'

'Burning,' repeated Willow, her nose twitching. 'I can definitely smell—' She broke off again and leant over the side of the bath.

'*Oh!*' she exclaimed, realising now what she had tipped off the stool when she'd reached for her mobile. On top of the towel she'd put ready to use was the tray of aromatherapy candles she'd lit earlier.

'*Oh, oh, oh!*' she said again, 'I seem to be on fire.'

Smoke was indeed coming from a blackened circle and small flickering flames were just taking hold with rivulets of melted wax running everywhere.

'What?' demanded Martha in her ear while Willow dithered. 'What do you mean you're on fire?'

Tossing her mobile to safety and wincing as it went skittering across the tiled floor, Willow scooped up a handful of water and doused the flickering flames. She then stepped out of the bath, but in her clumsy haste she somehow missed her footing as she reached for another towel and ended up falling sideways and nearly putting a hand down the loo as she tried to keep her balance. All the while she could hear her sister's voice calling to her from under the radiator asking if she was still there.

A towel now wrapped around her, Willow rescued her mobile.

'It's okay, Martha,' she said, 'no need to call for any hunky fireman, I've put out the fire.'

'How big a fire?'

'No more than a flame or two.'

'But in a bathroom? How is that even possible?'

'I'll tell you about it when I see you down at Mum's. By the way, Saturday or Sunday? Either is good for me.'

'I'll check with Mum which day is best for her and get back to you. Just don't go planning anything else meanwhile.'

The conversation finished, Willow emptied the bath, dried herself and put on her pyjamas. She then folded the ruined towel to take downstairs to put in the bin, grateful that that was all she'd damaged. The thought of having to tell her friends, Lucy and Simon, that she'd burnt down their house made her vow never to light another candle while she was housesitting for them.

She wasn't living here entirely for free; she paid her friends a nominal amount of rent on the grounds that she took good care of the house while they were away. They'd decided that once it was safe enough to travel again they would spend their last year of freedom before starting a family travelling the world. They had jacked in their jobs and simply taken off. They were currently in Kyoto in Japan before going on to Vietnam.

It was the kind of thing Willow would love to do if she had the money. Although knowing her, she'd probably get hopelessly lost.

'Bloody risky if you ask me,' her boyfriend, Rick, had said when she'd explained to him why she was lucky enough to be living so close to Victoria Park in London and in such a great house, considering her lack of funds.

Lucy and Simon could have earned far more money renting out the house through a letting agency, but then they would have had to get rid of their two beloved Siamese cats, Sirius and Cedric.

Every week Willow had to email Lucy with an update on the cats and her biggest fear was that one of them might escape through a door that she had accidentally left open. They were strictly indoor cats, apparently too pampered and valuable to be allowed to roam the neighbourhood.

Thinking about it, confessing to Lucy that she had nearly set the house on fire by falling asleep in the bath would be far easier than admitting she had lost one of the cats.

With her precious charges on her mind, she went to look for Sirius and Cedric. She found them curled up together in the shallow log basket by the radiator in the sitting room. They had proper beds to sleep in but rarely used them, preferring instead the empty log basket with a blanket to lie on.

When Rick came here, she had to keep the cats away from him because he was so allergic to their fur; it made him sneeze and his eyes itch. Which was why he liked her to spend time at his place, or for them go out.

They had met almost four months ago back in December last year – in the way that so many people met these days, by swiping right on Tinder.

He was the one who had swiped right first and after checking out his profile and liking what she saw (he had a nice smile that lit up his eyes), she swiped right to make a match. They then started messaging each other and a couple of weeks later they arranged to meet in a bar. The rest, as they say, is history.

But given how bad at sticking with a relationship she was (she could never get beyond the six-month mark), was Rick destined to be part of Willow's history, and not her future?

It was too soon to tell.

Those of her friends who had met Rick said he was a great catch, and even Martha, who never approved of any of Willow's boyfriends, described him as a keeper. Mum liked him too, and no doubt Dad, if he were still alive, would have given him the thumbs up too.

So why then could Willow not allow herself to believe that maybe she deserved this chance to be happy with Rick?

Chapter Three

It was a beautiful spring morning and with the tide out, wading birds were busy searching the mudflats for cockles to prise apart with their long probing beaks.

Coffee cup in hand, and aching in places a woman of sixty-three years of age had no right to ache, Naomi Miller shielded her eyes from the April sunshine and made herself comfortable on the bench at the end of the garden. The silvered wood of the seat gave her the best view of the shoreline; from here she could observe all the comings and goings of the beach, as well as the birdlife.

She and Colin had bought Anchor House thirty-two years ago, shortly before Willow was born and when Martha was already three years old. Back then she and Colin couldn't believe their luck in being able to afford a spacious five-bedroom Edwardian house like this with a large garden that stretched down to the beach. It had been a dramatic leap up from their terraced house in south London, and they had taken to life here in Tilsham Harbour like . . . well, like ducks to water.

That's what Colin used to say when anybody asked how they were enjoying their new life out of London.

'Oh, we've taken to it like ducks to water,' he'd tell them.

Not that Colin had been here all the time. From Monday to Friday he'd stayed in a small studio flat in London while working in the City, then straight after lunch on Friday he would drive down to Sussex to be with Naomi and the children. A lot of his weekends were spent sailing and he loved being out on the water, nothing gave him more pleasure. It was the sense of freedom he'd enjoyed, that and pitting himself against the elements.

It had been a great disappointment to him that his wife had never shared his love of sailing. Naomi had shown willing from time to time and gone out in the boat with him, but too often he would bellow some order or other which she would misunderstand and do entirely the wrong thing. She much preferred pottering around their little harbour, no more than an inlet really, in a small rowing dinghy. She was not a natural sailor, and to Colin's further disappointment, neither were his daughters.

It used to exasperate him that she didn't know one sailing boat from another. To her they were just boats with sails. Yes, she could tell the difference between the older craft made of wood and the fibreglass ones, but she couldn't put a name to them. And never saw any reason to do so. Perhaps it had just been her being stubborn and bloody-minded, which she knew she was apt to do.

Her interests lay more on terra firma, in particular the garden at Anchor House. Before they bought the house, the garden had been left to its own devices by the previous owners, an elderly couple no longer able to keep on top of it all.

Much of it had been overgrown and unusable, not to say unsafe with the smashed glass of the greenhouse and tumbling-down sheds. But gradually over time Naomi took it in hand

and turned it into a garden that was her sanctuary as well as somewhere for the children to play, when they weren't on the beach.

Through her love of gardening, Naomi also developed another passion, for collecting old gardening tools and equipment. She used to scour auctions and charity and second-hand shops for bits and pieces – old terracotta pots, galvanised watering cans and laundry tubs, wooden-handled tools, wicker baskets and trugs, stone troughs and urns, and old ornate wirework tables and chairs.

At first, she bought specifically for her own garden, but then, after amassing far more than she needed, or had room for, she decided to make a business out of it and rented a small shop in the village that had become available.

She called it All Things Gardenalia and oh, how she had loved that little shop. With the fashion for recycling and anything remotely vintage, she did surprisingly well and was constantly having to source new stock.

It had been a sad day when she'd taken the reluctant decision to close the shop because of the coronavirus crisis that had so devastated the world. She had sold some of the remaining stock online, but a lot of it still remained in the garage. One day she would get around to having a sort out and sell what she had left.

Colin would be appalled to see the state his once tidy garage was in now. It had always been his domain, where he had religiously put away their cars to spare them from the peril of being exposed to the salty air. Naomi was not so particular about such things and regularly left her car out to fend for itself.

'Standards have been allowed to slip,' she could imagine Colin saying.

More than two years on since his death and she could still hear his voice as clear as if he were right next to her.

She supposed she always would.

They had been out for dinner with friends in Chichester when he died. They'd been celebrating his sixty-sixth birthday, and when it was over, when they were putting on their coats, Colin had looked at her with a strange puzzled look on his face as though he'd suddenly remembered something important to ask her. Then thumping a hand to his chest, he'd closed his eyes with a grimace and gasped.

A big man – a bear of a man was the way he was often described – there had been no way of catching him, and he'd slammed against the table at which they'd just eaten, tipping it over on top of him as he dropped heavily to the floor.

The memory of Colin lying there amongst the debris of their empty wineglasses and coffee cups haunted her for months afterwards. It was such an undignified end to a man's life.

He had been warned by their GP, a personal friend of the family, to cut back on the amount of alcohol he consumed. He'd been told to watch his diet too. But he was old-school and refused to moderate what he ate, no matter how much Naomi nagged him. He was the kind of man who believed the usual rules didn't apply to him; he was untouchable.

'I'm going to die of something,' he would say when she tried to make him see sense, 'and I hope to God it happens before I go gaga!'

The perfect end for him would have been falling asleep in the conservatory after a day of sailing in his beloved boat, the *Marlow*. The name, at Naomi's suggestion, had been a combination of Martha and Willow's names.

The absence of his larger than life presence had taken some getting used to when he'd died, but she had not been what you would call heartbroken. Her life had not ground to a halt as people might have believed it would when they were paying their respects at the funeral. The way they'd offered their sympathy it was as if they thought she couldn't exist without Colin, that he had been everything for her.

The truth was, once the funeral was behind her, she had felt a gradual transformation of her old self into a new and stronger self. Her genuine self, she liked to think.

While it was true Colin had been the one to make all the financial decisions, which was his area of expertise after all, him being an associate director of an international investment company, she was the one who ran the show behind the scenes at home.

Yes, he was the star performer on stage, the one who held court and entertained their friends and his numerous work colleagues and clients, but she was the one backstage directing, producing and changing the scenery. She had accepted a very long time ago that there could only be one star performer in their marriage, and that was Colin. That was how some partnerships had to be.

She had been widowed for just over two years now and there wasn't a day when she wasn't reminded of Colin, but she refused to live in the past. Life changes and acceptance of that fact enabled a person to adapt and change as well. Maybe even for the better.

Her coffee finished, she saw that the curlews in the mudflats had now been joined by a couple of industrious redshanks. Dig, dig, dig, went their beaks.

Redshanks always reminded Naomi of her eldest daughter, Martha. It was the purposefulness of the bird that did it, the way it went about its business with such conviction. That was Martha all over – determined and focused. She set herself a goal and applied herself to it with unwavering intent. She was a doer, just like her father had been. In contrast, Willow was more like a wren – dainty and hopping around without any real direction.

As sisters they really couldn't be more dissimilar. It never ceased to amaze Naomi that two children from the same parents could be so utterly different.

Whereas Martha was dark-haired and tall with an oval face and hazel eyes, and a nose that she claimed was too long, Willow was smaller with a more petite build and her heart-shaped face was framed by blonde hair. Her eyes were blue, like Naomi's, and set wide apart. As a child she had always been picked to be an angel in the school nativity play, a role Martha had never been interested in playing. She always wanted to be the innkeeper announcing in a commanding voice that there was no room at the inn.

'Ahoy there!'

Leaning forwards, Naomi turned her head to the left from where the voice emanated. She knew without actually seeing him that it was Ellis Ashton, the new tenant of Waterside Cottage, her nearest neighbour.

Ellis had moved in at the end of February, just over two months ago. He was sixty-four years of age, widowed with a grown-up stepson living in Los Angeles and had recently retired as a client director for an asset management firm. His work had taken him to Frankfurt, Brussels, New York and latterly London, where he'd been temporarily renting a house in

Richmond. He'd then moved here to be nearer his mother, who was being looked after in a local care home.

'Ahoy to you too,' she said with a smile.

'Permission to come aboard?'

'Permission granted.'

Lifting the latch on the wooden gate, he pushed it open.

Now directly in front of her, Naomi could see that his denim-blue eyes matched the colour of his shirt and the sky above him. Bending at the waist, and in a very courtly manner, he kissed her cheek. Then with a smile – a smile that had not changed from the one she remembered a long time ago – he produced a bunch of pink and cream tulips from behind his back.

'I'm afraid I'm guilty of stealing them from my landlord's garden,' he said, 'but I wanted to give you something for making last night so special.'

'Thank you,' she said, blushing like a teenage girl at the memory of him cooking dinner for her and what happened afterwards. And which was the reason for her aching in so many places this morning.

Goodness, what would Colin have thought!

More to the point, what would Martha and Willow think?

Chapter Four

Tom Adams was on his way to work. It was now two days since Martha had secretly tested herself to see if she was pregnant.

He knew that his wife kept things from him, but then he kept things from her. Every couple kept shtum about something, he believed. Those who said otherwise were not being honest with themselves. To his way of thinking, it just wasn't feasible, or sensible, to pour out every worrying thought one ever had.

It was because he loved Martha as profoundly as he did that he didn't want to burden her with half of what went on inside his head. She had enough to cope with as it was with her longing to have a baby. They were only ten months into the process and already it was beginning to take its toll on her.

On him too.

They had always operated as a team, taking pride in the strength of their partnership. Whatever they took on, they gave it their combined two hundred per cent attention. There were no short measures with them. All or nothing. And that was what increasingly was worrying him.

He wanted a child as much as Martha did, he really did, but he didn't want to lose who they were in the process of creating a baby. He'd read up online how easily it could happen, and it frightened him.

'We won't become one of those awful couples that destroy their relationship by being obsessed with wanting a baby,' Martha had said before they found that things didn't fall into place as easily as they had assumed they would. She wasn't used to failing and he knew that was how she now viewed their inability to conceive at the click of their fingers.

How long before blame was apportioned?

And why did it worry him so much that he might be the one who was at fault?

Having a family had always been a part of the deal for them. When they were getting to know one another, they'd each raised the subject of children quite early on. Better to flush out the dealbreakers sooner rather than later, had been their mutual take on dotting the 'i's and crossing the 't's before committing to a serious relationship. He could remember how relieved they had both been when they'd tackled the subject and each heard the answer they'd wanted to hear.

They had married four years ago and had agreed to establish themselves as a couple before taking the step of becoming parents. They had everything planned, everything neatly figured out.

But then with all that had happened in the last few years Tom had suddenly not been so sure it was a good idea to bring a child into a world that could so easily be tipped on its axis. Previous generations had worried about war or a nuclear bomb destroying mankind, now it seemed that it could be something far more insidious.

His mother had caught the virus in the early stages of the

pandemic, before anyone really knew just how bad it was going to be. She had spent five awful weeks in hospital on a ventilator before she died. During that time neither Tom nor his sister, Lynn, had been able to see her in hospital. Their father hadn't been able to either. She had died alone, with only the kindness of an exhausted nursing team to watch over her.

Fifteen years older than Mum, Dad had always joked that he'd be the first one to check out. He'd been heartbroken at her death and he still hadn't recovered from losing her. In poor health anyway, and at Lynn's insistence, he had moved to live nearer her.

Tom felt guilty that his sister had so readily taken on the responsibility of keeping an eye on their father, but geography had rather dictated things. The family home had been in Harrogate, where Tom had grown up, and with his sister and husband living nearby in Northallerton, it had just seemed more sensible for Dad to remain in Yorkshire, rather than up sticks to move down south.

Tom had upped sticks himself when he'd graduated from Leeds University and left Yorkshire for a job in London as a graduate trainee accountant. He'd ended up specialising in forensic accountancy, which, with his nerdy propensity for detail, was a perfect fit for him.

Just over three years ago, he and Martha moved out of London and he took the plunge to start his own business. He rented office premises near Guildford where he and a small team could operate. Their client base had since grown at a very pleasing rate, even with the challenges of coping with a pandemic, and they'd just successfully been hired by a prestigious law firm to provide evidence in court against an insurance company accused of defrauding customers.

Martha had encouraged him every step of the way when he'd said he wanted to abandon his relatively secure and well-paid job in London and go it alone. He'd always be grateful for that, that she was happy for him to take the risk. A risk that so far was paying off handsomely.

In return for that support and encouragement he would love nothing more than to make her dream of having a baby come true. But how far would he go?

What if further down the line desperation kicked in and Martha proposed IVF?

The thought of that filled him with dread. Not just the outlandish cost, but the misery it could bring – hopes raised, only to be crushed with each failed attempt.

He hoped to God he could spare Martha that pain.

When he'd found the latest pregnancy test kit Martha had kept from him, not a word had he said to her about it. It wasn't the first time it had happened. She clearly wanted to keep him on a need to know basis, wanting to test herself in secret and then delightedly give him the good news if it was positive.

If he were honest, he wanted to be there with her when she did the test, to share the moment of discovery.

He hadn't been deliberately snooping through the bin when he'd found the kit, but he'd had his suspicions roused earlier in the evening when she'd disappeared straight upstairs to the bathroom the moment she'd arrived home from work. He had caught the unmistakable rustling sound of a bag. He knew her routine as well as his own, so any variation from the norm was like a klaxon going off.

So yes, he had looked in the bathroom bin when he was

cleaning his teeth while getting ready for bed. But only because he wanted to confirm what he thought he already knew.

At around three in the morning, he had woken to find Martha crying. She had claimed it was because she was suffering with the pain of her period, and maybe she was, but he suspected the tears were for another reason. He'd offered to fill a hot water bottle for her and while he was downstairs waiting for the kettle to boil, he had studied the calendar on the wall.

Now as he drove through the early morning traffic, Tom felt a wave of guilty shame, remembering the reason why he had looked at the calendar.

He had been counting up the days until Martha would be ovulating next.

Counting the days when he would be off duty.

Counting the days until it would start all over again and once more the pressure would be on.

Chapter Five

The 7.57 a.m. train from Cobham & Stoke D'Abernon station to London Waterloo was crowded and running thirteen minutes late. It was not an uncommon occurrence, but all the same, it annoyed Martha; she hated to arrive anywhere late.

The large man sitting next to her was taking up so much room he was spilling over into her seat. The intrusion into her personal space made her almost nostalgic for the socially-distanced days of the coronavirus. With no room to use her laptop, she took out her mobile to check her emails. Scrolling through them, she flagged up the ones she would deal with later and deleted anything of no interest. She was ruthless when it came to decluttering her devices. She was the Marie Kondo of screen technology!

Actually, she was quite a fan of the KonMari concept and when it first became popular, she had put it to good use at home with Tom. They were both naturally tidy people, another reason why they were so compatible, and had once spent a wet Bank Holiday weekend together systematically emptying all their cupboards, even the attic. They'd jettisoned anything they agreed was superfluous to their lives. Clothes they hadn't worn in ages, books they would never reread, cheap badminton rackets they would never use again, boxes of, well, just stuff that wasn't relevant to who they were now as people; it was all put into bin bags and either taken to the tip or put ready for their local charity shop. Neither she nor Tom had a sentimental nature, so the task wasn't difficult for them. By the time they'd finished, she had been filled with an extraordinary sense of empowered wellbeing. She'd felt thoroughly cleansed and more in control.

When the train finally pulled into Waterloo and she was hurrying along the crowded platform towards the underground, and remembering how upset she'd been the other night in bed – how pathetically useless she'd felt – she wondered if she needed to repeat the KonMari process. Would it make her feel more in control again? Because as things were, her inability to get pregnant made her feel powerless. She hated the growing sensation that she was up against some unknown force that was preventing her from having the child she so badly wanted.

She bought her usual latte from the coffee shop in the foyer of the building where Brand New Designs had their offices, and took the lift up to the tenth floor.

Settled at her desk, her computer switched on, she was ready for the day. Here at least she could throw her energy into thinking of something other than not being pregnant.

But it was not to be. At eleven forty-five she was asked to join the team in the main meeting room to discuss pitching for a new client who was in need of rebranding. Nobody knew who the client might be, not until Jason Dawson, the company CEO, clicked the top of his pen – always three times – and began.

'Topolino,' he said, 'originally a predominantly online company specialising in high-end baby and maternity products, but also sold through a number of exclusive outlets such as Harrods and Harvey Nichols. They became more widely known after Meghan and Harry's first child, Archie, was photographed wearing one of their blue-and-white-striped knitted jackets with the distinctive mouse logo on the collar. Topolino meaning "little mouse" in Italian, in case you didn't know.'

On the screen behind Jason, a photograph of baby Archie in said jacket appeared.

Murmurs of acknowledgement went around the table.

'As a result of the patronage, sales for their baby clothes, maternity clothes and accessories skyrocketed,' continued Jason, 'and they've since opened a number of stores in London, Bath and Cambridge. But here's the kicker, they recently made the mistake of—'

Staring up at the photograph of the adorable little Archie, Martha knew exactly what the kicker was and couldn't stop herself from blurting out, 'They've been accused of unethical manufacturing practices.'

Jason turned to stare at her and clicked his pen the statuary three times. 'Go on,' he said, his laser-beam attention on her.

Martha knew that Jason liked to have spontaneous input, but she was irritated with herself for displaying that she knew anything about babies when she didn't have one herself. Not a word had she said to any of her colleagues about wanting a child. Had she done so she was sure she wouldn't have had the promotion she'd recently been given. The others round the table were either never going to have families, or had their children years ago and were well past the baby and toddler stage.

'It was alleged they had used child labour in Bangladesh for a new line in maternity wear they were selling,' Martha said. 'As soon as the allegations came to light, they stopped using the factory and switched all production to the UK and to an existing factory in the Midlands where they had better controls in place.'

'Exactly so,' said Jason with a smile.

'Presumably by using the factory in Bangladesh production was cheaper for them?' said Steve, their creative director.

'And they've paid the price since,' said Jason. 'So now they feel the need for a rebrand.'

'Have they actually experienced a loss in popularity and sales?' asked James, their design consultant. 'Because often what shoppers say they'll do while professing outrage is not what they actually do in practice.'

'A valid point,' said Jason with three clicks of his pen, 'and while the drop in sales is minimal, image, or the perception of it, is all. Which means our job is to convince the client that we can put some shine back on what they fear is a tarnished crown.'

For the next forty-five minutes they tossed ideas back and forth until Jason called an end to the meeting.

'You were very well informed about Topolino,' he said when he followed Martha out of the room. 'Been researching baby stuff, have you?'

'I was buying a present for a friend's newborn,' she lied, her game face on. If this was Jason's not-so-subtle way of asking her if she was pregnant, or planning to be, a question by law he was not allowed to ask, he was crossing a line. But men like Jason were adept at crossing lines and could somehow always get away with it. Clever, dynamic and strikingly good-looking, and with an uncanny knack for seemingly knowing what she was thinking, he might have been a temptation for Martha in another life. But not now. Now she could see through the smoke-screen of his super-strength charm.

'I hope you found something nice,' he said with a slow smile, before sauntering off to his office.

I did, she thought, picturing the beautiful little jacket she'd bought, and which was hidden in the spare room at home. She'd bought it before the recent allegations had been made about Topolino and she very much hoped it had been produced as ethically as the company now claimed all their clothing lines were.

Lunch was a hurried cup of miso soup heated in the office microwave, and then it was another meeting with an existing client, an online betting website that needed to be seen as advocating responsible gambling while at the same time inviting their core audience – people who couldn't afford to lose money – to gamble even more.

It was not the most creative or inspiring of days, she thought that evening when she was on the crowded train home. When you had a business to run, you couldn't pick and choose your clients, Jason frequently said. Martha wasn't so sure about that. In this day and age, shouldn't they be more ethically minded, a bit more discerning? Jason had a thing about 'keeping it real' but at the same time he would play the game by whatever new rules he'd been handed.

Her father would have agreed one hundred per cent with Jason. Business was business. You did your best for the client, and for those who worked for you, and you didn't judge. It was a dog-eat-dog world out there and not for the fainthearted.

Martha had idolised her father from an early age and had wanted to be just like him, full of drive and energy. He'd made everything fun, and possible. 'There's no such thing as can't,' he had drilled into her. 'Everything in life is up for grabs. You just have to believe it's yours for the taking.'

Martha had believed him and had done everything she could to be the success she knew he wanted her to be. He had been so proud of her when she'd graduated with a first-class honours degree in Business Studies, and prouder still when she'd subsequently completed her master's in marketing.

'That's my girl,' he'd said happily. 'Now you're officially more qualified than your old dad.'

With sudden sadness she thought how much she missed him. She missed his rock-sure belief in her, the way he'd bolstered her confidence if she ever doubted her capabilities.

She had ten minutes to go before getting off the train when her mobile buzzed. It was a text from Jason.

I'd like you to give the pitch to Topolino when the time comes.

Great, she texted back. **I'll look forward to it.**

Now why had he chosen her, she wondered?

Was he testing her? If so, she might fail as right now her mind was a complete blank when it came to any kind of angle. Which her father would say was a sign that she just had to recalibrate and approach the problem from a different perspective.

She was in her car and driving out of the station car park when she remembered her mother still hadn't returned her WhatsApp message about the weekend. It was the strangest thing, but for a while now Mum had been uncharacteristically bad at staying in touch. Previously she'd always been so reliably quick to reply, but not anymore.

Martha hoped her mother hadn't gone silent because there was a problem she was keeping quiet about. That would be so typical of Mum, not wanting to cause a fuss or a bother.

31

Chapter Six

Willow had been told by her supervisor at Acts of Kindness – AoK – that she had the potential to be one of their star performers.

'You have a natural way of speaking to people,' Kyle had said during her training period. 'People open up to you. Do you know why? It's because you listen, and you have empathy. And that's not something you can teach. So be sure to make good use of that skill.'

The trouble was, this so-called empathy of hers was working against Willow and consequently she wasn't hitting her targets. It was just a dry spell, she told herself; it happened to them all here. She had joined AoK just over three months ago, full of enthusiasm at the prospect of being a part of something that was helping to make the world a better place. It had seemed like the perfect job for her – flexible hours, a short walk away from where she was living, and being a member of a team that believed in what it was doing. But there was a downside to the job; too often she felt sorry for the people she had to call. Sometimes she even felt a bit ashamed.

'You have to think of the bigger picture,' Kyle had said when she had voiced her concerns. 'These are people who genuinely care about the causes they already support; all you're doing is giving them a little nudge to encourage them to increase their donations. Most people are only too happy to do it.'

He was right. Many of those who were 'continuous givers' saw it as their moral duty to increase the amount of money they donated. Just keeping up with inflation, was one way of looking at it.

Another way of looking at it, as a disgruntled ex-employee posted online, was that working for AoK was nothing more than working in a telemarketing call centre that didn't care how it extracted money from the public in the name of charitable giving, just so long as it did. Kyle's answer to this was: 'You have to believe in the cause and that the end justifies the means.'

Working in the charity sector, so Willow was finding, was more ruthless than she had imagined it to be. You had to focus on the reasons why you were making the call. There were sick children dying of cancer who needed treatment and the only way they would have that treatment was if more money was raised to fund research. There were millions around the world dying from hunger. There were all the homeless people. And then there were the animals that needed help, the abandoned dogs and kittens and the brutally abused donkeys who were worked until they dropped. Okay, for some, caring for animals didn't seem such a priority, but at AoK, raising money for the varied list of charities they represented, there was no distinction. Suffering was suffering. A need was a need. And their job at AoK was to be a part of the solution.

Working the same shift that evening with Willow were quite a few she knew, predominantly edgy urban creatives who saw themselves as modern-day Robin Hoods, taking from the rich to give to the poor. There were also a couple of aspiring actresses. The job was perfect for these girls. With hours to suit, they could work around auditions and earn more money here than if they waitressed. They could act their socks off when making the calls and regularly hit their targets.

Willow had to get her own act together and improve her success rate, or she'd be looking for another job. Turnaround of staff was fast. If you didn't make the grade, you were out so that somebody better could take your place. After all, as Kyle often liked to joke, they weren't running a charity here!

Kyle had warned her the other day that she wasn't sticking to the script when on the telephone, that she was pausing too much. 'The slightest hesitation from you,' Kyle said, 'and you give the donor the chance to take control of the conversation and turn you down. You need to be more assertive.'

Her sister would have no trouble with being more assertive. If Martha worked here, she would regularly smash her targets and put Kyle in his place while she was about it. But wishing she could be more like her sister was a waste of time. They were chalk and cheese, always had been.

Auntie Geraldine, Mum's oldest friend, and Willow and Martha's godmother, had once summed up the difference between the two sisters as Martha, who craved order and perfection, being the type who wouldn't lend anyone a book for fear of it being spoilt, or not returned. In contrast, so Auntie Geraldine said, Willow was the type who borrowed a book and would absently turn back the page corners, accidentally spill drinks on it, or drop it in the bath, or simply lose the book. All through accident, never by design.

Well, Willow couldn't disagree with any of that. She was

hopelessly careless and never knew from one moment to the next where her life would lead.

Seeing that Kyle was on the warpath and doing his hourly check on their progress, Willow readjusted her headset and dialled the next number on her list. She never liked it when Kyle stood over her, or worse, listened in; it made her self-conscious and more liable to mess up. For now, he seemed more intent on observing Stefan, the newest member of the team.

When Mrs Tate answered the telephone in Matlock, Derbyshire, Willow set to with the script. But five minutes into it, she didn't know which upset her more, explaining how badly the poor donkeys in India were treated, how they were beaten and starved and left to die on the roadside, or hearing the apologetic sadness in the trembly voice of the donor, an old lady who couldn't afford to increase her standing order.

'Just another pound a week would do so much good for those horribly abused donkeys,' Willow wheedled. She couldn't have felt worse if she were actually mugging the woman in the street and stealing her handbag.

'I wish I could,' Mrs Tate said, 'I really do, but I only have my state pension and there are always so many bills to pay and I don't even have the money to have the washing machine repaired.' She sounded like she was on the verge of tears and Willow couldn't bear to upset her any more. If it were in her power, she'd send the old lady the money to buy a new washing machine, maybe even offer to do her ironing for her.

'I'm terribly sorry to have bothered you, Mrs Tate,' she said, almost in tears herself. 'Please don't worry about the donkeys; you're already doing a wonderful job for them and I'm sure they appreciate your help. Goodbye.'

'Goodbye, dear. And thank you for being so understanding.'

A lump in her throat, Willow ended the call. She had to steel herself before dialling the next number on her list. Why was it she now always seemed to be landed with the donors who didn't have any money? Just once it would be nice to speak to somebody who was rolling in cash and happy to share it with the less fortunate and abused.

Maybe that was what was wrong with the world, the haves kept it to themselves and the have-nots knew what it was to go without and wanted to help, even if they couldn't.

Willow didn't mind people being successful and rich, she wasn't one of those green-eyed misery-guts; far from it, good luck to them, she thought. After all, her own family had always been comfortably off and she had enjoyed what many would call a privileged upbringing.

She didn't like to think what Dad would make of her doing this job. 'Hardly a career, is it, sweetheart?' she could hear him say, giving her one of his tolerant smiles. 'What better purpose in life than to help make the world a better place?' she imagined herself saying back to him.

Funny how Martha never felt the need to justify herself, whereas Willow frequently did. But then Dad had never approved of what he called QLC, Questionable Life Choices – he would view this latest job of Willow's as decidedly questionable. 'The future,' he would say, 'you must always look to the future and ask yourself what you want yours to be.'

That was another difference between Willow and Martha. Martha had always known what she wanted – an amazing career and an amazing husband, and when the time was right, a couple of amazing children. In contrast Willow had never really known what she wanted. She still didn't.

'Daydreaming again, Willow?'

'Just waiting for the donor to pick up the phone,' she lied to Kyle who had magically appeared by her side.

When he'd moved on to check on somebody else, she dialled the next number and waited for Miss Evans of Penarth to answer. When she did, Willow threw herself into her opening lines from the script.

'Good evening, Miss Evans, I hope you're having a pleasant evening and that I'm not interrupting anything important, but I wonder if I could ask you to consider—'

The line went resoundingly dead in Willow's ear.

Okay, she told herself, the next call would go better. Thankfully it did, as did the following call, which resulted in a continuous giver saying he wanted to make a sizeable donation to the charity to which he'd been donating for several years.

At eight-thirty, she finished work on a high and was surprised to find Rick waiting for her outside the building. As always when she saw him, and took in his handsome face, neatly cut hair, and smart suit, she had to pinch herself that he was her boyfriend. She was sure she wasn't Rick Falconer's usual type, any more than he was her usual type. Her last boyfriend had been a motorbike courier who'd spent his days whizzing around London delivering packages and his evenings playing bass guitar in a band. His hair had been nearly as long as Willow's. The boyfriend before that had been a chef with his own vegan burger van which he took to music festivals. Which was where she'd met him. Rick, at thirty-eight, was a very different kettle of fish and looked much more the type who would have a clever, well-dressed girlfriend who was as ambitious as he was. The polar opposite to Willow.

'What are you doing here, Rick?' she said.

'Taking you for dinner, that's what.'

'But you never said anything when we spoke last night.'

He smiled. 'That's what you do when you want to surprise your girlfriend and celebrate a milestone date. You don't let on.'

'Milestone date?' she repeated. Oh Lord, what had she forgotten?

'It's four months today since we met and I'm taking you somewhere special to eat.'

'Oh, how lovely,' she said, touched by how he sweetly romantic he was. 'But I'm not dressed for anywhere special,' she added, tugging at her baggy dungarees and denim jacket.

'That's not a problem,' he said. 'Come on, let's go. I have another surprise for you. One I really hope you're going to say yes to.'

'Tell me now,' she said, as he slipped his hand through hers and steered her towards his BMW, which he had left parked on double yellow lines.

'No,' he said, 'you have to wait.'

He opened the passenger door for her, then closed it gently once she was safely inside. He was like that; the perfect gentleman. It was also his discreet way of making sure she didn't slam the door shut as she was prone to do. She never meant to do it, but then there were plenty of things she never meant to do, and she still did them. Like nearly setting her friends' house on fire the other evening. Or not remembering that Rick didn't drink tea or have milk in his coffee. It was unfortunate that he took it as a personal slight, but as she told him, she was hopeless with trivial details like that.

He had laughed when she'd admitted to having a sieve for a brain, that she could never remember a date, never mind a telephone number. Numbers just happened to be his 'thing', he'd said, and after she'd owned up to having got her finances into a bit of a pickle (a euphemism for being overdrawn), he had offered to go through her credit card and bank statements with her. He had been an enormous help, finding standing orders and direct debits she had forgotten to cancel, some of them from ages ago. She had been so grateful to him, but had also felt a bit silly for not spotting these things herself.

She had a modest trust of money Dad had left her in his will, Martha too, but until she was thirty-five, she could only access the interest, which had been their father's way of ensuring she didn't immediately fritter away the money. Presumably he'd hoped by the time she was thirty-five she would have become the responsible adult he wanted her to be. A responsible adult like Rick, she thought with a smile.

Rick worked in financial services and was an IT Operations Manager. She didn't have a clue what that really meant, but he seemed to enjoy it. He wore a suit Monday to Friday and seemed to earn a terrific amount of money. Dad would have approved of him. She sensed that Mum and Martha were quietly relieved that finally she had found somebody sensible to date, somebody steady with some security and with a proper future. Somebody who would be able to take care of her.

That's what Dad had once said. 'Martha will always be able to take care of herself, but Willow needs someone to look out for her.'

She had overheard him saying this to Mum and Mum had said, 'I think you'll find it's the other way around, all Willow needs is somebody for her to look after.'

*

When they arrived at the restaurant, Rick had plucked an expensive-looking carrier bag out of the boot of his car and given it to her. To her astonishment there was a beautiful black dress inside the bag and a pair of sexy high-heeled shoes for her to change into. 'I said it was a special evening,' he said when she'd returned from the ladies now wearing the dress and shoes. 'And you look every bit as special as I knew you'd look in that dress.'

'I've never worn anything quite like this before,' she said, glowing in his admiration. 'I feel so different. Not like me at all.'

'You look perfect,' he said. 'And very sexy. I'm wondering now whether to abandon dinner and just take you straight back to my place and undress you.'

She giggled. 'And what a waste that would be,' she said, 'after all the trouble you've gone to. And anyway, I'm starving.'

It was much later and after she'd told Rick about the generous donor she'd nailed down towards the end of her shift, and which meant she hadn't just met her week's target, but far exceeded it, that he told her what his surprise was. He'd made her wait right until their dessert was served, despite her pleas for him to tell her.

As his hand crept across the table to take hers, for a crazy moment she thought he was about to spring a ring on her and propose.

'I want you to move in with me,' he said, his hand then reaching up to her hair and tucking it behind her ear. 'I think we both know that's the stage our relationship has reached now, don't we?'

Chapter Seven

Along with a small task force from the village, Naomi was helping to give St Saviour's a spring clean. They had secretly agreed to wait until Veronica Carlyle, their vicar, had gone away for a three-day Christian Leadership conference before they undertook the job. It was a case of while the cat was away the mice would play. With Veronica around their progress would be seriously hampered by her worrying about Health and Safety issues; she was a real nit-picker for doing things by the book.

St Saviour's didn't attract the number of tourists that nearby Holy Trinity in Bosham did, which had the honour of being the oldest known place of worship in West Sussex, but records showed that St Saviour's was probably built in the late eleventh century. With fourteenth-century windows and some nicely carved Elizabethan pews, it was a simple country church and Naomi was inordinately fond of it. It was where Willow had been christened, and where Martha and Tom had married, and of course Colin's funeral had been conducted here, before his body was taken away to be cremated. It had been a full house for him, every one of the Elizabethan pews filled, which would have pleased him immensely. He did always like to be the centre of attention. Doug from the sailing club had given the eulogy and said that Colin, being Colin, had gone out on a high. 'For anyone who had known him,' Doug had said, 'making such a dramatic exit from life was wholly in keeping with the man he'd been, enjoying himself right to the end. We'll all miss him.'

In the time since, Naomi had often wondered how Colin would have lived his life had she died first. Certainly, coping with anything of a domestic nature would have thrown him. A long-held complaint of Naomi's had been his apparent inability to locate the dishwasher or vacuum cleaner. Not for them a modern marriage of a husband pitching in with the cooking or washing; those duties had been assigned to Naomi from the start, admittedly with the help of a cleaner once a week when she'd opened her shop.

She was glad Martha and Tom had a different approach to balancing their relationship; they had worked out a more equal way of sharing the roles. She hoped that Willow would be as fortunate with whomever she chose to spend her life.

For now, it seemed that Rick might be that man. Good-looking and caring and thoroughly level-headed, he had all the attributes any parent would want for their daughter. But would Willow, who was so fickle when it came to boyfriends, stick with him? Or would she grow bored of what might seem like a safe option compared to previous relationships she'd experienced?

Over the years Naomi had learnt not to become too emotionally invested in any of the boyfriends Willow had brought home for her and Colin to meet. Colin had dismissed them all as no-hopers with as much get-up-and-go as a wet paper bag. Naomi had often wondered if Willow had deliberately chosen those boyfriends to provoke her father. Had she waited until her father was dead to find the right man, when he wouldn't be able to crow triumphantly? 'Aha, at last, she brings home somebody with a decent haircut and prospects!'

Naomi hated to admit it, but privately she had thought more or less the same thing when she'd first met Rick. As shallow as it sounded, she'd approved straight away of the car he drove and the box of Lindt chocolates he'd given her, along with a bottle of Prosecco. Over lunch, he'd complimented her on the meal she'd cooked, and chatted easily with Martha and Tom. He had clearly wanted to make a good impression, and had succeeded.

'I can't believe it; she's actually going out with a fully-formed adult!' Martha had pronounced after that first meeting with Rick.

It was generally agreed that if he stayed the course with Willow, Rick would be a welcome addition to the family. Would there be the same agreement, Naomi wondered, when she introduced Ellis to her daughters?

As yet they knew nothing about him. And all anyone in Tilsham knew was that Naomi and Ellis had known one another a long time ago. If it were down to her, she would prefer to keep things the way they were, with no one the wiser; it was simpler that way, because once the genie was out of the bottle – once she told Martha and Willow about Ellis – everything would change.

Armed with a long feather duster, she climbed the stepladders she had placed in front of one of the side windows. She had reached the top when she heard voices behind her, over by the font. One of the voices belonged to Jennifer Kingsbury, the chief organiser of today's covert spring clean.

'Hello, Mr Ashton, have you come to help?'

Not trusting herself to turn around, Naomi concentrated hard on reaching for the large gothic-style cobweb that was draped around the stonework tracery above the window.

'I have indeed,' she heard Ellis reply. 'I caught a rumour that it was all hands on deck here.'

'How very kind of you.'

'So what can I do? Your wish,' he said grandly, 'is my command.'

At his words Naomi suddenly felt light-headed and in danger of falling off the ladder. He had said those words to her last night when, once again, he'd taken her by the hand upstairs to his bedroom. He had been about to draw the curtains, but she had stopped him. 'I don't know about you,' she'd said, 'but I can't recall the last time I made love in the moonlight.'

'Then your wish is my command,' he'd said.

Afterwards, and with the room lit only by the moon streaming its impossibly romantic silvery light through the window, they'd lain in each other's arms.

'I wish it could be like this always,' she'd said.

'Why shouldn't it be?'

'Because . . . because everything always changes, doesn't it?'

'Maybe it will change to something even more wonderful.'

Remembering the intensity of his words, of the tenderness of his mouth on hers, the way her body responded to his, she held on even more firmly to the stepladder.

In response to Ellis's question, there followed a chorus of eager female voices – some of them quite girlish – rushing to request his help in their assigned tasks. Most vocal were Katie Murdoch and Linsey Bales, who claimed they needed a strong man to help move the two bookcases in the book corner.

Jennifer vetoed their requests and proposed that Ellis helped her shift the furniture in the vestry.

'Happy to oblige,' he said cheerfully. 'Oh hello, Naomi,' he remarked as he passed the stepladders. 'I didn't see you up there. How are you?'

'I'm fine, thank you. And you?'

'Never better. Would you like me to do the high bits for you?'

'Oh, that's quite all right, I can manage. It's very generous of you to help us.'

'It's my pleasure.'

Jennifer was having none of the small talk. 'Chop, chop, Mr Ashton,' she said briskly, 'onwards to the vestry where I'm going to make full use of you.'

'Is that so?' he responded with a wink up at Naomi. 'But please, call me Ellis.'

It was all Naomi could do to bite down on the laugh that was threatening to burst out of her.

That evening, perched on a stool in Ellis's cosy kitchen, Naomi watched him add two sirloin steaks to the frying pan on the hob, then return his attention to the lime and honey dressing he was making. She could happily watch him moving about his kitchen for hours at a time. Whenever she was in his company, she felt something within her loosen, an undoing of the tangle of knots inside her. Being with him made her feel that for the greater part of her life she had sleepwalked through it.

It still amazed her that he was here in Tilsham, that of all the gin joints in the world, he'd shown up in this one. At sixty-four he was still an attractive man and in good shape. He had kept a full head of hair that was a pleasant shade of light grey and his beard, closely trimmed, was the same colour, if a little darker in places. She supposed in modern parlance he would be called a silver fox.

Glancing up from what he was doing, he gave her a long, searching look.

'What?' she said.

'I was thinking of today, with you up that ladder in the church and our subterfuge.'

'And?'

'And that it's only a matter of time before we give ourselves away, and that when people have put two and two together, they'll wonder why we've been so secretive. They'll think we had something to hide.'

'But we do.'

He frowned at her tone which was more severe than she intended. 'We're doing nothing wrong,' he said.

Not now we're not, she thought with an imperceptible tightening of the tangle of knots inside her.

'Don't you want your friends and family to know about me . . . about us?'

'Of course I do,' she said. 'It's just that I enjoy what we have. It's so wonderfully uncomplicated as things are. Just you and me.'

'Meaning?'

'Meaning that as soon as I tell Martha and Willow, everything will change. You'll be horribly scrutinised. Your every motive will be questioned.'

The dressing mixed, he drizzled it over the salad leaves he'd already placed in a large pottery bowl. 'I have nothing to hide,' he said. 'And I'd expect nothing less than your daughters to be suspicious of me. They need to know their mother isn't going to come to any harm with some stranger.'

'You're not a stranger,' she said faintly.

'I am to them.'

'But they wouldn't need to know the whole truth, we could gloss over a few details, couldn't we? I wouldn't want them to think—'

'Badly of you,' he finished for her. 'I wouldn't want that either. I thought we'd covered all that?'

'And there's your stepson to consider as well,' she went on stubbornly, reluctant to accept that he was right. 'He might have strong views on you being with someone other than his mother.'

'I've told you before, Lucas has his own life in Los Angeles and has always made it clear that I shouldn't live in the past.' He came over and put his arms around her. 'But that doesn't mean I don't appreciate your concerns. I do. You've lived here in a close-knit village for more than thirty years and everyone knows you as one half of a couple, the wife of a man who was hugely liked and admired. Who am I to think I could step into his shoes?'

'Don't say that.'

'But I'm sure it's what a lot of your friends will think. Particularly your daughters. But sooner, rather than later, we need to be honest.' He kissed her lightly on the lips. 'I just want there to be a *real us*.'

'As opposed to a *secret us*?' she said, tilting her head back a few inches so she could look at him.

He smiled. 'Exactly. Unless you think I'm rushing you, that this has happened too quickly? If that's how you feel, you must say, and we can put the brakes on. I've always regretted that I let you slip through my fingers all those years ago and I don't want to repeat that mistake.'

'I don't want that to happen either, but I'm worried that by telling my daughters about us it will break the spell.'

'Then we must do all we can to ensure we keep the magic going. But first things first,' he said in a brighter tone, 'you need to convince me that it's not just my body you want. That's it's my mind too.'

She laughed. How she loved that he could do that to her. That he could brush away her worries so effortlessly with his gentle humour. She placed her hands around his neck and allowed herself to forget about Martha and Willow who were coming to see her on Sunday and specifically, how they might react to her telling them about this perfectly wonderful man who made her feel so young and free again. She had cowardly put off answering her eldest daughter's message about them coming down to Anchor House for as long as she could, sensing that it was a turning point. The last time they had visited was shortly before Ellis moved in and in the weeks since, she had carefully avoided mentioning that there was a new tenant living next door.

She really didn't relish the prospect of sharing Ellis as she now reluctantly accepted that she should. She liked having him to herself. It felt like this was the first time she'd had anything that was just hers.

It was also the first time she'd had a good secret to keep, and not one that made her feel ashamed.

Chapter Eight

Ellis had always regarded himself as a mild-mannered man. Which he knew was a character trait invariably mistaken for weakness. If you were trying to sell yourself on a work CV or an online dating website, describing oneself in such terms would probably be the kiss of death. It didn't sound exciting enough; it gave rise to the suspicion that you lacked backbone.

Funny that not having a temper should be seen as a negative attribute, but he was just one of those people who rarely allowed things to reduce him to a state of apoplexy. Or perhaps he'd just been lucky in life, that he hadn't been tested to the point that he'd been in danger of losing his self-control. It wasn't that he allowed people to walk all over him; far from it, he merely had a knack for quietly resolving a tricky situation. Of course, who knew how he would react if he was attacked, or somebody he cared about was threatened? Perhaps then the monster within would rise up and reveal itself.

He believed that it was his ability to keep his emotions in check that had helped him care for his wife four years ago when cancer had finally robbed her of her life.

Their marriage had been a happy one with scarcely a cross word exchanged between them. They'd been set up to meet at a dinner party given by mutual friends who had decided that Diana had grieved long enough for her husband, who had died in a car crash three years previously. They had also decided it was high time Ellis settled down. To everyone's satisfaction, he and Diana had hit it off and before the evening was over they'd swapped telephone numbers.

At the time Diana's son, Lucas, was ten years old and Ellis was in his late thirties with no previous experience of children. A relationship with Diana had the potential to be a minefield of complex challenges, but it hadn't been like that at all. Lucas was an easy-going child and accepted Ellis into his mother's life quite readily. Had he not, who knows whether things would have gone as well as they had.

Ellis's mother, Rose, had been delighted at last to have a grand-child and loved Lucas as though he were Ellis's own son. As did he. Amongst the many framed and treasured photographs which Rose had brought with her to make her room here at the care home feel more homely were several of Lucas, charting his years from young boy to teenager to adult. She was so very proud of him.

Sitting in the stuffy, overly warm room where Rose was fast asleep, Ellis hoped she found the pictures a comfort. For him, the collection of photographs was a poignant reminder of her life coming to an end. Ninety-six years of age, she was now painfully insubstantial, as though the slightest of breezes would blow her away.

Physically she had never been a big woman, but mentally she had been a colossus, and an inspiration to many. A school-teacher all her working life, she had taken to mentoring troubled teenagers in her retirement. She believed everybody deserved not just a second chance, but a third and a fourth, or however many chances it took to find one's place in the world. Anyone who knew Rose Ashton had had nothing but respect for her.

The nursing staff here at West View Care Home were wonderful and Ellis didn't give a damn how much it was costing him to have Rose so well cared for. It had been a sad day for him when she had admitted that she could no longer look after herself, that she had begun to feel worryingly unsteady on her feet. Always a pragmatist, she had refused point-blank his suggestion that she live with him in Richmond.

'If you think I'm going to let you take me to the lavatory, you have another think coming!' she'd fired back at him. Her body might have been failing her, but her mental faculties and the ability to assert herself were not. 'No son deserves that punishment inflicted upon him.'

It didn't matter how often he assured her that he wouldn't be embarrassed by taking her to the bathroom, that he had done it for Diana, she was adamant that that was different. 'Diana was your wife; intimacy was an established bond between the two of you. No such thing should ever exist between a mother and a son and that is my final word on the subject.'

There was no persuading her and with her mind also made up on the location where she was to spend her final days, he set about researching care homes on the West Sussex coast. It was here that she had lived as a child and where she had met Ellis's father. Dying in Borehamwood, where she had lived for the last sixty-odd years, was apparently unacceptable.

The only care home he'd found that he felt sure would look after Rose well enough was inevitably the most expensive. He took her to view it and she gave it her seal of approval. She had been here since early February and despite the quality of care provided, it was clear that she was failing fast.

Which was why he'd taken the step to move down to West Sussex so he could spend as much time as possible with her while he still could. Retirement had been just around the corner for him anyway, so he decided to quit a couple of years earlier than planned. Financially he had everything in order and with no real plans in place since returning to London from New York, he looked for a modest property to rent a short drive away from Rose. Waterside Cottage had fitted the bill perfectly.

On a bitterly cold February morning, two days after he'd moved in, he had stood at the end of his new garden surveying the beautiful harbour view the cottage afforded him. The tide had been in, which meant there was only a narrow strip of shoreline between him and the water's edge. To his right, and in the distance, he saw the lone figure of a woman in a red hat and a red puffa jacket, hands pushed into pockets, walking along the shoreline. He had the strangest feeling that he recognised her, that he *knew* her. It was something about the way she moved, her head held high, her unhurried pace steady and even as though she had all the time in the world. Curiosity made him stay where he was until he'd figured out why he was experiencing the sensation he was. She was steering a course towards the house next door when it came to him.

'Naomi?' he called out, hardly able to believe his eyes. 'It is, isn't it?'

She slowed her step and looked over to him. 'I'm sorry, do I know—' Then she let out a gasp and put a hand to her mouth. 'Ellis? What are you doing here?'

'I'm living here.' He gave the gate a tap, as though claiming ownership of it. 'I moved in two days ago.'

She stared and stared at him. 'I've . . . I've been away,' she said. 'I only got back late last night. I saw lights on in the cottage and wondered if the new tenant had moved in. I . . . oh, my goodness, I can't believe it!' She shook her head. 'I'm sorry, I'm prattling on. It's the shock.'

'Take a breath,' he said with a smile, while opening the gate and joining her on the shingle.

That was two months ago. Two extraordinary months during which it was as if they had turned back the clock. He hadn't known such happiness in a long time. It made him realise that he had been doing no more than existing since Diana had died, merely taking each day as it came. Now he felt as though he had been given a second chance to live his life to the full.

The sound of his mother clearing her throat roused him from his thoughts. Turning from the wall of photographs he'd been looking at, he was surprised to see that Rose's eyes were wide open and fixed on him.

'How long have you been awake?' he asked, leaning forward in his seat and reaching for her hand.

'Long enough to wonder what you were thinking about.' Her voice was surprisingly firm and quite at odds with her frailty.

'I was thinking about Naomi,' he said.

'I thought so.'

He smiled. 'What gave me away?'

'The happiness on your face. Why don't you bring her to meet me one day? If she'll come.'

'I'm sure she'd like to meet you.'

53

'Well, ask her before it's too late.'

He gently squeezed her ghost of a hand. 'Don't talk like that.'

She ignored his comment, just as she always did whenever he admonished her for talking about dying. 'Do her daughters know about you yet?' she asked.

'No.'

'So you're still her secret lover.'

'That makes me sound a lot more interesting than I am.'

'What about Lucas, have you told him?'

'The moment hasn't felt right yet.'

She narrowed her eyes, making him feel like he was a child again and caught out for not being entirely truthful.

'Are you waiting for Naomi to take the first step of making things official before you do?' she said.

'Stop being so wily.'

She tutted. 'The pair of you need to get on with putting the past behind you so you don't sacrifice your future. I want to die knowing you're happy.'

'It's only been a couple of months, Mum. And please don't talk about you dying, you know I don't like it.'

'We both know why I'm here, so there's little point in being squeamish about it. Now be honest with me, are you worried Naomi will allow her guilt, for what you two did all those years ago, to wreck things? Because if you are, you need to convince her that past sins are just that, they're mistakes one makes in the past and they should be left there. They should not be allowed to ruin a person's future.'

'You're in a feisty and interrogative mood today,' he said, not answering her.

'Stuck here I have a lot of time to think about things.'

Driving back to Tilsham later that afternoon, Ellis contemplated his mother's words about past sins. Everybody had them, it was just how adept one was at letting go of them. And that largely depended on how strong a conscience one had.

Chapter Nine

Finished in the bathroom, Tom switched off the light. Martha was already in bed and despite it being well after midnight, she was staring intently at the screen of her laptop.

'Is that work?' he asked, pulling back the duvet on his side of the bed and getting in.

'No. I'm house-hunting,' she said.

'Why, you're not thinking of us moving again, are you?'

'Not for us, silly, for Mum.'

'Has she asked you to find her a house?'

'Not yet she hasn't.'

'Martha, what are you up to?'

She twisted her head round to look at him. 'When we go down on Sunday, I'm going to persuade Mum that it's time to downsize and live nearer to us. You've known ever since your father moved to be nearer Lynn that I've wanted my mother to do the same thing. I'd just feel happier if she wasn't so far away.'

'She's not that far from us.'

'The distance is enough to be a nuisance should there be a problem. She knows how I feel. When you lost your mother, I told Mum then that she should think about selling Anchor

House to make things more convenient for us all. She'll have to do it one day, when she's too old to cope on her own.'

Tom pulled a face. 'I think she's a long way off that. What's more, she loves her home, you know that.'

'But having her close by would be just so much more practical. Especially . . . when . . . you know, we have a baby.'

He knew why she'd hesitated; she'd been on the verge of saying *if* we have a baby. 'But won't *you* miss Anchor House?' he asked. 'It's your childhood home. You've always said how much you loved growing up there.'

'Of course I'll miss it, so will Mum, that's why it's important I find her something she'll love just as much.'

Tom wasn't convinced. 'Are you sure it's a good idea to present her with something that will make her feel as though she has no choice in the matter? Wouldn't it be better to sow the seed of an idea and let her take it from there?'

'But that could take forever. You know how slow and stubborn she can be. She can really dig her heels in when she wants to.'

He smiled. 'I know somebody else just like that.'

She smiled too. 'But you do see, don't you, I only want the best for her? And apart from anything else, I really believe this is what Dad would want me to do, to take care of Mum.'

'That's as maybe, but unlike my father, your mum is in good health, has never once complained that she finds Anchor House too big for her and, to my knowledge, she hasn't ever said she finds the distance between us inconvenient.'

'But that will change once she's a grandmother. She'll be keen to spend as much time with the baby as she can, therefore nearer would be so much better.'

'I'm just suggesting that we shouldn't make the mistake of getting ahead of ourselves.'

Martha flipped down the lid of her laptop. 'Since when has putting plans into place been considered getting ahead of ourselves? Sensible plans that will benefit us all, I might add.'

Tom knew when to quit and so he raised a hand in surrender. 'Fair enough, it's your mother, you know best.'

In essence he accepted that Martha was right, that as a couple they did always think of the future and plan accordingly. They were of one mind in that respect. However, in this instance he wasn't so sure he was fully on board with her reading of her mother's situation. He also thought it would be a great shame for their child – hopefully their *children* – to miss out on visits to their grandmother at Anchor House and the beautiful little harbour village of Tilsham. It would always be something for them to look forward to with idyllic days spent crabbing in the rock pools, paddling and swimming and maybe even learning to sail. But maybe he was being overly sentimental and Martha, quite sensibly, was being more of a pragmatist.

Probably this wouldn't be on her radar so soon if two things hadn't happened – her father's death from a heart attack, and Covid-19. Losing his own mother to that awful virus had brought it home to Tom just how easily life could be changed, so he could understand Martha's concern for her mother, her need to protect and do what she believed was the right thing in the absence of her father. But he doubted it would be as straightforward as she believed it would be. There was also Willow to factor in. How would she feel about parting with her childhood home?

Chapter Ten

When she and Tom arrived at Anchor House, Martha saw that Rick's BMW was already parked on the drive, and in the space she usually used. Given what she wanted to discuss with her mother, she would have preferred, on this occasion, for Willow to come alone. As much as Martha regarded Rick as a thoroughly good influence on her sister, he wasn't a proper member of the family yet and therefore she didn't think he should be privy to their every conversation. Family business was family business.

Out of the car, her tote bag slung over her shoulder, inside which she had a selection of printed property details, she carried a large bouquet of peonies, one of her mother's favourite flowers, and led the way round to the back of the house. Either side of the brick path, where Mum had placed pieces of driftwood, grape hyacinths, snowdrops and daffodils, some of them just going over, added splashes of spring colour.

On the terrace, in the shelter of the glass-covered verandah that faced the sea and stretched nearly the entire width of the house, Rick was in the process of opening a bottle of Prosecco and Willow was placing glasses on the table, which was set ready for lunch. As soon as the weather was warm enough, Mum loved to entertain on the verandah. In her inimitable way, she had made it a very welcoming place, not only with a long rectangular table that could seat ten, the top of which she had painstakingly covered with a mosaic of broken crockery and old tiles, but with old wicker chairs made more comfortable with plump cushions and colourful throws. A bougainvillea planted in an old stone urn grew at one end and ever since Mum had planted it, more than a decade ago, it had thrived in the sheltered sunny spot.

'Hi Tom! Hi Martha!' Willow said gaily. 'Ooh, aren't those flowers gorgeous? Far prettier than the roses Rick and I bought. Clever you for finding them.'

Leaving Tom to chat with Willow and Rick, Martha stepped through the open French doors to the kitchen. Her mother was standing at the sink, topping and tailing green beans.

'Hello, Mum,' she said, kissing her cheek. 'You look nice. Is that a new dress? Oh, and your hair! You've cut your hair!'

'No flies on you,' her mother said, kissing her cheek in return. 'I had it done yesterday. I felt I was in need of a change, a bit of shaking up you could say.' She laughed. 'Do you like it?'

'The dress or the hair?'

'Both, I suppose. I bought the dress in Chichester, the necklace as well. You don't think it's too young for me, do you? Not too short?'

'Not at all. I . . . I don't think I've ever seen you in that soft buttery shade of yellow before, and the chunky pearls go nicely with it. The hair's going to take some getting used to.'

'Well, as I said, I felt in need of a change. Are those beautiful peonies for me?'

Martha smiled. 'Of course. Shall I put them in water?'

'Please, and thank you for always remembering how much

I love them. If you fetch that large jug over from the dresser, I'll fill it.'

'Is this new as well?' asked Martha, picking up the surprisingly heavy glass jug and giving it to her mother. 'I don't remember seeing it before.'

'You know me, I can't resist a bargain. I saw it in a charity shop and thought it rather splendid and just perfect for big blowsy flowers like peonies and hydrangeas.' She handed it back to Martha. 'Just plonk the flowers in, I'll arrange them properly later. You go and join the others in the garden. I'll finish these beans, then I'll be ready to join you all for a glass of fizz. I'm parched.'

Removing the cellophane from around the flowers, Martha thought that it wasn't only her mother's appearance that was different. Her voice was different too; it was brimming with vitality. In fact, her whole demeanour was vibrating with a peculiar high-spirited energy Martha couldn't quite identify. Had her mother already enjoyed a glass or two of fizz? If so, it might work in Martha's favour when the right moment presented itself for her to bring up the subject of selling Anchor House.

Or was it possible, she thought, as she went out to the terrace, that Naomi was way ahead of Martha? That her need to shake things up was a sign that she was already thinking of the future?

*

As perfectly delicious as the meal was – the garlic and rosemary-infused spring lamb was tender and slightly pink, the new potatoes glossy with butter, the green beans and caramelised baby carrots perfectly cooked, and the gravy silky smooth – Naomi was struggling to enjoy the meal.

In her head she had everything she wanted to say seamlessly worked out, but it was picking the right moment to break her news to the girls that was proving more difficult. 'Don't force it,' Ellis had said, 'just let the conversation flow and you'll say what you need to quite naturally.'

Really it wasn't a big deal. So what if she had met somebody? It happened all the time. Why not to her? Because, no matter their age, children were children and they simply could not conceive of a parent being anything other than a boring old parent. They weren't meant to change or behave differently.

That much was obvious in the way Martha had reacted to her hair. When Naomi asked her hairdresser yesterday to give her hair a complete makeover, Sandy, her stylist for more than eight years, had asked her if she was sure. 'I couldn't be surer,' Naomi had replied. 'I want to be a new me.'

While the girl had set about the business of colouring and then chopping away the unwanted hair, Naomi had watched in fascination as it fell to the floor. When she left the salon with a smart smooth bob, she felt a lifting of her spirits and about twenty years younger. Her shoulder-length hair – how Colin had always liked it – was now a thing of the past. With a definite spring in her step, she went straight into a neighbouring boutique and tried on the linen dress she had seen in the window earlier. Staring at her reflection in the fitting-room mirror, turning her head to the right, then to the left, and checking how the dress looked on her, she had felt ridiculously pleased with herself.

At home, and as he said he would when he was back from

62

visiting his mother, Ellis called in to see her. 'Wow!' he'd exclaimed. 'Don't you look amazing!'

She hadn't needed to ask him if he meant it, she could see it in his face, and in the way he put a hand to the now exposed nape of her neck and kissed her.

As though the new dress and haircut had given her the necessary courage, she told Ellis that she had decided to tell her daughters about him.

'I'm glad,' he'd said. 'I don't want us to hide anymore. I want us to start making plans for our future. Our together future.'

'So do I,' she'd said happily.

But here she was, and still she hadn't told Martha and Willow about Ellis. The trouble was, she didn't feel it was right to tell them in front of Tom and Rick. She wanted their reaction to be contained to just the three of them. But how to engineer that? Perhaps she could hint that the girls should help her clear the table and then corner them in the kitchen. Except Tom would never stand for that; he would always say that Naomi had done quite enough in cooking the meal, that she should leave the clearing up to them.

Roused from her thoughts, and glancing across the table and through the centrepiece of a large candelabra she had decorated with ivy, she suddenly became aware of a big smile on Rick's face and his hand clasped firmly around Willow's. 'I've asked Willow to move in with me,' he said, 'and I'm delighted to say she's said yes.'

Naomi wasn't at all sure how to respond. What was the etiquette in this situation? The way Rick had said what he had, it seemed as though they were meant to offer their congratulations.

'But, Willow, what about Simon and Lucy's house?' asked

Martha before Naomi could say anything. 'You can't just aban-don it. Or their cats.'

'Would you believe it, they've had a change of plan and are coming home earlier than originally thought.'

'The timing really couldn't be more perfect,' said Rick, still smiling.

There was a slight lull in the conversation and Naomi won-dered if she should take advantage of it when Martha said, 'Talking of the time being right, I have something to—'

Willow gasped. 'You're pregnant!'

Next to her, Naomi heard Tom's sharp intake of breath and on the other side of her Martha looked across the table at her sister. 'No,' she said coolly, 'I'm not pregnant. And I don't know why you would rush to assume I was.'

Willow's expression dropped. 'Oh, I'm sorry. I thought you and Tom . . . I just thought that maybe . . . oh, honestly, me and my big mouth. Just ignore me.'

'I would if you'd keep quiet,' muttered Martha.

Naomi knew that her eldest daughter wanted to start a family and for a moment she too, just like Willow, had leapt to the same thought. It was not a topic of conversation that Martha openly discussed, other than to say that she and Tom had decided they were now in a position to have a child. Naomi had certainly never pushed the subject, preferring instead to accept that when there was something for Martha to share, she would.

To fill in for the sudden drop in mood around the table, Naomi offered seconds before it all went cold, and while Tom and Rick both came to the rescue and took her up on the offer of more lamb and potatoes, she said, 'So, Martha, what was it you were going to say?'

Her face set, Martha said, 'Willow and I have talked about this, as did you and I, Mum, a while back, and we really think now is a good time for you to consider moving from here so you can be nearer us. You know how much we worried about you after Dad died and then when we all went into lockdown.'

'I've told you before that there's no need to worry about me,' Naomi said, her expression as neutral as her voice. 'Although that's not to say I don't appreciate your concern,' she added.

In all probability it would have been Martha who had instigated things and Willow would have been jockeyed along, but Naomi couldn't help but feel disagreeably cross at her daughters for colluding behind her back the way they had.

'Wouldn't you like a smaller and more manageable house, though?' said Martha

'No. And when the time comes, when there are grandchildren, trust me, the more space there is, the better.'

'But wouldn't you like to live nearer your grandchildren,' Martha persisted, 'when that day comes?'

No two ways about it, the girl was her father's daughter; once she was set on a course, there was no dissuading her. Colin had been just the same. Many a time both he and Martha had, and for quite different reasons, buzzed about the house like angry bluebottles relentlessly hurling themselves against the window looking for a way out.

'But it's my home,' asserted Naomi. 'It's your home too.'

'Of course it is. But only earlier in the kitchen you said that you felt the need to shake things up. What better way to do that than move somewhere new that would give you new horizons to explore with lots of new possibilities? And with the added advantage of being nearer to Willow and me.'

Naomi didn't trust herself to speak, so she filled her water glass and took a sip from it.

'I don't think it's anything you should rush into, Mum,' said Willow. Avoiding her sister's eye, her tone was placating.

'Maybe it's something to think about in a few years' time,' said Tom, ever the diplomat. 'Just something to mull over. There's no rush.' He turned to Martha. 'Is there?'

'I know I'm a relative newcomer to the family,' joined in Rick, 'so maybe I shouldn't say anything, but this is an exceptionally beautiful house and the location is stunning.' He twisted round in his seat and indicated the garden and, beyond it, the view of the sea glittering in the bright sunshine. 'And if it were mine, I would only give this up if I really had to.'

Naomi smiled gratefully at Rick. 'Thank you,' she said. 'I couldn't have put it better myself.'

To Naomi's left, Martha slowly sat up straighter. 'Well, Rick,' she said quietly, 'as you rightly say, you're a newcomer to the family, technically an outsider, so on this subject maybe you should keep your opinions to yourself.'

'Martha,' warned Tom. 'That's uncalled for.'

'Yes,' agreed Willow, 'there's no need to be rude to Rick. He's only trying to offer another viewpoint.'

Rick raised his hands. 'Hey, it's okay, I should have kept quiet. I apologise. How about Tom and I clear the table and leave you three girls to chat amongst yourselves? How does that sound?'

'Good idea,' said Tom, on his feet and gathering up the empty plates. He probably couldn't wait to escape.

While the two of them ferried everything inside, Naomi bided her time. She was trying very hard not to overreact, to keep her angry disappointment in check. Just how ancient did her daughters think she was? Did they have a care home lined up for her as well? It was so ludicrously absurd she could almost laugh. Hearing the French doors behind them being discreetly shut, she took a deep breath.

'I appreciate you both giving my welfare so much thought,' she began, 'and I'm sure you believed you were doing the right thing, thinking about me in my old age, but—'

'It's not about you being old, Mum,' Martha cut in, 'it's about accepting that life changes.'

'I couldn't agree with you more.'

'Well then, when you become a grandmother won't you want to be on the doorstep so you can spend time with your grandchild?'

Naomi frowned. 'I thought you said you weren't pregnant?' Immediately she regretted the comment; it was needlessly hurtful to her eldest daughter.

'I'm not,' Martha said evenly. 'But I hope that I will be one day in the not too distant future. And it's that "one day" that I'm thinking of. Because one day you will be less able, Mum, and I want you near to us so we can look after you. It's what Dad would want for you, isn't it?'

Naomi turned to look at Willow. 'Is this what you want for me too?'

Willow's face had none of the certainty that her sister's had. 'I just want you to be happy, Mum,' she said.

'And I am happy. Living here. In the house where you both grew up, and which I love.'

'But you could be happy in a sweet little cottage with a more manageable garden, couldn't you?' As though gaining in confidence, Martha went on. 'Don't be cross with me, Mum, but

I went online and found some beautiful houses for you to consider. There's one that is literally just a few miles from Tom and me. It would be perfect. It has a nice-sized garden which you could soon make your own and four bedrooms, so you'd have plenty of space for visitors. Including,' she added, with a smile, 'your grandchildren.'

Feeling as though she were being thoroughly ambushed by Martha's reasonableness, Naomi forced herself to remain calm. 'There was no need for you to research property on my behalf,' she said, 'and please don't think you can bully me like your father did.'

'Dad never bullied anyone!' Martha remonstrated.

Naomi sighed, regretting once again her choice of words. Staring out to sea where a number of boats were sailing towards the sharp line of the horizon, she decided there was only one way she could convince her daughters that she was happy right where she was and what was more, she had plans of her own. It was not how she had wanted to break the news, but she had been backed into a corner.

'Girls,' she began, 'there's something I have to tell you. You see, I've met somebody. His name is Ellis, and this might come as a shock to you, but we're very much in love. So you really don't need to worry about me.'

Chapter Eleven

It was now May and a week had passed since they'd all been down at Anchor House and Mum had dropped her extraordinary bombshell.

In the days that followed, Willow was bombarded with texts and emails from Martha. She refused to acknowledge any of them until her sister apologised for being rude to Rick. Which eventually she did. Her tone on the phone was grudging, but Willow, who really didn't like conflict, accepted the apology with good grace. Rick had claimed he hadn't been offended by what Martha had said to him, but he must have been. He'd been made to feel he didn't belong. 'How can I make it up to you?' she'd asked several times.

His response was the same. 'The only thing I want you to do is move in with me.'

It was so sweet how eager he was for her to do that; he couldn't wait for Simon and Lucy to fly back home.

For the time being, and instead of staying the occasional night with her, Rick now spent most nights with her. He kept his clothes on the bed in the spare room and was fastidious about shutting the door to keep out Simon and Lucy's cats.

This morning, and having walked to Victoria Park, Willow

and Rick were enjoying a lazy al fresco Sunday brunch at her favourite café overlooking the lake. She had just asked Rick if he would come with her to what Martha was grandly calling a family conference that afternoon.

'But I'm not family,' he said, sipping his black coffee. 'Martha won't want me there. She's made her views very clear on that score.'

'But I want you there, with me.'

He shook his head. 'Your sister has her agenda, family business is family business, and I have to respect that.'

'Not many men would be so understanding,' Willow said.

'Hopefully your sister will think the same and award me a few brownie points. But you know, I'm not so sure it's even a good idea for you to go. All Martha is likely to do is complain that your mother doesn't know what she's doing. I should like to know what gives Martha the right to be so high-handed.'

'It's just her over-the-top way of showing concern. She's always been like it. It's a character trait she inherited from our father.'

'Whereas you,' Rick said with a smile, 'are more like your mother, I hope.'

Willow smiled back at him. 'I am.'

'So, like I say, why go to your sister's and be harangued for the afternoon. What good will it do anyway?'

'Well, it is quite important, isn't it? It's not every day your mother announces that an old friend has moved into the house next door and they've fallen in love. And Dad's only been dead two years; it's all a bit sudden. How would you feel if it was your mother?'

The smile gone from his face, Rick flinched.

'Oh, I'm sorry,' Willow said, 'that was insensitive of me.' Rick never spoke about his parents, other than to say they were both dead. She often tried to get him to open up about them, but he never did.

'It's okay,' he said.

'No it's not. I have to learn to be more careful with what I say. Look how I trampled all over Martha's feelings last Sunday when I jumped to the conclusion that she was pregnant. Honestly, I could kick myself sometimes.'

He leant across the table, put a hand to her hair and wound a lock of it around his fingers. She loved the way he did that, so gently and so uninhibitedly. 'I thought it was cute the way you showed how pleased you were that you thought you were going to be an aunt,' he said. 'I assume having children is something you're keen to do.'

For once she tried not to blunder in with her answer; this was awkward deal-breaker territory. Until now the subject had never come up between them, but now it had, and there was no way of ignoring it, much as she'd like to. 'I suppose so,' she said with a small shrug, 'when the time is right. What about you?'

'I'd love to be a father. I can't think of anything better. And you know, sometimes it's wrong to over-plan these things.' The smile returned to his face. 'Sometimes you just have to let nature have its way.'

Willow thought of her sister. 'Sometimes nature isn't very kind. I'm pretty sure Martha and Tom have been trying for a baby for a while now, but it doesn't seem to be happening for them.'

'They're probably trying too hard. I suspect your sister is used to things happening at the click of her fingers.'

71

He was right. That's exactly how it was for Martha. Everything had always come so easily to her. Even so, Willow did feel genuinely sorry for her sister. It must be horrible being like Martha and wanting something so very badly but being denied it. Maybe that was why she had been so full-on last Sunday. Wanting to organise Mum's life was perhaps some sort of displacement activity for her. Willow could see the sense in having Mum closer to them both, but it was much too soon.

And now there was a man called Ellis Ashton in Mum's life. Very likely he was the reason she'd had her hair cut and had bought that pretty new dress, and, it had to be said, had looked so radiant. Willow had thought it was the colour of the dress that had made her mother look so well, but now she thought it was because she was in love. Or imagined herself to be in love. That was something Willow knew all about, thinking she loved someone.

She really didn't know what to make of it all. Mum had never done anything particularly wild or out of character, she had always just been Mum – caring Mum, gentle Mum, considerate and patient Mum, and always there for them as a family. That's what a mother did, was what Willow believed. It was one of the reasons why she had answered Rick's question as carefully as she had. She didn't think she could ever be as good a mother as Mum had been.

Breaking into her thoughts, Rick said, 'Why don't you message Martha and say you can't make it this afternoon, that you've decided to spend it with me? The subtext being she needs to let your mother get on with enjoying herself.'

'Oh, I don't think I could do that. Besides, I want to discuss the situation with Martha. We need to know more about this man who's popped up from nowhere and we also need to decide when and how we're going to meet him.'

'You could ring her and do that. Don't you want to spend the afternoon with me? I thought we could try out that new gym together. They have a good offer on at the moment.'

The last thing Willow wanted to do was join a gym; it just wasn't her thing. 'Why don't you try it while I go and see Martha?' she said. 'If I don't go, she'll only keep pestering me.'

Letting go of her hair, Rich pursed his lips and suddenly he seemed so desperately disappointed, as though he'd really been looking forward to being with her.

She was about to change her mind and say she'd ring Martha, just as he'd suggested, when he shrugged. 'No,' he said, 'you go and enjoy yourself. But don't let your sister bully you into doing anything you don't agree with. Promise?'

Relieved that he didn't look so disappointed now, she said, 'You're always looking out for me, aren't you?'

'Somebody has to.'

'Have you spoken to Mum in the last few days?'

The way Martha phrased the question it sounded like an accusation, as if Willow had broken some unwritten rule.

'Yes.'

'And?'

'Well, understandably she wanted to know what I thought about her news, having had time to think about it.'

Martha tutted. 'As though a few days and some sleepless nights would resolve anything.'

Willow hadn't experienced any sleepless nights, but as they stood in the kitchen waiting for the kettle to boil, she suspected her sister had. She wasn't her usual immaculate self, her hair needed washing and her nail varnish was chipped, and she definitely looked tired. 'Everything all right, Martha?' she asked.

'What an absurd thing to ask! Of course I'm not. I'm worried sick about Mum. I mean, what's got into her? Dad hasn't been dead two minutes and she has some new man in bed with her.'

'He's been dead two years,' Willow said gently, 'and we don't know that he's . . . that they're—' she broke off, unable to say the words that would conjure up the unwanted image of her mother having passionate sex.

'Two years without Dad feels like two minutes to me,' said Martha adamantly, 'and she's replaced him with a man whom we know nothing about.'

The kettle now boiling, she set about making two mugs of instant coffee. That was another sign that proved to Willow that Martha wasn't herself. Normally she would make proper coffee and fuss about with a cafetière, timing exactly when to push down on the plunger. Or she'd use Tom's expensive machine that was just like the one Rick had.

'Where's Tom?' asked Willow, aiming for something commonplace to say when they went out to the garden to drink their coffee.

'He's gone for a run. He's of the opinion that I'm making a mountain out of a molehill and need to calm down. And since I can't do that, pounding the roads in his running gear gives him the peace and quiet I'm not giving him at home.'

'You don't think he might be right? What if it had been Mum who'd died, and Dad had found somebody new?'

'He wouldn't have done it the way Mum has. He'd have been totally upfront and introduced us to the woman from the start.

But Mum . . . Mum says she's been seeing this man since the end of February and not said a word. She's deliberately kept him as a secret from us. Why?'

'Perhaps to avoid what's going on now.'

Martha tutted and shook her head as though Willow had just said something particularly stupid. 'Don't you care? Doesn't it upset you that she's lied to us?'

'I hadn't really thought of it like that. You won't like it, but I'm more curious. I think we should arrange to meet him. And soon.'

'Well *duh*, of course we're going to do that. I've already insisted that we do. We need to make our position very clear to him and demand to know what they're planning to do.'

Not sure exactly what her position was, Willow said, 'What if he's nice and we really like him?'

Martha snorted. 'You always did want to hang on to the hope that Father Christmas and the Tooth Fairy were real.'

Remembering how Martha had sat her down one day and told her the truth about Christmas, that Santa didn't exist and it was Mum and Dad who filled her stocking and put the presents at the end of her bed on Christmas Eve, Willow drank her coffee and said nothing. She was glad now that Rick hadn't come with her. She wouldn't have wanted him to see her sister like this. Come to that, she didn't like it either; it was unnerving seeing Martha so angry and upset. So not herself.

'And what the hell did Mum mean when she said we weren't to bully her like Dad did? Dad never bullied her. He was just impatient at times.'

'He did have a tendency to shout and be a bit dismissive,' Willow said. 'Maybe that's what Mum meant.'

'He wasn't dismissive, he just wanted to get things done. Somebody had to make the important decisions for the family and frankly if it had been left to Mum, she would have dithered around for ages trying to decide what to do. You're just the same.'

'Thanks for that.'

'You know what I mean, you're so busy sitting on the fence trying to please everyone, you're unable to make up your mind about anything. It's why you've had so many boyfriends, one minute you like them and the next you've decided you don't. Give it time and you'll probably do the same with Rick, won't you? And talking of Rick, I'm surprised he didn't come here with you so he could stick his oar in like he did at Mum's.'

Stung that her sister was taking out her frustration on her, Willow said, 'Please don't start all that again. He was merely trying to add some objectivity to the discussion.'

'I'd feel better if it was someone we knew that Mum has fallen for,' said Martha, ignoring Willow's defence of Rick, 'like one of Dad's old friends who we've known for years. At least then we'd trust him, wouldn't we?'

Chapter Twelve

'What I find so extraordinary,' said Naomi as she stared disconsolately out of the kitchen window, 'is that I don't think it ever crossed their minds that I might meet somebody. Or that I might have a life of my own.'

Standing behind her, Ellis's hands gently massaged her shoulders. 'That's because they see you through a very narrow lens,' he said. 'You're their mother, therefore you have only the one dimension as far as they're concerned.'

She turned around to face him. 'I know that. I just didn't expect Martha's censure to be so wounding. It was perhaps foolish of me, but I had harboured a fragment of hope that they might be pleased for me, and to have that hope so thoroughly dashed makes me fear the worst.'

'Don't think of it as dashed, merely a little bruised. They need time to come to terms with your news, that's all.'

'You're right, of course, but what I can't get out of my head is that look of horror followed by utter disgust on Martha's face. It was as if I'd just confessed to being a child-killer, or something equally heinous. And now this text from her demanding that she and Willow meet you.'

'Is it a demand?' queried Ellis. 'Or have you turned her request into something more unfriendly? And isn't it better that they want to meet me? We always knew this moment would come.'

She gave his chest a small playful thump. 'Do you have to be so reasonable?'

He smiled. 'Would it help if I wasn't?'

'Enormously so. It would make me feel I have every right to be thrumming with an excess of righteous indignation!'

Laughing, he kissed her. 'How about we put all that thrumming energy to better use and go for a walk, followed by an early supper at the pub?'

'Is this us going public?' she asked.

'Why not? You said that once the girls knew about us, then we could tell people here in the village.'

'Are you sure it's what you really want?'

'I'm one hundred per cent sure. And just to allay your fears, I'm not going to behave like a lovestruck teenager intent on snogging you in front of everyone.'

She shuddered. 'What an appalling thought.'

'I wouldn't say it's that appalling,' he said, 'me wanting to kiss you.'

'Sorry, that wasn't quite what I meant.'

'I know. I also know how to behave as a gentleman. So how about it? Shall we give the village something to talk about?'

'First things first, I need to reply to Martha, and that means finding a day when we're both free and then we have to decide where to meet.'

'I'll fit in with whatever is convenient with you. Why don't you suggest Martha hosts the get-together, that way she'll feel in control of things? It means also we can choose when to leave if you feel we're being cross-examined a bit too aggressively.'

Naomi sighed. 'This is just what I dreaded. All this plotting and scheming and second-guessing.'

'It's only for now. Just a short-term measure to help your daughters come to terms with the realisation that their mother is a fantastically desirable woman who still wants to have some fun in her life. They'll come round; you'll see.'

'I wish I had your certainty,' she said, smiling at his description of her. 'I suspect it's not going to be as easy as you think.'

'If you want something badly enough, it's worth fighting for. And,' he added, 'I most assuredly will fight for you.'

The late afternoon sun had lost its warmth and so each wearing a fleece, they set out along the shoreline. There were a few day-trippers about, including a young couple with two young children and a frisky spaniel on a lead. Further along the beach, as they were about to take the path that led to Bosham, Naomi recognised the familiar outline of Jennifer Kingsbury trudging towards them. Waddling along at her side was Bentley, her overweight Labrador.

'Here we go,' said Naomi under her breath.

'Options as I see them,' said Ellis, 'turn and run, or brazen it out. What's it to be?'

For answer, she slipped her hand through his. 'Time to brazen it out.'

As the gap between them and Jennifer closed, he squeezed her hand. 'You lead,' he murmured, 'I'll follow.'

'Hello, you two,' said Jennifer, her gaze fixed firmly on their faces as though trying to ignore their hands. 'Out for a stroll?'

'That's right,' replied Naomi.

'And then supper at The Ship later,' said Ellis.

'That's nice,' said Jennifer. She somehow managed to make it sound anything but nice. But then, along with plenty of other women in the village, Jennifer had always thought so highly of Colin. On any number of fundraising committees together, the two of them had been stalwarts of the parish council, and all-round pillars of the community.

In private, Colin had often made fun of Jennifer, referring to her as one of his groupies. He'd never had any trouble twisting people, particularly women, around his little finger to do his bidding. Even a notoriously indomitable woman like Jennifer, who had no time for smooth-tongued charmers. That Jennifer would be unwilling to acknowledge what was staring her in the face – Naomi and Ellis clearly holding hands and what that implied – never mind approve, came as no surprise to Naomi. This, of course, was just the start of what was to come.

With Bentley wagging his tail and looking up at Ellis, Ellis let go of Naomi's hand and bent to stroke the top of the dog's head. It was then that Jennifer's expression changed. Her lips stretched into a wide smile and she gave Naomi an incongruous wink.

A wink! Naomi would have been less shocked if Jennifer had bitten her!

Straightening up, Ellis returned his hand to hold Naomi's again.

'Well then,' Jennifer said briskly. 'Enjoy your evening together.' Giving Bentley's lead a small tug, she continued on her way. She had only gone a few steps when she called back over her shoulder. 'About time the pair of you stopped skulking around and came clean. Good luck to you, I say!'

'I told you, didn't I?' said Ellis when they had walked on and were out of Jennifer's hearing. 'I knew we must have given ourselves away.'

'I wonder who else knows?'

'Who cares!' he exclaimed happily. Catching her up in his arms, he swung her round to face him and hugged her. 'Who cares what anybody thinks?'

His delight was infectious, and she found herself laughing. Maybe everything was going to be all right after all.

Her optimism was short-lived. Later that evening, when they were back from the pub having run the gauntlet of curious stares from a handful of locals, and they were sitting companionably in the sitting room with a glass of wine watching a repeat of *Endeavour*, the telephone rang. Naomi went to answer it and was, once more, taken by surprise. It was her oldest friend, Geraldine.

'Now then,' Geraldine said after a cursory attempt at small talk, 'just when were you going to tell me about this boyfriend of yours?'

'Goodness, how on earth do you know about him?'

'How do you think? Martha called me.'

'And I suppose as her godmother and honorary aunt, she felt the need to confide in you, and in turn you would then talk some sense into me? Am I right?'

'More or less.'

'So what precisely did she tell you?'

'That you've been secretly carrying on with some chap who's renting the house next door to you.'

'How marvellously sensational you make it sound.'

'You don't deny it?'

'Certainly not. And if you're about to ask why I didn't tell you, I felt it was nobody's business but my own until I was ready to tell anyone about him.'

'How very unlike you you sound.'

'And maybe that's the point. I want to be a new and different me.'

'Martha also said you'd had some kind of a makeover.'

'Heavens, hold the press, I had my hair restyled and bought a new dress!'

'All symptoms of something more profound going on.'

'It's called not wanting to be considered merely a widow anymore. You have no idea how draining that is.'

'But I still don't understand why you didn't tell me. Fair enough you didn't want to upset the girls by appearing to replace Colin so soon, but why keep me, your oldest and closest friend, in the dark?'

'Because I wanted something that was entirely my own. And if I'm really honest, I got a kick out of the secrecy. Which I don't expect you to understand.'

'No, I don't think I do.'

'And did Martha tell you that she had decided it was time for me to downsize to some poky little place on her doorstep so I can be a handy babysitter when the time comes? Did she? I don't know why she doesn't just find me a care home, or better still, an undertaker and have done with it!' The heated dismay in her voice spilled over. She was suddenly furious that she was having to justify and defend herself to her oldest friend.

'Now you're just being hysterical,' said Geraldine. 'But really, would it be such a bad idea to downsize and be nearer Martha and Tom?'

'If your daughter were treating you this way, how would you react?'

Geraldine had the grace to laugh. 'I'd tell Hilary to sling her hook and to hire an au pair if she was after cheap childcare! But never mind all that. Tell me something about this man.'

'Didn't Martha tell you his name?'

'No she didn't, I had to end the call before she reached that point in her tale as I had somebody knocking at the door. Why? Is it somebody I know?'

Naomi closed her eyes and took a deep breath. 'It's Ellis.'

There was a long pause, and then: 'Are you telling me you're seeing Ellis Ashton?'

'I am, and I feel exactly the same for him now as I did all those years ago.'

'Do the girls know anything of your history?'

'No. And it will remain that way.'

'Yes,' said Geraldine, 'I would imagine that would be best.'

Chapter Thirteen

Willow was frantic with worry. Cedric had been missing for over a week now and Simon and Lucy were due home any day and what on earth was she going to tell them? She certainly couldn't tell them the truth, that when she returned from seeing Martha to discuss The Mum Situation one of the cats was missing. She hunted everywhere in the house for him with Sirius following her. Rick couldn't say with any certainty when he'd last seen Cedric, but he did admit to leaving the front door ajar when he'd come back from trying the new gym.

'It was open for no more than a few seconds,' he told her, 'while I fetched in my gym bag which I'd left in the boot of the car.'

His admission had brought her out in a cold sweat. It was the Golden Rule, as laid down by Simon and Lucy, that under no circumstances was the front or back door to be left open if the cats weren't safely shut inside a room in the house.

'Sorry,' he'd said. 'I didn't think a few seconds would matter. But when you think about it, it's a bit cruel to keep a pair of moggies locked up and deny them the chance to be outside enjoying what they do best, killing birds and mice.'

Willow had tried to explain that they weren't ordinary cats;

they were special Siamese cats that had cost her friends a lot of money. And that was quite apart from the sentimental attachment they had to Cedric and Sirius.

'They couldn't be that attached if they left them for months on end to go off travelling around the world,' Rick had argued.

'But they trusted me to take good care of the cats in their absence,' Willow had said, close to tears, 'and I promised no harm would come to them.'

'Then you shouldn't have gone off to your sister and left me in charge of them. Especially when I'm allergic to the blighters.'

She hadn't expected that from him, but maybe he was right. If only she had put her sister off as he'd suggested and gone to the gym with him, she wouldn't be in the mess she was now. And in point of fact, it hadn't done much good spending the afternoon with Martha, because all her sister had done was complain about Mum lying to them. All that moaning she'd been forced to listen to and then the shock of discovering Cedric was missing. She'd had better days.

Since then she had trawled the neighbourhood looking for Cedric, knocking on doors and collaring people in the street to ask if they'd seen a Siamese cat. Nobody had. He had completely disappeared.

'I think we have to face facts,' Rick said now as she sat at the kitchen table following another fruitless search. 'Without any experience in roaming the streets, Cedric will have been run over almost immediately. Do you know if he was chipped?'

'Yes, he was. Both cats were.'

'Then I suppose there's a chance you might hear something from a vet.'

'But it would be Simon and Lucy who the vet would contact, not me. Oh, what am I going to do?' she said miserably.

'We'll tell them the truth,' he said, crouching down in front of her, 'that it was my fault by leaving the door open.'

'No,' she said, 'that won't do. Cedric was my responsibility; I can't let you take the blame.'

Taking her hands in his, he raised them to his lips and kissed them. 'I had no idea you were such a brave little stoic. But the good news is that you'll be leaving here very soon and coming to live with me where you won't have any cats to worry about. You'll just have me to worry about,' he added with a smile. 'And I think you'll agree, I'm much better housetrained than a cat. No hairs on the furniture and no litter tray to deal with.'

Thinking how tidy he was, that even when he cooked a meal, he never made a mess in the kitchen, she managed a small smile in return. 'You know what really marks you out from all other men I've dated?'

He feigned a look of shock. 'My God, you mean I'm not the first man in your life?'

Shaking her head, she said, 'I'm afraid not.'

'But tell me what marks me out as special then?'

'You never ever leave the loo seat up.'

He laughed. 'What can I say? Other than that must make me perfect.'

'Perhaps it does,' she said, marvelling at how handsome he was and that she still couldn't believe he cared for her the way he did.

'No perhaps about it,' he said. 'Which means that together we make the perfect couple.'

Pushing Cedric and her friends from her mind, and flinging her arms around Rick, she kissed him. 'Thank you,' she said.

He looked at her, surprised. 'What for?'

'For . . . for everything.'

'Which reminds me, I have something for you. A small present.'

She frowned. 'You can't keep spoiling me with presents.'

'But I like giving you things. Would you deny me that pleasure?'

'No, but I feel guilty that you keep buying me so many lovely gifts when I can't afford to return the gesture.'

'I promise you that doesn't bother me at all.' Getting to his feet, he left her alone in the kitchen with Sirius eying her balefully. *'What have you done with Cedric?'* his unblinking, reproachful gaze seemed to say.

'Here it is,' said Rick when he was back with her.

She took the prettily wrapped box from him. For a crazy moment she had wondered, just as she had that night at the restaurant when he'd asked her to move in with him, if he was about to give her a ring. But judging from the flatness of the box, she ruled that out, and with a degree of relief. It was a thought she didn't want to explore too deeply.

'Go on, then,' he urged her.

She did as he said and pulled on the ribbon that held the wrapping paper in place. When she had the box open, she saw that he had given her a necklace.

'It's beautiful,' she murmured, taking in the fineness of the gold chain and exquisite little four-leaf clover pendant, also in gold.

'Do you like it?' he asked.

'Rick, I love it, it's so pretty.'

'Just like you. Here, let me put it on you.'

Scooping up her hair for him, he put the chain around her neck. He then turned her round to face him. 'Perfect,' he said. 'Just as I imagined it would look on. And the four-leaf clover is to bring us luck.' He smiled. 'Not that we need it.'

'Everybody needs luck,' she said. She more than most, with the prospect of telling Simon and Lucy about Cedric.

Chapter Fourteen

In the bathroom and out of the shower, Tom dried himself with a towel, then wiped the mirror above the vanity unit so he could see his face in order to trim his beard. Even though it didn't really need it. It was a delaying tactic. A way to put off getting into bed and what awaited him there.

He knew he wasn't the first man to feel that the fun had been systematically drained out of having sex in the pursuit of creating a baby, but he wasn't proud of himself for feeling this way. He secretly longed for the days when a shag was just a shag. When lust could spring from nowhere and be satiated spontaneously and with passion. When he and Martha could lose themselves in the moment and without a care in the world. Other than for her to make sure she took that small pill every morning that would stop the careless creation of an unwanted child.

Whatever exhaustion or negative emotions he might feel at the rigorous and wholly unerotic nature of their current sex life, he was determined not to let it show. He had to keep in mind what they were trying to achieve. It would all be worth it in the end. He just hoped it would happen this month. If they failed this time round, he knew the next step – the only logical next step – was for them to seek medical help.

According to what Martha said, and what he'd read online, most couples would have already spoken to a doctor by now. Tom didn't normally drag his feet, he was like Martha in that respect, but in this instance, it was all wrapped up in his fear that he might fail Martha. Common sense told him that he might well be firing on all cylinders just fine, and it could be Martha's body that was at the heart of the problem, but if that was the case then he wouldn't be able to bear seeing how much that would distress her. If there was a bullet to be taken, he would sooner be the one who took it as he felt sure he would be able to cope with it better than Martha. She was one of the strongest and most clear-thinking people he knew, but he worried that she wouldn't be able to accept a diagnosis of that order objectively. He knew it would eat away at her.

Irrational behaviour was not something Martha went in for, that was more Willow's territory, but there was no getting away from it, Martha's response to her mother's news had made her behave irrationally. Her reaction far exceeded anything he might have expected. Not that he had previously put any thought into what would happen if his mother-in-law did announce that she had met somebody, perhaps because he hadn't thought she ever would; she seemed so quietly content with life post Colin.

Colin had always struck Tom as being at the centre of the Miller family; the lynchpin. That was how Martha had regarded him, that much was true. Another man in Tom's position might have imagined that he would partially fill the gap in the family left by Colin's death. But Tom had been astute enough to know that while Naomi had indeed occasionally turned to him for advice, it was Martha who had seen herself stepping into Colin's shoes as head of the family. For his part, Tom had been happy to play a supporting role to his wife, and to Naomi and Willow. It was recognising one's role in a marriage – and within a family – that was ultimately the key to a couple's happiness.

As far as he could see, that was what had made Naomi and Colin's marriage the success it had been; they had each carved out their roles and been happy with the arrangement. In the same way Tom had accepted that Martha hated to cook, and he loved to cook. In turn, she had never minded that he was hopeless at DIY and that she knew her way round a toolkit better than he did, thanks to her father having taught her the basics at a young age. Friends had teased him about this, but in no way did he feel emasculated by his wife's prowess with a drill and a monkey wrench. 'We all have our talents and should know our strengths and weaknesses,' he would say. As Martha would be the first to point out, she didn't know a roux from a bechamel sauce, and never planned to.

His beard trimmed, his teeth cleaned and wearing a pair of knee-length pyjama bottoms, he hung up his damp towel on the radiator and conceded that he couldn't put off going to bed any longer. It was show time.

But when he opened the door, he was greeted with Martha looking like sex was the last thing on her mind.

'Can you believe it,' she said, waving her mobile phone at him. 'Willow now says she can't make it on Saturday. She's decided that that's when she's moving in with Rick instead of meeting Mum's fancy man.'

The words 'fancy man' jarred with Tom, but he let them go. For now, the man they had yet to meet was the enemy in Martha's mind and Tom would be foolish to think otherwise.

'Can we change it to Sunday?' he asked.

'No, because Willow says she'll be sorting out her things at Rick's. Why does she always have to ruin things? Now we'll have to wait until the following weekend.'

'Well, it's just one of those things, isn't it?' he said, getting in the bed beside her. 'Or why don't we suggest an evening next week?'

'I tried that as well and Willow claims to be working the evening shift all next week.'

'Then there's nothing else for it, we have to be patient and wait for your sister to be free. It's no big deal.'

Martha frowned. 'How can you say that when it's an immensely big deal? This is my mother we're talking about, who has some strange man getting his hooks into her. Honestly, I could throttle my sister sometimes. I swear she's being deliberately awkward, putting this meeting off.'

'Why would she do that?'

'Head in the sand syndrome. If she can't see the problem, then in her mind it doesn't exist.'

'Then why don't we meet up with your mother and her chap without Willow?'

'No. I want it to be a united front, you, me and Willow. Together.'

'What about Rick?' It was a loaded question, but he'd risked it anyway.

'Hmm . . . I suppose so. I don't have much choice in the matter, do I?'

'It would be an olive branch after—'

'There's no need to say it,' Martha interrupted him. 'An olive branch to smooth over the way I spoke to him at Mum's. I get it.'

'There again,' said Tom, trying to be helpful, 'just the two of us might seem less confrontational. For your mother's sake, if nothing else,' he added, knowing full well that with or without Willow, Martha would inevitably take a confrontational stance.

Giving him no more than a sigh for an answer, she put her mobile on the bedside table and switched off her lamp. She then turned to look at him. 'According to my temperature chart, I'm at my peak fertility window.'

'Right,' he said with what he hoped was his best attempt at a smile of enthusiasm, at the same time extinguishing the light from his bedside lamp. 'We'd better get down to business then.'

'I'm not sure I can,' she said in the dark when they were both lying down, their faces almost touching. 'Not with worrying about Mum and—'

Hearing the unhappiness in her voice, he hushed her with a kiss. 'Leave it to me,' he said, wanting desperately to give her the one thing he knew she so badly wanted. If he could do that, then maybe it would take her mind off worrying about her mother having a boyfriend. She might even learn to be pleased for her.

*

It was almost midnight and with Rick fast asleep in bed, Willow had locked herself in the bathroom.

She was in a state of shock, unable to believe what she was seeing. There had to be a mistake. This couldn't be happening. It really couldn't. The kit had to be faulty. Or more likely, she had done something wrong.

But even as she tried to convince herself that she couldn't be pregnant, she pieced together her suspicions and the reasons she had bought the kit in the first place – two missed periods and a definite urge to throw up in the last few days.

Only a few days ago her biggest worry was breaking the awful news to Simon and Lucy that Cedric was missing. Now this!

But how? How could it have happened? She was never careless about these things. *Never!* And what on earth would Rick say if he knew? More worryingly, what about her sister, what would Martha say if she guessed?

It had been bad enough earlier this evening when Martha had been sounding off at her on the phone because Willow couldn't make it down to see Mum at the weekend as that was when she was moving in with Rick. But if Martha knew that Willow had been careless enough to get pregnant when she and Tom had been trying all these months to conceive, she would be doubly annoyed with her. Not just annoyed, but upset. Very upset.

Which meant there was nothing else for it, Willow had to keep her pregnancy a secret. It would give her time to think. But what was there to think about? She couldn't keep the baby, could she? No way could she take care of a child when she was so useless at behaving like a responsible adult. A responsible adult who had proper savings and a pension plan and ISAs fully topped up. All she had, apart from the trust Dad had left her, was a bank account that fluctuated between black and red as easily as the wind changed direction.

Nobody in their right mind would trust her to raise a child.

But she wasn't alone, was she? She had Rick. Unlike her previous boyfriends, Rick was decent and dependable, and he couldn't do enough to show her how much he cared for her.

What was it he'd said about having children? She thought back to the conversation they'd had.

'I'd love to be a father.' That's what he'd said. Or something very like it.

But would he want to be one right now? The thought of telling him that she was pregnant made her stomach churn even more than it was already.

What a mess she kept making of her life. Would she never learn?

Chapter Fifteen

Ellis observed his mother's face light up at the sight of the colourful anemones Naomi had picked from her garden first thing that morning.

'They're beautiful,' Rose said, 'how kind of you. Now shall we send Ellis off to find a vase while we get to know each other?'

'No point in asking if I have any say in this, is there?' he enquired.

Both Naomi and his mother said no.

With a smile on his face, Ellis left the room to go in search of somebody who could provide a vase. It was clear that Naomi meeting Rose was going to go a lot better than when he finally met her daughters.

Once Naomi had told Martha and Willow about him, Ellis had anticipated an immediate showdown, but it seemed they couldn't organise themselves to be in the one place at the same time and so the date kept being shifted. He knew from the way his stepson behaved that this was common practice amongst the younger generations. Even with all the available technology they used, it seemed that the simple act of putting a date in a diary and sticking to it was fraught with difficulty.

Each time he tried to speak to Lucas in LA, it was never quite the right moment. 'Sorry, Dad,' he'd say, 'gotta run, I have a meeting. I'll call you later.' Sometimes he did, several days later, but often he forgot. For a while now Ellis had been trying to nail Lucas down for a proper chat, to tell him about Naomi. He wanted, out of respect for Diana, Lucas's mother, to do the thing correctly. A text or an email didn't feel right. Perhaps that was just him being old-school. Him being an old duffer.

Which ironically was the last thing he felt. He felt vibrantly alive, as though life was now overflowing with wonderful opportunities. Opportunities that he wanted to grab hold of and enjoy to the full. With Naomi.

It still didn't seem possible that their paths should have crossed the way they had. Thank God his mother had insisted she wanted to live out her last days here on the West Sussex coast. When he thought of the miraculous coincidence of choosing to rent a cottage that was slap-bang next door to where Naomi lived, he could almost believe that fate had intervened, that it was meant to be, how it had always meant to be.

He'd felt something similar at Geraldine and Brian's wedding all those years ago when, after losing touch with her, he'd spotted Naomi amongst the guests. It had been a complete fluke him actually being there in the first place; a new girlfriend had invited him to accompany her and hadn't even told him whose wedding it would be, other than to say the groom was a cousin of hers. As much as the wedding was a lasting memory for him, he couldn't remember the girl's name, but then it had been a short-lived relationship, if you could even call it that. He'd ended it the next day in fact.

It wasn't until the marriage service was over and guests filed out of the church and they stood around in the wintry cold while the photographer took an age taking the required photos, that Ellis spotted Naomi beneath the extravagantly large brim of a navy-blue hat she was doing her best to hold on to in the blustery wind. From the moment he had realised who the bride was – that it was Naomi's best friend from their university days together – he'd craned his neck in the pew to see if she was there, but had drawn a blank. She later told him that she'd been seated at the front and hidden from view by a pillar.

Leaving the girl he'd come with chatting to a group of other guests, the photographer still ordering people about to have their picture taken, Ellis had gone over to say hello to Naomi. Such was his delight at seeing her again, he was tempted to approach her from behind, put his hands over her eyes and say, 'Guess who!' But he checked himself and instead approached with the words, 'Hello Naomi, long time no speak.'

'Ellis!' she'd exclaimed, 'what a surprise to see you here.'

'A good surprise, I hope.'

She smiled. 'A lovely one.'

They did the usual thing of kissing cheeks, no small feat given the size of her hat, and saying that neither of them had changed, then asking exactly how long it had been since they'd last seen each other.

'It must be five years,' she said.

'Seven,' he said.

'Really?'

'Really,' he repeated. 'And that's some hat you're wearing,' he added as a gust of wind nearly ripped it from her head and she had to hold on to it with a gloved hand.

'It was an absurd choice, especially given the weather,' she said.

'I think it's great and easily marks you out as the most strikingly beautiful woman here.' To his satisfaction he saw her blush.

'Don't let the bride hear you speak like that,' she said, 'no one is supposed to gain more attention than her.'

'And talking of the bride, I had no idea whose wedding it was until I saw the order of service and Geraldine walk up the aisle with her father.' He then explained the hows and the whys of his being there.

'Where *is* your date?' she asked.

Who cares? he wanted to say, *now that I know you're here.* He indicated over his shoulder to where he'd left her.

'She's pretty,' Naomi said, 'but then you always did pick a pretty face.'

Ignoring the comment, he said, 'It really is great seeing you again. Why didn't we ever stay in touch?'

'I suppose you graduating a year before I did meant our paths then went off in separate directions.'

'I wish they hadn't,' he said softly. 'We always had so much fun together.' A flood of memories came rushing back to him – of student parties that went on till dawn, of incomprehensible treasure hunts that involved most of them getting hopelessly lost, and of a skiing trip that ended with one of their group of friends being airlifted to hospital with a broken wrist and leg.

She smiled, but it was tainted with sadness. Or was it regret? Or was that wishful thinking on his part?

'Seeing you again makes me realise I should have made more effort to—' he broke off.

'To do what?'

'To make sure we were more than just friends,' he responded boldly.

'You never implied that was what you wanted,' she said, her voice low, her gaze sliding away from his.

'The time was never right. Either you were seeing somebody, or I was. Dare I hope that the time might be right for us now?' Again, he was being bold.

Before she had a chance to reply there came a loud voice from behind Ellis. 'Darling, so sorry to leave you in the lurch like that, but it turns out the duties of a best man are manifold. Remind me never to do it again!'

The owner of the voice was now standing next to Naomi and looking extraordinarily pleased with himself. And well he might, thought Ellis when Naomi introduced him as her husband, Colin. With her hands encased in gloves to fend off the cold, her ring finger had been hidden from him.

'Where do you fit in, then?' asked Colin, with the kind of overly firm handshake that was designed to establish the ground rules. 'Bride or groom?'

'The groom, sort of. Naomi and I are university buddies,' answered Ellis pleasantly.

'Is that so?'

'Ellis graduated the year before I did,' joined in Naomi, 'and this is the first time we've seen each other since then.'

'I think the last time we were together was the night of that fancy dress party, the one when you were dressed as Frida from Abba—'

'And you were dressed as Johnny Rotten.'

They both laughed. Just as they always used to. But a glance in Colin's direction warned Ellis that two old friends tripping down Memory Lane might not be such a good idea. Not if the proprietorial arm around Naomi's shoulder was anything to go by. The gesture was clearly made to stake out the territory. Which made Ellis wonder why. Why did this man feel threatened by an old friend chatting to his wife?

Under ordinary circumstances Ellis might not have stuck around to the end of the wedding reception, which was held in an upmarket country hotel, but on this occasion he wanted to talk some more with Naomi. He couldn't stop thinking about that look of sadness – or regret – on her face.

When the meal was over and the disco started up, he danced with the girl he'd come with. 'It's Raining Men' by the Weather Girls was followed by David Bowie's 'Let's Dance', and then Culture Club's 'Karma Chameleon'. Excusing himself, he went to find the bathroom and when he returned to the disco he saw that his date was dancing with somebody else. He then spotted Colin propping up the bar with a crowd of other men and seizing his chance, he sought out Naomi. He found her talking to the bride, Geraldine, who expressed her happily drunken surprise at the coincidence of him being there.

'It's just like old times,' she declared, 'us all being together again!'

Except it wasn't. Everything had changed.

'The dancefloor beckons,' Ellis said, extending his hand to Naomi. 'Shall we?'

She hesitated.

'Can't beat a bit of Phil Collins,' he pressed.

'Go on, Naomi,' urged Geraldine, giving her a shove. 'There's

101

no chance of Colin dancing with you, not now he and Brian have settled themselves in for the night at the bar.'

They'd just made it to the dancefloor when 'You Can't Hurry Love' segued into a drop in tempo to Stevie Wonder's 'I Just Called to Say I Love You'.

'Have you been married for long?' he asked as they came together in a careful embrace.

'Two years,' she said.

'Any children?'

She shook her head. 'Not yet.'

'In the pipeline, then?'

She didn't answer him.

'I don't like to pry, but you don't seem as happy as I remember you. Is there something wrong?'

He felt her body tense in his arms, and he took that to be a yes from her. Very gently he drew her a few inches closer to him. 'You can always talk to me,' he said, his lips close to her ear. 'It will go no further.'

When he heard a stifled sob from her, he looked over to the bar to check that Colin was still there and whispered again in Naomi's ear to follow him.

It was Naomi who led the way outside, to the garden. Picking up a lantern lit with a candle, one of many that lined the pathways, while he helped himself to an opened and abandoned bottle of Champagne, she took him to a summerhouse. She closed the doors, put the lantern on a table and reached for the bottle in his hands and took a swig. Followed by another as she sat down on a creaking wicker sofa draped with woollen blankets and a couple of large cushions. He sat down too, and taking the bottle from her, drank from it.

'It's Colin,' she said. 'He's . . . he's been unfaithful to me.'

'Is he aware that you know?'

'Yes. For some reason he felt the need to confess that he'd slept with his secretary. He's promised it meant nothing, and that it will never happen again.'

'Do you believe him?'

She shot him a look in the flickering candlelight. 'I want to.'

'It'll take time for you to learn to trust him again,' he suggested. 'Or more precisely, he needs to win back your trust.'

'You're the only person I've told.'

He was surprised. 'Haven't you told Geraldine? You used to tell her everything.'

'I couldn't have said anything to her, not when she was about to get married. She and Brian are so fond of Colin, particularly Brian. They were at school together.'

'I hope Brian's up for the challenge of being married to Geraldine,' Ellis said. 'My abiding memory of her was that she was pretty formidable.'

'She hasn't changed. Nor have you, I'm pleased to say.'

Unable to say the same of her, that he could never recall her being so weighed down with sadness, he passed the bottle back to her. It was like a game of pass the parcel.

When she'd taken another swig, bubbles frothing down her chin, she said, 'Have you ever cheated on a girlfriend?'

'No,' he answered, his hands twitching to wipe her chin.

'Me neither. But . . . '

'But what?'

'I don't think I'd better say.'

He swallowed and watched her wipe her chin with her hand. 'Perhaps not.'

103

The silence between them lengthened. 'We never once kissed when we were students, did we?' she said.

'Not that I remember,' he said lightly, his gaze on the glowing lantern. 'I'm sure I would recall it if we had.'

'I always wanted to know what it would be like,' she murmured.

He turned to look at her. 'You did? Why didn't you ever say?'

'Because as you said earlier, the time was never right for us.'

His every instinct told him that he should call a halt to their conversation, that the words they were exchanging were too loaded with want and need to lead them anywhere but regret.

But a far greater instinct made him take the bottle from her and put it on the table next to the lantern. Then tracing a hand across her cheek, he kissed her. Just as he had wanted to when they'd been students. And today when he'd spotted her hiding beneath that large brimmed hat. Funny that his desire for her had never quite left him.

They should have stopped after the first kiss, and after the second and third. But by then an unstoppable force had taken hold of them and throwing the woollen blankets on the floor, he unzipped his trousers while she removed her tights and silk underwear. The lower part of her dress fitted her so tightly he joked it was like trying to remove a surgical glove from her as he hitched it up over her thighs. He made love to her in a glorious explosion of breathless passion, not caring what the consequences would be. He didn't give a damn what Naomi's motives were for wanting to cheat on her husband with him. So what if this was her way of exacting revenge? He didn't care.

If there was a price to pay, and there usually was, so be it.

*

At the sound of a care assistant asking him if she could help him, Ellis was catapulted back to the here and now. He made his request and a vase duly found for the flowers and filled with water, he returned with it to his mother's room.

'There you are,' Rose said as he put the vase on the sideboard next to the television she seldom watched. 'We were beginning to think you'd found somebody better to chat with.'

'I was giving you time to gossip about me,' he replied.

'And don't think we haven't done just that,' said Naomi with a laugh.

About thirty minutes later, and with a small wave of her hand, Rose said, 'It's been lovely having you both here, but now I'm tired and should like to sleep. Do come again, Naomi.'

'I will. I promise.'

'I've enjoyed having somebody new to talk to.'

'Thanks for that vote of confidence, Mum,' said Ellis, going over to kiss her goodbye.

'Take Naomi somewhere nice for lunch,' she said, her head already tilting to the side as exhaustion overtook her. 'And get on with planning the rest of your lives.'

'We'll try,' he said, kissing her once more.

Chapter Sixteen

'Everything all right, Martha?'

At Jason's question, and his appearance in the doorway of her office, Martha gave a small start, which she tried to conceal by clearing her throat, and then coughing. How long had he been standing there? Probably long enough to know that she hadn't been working, that she had been staring out of the window watching a pigeon building a nest on the ledge of the office building directly opposite. The gap between the two buildings was no more than a couple of yards and Martha had often wondered how difficult it would be to lay a plank of wood from one window to the other and use it as a secret escape route. If one felt so inclined.

With Jason now stepping inside her office and plainly in the mood for one of his 'chats', she wished wholeheartedly that she could escape. Or be like her sister when she'd been little. Willow had gone through a phase of believing that if she closed her eyes, she was invisible. It had driven Martha mad because no matter how much she told Willow that she could see her, her sister refused to believe her. Even if Martha resorted to pinching her, she would somehow force herself not to react. That ability of Willow's as a young child to deny truth in favour of make-believe was an early sign that she was destined always to stick her head in the sand and refuse to face anything she found unpleasant.

A hardened realist, Martha smiled back at Jason as he sat down and waited for him to state the reason he had wandered into her office. As if she couldn't guess.

'How's the pitch going for Topolino?' he asked.

Yep, there it was.

'I don't have anything concrete right now,' she said, 'I'm just tossing a few ideas around at the moment.'

'Care to share them?'

'Well, the good thing as far as I can see is that by acting as quickly as they did, they've minimised the damage to their reputation. So that's the angle I want to pursue, the speed with which they moved to put their house in order. I'm thinking that we should definitely make a big thing about their efforts to monitor all aspects of their supply and production chain. No stone unturned, that kind of thing.'

'Sounds good,' he said, getting to his feet, 'let me know when you have anything more specific. Oh, and keep me posted on the nest-building project going on out there,' he added, throwing a look at the window.

Damn! She needed to get her act together. And fast. No more gazing out of windows and being distracted by thoughts of wishing she was pregnant.

And no more thinking about Mum and what the hell was going on with her. With any luck this imagining to be in love was just that, a trick Mum's mind was playing on her. It was probably a form of delayed shock at Dad dying so unexpectedly; a need to fill the void his death had created in her life. So maybe this was something they just needed to humour her over, let the moment run its course and then Mum would realise the mistake she had made. Or the mistake she was in danger of making. After all, she was an attractive proposition; a widow who lived in a beautiful house and who had, thanks to Dad's diligence, a sizeable financial portfolio at her disposal. But if this Ellis character was an opportunist on the lookout for a wealthy widow, he'd better think again!

All would be revealed at the weekend when they would finally meet him. Willow had at last agreed that she could spare the time to meet this coming Sunday, but had thrown a spanner in the works by saying the weather was going to be really warm and wouldn't it be so much more fun to be at Anchor House, and with the beach to enjoy, instead of being at Tom and Martha's, as she had originally planned? Rick had apparently been keen to spend the day at Mum's, too. Tom had reminded Martha of the olive branch she was supposed to be extending, so had gone along with it.

Which, to put it mildly, had thoroughly annoyed her. It still did, and with a fresh wave of annoyance flaring within in her, she forced herself to relax. Fretting, as she knew from everything she read about trying to conceive, was massively counterproductive. *Deep breaths*, she told herself, *slowly in, slowly out*. On the out breath, she stood up and went over to the window. The pigeon was busy with a mouthful of twigs, adding them to the growing nest, making it perfect for when it would contain an egg, or maybe two eggs.

Watching the conscientious bird bobbing its head up and down as it went about the business of setting up home, Martha suddenly felt tearful. The thought of that bird preparing so carefully for its offspring, and in such a precarious spot, filled her with wretchedness.

Added to the physical ache of her unhappiness was the certain knowledge that her apparent inability to become a mother was turning her into a crabby bitch. Every thought in her head was a negative thought. Worse than that, she was consumed with a need to criticise and condemn those around her. She couldn't think well of anyone. Least of all herself. It was as if she hated the world right now.

Tom had suggested that maybe they should book a few days away, a mini-break. But she couldn't raise so much as a flicker of enthusiasm for the idea. There was nowhere she felt the need to visit. Nowhere. *I just want a baby!* she had screamed inside her head as Tom proposed a few days in Florence, or maybe Venice, or what about New York, a return to where they'd got engaged in Central Park?

Now, and watching the pigeon fly off to gather more twigs, and at the thought of Tom trying so very hard to please her, to show how much he loved her, her hatred for herself multiplied. Her arms folded across her chest, she thought how vile she had been to Willow on the phone yesterday evening. She had known it the moment she'd spat out the words – 'Oh, for heaven's sake stop going on and on about Rick being such a tidy freak! Count yourself lucky he's not a slob who leaves his toenail clippings on the carpet and empty pizza boxes under the bed!'

'I wasn't going on and on,' Willow had said.

'Yes you were, and before that you were boring me senseless about the cat you'd lost and how relieved you were that Simon and Lucy weren't as upset as you'd dreaded because Lucy was pregnant and that's why they'd come home earlier than planned. Well, whoopty-doo!'

That, of course, was the real cause of her anger and frustration, hearing of somebody else's ability to conceive. Not that Willow had actually gone on about her friend being pregnant; in fact Martha had had to drag that out of her sister.

'So why did they come home earlier than expected?' she'd asked Willow, sensing her holding back on something. She always could pick up on when her sister was keeping something from her.

Eventually Willow had said that Lucy was pregnant. The way she'd said it, a sort of mumbled apologetic admission she'd rather not share, because she was worried it would upset Martha, only added to Martha's irritation. It was Willow's obvious desire not to poke at her weak spot that was the worst of it. That her sister could be so sensitive made Martha feel a hundred times worse.

Why had she forced the admission from Willow? Why couldn't she have left well alone? As their mother used to say – 'Martha, sometimes you really are your own worst enemy. You need to learn when to stop digging yourself into a hole.'

*

With Rick at work, Willow was alone in his flat still in her pyjamas. A hand playing with the gold four-leaf clover necklace he had given her, she was browsing baby clothes on her laptop.

It was a stupid thing to do, but she hadn't been able to stop herself, and the more things she looked at, the more adorable they all seemed. Initially she had only wanted to find out what might be in store for her, like when the nausea would pass. But before she knew it, she had been sucked down a black hole and was scrolling through Bugaboo prams that came with eyewatering prices, and then teeny-weeny bodysuits and sleepsuits, and the cutest wrap-over jackets. Oh, and then there were the mittens, hats, leggings and tights and funny little bibs.

But there was more to babies than a sweet sleepsuit that made a baby look like a fluffy bunny rabbit, she warned herself. There was far more to it. There was actual responsibility involved, a lifetime of responsibility and grown-up behaviour. Was she capable of that?

She reckoned she had to be about nine weeks pregnant now. She still hadn't told Rick; she just couldn't bring herself to do it. To tell him would make it real and she wasn't ready for that. The truth was, she didn't want it to be real. She wanted to kid herself that she wasn't pregnant, that she hadn't messed up so spectacularly.

The thought was always there in her head that it would simply be better to end things now, to have the problem removed and to keep her life nice and simple and worry-free. Rick need never know. It would be her secret.

Snapping shut her laptop, she rose abruptly from the black leather sofa she had occupied for the last hour and crossed the room to the kitchen. She had known before she moved in with Rick that he liked things kept tidy, but since last weekend after moving in with him, she now knew that he was practically OCD about everything being put away. He didn't like the worktops cluttered with anything more than the kettle. Once a mug, glass, plate or piece of cutlery was used, it was placed straight into the dishwasher and from there it was put in the cupboard or drawer.

Being tidy and organised didn't come naturally to Willow, but she was determined to become better at it. As Rick said, how difficult was it to put the jar of coffee away after using it? Although, what was the problem with leaving it by the kettle where you knew you were going to use it an hour later? The same for the box of teabags. But this was Rick's flat and she just needed to adjust to his way of doing things. That's what couples did. And she had to admit, his open-plan, loft-style apartment was pretty cool. It even had a narrow balcony with just room for two chairs and a small metal table. They'd eaten supper there last night, which Rick had cooked. He'd done it all himself, banning her from helping. He said she'd made too much mess the evening before to risk letting her do it again. She'd laughed and told him that that was her cunning plan all along, to get out of ever cooking for him.

Now, as she made herself a mug of instant coffee – she didn't dare use his expensive machine for fear of making a mess, or worse, breaking it – her thoughts returned to the baby she and Rick had created and which was slowly but surely growing inside her. It was, she suddenly thought, like a time bomb ticking away inside her with the potential to cause an explosion of emotions if she made it known that she was pregnant.

Just telling her sister last night that Lucy was pregnant had been bad enough; it didn't bear thinking about how Martha would react if Willow admitted that she was also pregnant. She had only herself to blame, of course. She shouldn't have said anything to Martha about being so relieved that Simon and Lucy hadn't gone mad with her over losing Cedric; it had only then led to her having to explain why.

In contrast to Willow's panicky fear of being pregnant, Simon and Lucy could not be more delighted or excited at finding themselves expecting a baby earlier than planned. She was pleased for them and such was their infectious happiness she had almost blurted out her own news. 'Guess what, but I'm pregnant as well and haven't a clue what I'm going to do!'

And wasn't that the truth.

Chapter Seventeen

From the large balcony that led off from her bedroom, Naomi watched a sailing dinghy making its way out to sea by means of its motor. There wasn't a breath of wind to be had, and in the surprisingly sultry stillness of the May morning, the puttering noise of the engine carried easily across the smooth surface of the water.

It was on such a day that Naomi, along with the girls and Tom, had gone out in Colin's boat – the *Marlow* – to scatter his ashes. They'd taken it in turns to empty the urn, and with no breeze to speak of, there'd been no danger of Colin's ashes flying back in their faces – something that always seemed to happen in films – they had quietly said their goodbyes. Afterwards, and with Tom at the helm, and with the engine running, they'd made their way round the headland to Bosham harbour and had lunch at the Anchor Bleu. By the time they'd arrived back at Tilsham, the sky had darkened, and the first heavy drops of rain began to fall. Within minutes, thunder boomed overhead and for the next hour a storm had raged. Naomi had watched the lightning fill the sky and imagined Colin, always a lover of a grand gesture, stage-managing the lowering of the final curtain on his life.

Turning away from the sea view and the memory of that day, she went inside to finish getting ready, hoping that today wouldn't end in a storm. A storm of words and emotions, that was.

They arrived together a little after midday, just as Naomi had put the finishing touch of a vase of lilac blooms on the table on the verandah and Ellis was placing an opened bottle of white wine in the wine cooler. It would have been just the sort of scene Tom and the girls would have walked in on countless times before, except it would have been their father seeing to the wine. And Naomi wouldn't be a mass of fumbling nerves. So much so, she knocked over a glass on the table in her rush to greet them, sending it crashing to the ground. In the ensuing kerfuffle as Ellis bent to help her pick up the pieces, they not only bumped heads, but managed to cut themselves on the broken glass.

It was not the relaxed way she wanted her children to meet Ellis, but it did serve as an icebreaker. So with plasters applied and drinks poured, and formal introductions now superfluous, they sat down around the table. It was then that Naomi commented on Rick not being with Willow. 'I thought he was looking forward to a day by the sea,' she said, 'a chance to get out of London.'

'He . . . erm . . . he changed his mind at the last minute,' said Willow, her gaze sliding towards her sister.

'What Willow means is that he thought it best that it was just the three of us today,' said Martha.

'Really?' said Naomi. 'Why?' She could guess exactly why but felt a disagreeable need to hear her eldest daughter explain the reason why Rick's presence had been vetoed.

'This is a family occasion, isn't it?' Martha said. 'After all, it's not every day we're invited to meet our mother's new boyfriend for the first time, is it?'

'Indeed not,' said Naomi mildly, 'and I can promise you I do not intend to put you girls through the ordeal on a regular basis.'

'It's not an ordeal, Mum,' said Willow. 'Far from it.'

Ellis smiled at Willow. 'I'm delighted to hear that,' he said. 'I just hope I can put your minds at rest and assure you that my intentions towards your mother are strictly honourable, as old-fashioned as that might sound.'

'How very disappointing,' Naomi said with an abrupt laugh, and then immediately regretted her inappropriate joke when she saw the shocked expression on Martha's face. *Oh dear*, she thought with a heavy heart when she excused herself to go and check on lunch, this was going to be even more of an uphill struggle than she'd anticipated. How on earth would she ever win Martha round?

Willow was always going to be more amenable to accepting somebody new into their midst, but Martha, so single-minded in whatever she thought or did, was a much harder proposition. It was that single-minded streak of hers that was both a strength and a weakness. Colin had been the same. By sticking resolutely to one belief, it left no room to accommodate either a change of heart, or the fact that one was wrong.

She had only been in the kitchen a short while, and was opening the oven to see if the olive and rosemary flatbreads she'd made were ready to take out, when Tom came in.

'Anything I can do to help?' he asked.

'Fancied escaping, did you?' she said. 'Or is this a previously agreed plan between the three of you?'

'Plan?' he repeated.

'Yes, the girls cross-examine Ellis on his own while you interrogate me?'

The snappish tone of her question plainly took Tom by surprise and she immediately apologised. 'I'm sorry,' she said, 'being on edge about you meeting Ellis is making me tetchy.'

'I think we're all a bit on edge.'

'Quite. But is it so bad for the three of you to imagine that I might not want to spend the rest of my life alone? That being with Ellis actually makes me happy?'

'Is that how you see things with him? Being together for . . .' his question fell away and he frowned, perhaps unsure how to go on.

Touched by his awkwardness, she said, 'You mean forever, until the day I die?'

'Lasting,' he said, his face brightening as though with relief that he had hit upon a better way of expressing himself.

'Lasting is the perfect way to describe how I feel about Ellis,' she said, and meaning it.

'Does he feel the same way about you?'

'Yes. And I can't tell you how liberating it feels.' Seeing his face colour at her admission, and sensing that he might be terrified she was about to share the unthinkable with him, that she was once again enjoying a full and active sex life, she hastily added. 'But if Martha asked you to speak to me in order to assess the state of my mind, to check that I'm still in full charge of my faculties, please do put her straight on that score.'

'Nobody in their right mind would think that you were anything but fully in charge of your faculties, Naomi.'

'Well, that's something at least,' she said, sliding the hot flatbreads onto a warmed platter. 'If you genuinely do want to

117

help, Tom, could you put that dish of hummus onto a tray, along with the little pot of olive oil and the one of rock salt, please?'

When he'd done that for her, and she'd checked on the paella on the hob, he said, 'You know that we just want you to be happy, don't you?'

'Martha doesn't give that impression. I think she'd much prefer for me to be miserable.'

He shook his head. 'That's not true at all. You know what she's like. She doesn't like change unless she's the one driving it, and you and I both know she idolised Colin, so anyone trying to replace him is going to be met with opposition.'

'It's not about replacing Colin,' Naomi said. 'It really isn't. It's about me seizing the chance for a new life.'

'Of course, but it's the perception. I can't speak for Willow, but for Martha I would say she's upset at the thought that Ellis, or any man, might eclipse her father's memory.'

Naomi sighed. 'I'm very lucky to have you as a son-in-law, Tom. You're so level-headed and sensitive to those around you.'

'It works both ways, I've always counted myself lucky to have you as my mother-in-law.'

Since they were being so open and it was just the two of them, so no danger of upsetting Martha, Naomi risked asking if there was any other reason why Martha was particularly uptight at the moment. She knew that Tom would know straight away what she was really asking.

'If you're wondering if she's pregnant, it's still what you might call a work in progress.'

'I see,' Naomi said. 'That can't be easy for either of you.'

'No,' he murmured, picking up the tray to carry outside and bringing an end to the conversation.

Adding the platter of flatbreads to the tray and picking up a jug of iced water, she said, 'Come on, let's go and rescue Ellis, heaven only knows what the girls are putting him through.'

When they stepped outside and Naomi saw the blatantly hostile expression on Martha's face her heart sank. Willow on the other hand, while playing with a pretty gold necklace around her neck, was smiling and listening to Ellis saying how much he was enjoying living in Tilsham.

'Perhaps it's because you have such excellent neighbours,' joined in Naomi.

'Or very easily charmed neighbours,' muttered Martha.

'I'll pretend I didn't hear that,' said Naomi with forced brightness, as though treating Martha's comment as a joke. 'Well, don't just sit there, you girls, help to make space on the table so Tom and I can put these things down.'

*

Throughout the meal, Martha found herself constantly cringing at her mother's over-the-top jolliness. But then hated herself for thinking so badly of her. Which only added to her annoyance that once again she was being so horribly unpleasant.

In any other situation she would probably like Ellis Ashton. He had, she couldn't deny, an easy way about him. Not pushy or trying too hard to make a good impression, just pleasantly genial as though he had nothing to prove. Except, as far as she was concerned, he had it all to prove.

Across the table, she observed him asking Willow about her job and what it entailed and found herself thinking that he had the sort of voice that caught one's attention. There was a warmth to it, a reassuring cadence that was almost hypnotic. Listening to him, she had a sudden mental picture of him being a hostage negotiator calmly talking a gunman into letting his hostages go free while handing over his weapons.

Those who had known Dad were always saying that Martha was so very like him – single-minded, clear-sighted and very determined. They were strengths and attributes she had always been proud of inheriting from her father, but what she didn't possess, and she was fully aware of this deficiency, was the ability to empathise. Mum had it, and so did Willow. Ellis probably did as well.

Tom had the capacity to be subjective, but mostly he viewed life through the same lens of objectivity as Martha did. He kept his emotions firmly out of the equation. Emotion only coloured one's perspective, was what they both believed. She had always loved that about him, that he understood the same clear-cut way of dealing with something as she did. It was why they seldom argued. They were both eminently rational. The trouble was she knew that recently she had allowed her emotions to get the better of her. It was, she was forced to accept, a throwback to being a young child when, so the family lore went, she had been a maelstrom of hot-headed emotion if she couldn't get her way.

Her teenage years had been full of angst and frustration that life seemed to be moving at what she saw as an infuriatingly slow pace. She had been in such a hurry to be an adult, and once she was, the world suddenly changed and she underwent a transformation, realising that her energy could be put to better use by keeping her emotions firmly under control. That was what was meant by being a grown-up, the ability to think logically and objectively. In contrast, Willow had always seemed to want to remain a child and view life accordingly.

Hearing Ellis now replying to something Tom had just asked him, Martha was once again drawn to the mellifluous sound of his voice, accompanied now by a burst of birdsong from the nearby lilac tree. She wondered how much of that persuasive voice of his he'd used to sweet-talk his way into Mum's life? And now into Willow's by the looks of things. Perhaps, she thought, stealing a look in Tom's direction, him too.

But smooth voice or not, how could Mum think it was right to replace Dad so soon? It was an insult to all those years of marriage. How could that be swept away so easily? Did they count for nothing? And why the hell did Mum have to look so gooey-eyed whenever she looked at Ellis? When had she ever looked like that before?

She certainly wasn't behaving like the woman Martha knew as Mum. This was a stranger sitting with them. An imposter who kept fiddling with her hair and smiling for no real reason. If Dad were here now, he probably wouldn't even recognise her.

Tearing off another piece of flatbread and dipping it into the dish of hummus, and hearing a lull in the conversation, Martha decided it was time she spoke. 'So, Ellis,' she began, 'tell us how you and Mum first met.' There were dozens of questions she wanted to ask Ellis, but this was as good a one as any to start with in getting to the bottom of just who he was and exactly where he had sprung from.

'I told you before how we met,' Naomi said with a small unnecessary laugh. 'It was aeons ago when we were students at university.'

'Yes, but *how* did you meet? And were you just friends? Or,' she added with heavy emphasis, 'more than friends?'

Chapter Eighteen

'All I'm saying is that somebody has to get to the bottom of things,' said Martha. 'I can't put my finger on it, but there's something that just doesn't add up. It's not so much what Mum and Ellis say as what they *don't* say.'

They were on their way back to Tom and Martha's, where Willow would then catch a train into London. It had felt like a long and tiring day for her and, too weary to respond to her sister, she stared out of the car window in the early evening light at the cow parsley that spilled over the narrow road that was taking them away from Tilsham. As a child, and if Mum was driving – she always drove at a slower speed than Dad – Willow would lean as far as she could from the car window to touch the hedgerow. She had loved the sensation of her hand brushing against the frothy flower heads. Although one day she was stung by a bee. Martha had told her how stupid she'd been and told her off for effectively killing the bee by making it sting her and then causing its death. Her sister, of course, never did anything as thoughtless or careless. That was Willow's speciality. She slid a hand down to her stomach to where proof of her latest act of folly resided.

It had taken a huge amount of effort throughout the day to

act as though she didn't have a care in the world. She didn't think she'd fooled her mother entirely though.

'You look a bit peaky,' Mum had commented when they'd had a few moments alone in the garden. Willow loved the fact that her mother had used the word peaky. Was she the only person in the known universe still to use that word?

'Funny you should ask, Mum,' Willow had wanted to say, *'I'm about nine weeks peaky.'*

What she actually said was something vague about having not slept well the night before. Which was true. Just as she and Rick were getting ready for bed he had told her that he'd decided not to go with her to Mum's. He'd explained that he felt uncomfortable at the prospect of being around Martha. 'I don't want to antagonise her any more than I have already,' he'd said. 'For the sake of your relationship I think it would be better for me to avoid her for the time being.'

Willow had tried to make him change his mind and come with her, but he'd been adamant. She hated knowing that he was so hurt by the way Martha had spoken to him and really she should take her sister to task for it. But the thought of getting into an all-out barney with Martha just didn't appeal.

According to a personality test Willow had once completed online, she was a Class 1 People-Pleaser. Which meant, so the test informed her, she would go to extreme lengths to avoid conflict. She would also rarely say what she genuinely felt for fear of causing offence.

But she had been honest when she'd told her mother that she thought Ellis seemed nice. There again, maybe she'd only said what she had because instinctively she wanted to please her mother and make her happy.

From the front of the car, Martha said, 'I'm going to give Auntie Geraldine another call when we get home.'

'Why?'

This was from Tom.

Switching her gaze from the passing hedgerows that were now giving way to suburban housing, Willow shifted position so she could see Tom's eyes in the rear-view mirror. She wanted to try and read his expression.

'Because I guarantee Geraldine will be able to shed some light on our mysterious Ellis Ashton,' answered Martha. 'He and Mum said that he was at Geraldine and Brian's wedding, so why have we never heard of him before? And why have we never heard his name mentioned by either Mum or her oldest friend who both, it turns out, knew Ellis at university?'

'There must be plenty of people they knew back then whose names have never cropped up in conversation with you and Willow,' said Tom.

It sounded perfectly plausible to Willow. But not to Martha.

'It seems to me that I'm the only one really looking out for Mum,' she asserted. 'And I stand by what I said earlier, that I strongly believe we're not being told the whole story. Call it a sixth sense if you like, but I swear they both became very shifty when I pressed the point on how well they knew each other. Did you see the way Mum looked at Ellis when he started to answer my question? It instantly made him go quiet.'

Privately Willow thought anyone, even the most innocent of people, would look shifty if they had Martha cross-examining them. 'I think we should give Ellis a chance to prove himself,' she suggested. 'What do you think, Tom?' Willow knew she was putting him on the spot, but if anyone could rein in Martha it would be Tom.

'Perhaps a quick word with Geraldine might be a good idea,' he said diplomatically. 'I can't see that it would do any harm.'

So long as Mum didn't hear about it, thought Willow.

'What if he asks Mum to marry him? Have you thought what that would mean for us?'

Willow inwardly groaned. Would Martha ever be quiet? 'That we'd have a stepfather?' she offered with impulsive flippancy.

'You'd be happy with that, would you? Happy too for him to have Anchor House if anything happened to Mum?'

'Hey, let's not get carried away, Martha,' said Tom. 'I can't see Naomi rushing into marriage. She's much too sensible for that.'

There was a huff of exhalation from the front passenger seat, which Willow interpreted as dissatisfaction at Tom's reasonableness. And very likely the idea that Mum was much too sensible to consider marrying Ellis.

After a lengthy silence, and just as Willow was closing her eyes to sleep, Martha said, 'I wish now that I'd acted sooner. If I'd suggested that Mum sell Anchor House to move nearer us immediately after Dad died, or during those months of the coronavirus, she would never have met Ellis again.'

Willow hadn't ever believed that Martha could persuade their mother to fall in step with her plans to move from Anchor House, not yet at any rate. But now that Willow was in the position she was – *nine weeks peaky* – she could see the attraction, if she did decide to keep the baby, of having Mum closer to hand.

'You never know,' said Tom, 'if your mother and Ellis do plan on making things more permanent, they might want to live somewhere new for them both so that Ellis isn't living in your father's shadow.'

'Yes,' agreed Willow. 'And if that's the case, maybe then we could encourage them to move nearer the pair of us. Somewhere in between us for instance.'

'You've changed your tune,' said Martha.

'I'm just trying to see things with a fresh perspective,' Willow said lightly, noticing that her hand had once again strayed unconsciously to rest against her stomach.

She noticed too at the very same moment that Tom was looking at her in the rear-view mirror. Immediately she lowered her hand to her lap in case he read anything into the gesture and guessed her secret. If he did, he would be sure to tell Martha and then heaven only knew what would happen.

Chapter Nineteen

Unable to sleep that night, her mind restless with replaying all the excruciatingly awkward moments experienced that day – yesterday, as it was now – with Tom and the girls, Naomi was downstairs waiting for the kettle to boil. It was gone three o'clock, another hour or so and the dawn chorus would start up.

She made herself a mug of tea and opening the cupboard where she kept the tin of chocolate biscuits, she took one out. Then another for good measure. She was in need of something comfortingly indulgent, and calories, as everyone knew, as she liked to joke, didn't count when consumed in the night or in the garden. She sat in the old rocking chair to one side of the Aga – the chair which had belonged to her grandmother, then her mother, and now her. Who, she wondered, of her two daughters would have it when the time came? Would Martha feel the chair should be hers because she was the eldest, but would Willow actually want it for sentimental reasons as opposed to a sense of entitlement?

With sudden wistfulness, she thought of all those times she had nursed the girls as newborns in this chair, then gently rocked them off to sleep. Maybe because she was the second child, Willow had been the easiest of the two to feed and settle.

She never woke up crochety or cried with angry, face-crunching intent. She was, as the visiting midwife once said, a dream of a baby. A dream of a baby who grew into a sunny-natured dreamer who was happy to drift along like a feather carried on the breeze.

While Colin had despaired of what he considered to be Willow's airy-fairy-ness and lack of direction, Naomi had instead cherished what she regarded as their youngest daughter's innate goodness. But she wondered now if that had been a mistake on her part. Had she shielded Willow too much from the real world, made her incapable of fighting for her place in it? There had been something slightly off-key about Willow yesterday. She had seemed tired and occasionally absent from the conversation around the table. More airy-fairy-ness, Colin would have said with a roll of his eyes.

In contrast to her sister's sweet nature as a baby, Martha had emerged from the womb with her fists flailing, ready to take on the world. Yet as Martha grew older, and for all her toughness and outward confidence, Naomi glimpsed a softer and more vulnerable child doing her best not to lose face or ever show weakness. From such a young age, and with Colin championing her, Martha had set her sights so high. But had that also been a mistake? Had it put too much pressure on her?

Children were so precious and parenthood so very precarious. Did anyone ever think they had got it right one hundred per cent?

Taking a sip from her mug of tea, Naomi recalled with fond nostalgia her daughters in all the various incarnations of their lives. In the semi-darkness, she saw their childhood shadows dancing around the kitchen. She heard their cries of delight as she unveiled the birthday cakes she'd made for them, their cries when they were hurt and their howls of indignation at some unfairness or other. She heard their laughter too when Colin played a practical joke on them. One of their favourite games when they'd been small was for him to adopt the role of the giant in *Jack and the Beanstalk*. For such a large man he had been surprisingly light on his feet and they never heard him creeping up on them, not until he was practically on top of them and they were shrieking with giddy terror at the words *Fee-fi-fo-fum, I smell the blood of a little-un*, which was his spin on the classic line.

She drank some more of her tea, took a bite of biscuit and switched her thoughts back to yesterday, in particular to when everybody had gone, and Ellis was helping her with the clearing up. They had planned for him to stay the night with her, but she'd suddenly had a change of heart and told him that it had been an exhausting day and if he didn't mind, she'd prefer to be alone. What she didn't say was that she needed time on her own to think. Time to convince herself that she was doing the right thing, that she hadn't rushed into things with Ellis.

If he had been disappointed by her request, he hadn't shown it. He'd kissed her goodnight and said that he understood. But did he? And was he right when he said that Martha and Willow just needed to adjust to the idea of him?

Or would there be, as she feared, too great a price to pay in loving Ellis? But hadn't she paid enough already? Had she made the sacrifice she had all those years ago only now to risk losing what she held most dear, her children's love?

For the greater part of her adult life she had hidden her real emotions beneath an impenetrable layer of calm acceptance that enabled her to keep the ship – her family – on an even keel. How fitting that Anchor House was their home, a place that was safely tethered to weather the storms of everyday family life. Perhaps it made her sound too pliant, but was that such a bad thing, to be the one who ensured Anchor House was their safe harbour, their one true constant?

It still dismayed Naomi that Martha had been so overbearingly adamant that the time had come for her to sell the family home. Of course she accepted quite readily that one day she would be too old to manage such a large house on her own, but that was far off in the future, and besides, who said she would live the rest of her life alone? But then just like her father had been, Martha was a great planner; she liked to have every i dotted and every t crossed, all eventualities covered. But life was not like that, and as that old saying went, while mankind planned, God laughed.

She dunked the last quarter of biscuit into her tea, then popped it into her mouth, thinking that there were myriad moments that changed or defined a life. Some were definitely more significant than others.

For her, the day of Geraldine and Brian's wedding would forever stand out as the one that would come to define her as a wife and mother for ever afterwards. Although it could be argued that it was Colin confessing that he'd slept with his secretary that was really the moment that defined Naomi's role in their marriage.

While the shock of his confession had torn the ground from beneath her, it was later that she wondered at his need to confess. He claimed it was because he needed to clear his conscience, that he couldn't live with the lie. Which was all very well, but had he not stopped to think of the consequences? What if

130

she had said his confession had destroyed all that she valued in their relationship and she could no longer remain married to him? Or had he calculated the risk involved and assumed that her capacity for forgiveness would mitigate his crime?

What he could not have factored into his thinking was Ellis showing up at Geraldine's wedding just days after he had sat Naomi down, taken her hands in his, admitted the awful thing he had done and then asked for her forgiveness. Appalled and sickened, she could barely bring herself to look at him, much less forgive him and had insisted that he sleep in the spare room.

For her friend's sake – having bought at the last minute the largest hat she could find to hide beneath – she had squared her shoulders, put on a united front with Colin and had smiled her way through Geraldine and Brian's wedding, just wanting it to be over.

But then Ellis had spotted her, and a collision course was set in motion and she had behaved in a way she would never have dreamt possible.

There was so much she shouldn't have done that day. She shouldn't have felt so pathetically sorry for herself and responded to Ellis in the way she had. She shouldn't have used him in order to hurt Colin, to pay him back for hurting her. *See, Colin,* she wanted to scream in his face as she kissed Ellis, *this is how it hurts.* But it hadn't hurt as Ellis had poured himself into her and her body had writhed in ecstasy beneath his in an explosion of angry desire.

Oh, it had been heady stuff! There on the floor of that summerhouse, for one euphoric beautiful moment, she had never felt more out of control, yet at the same time so utterly in control.

What she had thought would be a one-off moment of mad

revenge proved to be no such thing. She met Ellis twice more in the week that followed, taking an extended lunch break to meet him in a hotel that was equidistant from their offices in London, where he was now working after a stint in Manchester. Afterwards she would return to work with his scent on her, fuelling her desire for the next time she would see him, the next time when his touch would ignite her.

She may well have lost her head, but she hadn't lost her conscience entirely. With Colin still banished to the spare room, she would wake in the middle of the night full of remorse. This was not her. This was not the woman she thought she would ever be. Duplicitous. Revengeful. Reckless.

She came to her senses when a few days later she realised her period was now three weeks late. In all the emotional turmoil of the last week or so she had lost track of her dates, but when she checked her diary, she calculated she must have been pregnant before Colin's confession. The knowledge that she was pregnant made her accept that she could no longer behave like a spoilt child getting her own back on Colin. They were now going to be parents; it was time put away childish things.

The only person who had an inkling as to what had gone on between her and Ellis was Geraldine. She had seen them slipping away into the darkness the night of her wedding reception, and then spotted them later furtively rejoining the party inside. She claimed that there had been an unmistakable look of guilt about them when they reappeared, a look that shouted from the rooftops that they'd just had sex. Whether or not that was true, Colin had been too drunk to notice anything different about Naomi.

Geraldine didn't let on that she had guessed what had taken

place between Naomi and Ellis until she and Brian were back from their honeymoon. By then Naomi had explained to Ellis the reason why they must never see each other again.

'Are you sure the baby is Colin's and not mine?' he had immediately asked, and she'd explained why there could be no doubt.

'Trust me, Ellis,' she'd said, 'it can't be yours; the timing is wrong.'

The conversation had taken place on the telephone and she'd been deliberately and uncharacteristically brutal, telling him that it had been nothing more than a selfish act of revenge, her sleeping with him.

'I don't believe you,' he'd said. 'Yes, the night of the wedding that might have been true, but not in the days since. That was real between us.'

'You're wrong. None of it was real. We were both playing a part. Me the wronged wife, and you the—'

'No,' he said softly, 'don't go on. Please don't twist or denigrate what this last week has meant to me. Or what I hoped it might lead to.'

'Then, please, if that's true, if you really care about me, let it end now. Let me get on with repairing my marriage. Because it's the right thing to do. You're a decent man, Ellis, so I know you'll respect my decision.'

It said a lot about him that he did. She never saw him again, not until that day on the beach back in February.

Now, in the kitchen at Anchor House, and as the sky began to lighten and the first of the birds started to sing, Naomi feared that once again she might be forced to make a tough decision.

Would she have to put her children and their happiness before her own, or was there a way to have both?

Chapter Twenty

In the week since she'd been down at Mum's with Tom and Martha, Willow had been suffering with terrible morning sickness. Which was making it almost impossible for her to keep Rick from knowing she was pregnant.

Wiping her mouth after only just making it to the bathroom in time, she sat on the edge of the bath and pressed a cold flannel to her face. Her stomach still churning, she felt light-headed and drained of all energy. Why did women willingly put themselves through this? Not just once, but again and again.

'You going to be in there much longer?'

She started at the impatient tone to Rick's question the other side of the door and the forcefulness of the handle being jiggled. Thank goodness she'd locked herself in.

'Nearly done,' she said. No sooner were the words out than her stomach roiled and a gagging reflex had her leaping from the edge of the bath to bend over the loo again.

There was no disguising the awful retching sound she was making and once she'd stopped, there was Rick's voice again. 'Are you okay, Willow?'

'I think I must have picked up some sort of bug,' she murmured, when she reluctantly unlocked the door.

'What kind of bug?' he asked, staring at her. He had a strange unreadable way of looking at her sometimes, which in her current state thoroughly unnerved her.

She shrugged. 'The kind that makes you throw up,' she said, trying to sound as though it was no big deal.

The strength of his gaze intensified, then it moved to take in the inside of the bathroom as though she were hiding something in there. 'Are you sure about that?'

Don't tell him, she told herself. *Don't tell him, don't tell him, don't tell him!*

'I'm pregnant,' she blurted out. And then she burst into tears. Not just a pretty little wobble of a tearful weep, but a full-blown shoulder-heaving snorting wail of a sob.

With surprisingly gentle hands, he led her to his bedroom – she hadn't yet been able to think of it as theirs – and sat her down on the bed. Despite her wailing, she noticed he had already made it, the duvet perfectly smooth, the pillows invitingly plumped and neatly placed. She felt guilty sitting on the bed and messing it up.

Crouching in front of her in his work suit, he dabbed at her eyes with a tissue. She then pulled one from the box he'd put on the bed next to her and blew her nose, while he reached for the wastepaper basket for her to put the used tissues in.

'Why are you so upset?' he asked, his voice so laden with concern it made her want to start crying all over again.

'Because I'm not ready to be a mother,' she said. She blinked and looked away. 'Maybe I never will be. And . . . and I was frightened what you might say.'

'Frightened?' he repeated, his hands now placed on her knees. 'Why?'

She turned to look at him. 'Because it's an accident; it's not something we'd planned, and it's much too soon. We don't know if we're going to stay together, I mean we've only—'

'Hush,' he said firmly. 'You mustn't get yourself all worked up, it won't be good for the baby.'

But now the cat was out of the bag, she felt horribly worked up and wanted to scream and shout at the unfairness of it all. Why did bad things keep happening to her? She'd give anything to jump up from the bed and run. To run and run all the way to . . . To where precisely? *Anywhere!* Just somewhere she could hide and make this mess go away. 'But I don't know what to do,' she said in a choked voice.

'What do you mean? You're not thinking of getting rid of the baby, are you?'

'Do we want a baby?' she asked, not answering him. 'Do *you* want one? A real baby, not some hypothetical one-day-in-the-future baby. This is happening *now*.'

'Hey, I meant what I said when I told you I wanted a family, so I think this is wonderful news. I couldn't be happier.'

She looked at him doubtfully. 'You know that babies are very untidy, don't you? Within no time your immaculate flat will be turned into a tip. You'll hate it.' She was remembering all the times he'd tutted or sighed at some mess she'd made, or because she'd forgotten to put something away. How would he ever cope with the clutter that came with a baby? She didn't know that much about them, but she did know they came with a crazy amount of stuff – clothes, nappies, bottles, blankets, toys, prams and cots.

But he simply laughed at her question. 'Ours will be the tidiest baby ever!'

Not if she or he takes after me, Willow thought miserably.

The pressure of Rick's hands on her knees increased. He said, 'I can see that you've been worrying yourself sick how I would react, but you have to trust me when I say that I have never felt surer about a thing in my life.'

She frowned, thinking that she had never felt less sure about a thing in her life. It was all her fault, too. She should have carried on taking the pill, even though it had started to mess up her cycle and make her feel unwell at times. Rick had said it was probably because she had been taking it for so many years and he'd urged her to take a break from it, and then try a new one at a later date. Meanwhile he had taken care of matters, and as was so typical of him, he'd been very thorough in that department, never taking a risk. But somehow, one of his sneaky sperm must have made a break for it and escaped.

As if reading her mind, he said, 'No contraceptive device is one hundred per cent safe, Willow. We'll just have to chalk this up to one of those things. A happy accident,' he added with a smile. 'By the way, how many weeks do you think you are?'

'About ten.'

'As much as that and you didn't tell me before now?'

She swallowed. 'I was waiting for the right time to tell you.'

'Have you been to see a doctor yet?'

She shook her head.

'Well then, we'll need to put that right. But for now, I need to go to work, I have an important conference call. Why don't we eat out to celebrate this evening?'

'I'm on the evening shift again,' she said.

'Ring in and cancel. Tell them you've picked up a bug.' He

moved his hands from her knees to her stomach. 'Our Little Bug,' he said happily, 'that's what we'll call him or her from now on.'

He was standing up when she thought of something. 'Rick,' she said, 'we need to keep this a secret between us for now.'

He frowned. 'Why?'

On her feet too, she said, 'Because I don't want my sister to know I'm pregnant when she's not.'

His frown deepened. 'Look, you're going to have to sort this with your family. You can't always be pandering to Martha and worrying about her feelings. Ask yourself this, would she do the same for you?'

'Perhaps not, but that doesn't mean I shouldn't—'

'You need to put yourself first, Willow,' he interrupted her. 'No more letting your sister bully you.'

'She doesn't bully me.'

He scoffed at that. 'She does it all the time. She can't stop herself, and it really upsets me to see you always kowtowing to her. Didn't you say she was just like your father?'

'Well yes, but what's that got to do with anything?'

'Over lunch that day last month when Martha was bossing your mother about telling her she should sell Anchor House, your mother said that she wasn't to bully her like your father had.'

Willow had forgotten Mum had made that comment. 'Dad was just Dad,' she said, 'he was used to giving out orders at work and did it at home. It was no more than a habit with him.'

'That's as maybe, but understand this, I'm not going to stand by and let Martha dictate how you, or more to the point, how *we* live our lives. I gave her a pass when you had your last family get-together to meet your mum's new boyfriend by not going with you, but I won't be doing that on a regular basis.

138

Especially not now that I'm going to be father of your mother's first grandchild. It's time somebody stood up to your sister, and for you as well, Willow.'

'Okay, but can we just keep me being pregnant between us for a bit longer?' She gave him her best winning smile. 'Please?'

'How can I resist?' he said, kissing her forehead. 'Now I really have to go. And remember to cancel your evening shift, I'm taking you out for dinner and that's my final word on the subject.'

Chapter Twenty-One

Geraldine's arrival in the rain at Anchor House with a small wheelie case and a bottle of Bollinger could not have been a less welcome sight for Naomi.

'Have you been talking to Martha again?' she demanded of her oldest friend, while making no attempt to step back to let her in.

'I might have.'

'And I suppose you think a bottle of fizz is a peace offering, or some kind of sweetener to soften the argument you plan to have with me? If so, I'll warn you now, you've had a wasted journey.'

Her eyes dancing with mischievous delight, Geraldine smiled. 'My, my, what lovely big ruffled feathers you have, Grandmama. And since I don't plan to argue with you, least of all here on the doorstep for all and sundry to hear,' she tipped her head towards Waterside Cottage next door, 'why don't you stop acting like a stroppy teenager and let me in?'

Geraldine always had been the more assertive of the two of them, but just once Naomi wanted that dubious honour. 'Only if you stop acting like a bossy schoolmistress,' she said.

'But how can I when I've spent my entire working life being paid to be one?' said Geraldine with a laugh, thrusting the

Bollinger at Naomi and pushing her way inside. 'Now go and open that and let's sit in your beautiful conservatory and discuss what's put you into such a fearful mood.'

It was easier to do as her friend instructed and besides, what was the alternative, throw her out bodily? Which was physically impossible given Geraldine's size. Colin used unkindly to say that Geraldine was built like a Panzer tank and with as much subtlety to her.

The bottle open, along with a pot of stuffed olives, and Geraldine now back from the cloakroom where she had gone to freshen up, they sat in the conservatory with the rain pattering down on the glass roof above their heads.

'Why didn't you let me know you were coming?' Naomi asked her friend.

Geraldine raised her glass to her, then took a long thirsty swig. Followed by another even longer swig. 'That's better,' she said with the kind of lip-smacking relish an alcoholic might say after a period of enforced abstinence. Then: 'If I had asked if I could come and see you after visiting my sister over in Brighton, what would have been your answer?'

'I would have asked why.'

'Bingo! Because before our last chat on the telephone you would never have asked *why* I wanted to come and see you. You'd have simply asked me when and for how long and then written it on the calendar. But now you're clearly suspicious that I have a motive for wanting to visit my oldest friend.'

'Don't you?'

'Of course I do! I wanted to find out for myself what all the fuss is about.'

'Fuss which Martha is creating?'

'Partly. I hope you're going to let me meet Lover-Boy. I must say I'm curious to see him after all these years.'

'As if I could ever stop you doing something.'

'You sound so defensive. Which is usually a strong indication that you have something to hide. Has he changed much? Or is he still the handsome devil he always was? I guarantee he's aged better than Brian.' She laughed. 'But then let's face it, that wouldn't be difficult!'

'I'm afraid I'm going to disappoint you in that case,' Naomi said quietly. 'I've decided I'm going to end things with Ellis.'

Geraldine sprang forward in her seat. Had her glass not been nearly empty, she would have spilled the contents over herself. 'End it already, why?'

'It was never going to work out.'

'Says who?'

'Well, you weren't exactly full of joyful encouragement about the two of us when you knew, were you?'

'Oh, that was because I was madly jealous. I didn't want you having mind-boggingly good sex when Brian and I are such a boringly middle-aged couple we'd rather watch *Newsnight* than shag the bejeebers out of one another.'

From nowhere a bubble of laughter rose up inside Naomi and she laughed.

Her face deadpan, Geraldine said, 'I'm glad you think my dull sex life is a matter for merriment.' But then she smiled. 'So come on. Tell me all. The good bits, that is, then we'll get to why you've lost your nerve.'

'Who says I've lost my nerve?'

Geraldine tutted. 'It's written all over your frowny face. By the way, I like the hair. It's not dissimilar to how you wore it when we were students. And we'll read into that what we will,' she added with a raised eyebrow before draining her glass and holding it out to Naomi. 'Time for a top-up, followed by a rundown on Lover-Boy's sexual prowess. Oh, don't look so coy, you know jolly well you must have been bursting with hideous smugness and the raging desire to boast about what you were getting up to.'

Taking the bottle out of the cooler bucket on the table next to her, and refilling Geraldine's glass, and a more modest amount for herself, Naomi said, 'You came here with an awful lot of ready-made assumptions, didn't you.'

'Rather my stock-in-trade, I'd say. Have I made any incorrect assumptions?'

'Plenty! Firstly, you assumed incorrectly that I would want to share anything of an intimate nature with you.'

'You used to.'

'Yes. That was when we were young and silly and shared every jot and tittle. But we know better now.'

'Do we?'

'Yes. As adults, we know to respect that there are certain lines we don't cross.'

Geraldine shrugged. 'Can't say I've ever respected these so-called lines. I've always been honest with you.'

Yes, thought Naomi, *much too honest at times*. Geraldine had always prided herself on her robust frankness, which didn't necessarily go down well with everybody. She had once told Naomi that she had put on weight and that it didn't suit her. Naomi had been mortified, but without retaliating – by saying that was rich coming from Geraldine! – she had lost the weight and resumed her usual size ten and consequently received compliments from other friends on how well she looked. That was the mark of a true best friend, Naomi had concluded, the one person in the world who could be relied upon to speak the truth.

But in her current frame of mind, she wasn't entirely sure she wanted to be on the receiving end of Geraldine's particular brand of home truths. Last week she had gone for a walk with Ellis along the beach as far as the dunes and asked him if he'd really meant it when he'd said that if she thought they'd rushed into things, he would understand and give her some space. With sudden wariness in his eyes, he'd said of course he had.

'It's your family, isn't it?' he'd gone on. 'You're upset by their reaction to me?'

'Yes,' she'd replied. 'I don't want to be pushed into making a choice between you and the girls.'

'But you mustn't let them convince you that you have to choose.'

'It's not that, it's about considering their feelings.'

'In that case, I'll give you some space to work out exactly what it is you want.'

On returning home, he'd kissed her goodbye at her garden gate, and that was the last she'd seen of him. There had been no phone calls and no text messages. The ones she particularly missed were those when she woke in the morning when he hadn't actually spent the night with her. She missed those times in bed together too. But mostly she missed the companionship of him; the easy unconscious way they fitted together. How often did two people fit together as well as that? Did she really want to give that up?

'You know, I always wondered about you and Colin,' Geraldine said, rising from her chair and going to look out at the sodden garden through the rain and salt-streaked glass.

Roused from her thoughts, Naomi said, 'What do you mean you always wondered about us?'

Geraldine spun round. Her movements were brusque and sudden, there was no elegant finesse to her. There never had been. 'No marriage is perfect,' she said, 'but how would you sum up yours with Colin?'

'Where on earth has that question come from?'

'From a lifetime's friendship, that's where. So what's your answer?'

'I'm going to take a stab at you already thinking you know what the answer is?'

'I know what the glib answer would be, but as to the real one, I'm not so sure you're brave enough to say it out loud.'

'Are any of us? How would you sum up yours?'

'Oh, that's easy. Brian and I irritate the hell out of each other, and we bicker constantly. It's a habit, of course, and one we'll never break. It's part of the fabric of our relationship and has, if you will, seeped into the bricks and mortar and the very foundations of our marriage. It cements us together. Of course, it helps that he does what he's told, and I never complain about the amount of time he spends on the golf course or the hours he spends watching the wretched game on TV.'

It was interesting that after all this time, Geraldine should ask about her marriage to Colin. Why now? And more to the point, why had her friend never broached the subject when nothing else was off limits to her? 'You just said that there have been no lines between us that you felt you couldn't cross,' Naomi said.

Geraldine drank from her glass. 'I lied,' she said. 'There was always one non-negotiable line which I felt I had to respect:

your marriage.' Resuming her seat, she went on. 'You and Colin never bickered, did you?'

'No,' Naomi said. 'But then I'm not the bickering sort.'

'Too accommodating, that's why,' she said, helping herself to a stuffed olive from the dish on the coffee table in front of her. 'Although when you opened the door to me earlier, you were fair spoiling for an all-out fight, never mind a good-natured bicker.'

'True,' said Naomi with a smile.

'There must have been times when you felt like giving Colin a piece of your mind. I know I did. Brian too.'

Taken aback, Naomi said, 'Really?'

Her friend looked at her. 'Gloves off time?'

'Heavens, you mean you've been wearing a pair?'

Another olive eaten, Geraldine said, 'Colin was great. Life and soul. Never a dull moment. Always ready to lend a hand. Always quick to lead from the front. A dynamo of a man who never knowingly undersold himself.'

'That last bit sounds awfully like a criticism.'

'It was meant to be.'

Uncomfortable with the way the conversation was going, and thinking that she might actually prefer to be interrogated about Ellis, Naomi said, 'Are you sure you want to take this any further?'

'Oh, I think it's high time I did. You see, if I'm brutally honest I tolerated Colin because he was your husband. If I had known him in any other guise, I would have given him short shrift.' She raised a hand. 'No, no, hear me out. I need to say this, and I believe very strongly you need to hear it.'

'It doesn't sound like I have any choice.'

'He was overbearing,' her friend continued as though

Naomi hadn't spoken, 'and horribly patronising, especially towards you. I had to bite my tongue every time I heard him put you down. Oh, he didn't make it obvious that he was putting you down, but it was there in all sorts of little ways. He'd comment on a new dress you'd bought and say something like "Are you sure that colour suits you?" Or he'd—'

'Isn't that exactly what you'd say?' Naomi interrupted.

'No. I'd come right out and say the colour didn't suit you and give you the reason why. And do you remember that evening we were with you a few days after your first wedding anniversary, and the soufflé you'd made didn't rise? I've never forgotten how he tutted and cracked a joke about it being such a let-down and that he'd better give you a bicycle pump for the next time you attempted to make one.'

'It was a joke,' Naomi said, surprised that Geraldine should remember such a small detail from so long ago.

Her friend shook her head. 'You didn't see his face when you left the room, or hear what he said about you. I swear I could have slapped him. Even Brian commented on it when we drove home afterwards.'

'What did he say?'

'That he hoped the rest of marriage to you wouldn't be such a let-down. I was furious and was about to say something when Brian caught my eye and made a joke about you probably hoping the same thing about Colin.'

Naomi swallowed. 'All these years on and you remember that evening in such detail?' The only memory she had was her embarrassment at producing something so inedible.

'Wouldn't you, if Brian had said something like that about me?'

'Yes,' she said quietly. 'Yes, I would.' Unable to meet her

friend's gaze, Naomi looked at the small bookcase to her right, which she had stripped and painted many times over, depending on how the mood took her. It was currently a deep shade of teal with burnished copper accents. On the middle shelf was a framed photograph of Colin and the girls, his arms around their shoulders as he knelt between them.

Naomi could remember taking the picture, it was when Martha and Willow were ten and seven, and when they were happy to pose for the camera, their open grinning faces full of carefree joy, and not yet burdened with the adolescent need to hide from the camera.

As happy as they looked, Naomi also remembered the ugly row that followed. Colin had insisted that he take the girls out in the boat. Willow hadn't wanted to go; the poor girl was not a natural sailor, but Colin had brooked no argument. The only way Willow would go was if Naomi went too. They sailed out of the harbour towards West Wittering and not long after, the wind had sprung up, sending white horses racing across the surface of the churning water. Martha had been exhilarated, sensing adventure, and maybe danger too. But Willow had clung to Naomi, petrified that the *Marlow* would capsize. It really wasn't that rough, but to a young child with a vivid imagination who regularly suffered nightmares after watching anything with a hint of tension to it on the television, the thought that a huge wave could smash the boat to matchwood was all too possible, if not inevitable. It didn't help that she suffered from seasickness and long before they'd reached the safety of Tilsham Harbour, she had thrown up, and not over the side of the boat, as Colin instructed, but in it.

Colin made no attempt to conceal his anger, even saying that Willow should be made to clean up the mess. When Naomi said that wasn't going to happen, that she was taking Willow straight home to put her in the bath, he had been furious. Somehow, he'd contained his anger and unleashed it later when he arrived back at Anchor House, having cleaned the boat himself. He'd let rip, claiming, amongst many things, that Naomi pandered to Willow.

'She'll never learn to grow up if you keep treating her as a baby!' he'd shouted. 'It's your fault she's such a timid thing, you selfishly refuse to let her go so she can be more adventurous like Martha.'

'You can't expect her to be just like Martha, they're chalk and cheese,' Naomi had told him.

'And whose fault is that?' he'd demanded.

He'd been deaf to any form of reason, unable to accept that his youngest daughter could not live up to his expectations.

His vehement accusations made Naomi wonder if perhaps she was holding Willow back, that subconsciously she wanted to keep her youngest daughter as her forever-baby. The truth was, she had treated Willow differently to Martha. Just as Colin had treated Martha differently to Willow. Parents always liked to think they treated their children identically and with equal fairness, but rarely was that true.

'Brian and I knew that Colin had a temper,' said Geraldine, breaking into her thoughts. 'That he was one of those men who had to work at controlling it. You know, it probably drove him crazy that you didn't ever lose your temper with him. I bet he would have liked you doing that, if only so he could justify losing control.'

'You're making him sound like a monster,' said Naomi.

'Your words, not mine,' said Geraldine with a shrug. Then as nonchalantly as though asking what time it was, she said, 'Did Colin ever hit you?'

Chapter Twenty-Two

Ellis had spent a large part of his working life moving from one posting to another and as a consequence, he had any number of acquaintances, many of whom were scattered around the world, either still working, or now retired like himself. His close friends, though, he could count on the fingers of one hand, which was probably true of a lot of people. It was also true that since Diana's death he had not stayed in touch with them as well as he should have.

Right now, as he lay in the sand dunes, despite the slight dampness from yesterday's rain, his eyes closed against the brightness of the sun in the untainted blue sky, he thought how he would value chatting with one of those close friends. But what to say? 'Hi! You haven't heard from me in ages, but any chance I can bend your ear about something?'

He'd tried speaking to Lucas, at last nailing him down for a proper chat, but it turned out that Lucas was full of his own news. He'd just been promoted to a more senior level at work and his new role, so he told Ellis, would require him to travel to Europe. 'London is on the cards in the not too distant future,' he'd said, 'so I'll be able to come and see you and Gran.' Ellis was pleased for him, really pleased, but there was no getting a word in edgeways. Moreover, he hadn't wanted to bring the conversation down by offloading his own problems onto Lucas.

Problem, singular, that was.

Naomi.

He saw now why she had been so keen to keep their relationship secret. Hadn't she warned him that the moment they told anyone, specifically her daughters, everything would change, and not for the better?

But it was nonsense her thinking she had to make a choice, that it was either him, or her family. It was no more than an overreaction to a less than enthusiastic response to a mother having somebody new in her life. All children would be the same, instantly on their guard to protect their mother, or their father for that matter.

Although that wasn't strictly true. Lucas had never regarded Ellis as a threat to his relationship with his mother, but then he had been a small boy when Ellis and Diana had met, and perhaps therefore more amenable to the idea of having a new father. Had Lucas been a teenager it might have been a different story.

But really, what could Martha and Willow have against their mother being happy? Could they not understand that they were making her *un*happy by being resistant to change?

Ellis had readily agreed to give Naomi the time and space she claimed she needed, but he realised now that he hadn't meant it. He had merely said what he knew she wanted him to say, thereby portraying himself as being as patient and accommodating as she wanted him to be. But it turned out he was neither of those things. He was impatient to move forward, to put their relationship on a more permanent footing. He knew just how fragile life could be – as should Naomi – and he didn't want to lose this unexpected chance of happiness. The thing was, you could reach an age when you thought the best years of your life were behind you, then from nowhere you realise something so amazing it stops you in your tracks. And that something was that actually the best is yet to come.

Marriage. That was what he'd had in mind as he and Naomi had walked along the beach together when he'd last seen her, more than a week ago. He'd been on the verge of telling her he loved her and wanted to ask her to be his wife. He had even pictured them going ring-shopping together and planning for the future. He'd had it all falling into place in his head. Until that moment when she'd said she didn't want to be forced into making a choice between him or her daughters.

Would he be better off walking away now, before he wasted any more time hoping for Naomi to reach the decision he wanted her to? She had pushed him away once before; what was to stop her doing it a second time?

No, that wasn't fair. She had been pregnant with Colin's child and had acted selflessly and for what she saw as the best. From everything Naomi had shared with him, she had not regretted the decision, or more importantly doubted her certainty that Colin was the father. Ellis hadn't doubted her certainty either, because he knew she wouldn't betray him so cruelly, she just wasn't the sort. And now, having seen photographs at Anchor House of Colin and Martha the similarity between father and daughter was unmistakable.

As hard as it had been to walk away from Naomi all those years ago, he hadn't spent the rest of his days nursing a broken heart. He'd thrown himself into many a relationship afterwards, but nothing of any substance until he'd met Diana.

At the sudden loud and ugly cry of a seagull overhead, he opened his eyes and sat up. The tide was coming in, creeping inexorably towards him. Back the way he'd come, along the sweep of shoreline, he could see the mudflats had all but disappeared, the wading birds now gone.

Would he be gone one day too? Why would he stay if Naomi chose her family over him? The trouble was he liked it here. He felt at home in this small harbour village and enjoyed being part of the community that had been so welcoming; he felt it was somewhere he could put down roots. He also enjoyed having the sea on his doorstep, something he'd never experienced before. There was a reassuring constancy about the watery beauty of the shoreline and horizon beyond, and he often marvelled how little, in essence, it must have changed since the days when the Romans set up camp at nearby Fishbourne Palace.

The rental agreement on Waterside Cottage was only for six months and would be due for renewal before too long. Whatever Naomi's decision was, he would soon have one of his own to make. To stay or not to stay.

Chapter Twenty-Three

Martha hadn't heard from either her mother or sister since going down to Anchor House well over a week ago. She had texted and left messages on their voicemails but had received nothing in return. She was sure they were both deliberately avoiding her. Or was that conviction fuelled by guilt, or even paranoia on her part?

Their mother wasn't the sort to hold a grudge, nor was Willow for that matter, but Martha thought it very likely that in this instance Mum might still be annoyed with her for cross-examining Ellis the way she had. But to Martha it had been perfectly reasonable to ask the questions she had; she just knew it was what her father would want her to do. With a sad smile of remembrance, she thought of him interrogating every boyfriend she'd ever brought home. Not that there were that many. Tom had won her father's immediate approval though and had bonded over a beer and game of rugby on the telly.

Through the kitchen window and in the evening sun, Martha watched Tom out in the garden as he rode the sit-on mower he'd treated himself to this spring. It was his favourite new toy and she'd joked with him that one of these days he might just let her have a go on it. Not that she was that keen to mow the lawn, she was more than happy for him to do that job. Her task this evening was to cook supper. It was something easy – steaks with jacket potatoes and a watercress salad.

She wished her day had been as easy. With Jason away dealing with an existing client, she'd given her pitch to Topolino and had been painfully aware that it had lacked pizazz. She'd rolled out the usual spiel that a brand is a promise to a customer that their product and service was of the highest quality, before moving onto the nub of the matter, which was essentially an act of reparation in the form of a one-way-door offer. For an indefinite period of time, Topolino would pledge themselves to a scheme whereby for every babygrow they sold here one would be given to a child living in poverty in Bangladesh.

Judging by their restrained response – a restraint that was practically suffocating – she sensed she had blown it and when the meeting was over, she had disappeared to her office, shut her door and kicked her desk. Channelling Jason, she had kicked it three times for good measure.

With everything for supper now prepared, the potatoes pricked and in the oven, she tried ringing Willow again. The phone rang and rang and just as Martha was about to give up, she heard a voice that most definitely wasn't Willow's. Assuming she had somehow rung the wrong number, she was all set to end the call when the voice in her ear said, 'Is that Martha?'

'Yes,' she replied cautiously. 'Who's that?'

'It's Rick.'

'Oh,' she said, 'is Willow there?'

'No,' he replied.

Martha waited for him to expand on that, but when he didn't, she asked if he knew where her sister was and when she would be able to speak to her.

'She's working,' he said.

Not liking the abruptness to Rick's voice, and guessing he was still cross with her for excluding him from what she'd considered family business, she tried to placate him by keeping her voice light. 'I suppose Willow dashed out and forgot to take her mobile, then?'

'Something like that,' he said flatly. 'Was there anything else?'

Wow, he really was cross with her, wasn't he? 'Er . . . yes,' she said, reluctantly acknowledging that maybe she should make more of an effort to put things right between them. 'I think I might have inadvertently offended you, Rick.'

There was a pause before he responded. 'You think, or you *know* that you inadvertently offended me?'

'Okay,' she said, waving back at Tom as he waved to her from the garden on the mower. 'I know that I was rude that day at my mother's.'

'If it was only then, it wouldn't matter. But you keep doing it.'

Now it was her turn to pause before answering. 'Doing what?' she asked.

'Deliberately excluding me. Is it because you don't like me?'

The directness of his question left her momentarily grappling for something to say. Not so long ago she would never have believed he would be asking her this, or that she would find herself having to lie. 'Of course I like you,' she said. 'I think you're great for Willow. You're just the kind of boyfriend she needs.'

'You have a strange way of showing that.'

'I'm sorry if that's how you feel,' she said.

'It's not me you should apologise to, it's your sister. This time you've really upset her.'

This time? Martha bridled at his tone and his accusation. But at the same time, she had to accept that there was doubtless an element of truth in what he'd said. It was just a bit much hearing it from him. But it did explain why Willow wasn't returning her messages.

'And the thing is,' Rick said, just as she was about to apologise again, 'I don't want anyone upsetting Willow right now, not when she's—' He broke off.

'Go on,' she said, 'when Willow's what?'

'Forget it, I shouldn't have said anything. I promised Willow I wouldn't.'

Martha's senses were instantly on full alert. 'If there's something wrong with my sister, Rick, I think you should tell me.'

When again he didn't answer her, her concern grew. 'Willow's not ill, is she?'

There was a rustling in her ear, followed by a sigh. 'If I tell you, you have to swear you won't tell her that I told you.'

'Told me what?'

'That she's pregnant.'

Martha gripped the worktop in front of her and jammed the mobile hard against her ear. Once more Tom saw her at the window and waved, his face wreathed in a boyish smile of happy contentment in the golden sunlight. He looked so perfectly at one with the world. Whereas here, inside the kitchen, her world had just spun off its axis.

'Are you still there, Martha?' asked Rick.

'Yes,' she said faintly. 'That's . . . ' her words fell away as she fought to find the right ones.

Rick chuckled in her ear. 'I think what you're trying to say is that it's quite a surprise.' He chuckled again, shredding her nerves. 'A shock might actually be more appropriate. We're both still trying to come to terms with the idea of a baby. An actual baby! It's going to mean a lot of change for us.'

'Yes,' Martha finally managed to say. She swallowed. 'Well, I suppose I should offer you my congratulations.' She immediately regretted her choice of words.

'Yes, I *suppose* you *should*,' he said. 'But I think you ought to know the reason why Willow didn't want you to know about the baby. She was worried it would upset you; you being so desperate to have a child of your own. She really is one of the sweetest, kindest and most considerate of people. But then I don't need to tell you that.'

'No,' Martha said, 'Willow has always had a very generous and warm-hearted nature. She certainly puts me to shame.'

He made no attempt to dispute this. Instead he asked if he could pass on a message from her to Willow.

'Just tell her I called,' Martha said.

'But you will promise not to tell her that I let the cat out of the bag, won't you? I don't want to find myself in the dog-house. If that isn't too much of a mix of metaphors.'

'Of course,' she murmured, her throat tight with the weight of pain his blitheness was causing her. 'I'll wait for Willow to share her good news with me when she's ready.'

'Thanks for that. Oh, and not a word to your mother. Not yet. Let's keep this between ourselves.'

Martha agreed and ended the call.

She was halfway through a second glass of wine – not caring that it was a non-alcohol night – when Tom came in from the garden. His gaze caught on the glass in her hand. Then her face.

'You okay?' he asked.

'No,' she struggled to say. Her voice wobbled and she bit down on her lower lip. Turning away from Tom, she fought hard to stop herself from crying.

'Martha? What is it?' He crossed the kitchen and turned her round to face him.

'It's Willow,' she said, 'she's pregnant. Rick just told me.'

'Rick told you?'

Stumbling over her words, she relayed the conversation she'd had with Rick. 'He didn't mean to tell me. He said that Willow didn't want me to know, that it would upset me too much. And she's right, Tom. I feel miserable. I know I should be happy for her, but I'm not. I'm torn apart with jealousy. It should be me who's pregnant, not her! And that makes me the worst of the worst, a selfish bitch who can't be happy for her own sister. I hate myself!'

Taking the glass from her shaking hands, he took her in his arms. 'Don't speak that way about yourself. It's only natural that you're jealous. I could be wrong, but I'm guessing this wasn't planned on their part.'

'Willow's never planned anything in her life,' said Martha with a defiant sniff.

Tom released his hold on her and tipped Martha's head back so he could look at her. 'Well, that's true,' he said with a smile. 'Maybe that's been our problem; we've planned too much. Maybe we need to be more like Willow, just go with the flow.'

'You know that's never going to happen, don't you?'

His smile widened. 'It was worth a try.'

'I love you so much, Tom. Please don't ever doubt that when I'm being such a bitch.'

'I love the whole of you,' he said. 'Which means I accept at times you're not at your best. Just as I hope you love me, faults and all.'

She sank into his arms again and resting her head against his chest, she absorbed the slow and steady rhythmic beat of his heart. It had the soothing effect of slowing her own, which until then had been beating as though she were running fast.

His chin resting on the top of her head, he said, 'Did Rick sound happy about the baby?'

'Yes,' she said, recalling the sound of his laughter and how it had grated on her nerves. 'He claimed they were both in shock, but he didn't give me the impression that he was. It was almost as if he were bragging. But to be fair, my opinion might be clouded by envy,' she added. She kept to herself that her opinion of Rick was also affected by the way he had spoken to her, as though she were a naughty child who needed to be reprimanded and put in her place. Just who the hell did he think he was?

'They've been together for so little time,' Tom said. 'It will test their relationship beyond anything they can imagine. I know this is going to sound unkind of me, but do you think Willow might have done it deliberately?'

Martha tilted her head back. 'Done what deliberately?'

'Got herself pregnant to—'

'To trap Rick?' she finished for him when he hesitated.

'Yes. You and your mother have joked before about him being a keeper, that he was the first boyfriend Willow had had who was reliable and financially secure. What if she thought the same and decided a baby would be her ticket to a better life?'

Martha was shocked by Tom's suggesting something so cyni-cal, it was so unlike him. She rushed to defend her sister. 'Willow

160

doesn't have a devious bone in her body. I can't believe you'd even think such a thing.'

'I'm sorry,' he said, 'but the whole set-up just seems so improbable. The funny thing is,' he went on, 'that last time we were driving back from Anchor House, there was something about Willow that was different. I noticed several times her putting a hand to her stomach while she was talking. At the time I just thought she was feeling a bit unwell, but now it makes sense what she was really doing.'

Martha knew precisely what he meant. She too had seen friends who were pregnant do the very same thing – a hand unconsciously placed to protect their unborn child. She had even done it herself when she had hoped that she was pregnant.

Thinking back to that day at Anchor House, Martha couldn't remember there being anything particularly different about her sister, apart from her apparent change of mind when they were driving home about the possibility of their mother moving nearer to them. Willow had couched her U-turn in the context that if Mum and Ellis married, it would be better for them not to live in Dad's shadow at Anchor House.

But now Martha regarded her sister's change of stance with new understanding – Willow knew that she was pregnant and was cueing their mother up to help with future childcare. Just as Martha had been planning on doing. Maybe she had underestimated her sister. Maybe Willow was capable of planning something after all, and of being utterly devious.

Chapter Twenty-Four

Geraldine only stayed for one night, but as she herself frequently joked, a little of her went an awfully long way. Her departure yesterday afternoon had left Naomi feeling irritably unsettled. Even more out of sorts than before her friend's visit.

It wasn't that she was cross with Geraldine, it was herself with whom she was annoyed. For not being honest with her friend. If Geraldine had suspected she was lying when Naomi had said that of course Colin had never hit her – what a preposterous idea! – she'd had the grace not to push it. Instead she had turned her attention to interrogating her about Ellis. Which had been much safer ground, Naomi thought now, as she earthed up the potatoes that were pushing their way through the soil.

With her old gardening hat jammed onto her head, the noon sun in the crystalline sky was hot on her back and shoulders. It was almost the end of May and the day was one of those late spring days that shimmered with heat and the promise of summer. Occasionally a welcome breeze blew in off the sea, bringing with it a salty sharpness. Her arms were bare and really she should have changed out of this sleeveless top and put on one with long sleeves, but she'd been in too much of a hurry to get out here as soon as she'd eaten her breakfast, following another sleepless night.

Sleep had been bad enough before her friend's visit, but last night she had tossed and turned for hours on end. She should never have allowed Geraldine to rake up the past to the extent that she had. Had she put her foot down, she wouldn't now be feeling as though her life had been nothing but a sham. A sham of lies and pretence. And humiliation. She had lived with so many half-truths for so long – the myths of her own creation – she had come to believe them.

Not that she was the only one to have lived with the lies. Geraldine and Brian had evidently done so too. In all the years they'd been friends, Naomi had not once suspected what they truly thought of Colin. How many other friends had not held Colin in the high regard she had always thought they had? Had the condolences she'd received on his death been genuine, or merely yet more falsehoods prettily wrapped up in clichéd commiserations?

What she needed, she thought now, straightening up to stretch her spine, then resuming her digging, was to bury herself away. She felt such a fool. A stupid idiotic fool for believing her own lies. The lies she'd told through omission.

It would never have been Geraldine's intention to humiliate and embarrass Naomi by instigating the conversation they'd had, but that was how she felt, stripped bare of all pretence. In one fell swoop she had gone from thinking that everyone loved and respected the man to whom she'd been married, to suspecting that actually everybody knew the truth and pitied her.

Yet what exactly was the truth? That Colin hadn't been the

perfect husband everyone believed him to be? That behind closed doors, not even closed sometimes, he had been a patronising bully? Nobody was perfect, she used to tell herself; everyone had their share of faults. Hers would certainly run to a lengthy list. In her mind she pictured a dusty scroll of papyrus steadily unrolling as fault after fault was read out in a booming voice of condemnation.

Top of the list, in large bold type, would be **SELF-DECEPTION**.

She was an expert in that, having forced herself to see it as a strength, a virtue even. *For the sake of the family.* But actually, it was a sign of weakness and cowardice. Of which she wasn't proud. She would never allow her daughters to behave the way she had.

It first happened when Colin missed out on a promotion which he'd believed was his as a matter of course.

'I'm perfect for the job,' he'd said. 'Everybody reckons I'm a shoo-in.'

But when somebody was brought in from outside to do the job, and Colin then had directly to report to that person, he was furious. He arrived home from London at Anchor House that Friday evening in a foul mood. It was an understandable blow to his pride and Naomi did her best to absorb his disappointment. That's how she saw her role during that period, as a sponge to soak up the bitterness leaking from his fractured self-esteem.

His mood and temper worsened when the new man, a brash American (so Colin said) took up the position. Then one weekend, after several days of the girls being unwell with a sickness bug (they were five and two at the time), and just as Naomi had settled them in bed, Colin flipped. And over, of all things, the remote control. She came downstairs to find him hurling things around in the sitting room as he searched for it.

'This place is a sodding tip!' he shouted as he kicked over a basket of books and toys. 'Do you really think this is what I want to come home to after a stressful week at work?'

'And do you think after a week of looking after the children on my own, I need you to start behaving like a toddler having a tantrum?'

That was when his hand caught her hard on her cheek. Such was the sudden force of the blow, her head snapped back and she nearly toppled over. Shock sucked the breath out of her. Regaining her balance, she stared at him in stunned disbelief, her heart hammering in her chest.

'You hit me,' she murmured incredulously. She put her hand to her face, then looked at it and saw blood. It was coming from her mouth.

His eyes wide, his jaw slack, he stared back at her. And then he just seemed to crumple before her eyes. Suddenly he wasn't the Colin she knew; he was a small frightened boy who knew that he had just done something terrible.

She had seen his rage before when he'd shattered the screen of his laptop because it had lost a document he'd been working on, or when he'd yelled furiously down the phone at some poor devil in a call centre who wasn't dealing with a problem in the way Colin wanted. There were plenty of other occasions too when the red mist had come down – when his inner demon that he refused even to acknowledge had the better of him – but never before had he done something like this.

'I'm sorry, I'm sorry, I'm sorry!' he repeated, tears filling his eyes. 'Oh, my God, I didn't mean to do that. Forgive me, please. That's not who I am. I swear to God. It's the stress of work right now. It's—'

From upstairs came the sound of Martha calling for one of them to take her up a drink.

'I'll go,' Naomi said quietly, swallowing her shock and rubbing away any trace of blood from her face. 'You tidy up the mess you've made here.'

By the time she had dealt with Martha, and then Willow who also wanted a cup of water, Naomi had her composure fully reinstated. Downstairs, she found Colin in the kitchen hunched over the sink and staring into the darkness of the garden. Or maybe he'd been looking at the man staring back at him from his reflection in the window.

'I don't know what to say,' he said hoarsely, but without looking at her.

'Nor do I,' she replied. 'Apart from this: you must never lose your temper like that again. And never in front of the girls.'

He turned to face her. 'I swear, it won't happen ever again. You have my word.'

But it had And not just once.

Putting aside her spade and taking off her gardening hat, Naomi used her forearm to wipe the sweat from her forehead. With a dispirited sense of hopelessness, she surveyed the weed-free vegetable patch and wondered what it was all for.

The question was aimed not so much at the merit of her morning's toil, but at her life, and specifically what she had achieved in that life. Could it have been better spent if she had been honest and told the truth at all times?

And where should that honesty have started? With Colin's affair, or his temper and violence. Or with her infidelity with Ellis?

Why had she not possessed the courage to admit to the affair in the way that Colin had when he confessed that he had slept with his secretary? It could have been a simple tit-for-tat admission. See, two can play at that game!

But she hadn't done that for the simple reason she had been a coward. And worse, she hadn't wanted to relinquish her hold of the moral high ground. Remove that and she was no better than Colin.

Except she wasn't better than him and so when he occasionally lost control of his temper and lashed out at her, she accepted it as her punishment for her betrayal and the lies she told herself.

All of which made it sound as though their marriage had been unhappy. Which was far from the truth. Independently fuelled by guilt on both sides of the relationship, they had each made a huge effort to make things work. And so, swept along on the daily tide of family life, they had coexisted perfectly well, perhaps not as loving as some couples, but certainly better than a lot. If tenderness and passion and honesty were missing from their marriage, there had been an acceptance on Naomi's part that, for the sake of the children, the status quo tipped the scales in favour of staying together, of keeping up the pretence.

She never allowed herself to think of what might have been if she had responded to Colin's confession by ending their marriage on the spot and seeking a divorce. Nor did she think of what might have been if she hadn't been already pregnant with their first child when she slept with Ellis.

What tangled lives we lead, she thought as she pushed the wheelbarrow of weeds along the brick path and added them to the compost heap. Ripping off her gardening gloves, she decided she would plant the French beans when the day had cooled down, for now she needed a drink.

Some minutes later, and with a refreshing glass of orange juice in hand, she walked down to the wooden bench seat that overlooked the beach. It was some time since she had occupied the bench, afraid that Ellis might pass by and she would have to speak to him.

That was another example of her cowardice: hiding from Ellis.

He had done just as she'd asked, given her space to decide what it was she wanted. She now knew what that was, but was worried how he might react.

When she'd finished her drink, she placed the empty glass on the ground next to the bench and closed her eyes. Before long, and without meaning to, she was drifting off to sleep, the cry of seagulls and the voices of happy children playing on the beach slowly fading into the distance.

She woke from a restful sleep to the tinny sound of far-away music playing. It was the jingling siren call of 'Greensleeves' coming from the ice-cream van on the jetty in the harbour. The languid tune was so very synonymous with the long, slow days of summer.

After checking her watch, she realised she had been asleep for half an hour. Time for some lunch, she thought, getting to her feet. That was when she saw Ellis walking by and when he turned and looked at her.

Her jittery smile met his more cautious one, and in a heartbeat she knew now was the time she had to summon all her courage and tell him what she had decided.

Chapter Twenty-Five

'Martha,' Tom called out, 'it's your mother on the phone!'

Carrying the ringing mobile with Naomi's name clearly showing on the screen, he went in search of Martha. The last he'd seen of her she was back from a run and heading upstairs for a shower.

She had started going out for a run the moment she returned home from work. This had begun three weeks ago, the day after they'd learned that Willow was pregnant. Tom had suggested that they run together, but Martha had said she wanted the time to be alone so she could clear her head of work. Despite feeling the sting of her rejection, and knowing it wasn't just work she needed to clear from her head, he hadn't pushed it any further. In fact, it was probably what they both needed, an hour in the day when they could catch their breath and not think about work. Or their attempts to conceive.

Upstairs, and hearing the shower running in the bathroom, Tom wondered about answering the ringing mobile himself. The thing was, they had an understanding, just as they didn't open one another's emails or post, or read each other's texts, nor did they answer one another's mobiles. But ever since his mother's death and before that, Colin's, always at the back of

Tom's mind was the concern that the insistent ringing of a telephone signalled bad news, or some kind of emergency. Was this an emergency? Was Naomi in trouble and in need of their help?

As numerous scenes flitted through his mind, the mobile went quiet. If it was something important, he told himself, Naomi would ring again. More than likely it was a far more prosaic reason for her call, just the usual kind of family catch-up chat.

Although for the last month there had not really been any proper Miller family catch-up chats, which was in direct contrast to his own regular FaceTime calls with his sister and father. It seemed that for differing reasons, the Miller Girls – as Colin had often referred to his wife and daughters – were keeping their distance from each other. It was, Tom supposed, the combination of Willow's pregnancy which she wasn't telling anyone about and Naomi's relationship with Ellis that was putting a strain on family communications.

Tom felt sorry for Naomi. Privately he was of the opinion that if Ellis filled the void left by Colin's death and made her happy, good luck to her.

Martha didn't see it that way, of course. In her eyes, nobody was ever going to be good enough to replace her father. Which was understandable. It was anybody's guess what Willow really thought about Ellis; she was always so vague about things and could easily swap and change her views for no apparent reason. Having said that, there was nothing ambiguous about her change of heart regarding Martha's suggestion that Naomi sell Anchor House to move nearer them.

Tom was very fond of his sister-in-law; he always had been. He often felt like a protective big brother to her, and hand in hand with that was the occasional feeling of exasperation that she didn't have a clear sense of purpose to her life. But he had to applaud her thoughtfulness in wanting to keep her pregnancy from her sister; it was a typically kind gesture on her part. However, he felt less generous towards Rick for breaking the news about the baby to Martha the way he had. Had he done it deliberately to pay her back, as she believed? If so, it didn't bode well for the future for them as a family. It was a shame their opinion of Rick had altered so quickly and so dramatically. Did that say more about Tom and Martha, or Rick, he wondered?

He was still standing in their bedroom with Martha's mobile in his hand, when he realised the shower had stopped running some minutes ago. He tried to think when they'd last showered together, or more precisely, when they'd had good old-fashioned up-against-the-tiles sex in the shower and for the sole purpose of the erotic pleasure it gave, rather than the creation of a new life.

Would sex ever be like that for them again?

Despising himself for such a shallow and self-centred thought, he was about to go downstairs to start cooking supper when he heard what sounded like a yelp coming from the bathroom.

He went over to the door. 'You okay, Martha?' he asked.

When she didn't answer, and anxious she might have slipped and hurt herself, he opened the door. With her back to him, a towel wrapped around her head and another around her body, she was standing in front of the vanity unit. His gaze took in what lay on the top of it – the tell-tale ripped open packaging – and he knew straight away why she had let out a yelp. His heart went out to his wife, but at the same time he felt irrationally cross with Martha. *Stop putting yourself through this!* he wanted to shout. *Just let nature take its course.*

'Sweetheart,' he said, putting the mobile into his pocket and going over to her, 'please don't be upset.' He turned her round to face him, bracing himself for an outpouring of grief. For he knew that was what it felt like for her each month that came and went and with still no sign of a baby. To make her feel better, and although it really wasn't the step he wanted to take, he said, 'let's make an appointment tomorrow to see a specialist. We'll—'

He stopped himself short when he realised that Martha's face wasn't consumed with misery as he'd seen so many times before, but with something quite different.

She held up the white plastic stick. 'It's positive,' she said, her voice little more than a whisper, as though to say it any louder was tempting fate.

He stared at the stick and saw the line for himself.

'But I want to do a second test,' she said, before he could say anything. 'Just to be sure.'

He knew there was no point in talking her out of it. Not when he could see that she had a second kit already lined up. But deep down, he also wanted as much evidence as Martha did to prove that the first test hadn't given a false reading. That would be just too cruel. He said nothing of this, merely left Martha alone to follow the instructions and then came back into the bathroom when she said he could.

Holding hands, they waited together. It felt like a very long time since he had felt this emotionally close to Martha, as though finally she had lowered the barriers that each month of disappointment had erected between them.

'Do you suppose it's all that running you've been doing,' he said, 'it's relaxed your body?'

She shook her head. 'No, silly. We must have conceived well before I started running again.'

He smiled and checked his watch. 'Another fifty seconds,' he said. 'Oh, and I forgot to say, in all the excitement, your mother tried ringing you.' He pulled out Martha's mobile from his pocket and gave it to her.

'I'll call her later,' she said, barely looking at it. 'How long now?'

'Thirty-five seconds.'

'Will you tell her our news?' he asked, when a few more second had passed. 'Or should we wait?'

'What do you think?'

'I think we should wait.'

'For what? To be sure?'

'No,' he said, already feeling protective of the life they had created together, 'until we're beyond the risk of—'

'Don't say it,' she interrupted him. 'Please don't say anything to spoil this moment.'

'I'm sorry,' he apologised, wishing he'd kept his mouth shut. Then: 'Time's up,' he said.

Together, his arm around her shoulders now, they looked at the slender white stick and just as the first one had given a positive result, so did this one.

'We did it, Tom,' Martha said, her face wreathed in the brightest of happy smiles. 'We did it.'

'I knew we would,' he lied.

Chapter Twenty-Six

'You did what?'

'I just said. I went for a drink with a group from work after my shift; it was Stefan's birthday today.'

Rick slammed a drawer shut. They were in the kitchen and he was emptying the dishwasher, a job she should have done before setting off for work, but which she had forgotten all about. 'I don't care whose birthday it is,' he said, 'what did you drink?'

'I had just the one glass of wine,' she lied. 'One won't hurt the baby.' *Would two?*

'One might be all it takes,' he snapped. 'Is that what you want? For our child to be damaged? To be mentally impaired or deformed because you,' he swung round and jabbed the air with an accusatory finger just inches from her face, 'had *just the one glass of wine*?'

'There's no real evidence that it does any of that,' she said, doing her best to suppress a nervous giggle at the silliness of him mimicking the pitch of her voice. She could never understand why, but she often felt like laughing when Rick was in one of his moods. He seemed so childishly petulant at times; it reminded her of Martha. And her father.

Something else she didn't know with any real certainty was

if it was true what she'd just said, that there wasn't any evidence to prove that one glass of wine was harmful to the baby. But at the end of the day, it wasn't as if she was out every night getting off her head on tequila shots like she used to. Well, that was such a distant memory, she could scarcely recall it. It was as though that had been a different person. But she *had* been a different person back then; she wasn't the responsible grown-up she was now trying to be, and who was expecting a child.

The thought of that instantly sobered her up. Not that she was drunk; it would take more than two glasses of Pinot to do that. But standing here with Rick quietly fuming at her – actually, not so quietly; he was slamming cupboard doors now as he continued to empty the dishwasher – she couldn't help but feel like a slightly tiddly teenager all over again and being reprimanded by her father.

'Let me do that,' she said, wanting to please Rick, to stop him being in a bad mood. Especially when she knew she was the cause of it.

'No, you'll only put things in the wrong place like you always do.'

'You wanted me to do it before,' she said. 'So let me do the rest now.'

He whipped round. 'I said *no!* Are you deaf as well as stupid?'

'I'm sorry,' she said, stepping away from him in alarm. Then: 'I keep annoying you, don't I? Perhaps,' she added faintly, 'this wasn't such a good idea.'

He stared at her, his jaw set implacably, his gaze fixed so determinedly on her, she had to look away.

'What do you mean?' he finally asked. 'What don't you think is such a good idea?'

She swallowed. 'Living together. I just don't seem able to live up to your high standards.'

'But we're having a baby together.'

'Maybe that's a mistake too.'

Everything about him suddenly changed. The angry hardness that had been in him the moment she arrived back and he'd demanded to know where she'd been, was gone. Right before her eyes, he visibly softened, became the Rick that was kind and caring and who told her every morning before he went to work how much he loved her. The Rick who left yellow Post-its on the fridge door with baby name suggestions. The Rick who had already ordered a pram and researched which baby seat would be the safest option for their child.

'Don't ever say that,' he said, coming towards her. 'Our having a baby is the best thing ever to happen to me. The next best thing after meeting you, of course,' he added with a smile.

'But I can't do anything right in your eyes. And you called me stupid.'

He put a hand to her hair and tucked it behind her ear. 'Sometimes you do stupid things, that's all. Like not telling me where you were going after work. I was waiting for you to come home. I'd planned a special supper for us. I was worried about you.'

'But I thought you were going to the gym this evening.'

'I changed my mind. I came home early wanting to surprise you with a Thai takeaway I picked up on the way home. But you weren't here.'

'Why didn't you text me?'

'What, and have you think I was checking up on you? That's the last thing I'd want.'

She supposed there was some logic in what he'd just said, but she couldn't see it. 'Well, I'm here now,' she said brightly, and thinking how much she would enjoy some Thai food. But there was no sign of any foil cartons on the worktops, just a lingering appetising smell that was suddenly making her realise how hungry she was.

'I'm afraid I threw yours in the bin,' he said, as though picking up on her thoughts, as he so regularly seemed able to do. 'It was ruined by hanging around for you.'

'Oh,' she said, disappointed.

'Didn't you eat when you were with your friends celebrating Steven's birthday?' he asked.

'Stefan,' she said. 'And no, I didn't have anything to eat, it really was just a round of drinks we had. But not to worry, I'll make myself some toast.' If she was really careful she could do that without making too much of a mess in Rick's pristine kitchen, and winding him up further.

'Absolutely not,' he said, placing his hands around her face and kissing her forehead. 'I want you to go and run yourself a bath and while you relax, I'll rustle up something nutritious and tasty for you and the baby. That,' he went on, 'is my way of saying sorry for calling you stupid.' He tilted her head up. 'Am I forgiven?'

Relief flooding through her that he was no longer cross, she smiled. 'Yes. Am I forgiven for not telling you where I was going after work?'

'Forgiven and forgotten,' he said. 'Go on, off you go and enjoy your bath. I'll give you a shout when your supper is ready.'

'I'm so lucky,' she said later when she and Rick were lying on the sofa together. One of his hands was absently playing with her hair as they watched the latest episode of *Line of Duty*.

'Why's that?' he asked.

'No real reason,' she replied, 'I just felt like saying the words out loud.'

'You are funny,' he said.

She snuggled in closer to him. 'But then that's why you love me, isn't it?'

'If you say so.'

She could tell he wasn't really listening to her; his attention was focused on the enormous screen that took up most of the battleship-grey breeze-block wall. The TV was so large it almost felt like Steve Arnott and Kate Fleming were in the room with them. Her own attention wavering from the complexity of the plot – she'd lost her grip on it several episodes ago – she tried to imagine a baby in this freakishly tidy apartment. It was bad enough the clutter Willow had brought with her when she moved in (most of which had been shoved into a cupboard), heaven only knew what a child would do to it. She knew from friends that babies gathered stuff to them faster than a snowball rolling down a mountainside.

'I was thinking,' said Rick, his hand still winding a lock of her hair around his fingers, 'that it might be better to chuck in your job now rather than keep going until you're the size of a hot-air balloon.'

'Hey,' she said with a playful kick of her foot against his, 'who says I'm going to be the size of a hot-air balloon?'

'Okay, an inflatable dinghy.'

'Not that either!' she said.

'Seriously though, why carry on with a job which will just wear you out and which doesn't even pay that well?'

'It might not be a huge salary, but it's better than nothing,' she said. She kept to herself that she would miss the camaraderie of her work colleagues. It had been fun this evening at the pub after their shift when they'd all had a jolly good grumble about how impossible it was to reach their daily targets.

'But we have my salary,' Rick said. 'It'll easily stretch to cover us both.'

'And don't forget the baby,' she reminded him.

'How could I?' he said happily. He then pointed the remote control at the screen and paused it. 'Why not stop working and enjoy some time at home preparing for our Little Bug? You could decorate the nursery and start buying all those things we're going to need.'

'Don't you think it might be tempting fate to prepare so soon?'

He put the remote control down and put his hand to her neck. He gave the four-leaf clover necklace he'd given her a little tug. 'That's why I gave you this,' he said. 'To bring us extra luck. And didn't you just say how lucky you were?'

Thinking that sometimes luck wasn't enough, Willow was about to sit up, when he held her down.

'But it would help the odds enormously in our favour if you didn't go out drinking with your mates and keep it from me,' he said.

She frowned. 'I thought that was forgiven and forgotten?'

'I'm just reiterating the point that it was irresponsible of you, and if anything was going to tempt fate and make something go wrong, that's just the kind of thing that would. By the way, did you take your vitamin D tablet today and the folic acid supplement?'

'Yes,' she said, 'I took them both after I was sure I wasn't going to be sick again this morning.'

He stroked her cheek. 'Poor Willow,' he said. 'Hopefully you have only another couple of weeks of morning sickness to get through now.'

'It feels like an eternity,' she said before yawning hugely.

'Come on,' he said, switching off the telly. 'Time for bed. It's our big day tomorrow – ultrasound scan day!'

Alone in the bathroom while brushing her teeth, Willow wondered how she might react tomorrow morning when she saw their baby for the first time. She knew from everything she'd seen online, and from the grainy photo her friend Lucy had shown her, that at fourteen weeks, there really wasn't that much to see.

Lucy was four weeks ahead of Willow and was as pleased as punch about being pregnant. Willow still hadn't confided in her that she too was expecting. She was finding it harder and harder not to share her secret, but she'd promised herself that she would keep quiet for as long as she could in the hope that her sister might suddenly announce that she and Tom were going to be parents. To ensure she didn't accidentally blurt anything out, she had deliberately avoided responding to most of Martha's messages or phone calls. When she felt she had to reply, she kept it short and sweet.

In the last week or so there had been nothing from her sister, which was both a relief, and a concern. Was Martha okay? But to ring and ask might result in Willow blabbing that she was really sorry, and she really didn't mean to do it, but she was pregnant. She could picture the scene all too easily. More easily than imagining the small life growing inside of her.

Nobody knew better than Willow that secrets could be

a burden. Some, though, were easier to keep, not because they were insignificant, but because they were just too awful to think about. Those were the ones you could lock away so deeply you could almost kid yourself they didn't exist. Almost.

Keeping her pregnancy secret was one of the reasons why she had drunk the wine she had at the pub with Stefan and the others after work; she hadn't wanted to rouse their suspicion. Also, more than anything in the world right then, she had wanted a glass of white wine. She had practically had her tongue hanging out on the way to the pub, such was her eagerness. It would be just her luck to crave wine while pregnant and not something normal like pickled onions or coal! She smiled at the thought. Which was a mistake as frothing toothpaste then dribbled down her chin, giving her a small white beard.

Wiping her face and making sure nothing was out of place on the shelf above the basin, and that the sink wasn't speckled with toothpaste, she joined Rick, who was already in bed.

'You know what we haven't decided,' he said, 'is what we say when we're asked tomorrow if we want to know the sex of our child.'

Lucy and Simon knew they were expecting a boy and had already given him a name – Milo – but Willow wasn't convinced it was a good idea.

'I want to keep it as a surprise,' she said, sliding in beside Rick. She loved the expensive Egyptian cotton bedlinen he bought, it was so much nicer than her cheap Ikea sheets and duvet covers. He had the linen laundered every week and she could forgive him all his finicky ways for the pleasure this wonderfully extravagant luxury gave her.

'But it could be a surprise tomorrow,' he said.

She smiled indulgently at him. 'You're so excited, aren't you?'

He smiled back at her. 'Nothing wrong in that, is there?'

'Were you like this as a boy? Did you find your presents and sneakily open them before your birthday or Christmas Day?'

His face turned serious. 'No, I never did that.'

Hearing the change of tone in his voice, she said, 'You never speak of your parents, do you?'

'What's to say? I told you before that my dad died when I was sixteen and my mother two years later.'

'How did they die?' she asked.

'Why do you want to know?'

'Because I want to know more about them. And because they made you, and now you've made what would have been their grandchild.'

'Ah yes, the circle of life,' he said with what sounded like heavy irony. 'There's not much to say, other than they met, married and had me, then things went awry. My father lost his job, began drinking to drown his sorrow and shame and ended up dead in the gutter one day. I mean that literally. He stepped into the path of an oncoming car. Dead on impact. My mother never really recovered from the shock. She went to pieces and it was down to me to hold things together. You could say it forced me to grow up fast.'

'And your mother? How did she die?'

'She killed herself. I came home from university one weekend and found her dead in the bath. She'd slashed her wrists. According to the post-mortem, she must have done it the day before she knew I was coming home. That way the body wouldn't have been left to decompose for too long. It was considerate of her, don't you think? Less of a mess to deal with.'

Willow was shocked, not just at what Rick had shared with her, but by the flatness of his voice.

'I can't imagine how dreadful that must have been for you,' she said.

'No, you wouldn't be able to. Which is why I don't like talking about my parents. There's nothing to be gained from it, so please don't raise the matter again. And please don't tell your mother and sister about this, it's private. I don't want anyone else to know about it. Do you promise?'

'I promise,' she said.

As though to make it clear the conversation was over, he switched off the light.

Willow lay awake long after she'd heard his breathing slow to a steady rise and fall. How strange it was that within a few seconds she could now see Rick through completely different eyes. He was someone who had been badly hurt when young, whose family had been smashed to pieces and all he wanted, as an adult, was to recreate what he'd lost. It made sense of his obsession with keeping everything in order. Of his loving her and his happiness at being a father. She could see also why he worried about her, just as he had this evening, and why that worry had made him angry.

It reminded Willow of what Mum had explained to her once, that Dad had lost his temper the way he did at times because he too had lost his parents at a young age. Grief could do that, Mum said; it could have a lasting effect on a person, especially if they bottled it up and refused to talk about it.

Perhaps when Rick was more receptive to opening up to her about his family, Willow could help him to put it behind him. But for now, she would try harder to please him, to make him truly happy.

Chapter Twenty-Seven

'I can't believe it,' he said.

'What can't you believe?' she asked.

'That you said yes. I was convinced you'd say no.'

'Why did you ask me, then?'

Turning away from the silvery moonlight that was dancing towards them across the oscillating surface of the incoming tide, Ellis looked at Naomi. At the woman who had just agreed to marry him. One minute they had been sitting here on the sand quietly drinking Champagne to toast his sixty-fifth birthday the second the church bell had struck midnight, and the next they were on their feet and whooping like a couple of crazy teenagers. He hadn't actually meant to propose, but in a sudden moment of now-or-never madness, the words had just slipped out – *'Naomi, will you marry me?'*

'Because my heart had the better of me,' he said in answer to her question. 'Because since we started seeing each other again it's made me realise I've never been happier. And,' he added, 'it just feels right.'

'I feel the same way,' she said. 'Which was why it was so easy for me to say yes to you. But you know, another glass of Champagne and I might have been brave enough to propose to you. Or at least suggested we made things more permanent and official.' She smiled. 'Which wouldn't have been half so romantic as the way you did it.'

'All I did was blurt out the truth of my feelings. Would it have required bravery on your part to do the same?' he asked.

'I believe so,' she said with a small nod. 'Especially after the way I treated you, pushing you away because I was scared.' She shook her head. 'I turned into such a cliché and made myself thoroughly miserable into the bargain.'

His arm around her, he said, 'It was the sensible thing to do at the time, for you to ask me to step back, much as it pained me. Giving you space gave you the chance to think what you really wanted.'

'And that's to be with you,' she said quietly, her words washing over him as the tide crept ever nearer to where they were sitting.

Seated on her left, Ellis withdrew his arm from around her shoulder and reached for her hand. Since that day ten days ago at the end of May, when he had gone for a walk on the beach and spotted Naomi the other side of her garden gate on her wooden bench, she had, after sharing with him the decision she had reached, stopped wearing her wedding and engagement rings. It was a symbolic gesture that he didn't underestimate.

While sitting on the bench together that warm day, the sound of voices coming up from the beach and the screeching cry of seagulls overhead and motorboats chugging in and out of the harbour, she had apologised for shutting him out the way she had. She had then told him the truth about her marriage to Colin. He'd listened in horrified disgust, appalled at what she'd put up with.

'Whatever you do, don't pity me, or God forbid, judge me,' she'd said vehemently, when she had eventually fallen silent.

185

'After the way I cheated on Colin with you, I accepted that just like me, he was less than perfect. Then later, when the violence started, I accepted that for the sake of the children, putting up with his occasional loss of control was the price I had to pay for maintaining a stable and happy environment for them. Countless women, and men, would do the same as I did. Which doesn't make it right, I know, but I swore to myself that if he ever laid a hand on the girls, that would be it.'

Ellis wasn't an expert on the subject, but he knew enough to know that staying with an abusive partner was, in some circumstances, not an act of weakness, but of strength. Which only reinforced the opinion he'd already had of Naomi, that she was a woman of great inner strength and resilience. He hated the thought, though, that his affair with her, as brief as it had been, had made her feel that in some twisted way she deserved what Colin had done to her. Never would Ellis accept that that was right.

Holding her hand now, and stroking her finger that was indented from years of wearing the rings that had symbolised her union with Colin, Ellis said, 'If we're to be married, I'd like to buy you a ring; that's if you want to wear one. If you do, it must be a ring of your own choosing.'

'I'd sooner wear a ring of *our* choosing,' she said. 'But as lovely as your suggestion is, I think a ring can wait for the time being. We have more pressing decisions to make.'

He smiled. 'How very businesslike you sound.'

'I don't mean to be. But you said it yourself, the tenancy agreement runs out on Waterside Cottage next month, at the end of July, so how would you feel about moving in with me?'

'What about Martha and Willow; what will they think?' He knew that it troubled Naomi that his presence in her life had caused something of a rift between her and her daughters. Perhaps not a rift exactly, but certainly an upsetting of the family apple cart. He couldn't help but wonder if they might regard him differently if they knew what their father had really been like. Wouldn't they then welcome someone who would love and cherish their mother? Naomi had been adamant that she never wanted Martha and Willow to know that she had allowed Colin to do what he had, that it would undermine the very foundations of their family. But was it possible they knew anyway, if only on a subconscious level?

'I told you before,' Naomi said, breaking into his thought, 'I'm not going to let my daughters determine how I live my life. I nearly gave you up because I was worried about losing their love, which has always been the most precious of things for me, but if they love me and want the best for me, they'll come round to the fact that you and I love each other. And,' she went on after a slight pause, 'that we plan to marry.'

Staring up at the bulging moon in the inky-black sky that was studded with diamond-bright stars, Ellis hoped that was true. 'I suppose if I did move in with you,' he said, 'it would give you the opportunity to put me on a probationary trial.'

She rested her head against his shoulder. 'That works both ways, you know. You might decide that you couldn't possibly put up with my irritating habits.'

'Only one way to flush them out on both sides, in that case,' he said with a laugh.

'But how do you feel about living in the home that I shared with Colin?'

'I'm not going to ask you to sell it to pander to my finer feelings. I know how much you love Anchor House, how it's a part of you.'

'You haven't really answered my question, have you?'

'I'm very adaptable,' he said with a shrug. 'I've lived in many houses over the years; admittedly some I've liked better than others, but at the risk of sounding hopelessly corny, I'd be happy to be with you in an old caravan with a leaky roof.'

'Lord, let's hope it never comes to that!'

'I don't know,' he said, 'a caravan and the freedom to up sticks and go wherever we feel like going does have a certain appeal to it, don't you think?'

'I think that's called running away,' she said with a small laugh. 'But you know, I would never have had you down as such an old romantic.'

'I fear it's come with a receding hairline and a grizzled beard; all my edges have been softened.'

'I rather like your grizzled beard,' she said, 'it makes you look—'

'If you say it makes me look like a cuddly teddy bear, I shall throw you over my shoulder and dunk you in the sea.'

'You wouldn't dare.'

'No, I wouldn't, not when I'm now officially a year older; my back would probably give out.'

'Thinking of your birthday, I have an idea. In the morning, while I make you a birthday cake, why don't you move some of your things in from next door. How does that sound?'

'It sounds good. Especially the bit about a birthday cake. I can't remember the last time I had one made for me.'

'Then I shall bake you a cake to remember!' she said with another happy laugh. 'And guess what we should do now.'

'Go on.'

'We should go for a swim.'

'A swim, you say. In yonder actual sea just some few yards

from our feet and which is no doubt colder than the Champagne we've just drunk?'

'Yes,' she said with what sounded like a sparkle of challenging mischief in her voice. 'Just like that time when a bunch of us booked a long weekend in a holiday camp on the Norfolk coast at the end of the autumn term and we all decided that what we needed was a refreshing swim to wake us up.'

'God yes, it was bloody freezing. We must have been mad.'

'And do you remember how Andrea and Suzie kept complaining about the smell in their chalet?'

'I do. We were really mean to them because the rest of us pretended we couldn't smell anything.'

'Whereas the truth was it smelt like there was a rotting body hidden under the floorboards!'

They both laughed.

Then: 'That was the weekend I planned to ask you out,' said Ellis, 'but Stewart beat me to it.'

'And so you hooked up with Mandy instead,' said Naomi.

Ellis frowned. 'Was it Mandy?'

'It was. I remember thinking what an attractive couple you made.'

'Well, I think you and I make a much more attractive couple all these years on.'

Naomi smiled. 'So how about that swim?'

'I'm game if you are,' he said.

Within no time they had stripped off and, clasping each other's hands, they ran pell-mell into the sea. When they were fully submerged and gasping for breath at the coldness of the water, they swam to keep themselves warm. After some minutes of swimming in the still quiet, save for the lapping of waves on the shoreline, they swam towards each other. Linking her hands around Ellis's neck, Naomi kissed him. 'Thank you,' she said.

'What for?'

'For being mad enough to do this with me.'

'Happy to oblige the future Mrs Ashton. If that's how the lady would like to be addressed.'

She laughed and threw back her head with an expression of joyful abandon, the moonlight casting a silvery radiance over her face so that for a split second she resembled a glistening marble statue. 'It sounds perfectly wonderful!' she said.

And how gloriously uninhibited she was to him in that moment and how she filled him with the strongest of desire.

Kissing her throat, and then moving his mouth to just below her ear and eliciting a long drawn-out sigh, he said, 'You know that scene in *From Here to Eternity*, what do you think?'

She smiled. 'If a thing is worth doing, it's worth doing well, or not at all.'

'I'll do my best,' he said.

But acting out the roles played by Burt Lancaster and Deborah Kerr was not as easy as they thought. For a start the rushing waves got everywhere, as did the shifting sand and pebbles. And it played merry hell with Ellis's concentration, to say nothing of his staying power.

'It's no good,' he said reluctantly, 'these shoreline antics are for the young.'

So they hurriedly wriggled into their clothes and, carrying the picnic basket and empty Champagne bottle, they walked back to Anchor House, where never had the softness of a bed been more welcome.

Chapter Twenty-Eight

Once again Martha and Tom were on their way to spend the weekend at Anchor House. Their visit was timed to coincide with the annual village fête, which was invariably held in the middle of June, as it was this year. Held in Jennifer Kingsbury's beautiful manor house garden, it attracted a large crowd – not just local people, but from miles around.

As young children, Martha and Willow had loved the fête and looked forward to it with eager anticipation. Martha had particularly enjoyed the Punch and Judy show and would sit cross-legged in the front row, paying avid attention and calling out when prompted to do so. One year, much to Martha's mortification, Willow had burst into tears while all the other children had roared with laughter at Mr Punch's antics. Mum had had to scoop her up and then spend ages telling her that Mr Punch didn't really hurt Judy, that it was just a game they played. Embarrassed that her younger sister had caused such a scene, Martha had stood with her hands on her hips and tutted at Willow for being such a baby. 'There's nothing to cry about,' she'd said, 'they're only puppets, so they can't feel anything.'

The hands on her hips pose was one she had copied from their father. She used to practise in front of a mirror to get the

191

stance just right. She wanted so much to be like him, and to have the same sense of authority he possessed. From an early age, she knew that people respected her father and they always did what he asked of them.

She recalled the way she'd spoken to her sister that day, when Martha had only been about nine years old and Willow six, and as priggish as she must have sounded, her logic could not have been questioned. Would her own child be the same, she wondered? In her mind's eye, she had already skipped over the baby stage and moved straight to a child old enough to articulate a strong, cogent opinion.

Which currently was more than she herself seemed capable of. Since she'd had her pregnancy officially confirmed by her GP and had her first appointment with a midwife – she was now ten weeks – she appeared rather alarmingly to have lost touch with her ability to apply logic and reason. During the last year when her longing for a child had dominated most of her waking thoughts, her emotions had been disagreeably up and down. But there had at least been a manageable order to them; now, they were all over the place. Trying to keep track of her emotions was like herding cats.

For the most part her brain felt as though it was turning to mush and, completely out of character, she cried at the slightest thing. Last night an advert on the telly for a brand of washing detergent had reduced her to tears. Her undoing had been the sight of a small child upset because she'd spilled blackcurrant juice down her new dress shortly before her birthday party began. The girl's father had come to the rescue by using the newly improved washing detergent tablets and the closing scene showed the doe-eyed girl blowing out the candles on her cake and looking adoringly at her father. The stupid thing was, working in the industry she did, Martha knew perfectly well how the ad had been put together with one cynical aim in mind, to manipulate and exploit the target audience's emotions.

Her other problem, aside from crying at the slightest thing, was her absent-mindedness and inability to concentrate. Which put her at a distinct disadvantage in the office. She had actually left for work one morning still clutching her electric toothbrush, thinking it was her mobile.

Baby brain; that's what they called it. The official definition referred to a state of impaired memory and concentration, combined with a general lack of mental agility. It could be experienced not only during pregnancy, but after giving birth also.

On top of all that was the extreme tiredness that consumed her at times. Just the thought was enough to bring on a yawn. Not just any old yawn, but the jaw-breaking kind. Followed by another, and then another.

'Ready for bed?' asked Tom, turning to look at her with one of his gentle smiles.

'It's crazy,' she said, 'but it doesn't matter how much sleep I have, it's not enough.'

'Poor you,' he said. 'But just think, the next time we come down for the fête, we'll have the Beanie with us.'

She smiled back at him. How easily they had slipped into using the nickname Tom had come up with for their baby.

'And the Beanie will have a cousin too,' he said. 'What's the betting there'll be a new generation of Miller Girls; a mini Martha and a mini Willow?'

'Dad would have loved that,' she said.

'Yes,' agreed Tom, 'he would have. He used to say to me how

glad he was to have an ally, another man around to help even out the score, but I think deep down he was much happier having daughters.'

'I don't recall Dad ever once saying that he would have liked a son,' said Martha, before lapsing into silence once more and imagining mini versions of herself and her sister.

Having lost what she saw as her true self to the baby brain, Martha wondered if Willow was experiencing the same thing. Was she now even more forgetful? Or maybe for Willow, a baby brain was an improvement.

Martha immediately reminded herself that she had vowed not to harbour any negative thoughts this weekend – *negativity was not good for the baby.* Naturally she was reading up on how to do all she could to improve her child's chances of being born happy and healthy. There would be no harmful or destructive behaviour on her watch. To that end she was doing all the right things.

Listening to Mozart – check.

Eating the right food – check.

Singing to her baby – check.

Reading to her baby – check.

Having an optimistic and positive outlook – check. Well . . . sort of.

In truth she had yet to master being wholly positive. She had never really been what you might call a cockeyed optimist, that was much more her sister's speciality. Instead she had tended to look for problems before they happened, on the basis that she was then better equipped to deal with them when they did occur. Knowing how to deal with all eventualities was what enabled her to sleep at night; it was what kept her positive. She needed to be proactive, rather than simply go with the flow as Willow did.

So whatever jealousy or resentment Martha had harboured following Rick's admission that Willow was pregnant, she was now doing her utmost to put that behind her. All that mattered was that she and Willow were having babies at roughly the same time, and that was a sisterly joy to be shared.

Except what still rankled with Martha was Rick's voice on the phone that day. He had openly criticised her, and in a way that nobody ever had before. She hadn't told Tom the extent of what Rick had said, and maybe that was because it would mean having to admit to the possibility that Rick was right.

Another admission she was determined to keep to herself was that she wasn't looking forward to seeing Rick again today. She had gone from thinking that he was an ideal boyfriend for her sister to thinking the opposite. She didn't want a brother-in-law who was prepared to be so confrontational with her. Would he have another go at her during this weekend?

The rational answer to that was to ensure she gave him no reason to criticise her; to be, at all times, on her absolute best behaviour. She would not think the worst of anyone or anything. Which included Mum and Ellis. She was going to appear to be perfectly magnanimous about their relationship. To put up any resistance would probably only throw them closer together, whereas to accept it would allow the thing to run its course. Much like that time when Mum allowed Willow to dye her hair shocking pink during the summer holidays when she was a teenager. Dad had gone mad, but Mum had said it was better to let Willow get it out of her system.

They were only a few miles from Tilsham, passing along

lanes with verdant hedgerows and towering cow parsley, when Tom asked the question she knew he would. 'Have you decided when exactly this weekend we'll tell your mother and Willow our news?'

'This evening is still my preferred option,' she replied, 'when the fête is over and we're having supper. But who knows,' she added with a wry smile, 'I might just blurt it out.'

'I don't have a problem with that,' he said, 'and the sooner we do share our good news, the sooner Willow can admit that she's also pregnant, and then we can all relax. Do you think it's possible she might have already told your mother?'

'More than possible. Or maybe Rick has let the cat out of the bag again. He did seem excessively pleased with himself when he told me.'

'You can't blame him for that,' said Tom, 'I expect I shall sound just as smug when I tell people.'

'But remember what we decided,' she warned, 'no telling anyone at work, not for a good while yet.'

'It's okay,' he said, 'I know the drill.'

As they entered the village and saw the pretty flint-stone cottages either side of them decorated with colourful hanging baskets and bunting – a long-standing fête tradition – Martha unexpectedly experienced a shot of adrenaline course through her. She was accustomed to feeling this at work – a fight or flight response – but this was a new phenomenon for her when arriving home at Anchor House.

She reasoned that it was because she didn't really know what awaited her when they parked on the drive, and walked round to the back of the house to let themselves in. Before Dad died, she knew exactly what to expect; he'd greet her with one of his all-enveloping hugs and demand to know every scrap of her latest news. Meanwhile Mum would be chatting to Tom in a much quieter and more measured manner.

But now that didn't happen. Now it was as if Anchor House no longer really felt like home. And Mum wasn't Mum anymore. She was a stranger acting in a strange and totally unlike-Mum kind of way.

Martha had been grateful that Mum had never been one of those awful helicopter mothers who felt the need to control every aspect of her child's life. She had been much more inclined to stand back and let Martha and Willow get on with things, and without feeling they had to be constantly in touch. 'You must have your freedom,' she had frequently encouraged them. 'That's how you learn to cope in life.'

But as unfair as it might sound, Martha couldn't accept that Mum might feel the same way herself, that she now needed her own freedom to make her own mistakes and learn from them. Martha couldn't bear the thought of her mother making a fool of herself over some man she thought she loved.

The sight of Rick's BMW on the driveway – parked at an angle that made it awkward for Tom to park as neatly as he would have liked – caused Martha at once to feel less than positively towards him. And despite all her good intention, she was suddenly filled with the same sense of indignant outrage she'd experienced when Rick had taken her to task on the telephone.

Chapter Twenty-Nine

The weather, as everybody kept saying, could not be more perfect and the organisers of the Tilsham Village Fête could once again breathe a collective sigh of relief that the event wasn't going to be ruined by a downpour.

As always, Naomi was in charge of the cake stall and as soon as the vicar had declared the fête open, a rush – a veritable stampede – descended upon the heavily laden trestle tables to snap up the best baked goods. The more determined and experienced had placed themselves close by to be sure of not missing out.

For the last hour, and with occasional help from Katie Murdoch and Linsey Bales, Naomi had been so busy serving customers there had been no time for her to worry about the task that lay ahead for her that weekend – that of finding the right moment to tell Martha and Willow about her plans to marry Ellis. Their arrival this morning at Anchor House had been taken up with them settling in and having a drink before coming here to help set everything out. But later, when the distraction of the fête was gone, she would have to break the news to them.

She was aware that many people would question the very idea of marriage; why not simply live together? It was certainly an option, but she genuinely liked the thought of being married to Ellis. She wanted to make that commitment to him, just as he did to her. As he said, it just felt so right, as though they should always have been together.

Ellis was sure that Martha would insist on Naomi having a pre-nup; in fact he had suggested it was something they should arrange themselves anyway, that they should pre-empt matters.

'If we have everything buttoned down nice and tight,' he'd said, 'it will help to put Martha and Willow's minds at rest that I'm marrying you for all the right reasons and not material gain.'

With the barbershop quartet belting out a medley of songs over by the ornamental fishpond, Naomi took a handful of hot sticky coins from a young girl in exchange for a paper plate of fairy cakes wrapped in clingfilm. When the girl had gone, Naomi scanned the surrounding stalls for any sign of Martha and Willow. The last she'd seen of them was when they'd met up with some old friends from the village who, like them, were down for the weekend. As a group, they had gone in search of a drink, probably a glass of Jennifer's famously potent Pimm's which she made herself. It didn't matter how many times she was asked for the recipe, Jennifer refused to divulge the exact ingredients and quantities used. All anyone knew was that its strength was not to be underestimated.

When the barbershop quartet came to the end of their set, the tannoy system burst into life with a loud crackle and Ellis announced that there were now donkey rides available in the orchard and the tug of war to look forward to, followed by the Punch and Judy show, and the three-legged race, as well as plenty of raffle tickets on sale to buy.

'Don't miss this chance to win tickets for two for the

Chichester Festival Theatre,' he urged the crowd, 'or dinner for four at the Millstream Hotel in Bosham. There's also a jeroboam of Champagne, and who wouldn't want to win that?'

'Ellis is a very good MC, isn't he?' said Willow, who had materialised out of nowhere and on her own. She was dressed in a diaphanous maxi-length dress the colour of clotted cream, and on her feet – her toenails sparkly with pink glittery nail varnish – were diamanté flip-flops. Over her shoulder was a faded denim bag decorated with an embroidered rainbow and threaded through her blonde plaits were daisies she'd picked from the lawn at Anchor House. She looked so young, almost childlike; Naomi was reminded of all the times she had brushed Willow's hair for school in the morning.

'He wasn't at all sure about accepting the job when he was asked to do it,' she said, suddenly nostalgic for those days when the girls had been children, 'but as everyone in the village knows, nobody refuses a request from Jennifer.'

'Did he know that Dad used to do it?' Willow asked, after eating a strawberry from a small biodegradable tub in her hands – the vicar had insisted this year that they had to be as plastic-free as possible.

'Yes,' said Naomi. 'I told him. Jennifer did as well. It seemed only fair.' She kept to herself that Jennifer had joked about Ellis having an appealingly sexy come-to-bed-with-me voice that was guaranteed to seduce the punters into spending even more money than they usually did.

'So things are still going okay between you and Ellis?'

Naomi felt her face blushing like a schoolgirl at her daughter's question. 'Yes,' she said. 'More than okay. Is . . . is that a problem for you?'

'No. Or at least I don't think so. It does seem funny though, you being with a man who . . . who isn't Dad. Does everyone in the village know about the two of you now?'

Naomi gave a hesitant smile. 'I would imagine so.'

'Well,' Willow said with a sigh, 'I suppose that makes it all the more real, doesn't it?'

'You sound like you would rather it wasn't.'

'Oh, ignore me,' she said with a shrug, at the same time scooping up another strawberry and putting it in her mouth. 'I'm all over the place at the moment. Although Martha would say no change there then.'

Naomi smiled. 'You seem very much on the ball to me, darling. Where are the others?'

'I left them having a go on Bash the Rat. I think Rick and Tom were keen to have a mine's-bigger-than-yours contest. Oh, and I bumped into Finn.'

'How is he?'

'Just the same as he ever was.' She frowned. 'But if his name comes up in conversation later, best not let on to Rick that he was a boyfriend of mine though. No point in . . . well . . . you know.'

Naomi smiled. 'I shan't say a word.'

Her head tilted back, Willow sniffed the air as an appetising waft of frying onions drifted over from the hot-dog stall run by the PTA from the village school. 'Do you want me to fetch you anything to eat or drink?' she asked.

'No thanks. For now, I'll pinch one of those strawberries, if you don't mind,' Naomi said. 'By the way, have you warned Rick to go easy on Jennifer's Pimm's?'

Willow held out the tub to her. 'I tried, but he laughed at

my warning, said it would take more than a bit of pepped-up lemonade to catch him out.'

'Just as well you're staying the night, then,' Naomi said with a smile.

After serving another customer, there were just the not so attractive-looking cakes left to sell now – an overcooked fruit loaf that was as heavy as a brick and a few fairy cakes which had probably been iced and decorated by a heavy-handed child – Naomi turned back to her daughter.

'It's so lovely being here today,' Willow said as she watched a group of giggling girls walking by while licking ice-lollies. 'I love that nothing ever seems to change in Tilsham.'

There was a wistfulness to her voice, which made Naomi look at her more closely. Often when somebody spoke of enjoying a particular kind of status quo it was because it gave them a sense of stability that was missing in their life. Did Willow regret moving in with Rick? Was Willow about to do what she always did at this stage in a relationship, bail out?

'Nothing really stays the same,' Naomi said carefully, 'it might look like it does on the surface, but there are plenty of changes going on here.' It was on the tip of her tongue to say, *look at me, look how I've changed*, but she thought better of it. Instead she said, 'If the vicar has her way, there'll be no Punch and Judy next year. She thinks it's past its sell-by date and sets a bad example to children.'

'I suppose she has a point,' Willow said after a small pause. 'I never really liked it as a child. The puppets scared me.'

'I remember it made you very upset one year.'

Willow stared off into the distance, as though bringing the episode to memory. 'I expect I was just being silly,' she said. 'Dad and Martha were always telling me I was too much of a cry-baby.'

'You were no such thing. You were just more sensitive than your sister, that's all. Oh look, here come the others.'

'Anything decent left for us to eat?' asked Tom as they all gathered in front of the trestle tables. He looked with disappointment at the unappealing cakes that were left. 'I guess not,' he said, answering his own question.

'Don't worry,' said Naomi, 'I have a cake in the larder back at home which I made specially for you. It's your favourite.'

Tom's expression brightened. 'Your version of Mary Berry's chocolate cake?'

'The one and the same.' She loved to please Tom; he was one of those people whose gratitude shone out of his face.

'Is the fête always as well attended?' asked Rick.

'Yes,' replied Naomi. 'What's more, we're consistently lucky with the weather. I can't recall the last time we had rain to contend with.'

He looked about him at the assorted stalls – at the plants, books, white elephant, bottle tombola, bran tub and the numerous local artisan craft stalls. 'It must be quite the money spinner,' he remarked. 'Where do the profits go?'

'It's split evenly between the church and the village school,' Naomi answered him, just as the tannoy system crackled into life again and Ellis announced that the tug of war was about to take place.

'All are welcome to take part,' he informed the crowd. 'Ladies, don't be shy, you can have a go as well! Children too!'

Tom turned to Rick. 'How about it, Rick, are you game?'

Downing the last of his Pimm's, Rick laughed. 'Don't tell me, this is some kind of quaint initiation for a new member of the family?'

'Not at all,' said Naomi, sensing that Rick didn't much care for the idea. Maybe he was finding a humble village fête a bit too parochial. There was, she noticed, a slight air of belligerence to his manner which hadn't been there before, but perhaps that had something to do with Jennifer's lethal Pimm's. 'We've all done it in our time,' she explained. 'How about you, girls? Are you going to join in like you usually do?'

'What do you reckon, Martha,' said Willow, 'shall we? Just to show these boys what we're made of.'

With an abruptness that took Naomi completely by surprise, Rick let rip with an almighty scoff of disapproval.

'Are you out of your mind?' he demanded. 'In your condition!'

His words had the instant effect of freezing them as if in time. It was Willow who spoke first and unlocked the moment.

'You promised you wouldn't say anything!' she said. 'You *promised!*'

'Oh, what does it matter?' he said. 'We couldn't go on hiding it for very much longer, could we?'

'Hide what?' asked Naomi. Although she had a pretty good idea what the answer was.

'Willow is pregnant, Mum,' said Martha, matter-of-factly.

Willow gasped. 'You knew?'

'Yes, Willow, I knew. Rick told me weeks ago.'

Her eyes wide, Willow stared at him. 'Why? Why did you do that when I said we had to keep it a secret? Oh Rick, how could you? And how could you keep that from me?'

'Like I said, what does it really matter?'

'It matters because . . . because Martha's my sister and I didn't want her to be upset by me being pregnant and her not. I told you that! I told you that repeatedly!'

'Come on, Willow,' he said, 'see for yourself, your sister's not upset. She's happy for us. Isn't that right, Martha?'

Her heart going out to her eldest daughter, Naomi wanted to intervene, to make Rick with his blithe belligerence hold his tongue. But before she could step in, he was off again.

'The only one who is upset is you, Willow,' he asserted, 'and you know it's not good for the baby for you to be all worked up like this. Don't make a scene. People are looking.'

'I don't care!' Willow's voice had risen to a childlike squeal and Rick was right, people were glancing their way. 'You shouldn't have said anything,' she persisted. 'You really shouldn't have.'

'Willow, it's okay,' said Martha. 'I know why you didn't want me to know that you were pregnant, and that was really sweet of you, but the thing is,' she exchanged a quick glance with Tom, 'I'm pregnant too.'

'Really?'

'Really?'

Naomi's voice chimed with that of Willow's.

'Yes,' said Martha to them both.

The sisters stared at each other and in one of those moments so evocative of when they were children – when it was impossible to know whether their disagreement was going to escalate or fizzle out – they suddenly grinned and hugged each other.

Thank heavens for that, thought Naomi with relief. Then catching Tom's delighted expression, she smiled at him. 'Congratulations,' she said.

In contrast, Rick's expression was less easy to read. It was almost as though he were disappointed, which didn't make sense at all.

Chapter Thirty

When the fête was over, they all pitched in to help dismantle the stalls and tidy up Jennifer Kingsbury's garden. All the while both Rick and Tom insisted Willow and Martha left any heavy lifting to them. Afterwards, together with Mum and Ellis, they slowly meandered their way down the main street of the village back to Anchor House.

Passing the pub, and the seating area that was decorated with bunting and looked out over the harbour, Willow could see that it was packed with many who had attended the fête. Her old friend, Finn, was there too with his parents and their cute sausage dog. The pub was where Dad had always gone after the clean-up operation at Jennifer's, whereas Mum had often preferred to go home and relax in the garden with a cup of tea before cooking supper.

A group of villagers called over to Mum to join them for a drink.

'It's been a long day,' she answered with a cheery wave, 'I'm homeward bound, thank you!' She then turned to the rest of them. 'But if you'd all like to go and have a drink, don't let me stop you.'

The deliciously tantalising image of a glass of ice-cold cider and a bag of crisps popped into Willow's head, but she knew that Rick would veto it, just as he did the glass of Pimm's she'd earlier fancied. But then a sneaky thought occurred to her.

'Seeing as Martha and I can't have a proper drink,' she said, 'why don't you boys go for one; you too, Ellis?'

'That sounds like a good idea to me, Willow,' said Mum. 'You girls and I can put our feet up and enjoy a slice of that cake I made.'

'Well, I for one could murder a beer,' said Rick approvingly.

Tom and Ellis looked less keen; perhaps Tom was anxious he'd miss out on Mum's chocolate cake.

But Martha urged him to go. 'Go on,' she said, 'go and enjoy some non-baby talk. Because that's what we'll be doing for the rest of the evening.'

'Bring me back some salt and vinegar crisps,' Willow called to Rick as they parted company.

'I have crisps at home,' said Mum.

'But they'll be those Kettle crisps. Or those healthy baked vegetable ones, which never quite hit the spot.'

'I thought you liked them?'

'Nothing beats a proper salt and vinegar crisp, Mum. Nothing.'

'Especially when you're pregnant,' said Martha with a smile.

'I'll make a note of that,' Mum said, linking her arms through Willow's and Martha's as they continued walking home.

It made Willow think of the day when they had walked to St Saviour's for Dad's funeral service. When it was over, and sitting in painful silence in the back of a large black car that smelt cloyingly of pine, they had followed behind the hearse that carried Dad's body to the crematorium in Chichester.

She could not say hand-on-heart that she had loved her father, certainly not in the same way that Martha or Mum had, but his death had saddened Willow. Perhaps because she hated to see her sister so upset, their mother too.

Willow had always been conscious that she could never please her father the way Martha did. In fact, the last time she had seen him he'd had a go at her for not sticking at yet another job.

'You don't stick at anything, do you, Willow?' he'd said. 'For the life of me I don't understand your mindset. Is it because you always think you can drift back home if things get really bad? Because let me tell you, you'll get nowhere in life thinking like that. You have to accept that you need to stand on your own two feet. You have to take responsibility for yourself. Like Martha.'

It had taken him longer than usual to get to those two little words. *Like Martha.* They had been flung at her for as long as she could remember; the constant comparison to her big sister. Willow never blamed Martha for being the poster-girl for perfection. She had only to imagine herself in her sister's shoes and think how hard it must be to be so perfect – the one who always studied hard and achieved A-stars for everything – for her to be glad she was the very imperfect sister.

No, not for a single minute did Willow resent Martha for being the apple of their father's eye. Goodness, she was far happier being the also-ran of the family, when nothing was really expected of her.

As soon as they were back at Anchor House, Willow opened the fridge and was rewarded with the sight of an open bottle of Pinot Grigio.

'Er . . . correct me if I'm wrong, but I thought you were pregnant and therefore, like me, not drinking alcohol,' said Martha.

'Just one,' said Willow, already opening the cupboard where

the glasses were kept. 'One teeny glass won't hurt the baby. Mum, I bet you had the odd drink now and then when you were expecting us, didn't you?'

'It's true I did. But it was different back then. We were all a bit more relaxed.'

'Well, we turned out just fine, didn't we?' said Willow, pouring wine into a glass. 'So I'm going to risk it. But please don't let on to Rick,' she added. 'I know he has my best interests at heart, and the baby's, but honestly, it's such a bore having to follow all his dos and don'ts. I swear I don't know what I'm allowed to do half the time.' She held out the bottle. 'Martha?'

'Oh, go on, then,' her sister said. 'But just a very small amount.'

'Mum, how about you? Or should that be Grandma-to-be, are you going to join us?'

'Absolutely!' she replied. 'How could I not join you in drinking a toast to your wonderful news?'

They took their glasses out to the garden and instead of sitting on the verandah in the shade, they opted for the group of deckchairs on the lawn that was still catching the late afternoon sun.

'Mum, I know you'll be chuffed about Martha being pregnant,' said Willow, after they'd settled themselves and chinked their glasses, 'but how do you really feel about me having a baby?'

'Goodness, what an extraordinary question! I'm delighted for you, of course I am.'

Willow wished guiltily that she could say the same herself. 'I don't think Dad would have been so delighted, would he? I mean, it's just another example of me not getting something right.'

Both her sister and mother stared at her.

'Look,' she said, 'you might just as well know, my being pregnant wasn't planned. I was as shocked as you both must be. I don't even really know how it happened.'

'Do we need to show you with the use of diagrams?' suggested Martha with a raised eyebrow.

Willow shook her head. 'No need. What I'm saying is that we were being careful . . . you know . . . taking precautions, and yet somehow I ended up pregnant. I'm seventeen weeks now and I can even feel the baby moving inside me, a sort of weird fluttering sensation. I have a blurry scan photo of the baby too, but . . . but it still doesn't feel real.'

'Seventeen weeks,' repeated Mum. 'You don't look it.'

'Maybe that's why it still doesn't feel real for you?' suggested Martha.

'Could be,' Willow said vaguely.

'Well, however it happened,' said Mum, 'it's where you are now, and you have plenty of time to come to terms with being a mother. I must say, Rick seems very happy about it.'

'He is. Ridiculously so.' Willow looked at Martha. 'I'm sorry the way you heard about me being pregnant from Rick. I genuinely had asked him not to tell anyone. I suppose he was just bursting to tell somebody the news. Were you very upset?'

'Yes,' said Martha after she'd taken a small sip of her wine.

'I'm sorry. That was exactly what I was trying to avoid. Why didn't you tell me that you knew?'

'Rick asked me not give him away.'

'I wish you'd ignored him. I hate the idea that you felt the need to keep something from me.'

'Said the pot to the kettle!'

Willow laughed. 'Bang to rights. But you know why I didn't say anything, I was thinking of you.'

'Which was very thoughtful of you,' said Mum, 'but now you need to think more about yourself; you too, Martha. This is a special time for the pair of you, and my advice is to make the most of it, as you'll never experience a first pregnancy again. Whatever help and support you're offered, take it. Including from me,' she added with a smile.

Staring into her wineglass, then taking a long sip, Willow tried to take some comfort from her mother's words. She so badly wanted to, but she couldn't. She felt such a fraud sitting here being congratulated for something she hadn't planned or wanted. Did that make her a bad person? She supposed it did. It was so different for her sister. A baby had always been a part of Martha and Tom's plan.

'So Mum,' said Martha, 'now that you know you're going to be a grandmother twice over, what do you want to be known as?'

Willow smiled to herself. How typical of Martha to be thinking that far ahead.

'I refuse to be called Nanna,' Mum said with a laugh. 'I always think that makes one sound decidedly ancient.'

'What about Mims?' offered Martha.

'Or Glam-ma?' suggested Willow. 'Would that make you feel less ancient? Or better still, what about Glammy? And then there's Ellis to consider.'

'What about Ellis?' Martha said sharply.

'Well, if he's going to be . . . erm . . . a permanent fixture, he'll also need a name.' Seeing the frown of disapproval on her sister's face, and knowing that she'd caused it, Willow appealed to their mother. 'Won't he, Mum?'

211

'I don't think we need to worry about that just yet, do we?' responded Mum after the briefest of pauses.

'I disagree,' said Martha. 'I think Ellis should be discussed.'

'You make him sound like a problem that requires fixing,' said Mum, slowly turning her wineglass round in her hands.

'At the very least I think we need to know where we stand with him. Isn't that a reasonable request?'

Wishing she hadn't mentioned Ellis, Willow took another sip of her wine and listened to a blackbird singing from a branch in the lilac tree. The sweetness of its song was so much nicer than the questioning tone of her sister's voice.

'It's perfectly reasonable, Martha,' said Mum. 'And actually, Ellis and I planned to share our own news with you this evening. You see, he's asked me to marry him and—'

'Tell me you haven't said yes,' Martha interrupted abruptly.

'That's exactly what I said.'

'But you can't! How could you even contemplate marriage? What would Dad think?'

'I'd like to think he wouldn't want me to spend the rest of my life alone.'

'But you're not alone,' Martha asserted. 'You have us.'

'And you girls both have your own lives to lead. Am I not allowed the same thing? Am I not allowed to have somebody special in my life too? And Ellis is special; he makes me happy in ways I haven't felt in a long time.'

Martha scoffed at that; her expression unattractively severe as she narrowed her eyes and chewed on the inside of her lip.

Conscious that she should contribute in some way, that by remaining silent Mum might think she agreed with her sister, Willow said, 'If you do marry Ellis, where will you live?'

Her mother looked at her with a small smile of gratitude. 'Here, of course.'

Martha made another scoffing sound, but thankfully didn't say anything.

'You wouldn't want to live somewhere new, then?' Willow asked. 'Where you could both start afresh?'

Now Martha did speak. 'What Willow is trying to say is, wouldn't you prefer to live nearer the two of us so you can spend more time with your grandchildren?'

'No,' Mum said with finality. 'I love living here and I think your children will love it too, in time. Just as you two did. Now then, there's something else you should know. The rental agreement runs out on Waterside Cottage next month and I've suggested to Ellis that he moves in with me.'

'Lucky Ellis, he's got it made, hasn't he?' muttered Martha.

'No,' said Mum with quiet dignity, 'I think you'll find it's the other way around. I'm the lucky one.'

At the sound of voices approaching along the beach – male voices – Willow felt a bolt of alarm. She hurriedly downed what remained in her wineglass and sprang guiltily from the deckchair.

But it was impossible to spring – innocently or guiltily – from a deckchair and by the time she had scrabbled inelegantly from it in a pantomime of clumsiness, Rick, Tom and Ellis were heading up the garden. Without really thinking what she was doing, only that she had to get rid of the evidence of her illicit drinking, Willow tucked the glass out of sight behind a bush.

'Not a word,' she murmured to her mother and sister, who both looked at her as though she were mad. Well, it would be Rick who would be mad with her if he knew what she'd been up to.

Chapter Thirty-One

The next day, following a barbecue in the garden at Anchor House and a walk to Bosham and back, and after Rick and Willow had already set off for London, Tom happily handed over the car keys to Martha so she could drive them home.

'I like you being pregnant,' he said, putting on his seat belt, 'it means I have months and months of you being the designated driver.'

'Hey, don't think it gives you a free pass to drink a keg of beer over lunch and then doze off in the passenger seat,' she said, pipping the horn as a final farewell to her mother. Ellis was there too to wave them off.

'A couple of beers does not constitute a keg,' Tom said good-humouredly. He had to admit though, after all that good food, beer and sea air, a nap wouldn't go amiss. Especially as he hadn't slept well last night. Not with Martha tossing and turning beside him. But as much as he fancied a nap, he knew that Martha would want a post-mortem on the weekend. Experience told him that it was always better for her to unload sooner rather than later. So once Tilsham was behind them, and to fight off the need for sleep, he decided to broach the subject himself.

'Come on, then,' he said, 'tell me what you're thinking.' He saw her hands tighten their hold of the steering wheel.

'Not if you're going to take that tone of voice with me.'

'What tone would that be?'

'The one that says you know best.'

'This might be one of those rare instances when I do.'

She tutted.

'For what it's worth, the way I see it is you're going to have to give your mother the benefit of the doubt, not just for her sake, but yours too.'

'Benefit of the doubt,' she repeated, 'you mean leave her to make a terrible mistake?'

'How do you know it would be a mistake for her to marry Ellis?'

'Because she's rushing into this without thinking it through. It's as though she's acting like a lovestruck teenager, allowing herself to be swept along in the heat of the moment.'

'Isn't that what everybody does when they fall in love?'

'We didn't. We spent time getting to know each other before deciding we'd definitely found the person with whom we wanted to spend the rest of our lives. We lived together first, to be sure of what we were getting into.'

'That's true, but I knew well before we moved in together that I wanted to marry you. And you know, maybe when you're Naomi's age and have experienced a lot more of life and how relationships work and don't work, you know instinctively when you've met the right person.'

'Or you panic and think this is your last chance and grab the first man that barges into your life before he gets away.'

'Ellis doesn't seem the sort to barge in,' said Tom with a frown.

215

'And don't forget they knew each other a long time ago. They were friends then, so they already have a good understanding of each other; the groundwork has already been done.'

'And how would you feel if this was your father rushing to marry some woman you didn't know from a bar of soap? Wouldn't you be concerned at what he was getting himself into? Wouldn't you feel he was committing the ultimate betrayal of your mother?'

'Yes and no,' Tom replied as honestly as he could. 'Yes, I would want Dad to be happy and if marrying someone he was convinced he loved did that, or even if it was only for companionship, I would support him in his decision. And no, I wouldn't see it as a betrayal. Because it's not. It's about making the most of the life you have left. Losing Mum to Covid taught me that there's no knowing what's around the corner, so it's a case of seize the day while you can.'

When Martha didn't say anything, he said, 'Is it specifically Ellis you don't like, or the thought of your father being replaced? Because to me, Ellis seems a thoroughly decent guy and very mindful of your feelings. And Willow's. He was considerate enough to sleep next door and not with your mother last night. Didn't you think the same?'

Taking her eyes off the road, Martha briefly turned to look at him. From behind her sunglasses Tom couldn't see her eyes, but he could guess at the expression in them.

'For starters I expect it was Mum who suggested he didn't sleep with her while we were staying,' she said. 'And secondly, of course I hate the idea of Ellis taking my father's place. What daughter wouldn't?'

'Fair point. But does that mean you're never going to accept

Ellis, that you'll let your disapproval spoil your relationship with your mother, and in turn the relationship she has with our child – her grandchild?'

Again, she flicked her gaze towards him. 'Could you sound any more sanctimonious?'

'I probably could if I tried,' he said. 'But really, that's the bottom line of it, isn't it? By not accepting your mother's wish to marry again, you'll be cutting off more than your sweet little nose.'

She tutted. 'Don't be absurd, you know full well that I do not have a sweet little nose. I inherited my father's rather more well-endowed schnozzle, as he always called it.'

Tom risked a smile. 'And your father's tenacity to stick to your guns . . . I suggest boldly.'

His comment had the effect of lowering Martha's shoulders, which had risen with each crank of the dial of his reasoning with her.

'A trait,' she said, 'that you've always loved in me . . . I reply with grudging resignation.'

He laughed. 'Indeed I do. But I hate to see you unhappy, Martha. Particularly when we have so much to be happy about with our very own Beanie on the way.'

She sighed. 'I know you're right. But I just can't accept that Mum is going into this with her eyes fully open. Why doesn't she just live with him and see how things go? I told her that if she really is determined to marry Ellis, she has to have a pre-nup. It's what any sensible person in her position should do. You know as well as I do that Dad's portfolio left Mum very comfortably off.'

Tom knew all too well just how comfortable Naomi was, but he suspected that Ellis might be equally well-placed. 'What did your mother say to that?' he asked.

'Apparently Ellis has already made the same suggestion.'

'I hate to say it, but that puts him in an even better light, doesn't it?'

Without answering his question, Martha drove on in silence. Then just as Tom's eyes grew heavy and began to close, she served a curve ball and changed the subject completely.

'After a weekend spent with him, what do you think of Rick?' she asked.

'Well, he's a bit smooth at times for my liking, but he's clearly devoted to your sister. He can never do enough for her. And he certainly makes himself useful in helping your mother. Can you recall any of Willow's previous boyfriends being so thoughtful?'

A more honest answer from him would have been to say that there had been times over the weekend when he'd had to guard against an unexpected feeling of jealous resentment towards Rick. But he wasn't prepared to admit to something so petty, not when he was ashamed of his reaction. Since Colin died, and on the few times Naomi had sought Tom out for help and advice, he had been only too willing to offer whatever assistance he could. He had done so because he had wanted to be of use to her and had consequently enjoyed Naomi's trust of him. Would that now change with Rick on the scene? Would Tom have to adjust to somebody else sharing that role that had been his following Colin's death?

'You don't think Rick overdoes the protective concern, do you?' asked Martha, stemming the flow of his thoughts.

'In what way?'

'His constant fussing of her. Didn't you find that irritating?'

'Most men would be criticised for not fussing enough. But you know your sister, if she doesn't like something, she simply walks away.'

'Pregnancy won't make that so easy, will it?'

Tom turned his head to look at Martha. 'Are you worried she might feel she's trapped now?'

'Yes, I think I am. Willow's a free spirit and much as it surprises me to say this, I'd hate for her to have her wings clipped. It would change her too much.'

'You don't think this is her time to emerge from her chrysalis and be the beautiful butterfly she was always meant to be?'

Martha smiled. 'How very sweetly put.'

'Less generous of me would be to say that maybe this is simply her time to grow up. She is going to be a mother, after all.'

At home, and while Tom was in the garden cutting the grass, Martha tackled the ironing which she'd been putting off for some days. While she worked her way through Tom's work shirts, she thought about her sister and Rick. She knew that she should be happy that Willow had found somebody who was so caring and so utterly determined to protect her and their unborn child. But . . .

But what? That she thought Rick cared too much? How could that ever be a problem?

The thing was, the more she saw of Rick, the more she thought there was something that didn't ring true about him. If she didn't know better, she would say it was all an act with him. He was playing a part, and playing it to the hilt, insinuating his way into their family and beguiling Naomi with his charm and helpfulness. Although there had been nothing charming about his manner at the fête yesterday afternoon when he'd revealed Willow's *condition* – that she was pregnant. For a moment he'd seemed quite different, almost surly. Was that his true self? Had, for a split second, the mask dropped?

As for his endless fretting over Willow, dictating what she could and could not eat and drink, that would drive Martha crazy if Tom ever tried that on her. During lunch today, Rick had insisted that anything Willow ate from the barbecue, which Ellis had presided over, was thoroughly cooked, that there was no blood seeping out of her burger or lamb chop.

'Sorry to be such a pain, Ellis,' he'd said, all ingratiating smiles and apologies, 'but I'd never forgive myself if any harm came to Willow or the baby.'

He'd then had the nerve to take over the barbecue, damn near burning everything for them all while banging on about salmonella and how somebody he'd known had been ill for months after eating a dodgy chicken drumstick while in Hong Kong. God, he'd sounded such an old woman and had made Martha want to eat the bloodiest burger she could get her hands on, which naturally she wouldn't, she wasn't stupid. But she could quite sympathise with Willow trying to have a sneaky glass of wine behind Rick's back. No, she didn't blame her sister for doing that. In her shoes, Martha would probably do the same.

In contrast Martha had been quite open with Tom about the wine she'd drunk in the garden yesterday afternoon, but it wouldn't be something she would do too often. Just as she wouldn't drink more than the odd cup of coffee. Which was a challenge at work, where mainlining super-strength caffeine was an essential part of the working day.

Returning her thoughts to Rick again, Martha wondered if her problem with him lay in the potential threat he possessed with regards to the balance of their family. By being the father of Willow's child, he had the power, and, Martha suspected, the motivation, to change things. Because if, through his encouragement, Willow emerged from her chrysalis, as Tom had called it, and finally become the adult it was high time she did, that would mean the dynamics between the two sisters would have to change. No longer could Martha play the Big Sister card.

The very fact that she was articulating these thoughts disturbed her. Perhaps because it was scarily true, and the truth was often at odds with the perception one had of oneself, or how one wanted to be perceived.

Rick was effectively holding up a mirror to Martha, and she didn't much like what she saw reflected back at her.

Chapter Thirty-Two

Two days after the weekend of the fête and when Naomi had broken the news to Martha and Willow that she was going to marry Ellis, he received a text from Lucas saying he would be in London on business that coming Friday.

In a flurry of messages, Lucas told Ellis that there was no need to meet him at Heathrow, he'd jump on the Express and go straight into London for the meetings he was flying over for. He would then hire a car and drive down to Tilsham. Ellis chose not to say anything about his own news, other than to mention that he had something to discuss with Lucas. As was typical of Lucas, he didn't press for any further information.

Now, and after nearly a year of not seeing each other, Lucas was upstairs in the guest bedroom at Waterside Cottage changing out of the smart jacket, open-necked shirt and chinos he'd arrived in. Downstairs, and as per Lucas's request, Ellis was making a pot of 'bog-standard tea'. Apparently, this was one of the few things he missed from England. That and Cadbury's chocolate and Mr Kipling's cherry Bakewell tarts, which Ellis had been quick to buy in readiness for his visit.

'It's a great little place you have here,' Lucas said, coming into the kitchen. He was now dressed in jeans and a Final Fantasy

T-shirt; his feet were bare. Funny how he'd always been like that, kicking off his shoes at the first opportunity and leaving his socks in the oddest places. It used to drive his mother crazy looking for where he'd put them. 'For the love of God, just put them in the laundry basket, that's all I ask!' she would say. In the end she gave up and left him to go sockless or wear unmatched pairs.

'I was lucky the cottage became available when it did,' Ellis said. 'I thought we could have tea in the garden. That okay with you?'

Lucas nodded and followed him outside where Ellis had already put the tray of tea things on the wrought iron table.

'It doesn't get more English than this, does it?' Lucas remarked after he'd stood for a while to take in the view of the beach. 'Even the sound of seagulls and the smell of seaweed lives up to expectation.'

'It probably feels a bit tame compared to what you're now used to, doesn't it?'

Lucas turned around and came and sat down. 'Not really. Everywhere has its own particular quality and charm.' He drank some of his tea, followed by a bite of cherry Bakewell, nearly polishing it off in one go.

'How's Gran?' he then asked.

'I'm sorry to say she's growing frailer by the day, but when I told her you'd be visiting, she immediately bucked up and started talking about having her hair done. She always asks after you. Never fails.'

'I'm sorry I haven't been a better grandson to her.'

'I shouldn't worry, you can do no wrong in her eyes.'

Lucas smiled. 'Gran always did spoil me rotten.'

'Just as it should be, that's the role of a grandparent. I thought we'd go and see her in the morning, if that suits you?'

'Sure. I'll fit in with whatever you suggest.' He wolfed down the rest of the cherry Bakewell and after passing him another, Ellis found himself on the receiving end of a penetrating stare.

'I get the feeling you're anxious about something,' Lucas said. 'You keep fiddling with your watchstrap and tapping the ground with your foot. Does it have something to do with what you mentioned in one of your texts, about having something important to tell me?' A small frown appeared between his eyebrows. 'You're . . . you're not ill, are you?'

From all outward appearances, Lucas didn't give the impression of taking anything in – such as a passing comment in a text message – but that was to underestimate him. He was acutely aware of everything that went on around him, he just didn't rush to respond in the way most people did.

'I'm fine, and plan to live for a good deal longer yet,' said Ellis. 'But you're right, there is something I'm a little anxious about. I'm concerned how you might react to what I'm going to tell you. The thing is, I've met somebody. Somebody rather wonderful. Her name is Naomi and I knew her from way back when. Long before I met your mother. We were at university together. I couldn't believe it when our paths crossed again right here on the beach. Since then it's been . . . well . . . it's been amazing. After your mother, I never thought I'd meet anyone who meant—'

'Whoa, take it easy, Dad!' interrupted Lucas with a laugh. 'No need to give me the whole smoochy love story in one breath.'

Ellis felt himself relax and took a sip of his tea. 'Sorry,' he said. 'Nerves had the better of me.'

'Why? Why would you think I wouldn't be happy for you?'

'Because you might think it was disrespectful to your mother. Disloyal even.'

'Is that what it feels like to you? Do you feel guilty that you've met someone?'

'No! Not at all.'

'Then what's the problem?'

Ellis laughed. 'You haven't changed, have you? You always do see things so clearly.'

'No other way to be. But honestly, Dad, I'm happy for you. Is it serious?'

'Yes. We plan to marry.'

'Cool, as well as a stepfather I'm going to have a step mama. Any chance I can meet her before I fly home?'

Ellis smiled. 'If you're amenable to the idea, I thought the three of us could have dinner together this evening. But if you'd rather not, I'd understand.'

'Give it a rest, Dad. Of course I want to check her out. Now give me the full low-down, though do me a favour, spare me any references to sex!'

Laughing, and deciding it was time to drink something stronger than tea, Ellis fetched a bottle of wine and some glasses and told Lucas everything.

When he'd finished talking, Lucas nodded. 'So, to sum up, all is hunky-dory between you and Naomi, but potentially there's a problem with your future evil stepdaughters who don't fancy you usurping their beloved daddy's place in their affections. I'm not sure I like the idea of them as my stepsisters.'

'They're not evil, they're just reluctant to accept such a huge change. And really, it's only Martha who is proving resistant. Their father died a couple of years ago, and for her it probably feels much too soon for her mother to be contemplating marriage again.'

'Can I meet the sisters while I'm here? After all, if we're to be family, meeting them before the actual day of your wedding might be preferable. When do you plan to tie the knot?'

'We haven't got that far yet. The more immediate plan is for me to move in next door with Naomi. Then we'll think about the details of marrying. I'm quite happy to be led by what Naomi wants.'

'Which means she'll be led by her daughters.'

'Not necessarily, although understandably she wants to be sensitive to their feelings, especially as they've both just announced they're pregnant. Do you really want to meet them, and their partners?'

Lucas shrugged. 'Yeah, why not? I'm not flying home until Monday evening. Maybe I can talk them round. I can be very persuasive when I want to be. And don't forget, I was in their shoes when I was a kid. I knew all the tricks to play on you when you became my newly minted stepdad.'

'What do you mean?'

'Guilt presents! I could get you to buy me more or less anything I wanted.'

Ellis laughed. 'You conniving little sod!'

'Yeah, every child knows every button to press. No matter what age we are.'

Chapter Thirty-Three

Willow would have been happy to go down to Anchor House to meet Ellis's stepson, but Martha had made it clear she would do no such thing.

'If we're being forced to meet him,' she had told Willow on the phone, 'then we'll do it on our own terms. Everyone can come to Tom and me. I've suggested to Mum that they come for lunch at one o'clock on Sunday.'

'We're not being forced,' Willow had pointed out in response to her sister's high-handedness, 'we're being *invited* to meet him, there is a difference.' Martha had ignored the comment and asked if Willow was going to bring Rick.

'Of course I am,' she'd said. 'Why wouldn't I?'

'I just wondered if he might have something better to do,' Martha had said. 'It would be perfectly understandable if he was thoroughly sick of us all.'

In the car now, as Rick drove them out of London, the address for Martha and Tom's house put into the satnav, Willow wondered what Lucas would be like. All they knew about him was that he was in his mid-thirties and that he lived in Los Angeles and did something clever in the world of digital media, which didn't really mean a lot to Willow. Odds-on he was one of those geeky types who only got excited when talking about software code, or computer games.

Thanks to Hollywood, she imagined that most people who lived in LA must be hugely successful and regularly hang out with the rich and famous. If Mum did marry Ellis and Lucas became Martha and Willow's stepbrother, would he invite them all to visit him one day? Again, thanks to Hollywood, Willow pictured him owning a fabulous house with a pool in which she could dangle her toes while sipping a cocktail against a backdrop of the Hollywood Hills.

She was probably being silly, falling for an absurd stereotypical illusion, in the same way that she wanted to believe that all Parisians lived in charming old apartments with tiny balconies looking out towards the Eiffel Tower. But then as a romantic idealist, she had always found dreams were so much nicer than reality.

Just as the reality of being pregnant was a long way from the glossy version she had seen in a magazine Rick had bought home for her. All those sparkly-eyed mothers-to-be with their hair tied back in sleek ponytails as they posed for the camera with their swelling bodies pushing against the Lycra of their yoga outfits.

Yoga and skin-tight Lycra couldn't be further from Willow's mind. Now that the nausea had passed, she was dogged by extreme lethargy. Given the chance, she could easily sleep sixteen hours a day. Ironically, and even though Martha was seven weeks behind Willow with her pregnancy, she had already gone through a stage of constantly feeling tired, but now, so she said, her usual energy levels had returned. Hopefully the same would happen to Willow.

Every time Willow yawned, Rick would urge her to give up

her job. Sometimes she was tempted to do just that, but then she would think of being alone all day in that spotless apartment with nothing to do. It was a shame she couldn't hibernate somewhere warm and cosy like a tortoise did and wake up when the baby was due.

Apart from wanting to sleep and sleep, she had developed a massive craving for salt and vinegar crisps. Ever since the day of the fête down at Mum's, she'd had a hankering for them. She was eating three or four packets a day. Usually at work so that Rick didn't know. If he did, he'd go on about the high levels of fat and salt she was consuming. Bless him, he kept making energy-boosting health drinks for her to take to work. Some of which were disgusting. Kale had no place in a drink in her view. Nor did beetroot.

On the Monday after being down at Mum's, Willow had met up with her friend Lucy and shared with her that she was pregnant. With Lucy being further down the pregnancy track than she was, Willow had been looking forward to sharing some of her worries with her friend, in the hope that she would be able to put her mind at rest. But that very evening after they'd been together for lunch, poor Lucy had had a miscarriage. There had been no warning, just awful stomach cramps that had Simon rushing her to hospital. But there was nothing that could be done to save the baby. Knowing how excited they had been at becoming parents, Willow was devastated for her friends. When she'd told Rick about it, he'd hugged her tight and told her not to worry.

'That's not going to happen to us, sweetheart,' he'd said. 'You mustn't dwell on their loss. But you must be more careful and follow all the advice and guidelines I give you.'

'But it seems so . . . so wrong,' she'd said, quickly checking

229

herself. She'd been on the verge of saying it was so unfair, but then Rick would want to know what she meant by that. And that was something she could never say to him, or to anyone for that matter. Because, as awful as it was, and even though she was now eighteen weeks, she still wasn't sure she wanted the baby she was carrying. Whereas Lucy most definitely had wanted hers. God forgive her, but Willow would have readily swapped places with her friend if she could. *Here, have my baby, you deserve it so much more than I do, and you'll be a much better mother than me.*

'I want you to promise me you won't drink any alcohol behind my back today,' Rick said, crashing into her guilty thoughts. 'Not like you did last weekend.'

Willow squirmed in her seat at his mentioning that again. He hadn't said anything at the time in the garden in front of everyone, but later that night when they were in bed, he'd taken her to task. 'I could smell wine on your breath when I came back from the pub with Tom and Ellis,' he'd said crossly. 'I just don't understand why you would be so stupid and so recklessly selfish as to risk it.'

'It was Martha's idea,' she'd lied, hating herself for blaming her sister.

'I might have known,' he'd said. 'But I expected better from you. You need to remember that it's not just your baby inside you, it's mine as well. I have a right to insist that you're careful.'

'Don't worry, I have no intention of drinking any wine today,' Willow said now in answer to his request. 'It only happened that day because Martha and I were celebrating with Mum. And as I told you, it was a very small glass of wine, no more than a thimbleful. I was just entering into the spirit of the occasion. It was a special moment for us Miller Girls, you know.'

'Well,' he said with a smile, 'don't get any ideas about doing that again today. And be careful what you eat. Especially if it's a barbecue like last Sunday.'

'Yes,' she said tiredly, wishing he would stop treating her as if she were a child. She knew he meant well, but the more he fussed over her, the more she longed to be free of his endless nagging. What she wouldn't give to be her carefree, irresponsible self! To stop being this boring stranger she was now expected to be. It wasn't who she was, it really wasn't.

Willow wasn't the only one not to be her true self; Martha was also behaving differently. She had asked Willow to be sure to arrive before the others, for what purpose Willow didn't really know, other than to lend a hand with anything that needed doing. But each time Willow offered to do something, she was told not to fuss by Martha, who was flapping about like a demented whirling dervish. A state of affairs that couldn't have been more at odds with her expensively fitted kitchen, which was show-room smart at all times. Even today when guests were due any minute for lunch. Willow had never thought about it before, but Martha and Tom would probably feel very at home in Rick's apartment where there was never anything out of place. Other than Willow, that was.

'I just want things to be right when they get here,' Martha said, when Willow asked her if there was anything wrong. 'And just look, the weather's on the turn. So bang goes my plan to have lunch in the garden!'

'Don't worry, what will be, will be,' said Willow, helping herself to a cheese straw from a dish on the worktop. Her comment elicited a scornful tut from Martha, prompting Willow to ask, for the umpteenth time, what she could do to help.

'For heaven's sake, do stop trying to be so bloody helpful!' snapped Martha. Then she sighed. 'I'm sorry, I shouldn't be taking my mood out on you.'

'Oh, I don't mind. But I wish you'd tell me what's making you so on edge?'

'I'd have thought that was obvious. Having Mum and her boyfriend and his stepson here for lunch is hardly normal, is it? It's completely . . . completely unnatural.'

'You didn't have to invite them. We could have gone down to Anchor House. Or claimed we were both busy.'

'I know that!' snapped Martha again. 'But that doesn't stop it feeling weird and frankly, just plain wrong.'

What Willow found more wrong and unnatural was the unfamiliar sensation that for the first time ever, she was the sensible calm sister, and Martha was the flighty one who was all over the place. Putting her arm around Martha's shoulders and feeling how stiff and uptight her body was, she said, 'It's bloody bonkers, that's what it is, but we'll get through it. Together.'

'I should never have suggested they come here,' Martha said faintly, while staring out of the window. 'But I thought I'd feel better about meeting this stepson of Ellis's on my home turf. You know, putting them on the back foot, but so far I'm the only one on the back foot.'

'You'll be fine. You've just put too much thought into this. It really isn't a big deal. It's just lunch with—'

'Mum's new family!' interrupted Martha.

'Potentially *our* new family,' said Willow, 'which is kind of interesting, if you look at it objectively.'

'I'm not sure interesting is the word I'd use. Or that it's possible to be remotely objective when it comes to what Mum is doing.' Frowning, Martha said, 'What do you really think, is it going to rain?'

'No idea,' said Willow, looking outside at the cloudy sky. 'But even if it buckets down, we can just come inside, can't we?'

Abruptly Martha leant forward and rapped on the window with her knuckles to attract Tom's attention. With Rick's help, he was setting out the cushions on the rattan garden furniture on the patio. He turned around to look enquiringly at Martha through the window. She pointed up at the sky. Willow knew what she was trying to indicate to Tom, but he merely shrugged. There again, that might have been his answer, that he couldn't predict the weather any more than Willow or Martha could.

What Willow couldn't predict either was how the afternoon would unfold. She just hoped that everyone would get along, that there would be no awkwardness. For Mum's sake mostly, because, and despite what Martha might think, none of this could be easy for her.

Chapter Thirty-Four

It had started to rain shortly after they'd arrived at Tom and Martha's, so they were eating in the dining area of the kitchen, which was large and fitted with charcoal-coloured units and white marble worktops, resulting in a very striking look. The walls were painted in a dramatically dark grey colour, and always when she came here Naomi felt as though she were in a still-life painting. She couldn't help but feel slightly out of place, as if she might be spoiling the sophisticated effect.

The circular copper-topped table they were seated around had been custom-made to Martha's specific instructions and placed at the centre of it was a hefty glass vase containing three tall dark purple irises and, because with Martha no detail was overlooked, the paper napkins were the same rich hue. Naomi had to admire her eldest daughter's flair for elegant scene-setting. In contrast, her own style had always been a rather more ad hoc affair, a bit of this with a bit of that thrown in. An eclectic jumble, some might say. Characterful, she liked to think.

Naomi had taken to him straight away when Ellis had introduced her to his stepson. He may not have inherited any biological genes from Ellis, but Lucas had acquired his easy-going manner and one or two of his mannerisms, like the way he sat back in his chair, his head tilted ever so slightly to one side while quietly assessing his surroundings. And let's face it, he had a lot to take in, with the prospect of a new stepfamily thrust upon him.

Aware that Lucas was another important piece of the jigsaw when it came to her relationship with Ellis, and the coming together of their two families, Naomi knew that Ellis had been as nervous as she was about today. They both badly wanted Martha and Willow to like Lucas, and equally for him to like them. She could see that Willow had already bridged that initial awkward moment on meeting Lucas, but then that was one of her great strengths, always able to connect with people and put them at ease.

'It was really kind of you to invite us here today,' Lucas said to Martha, 'and to cook such a great meal. I think this is the best chicken Kiev I've ever tasted.'

'It's Tom you need to thank, not me,' she said. 'He's the chef, all I did was chop and clear away.'

'But darling, you do it so well,' said Tom with a wink.

She rolled her eyes. 'Did I mention that he's also incredibly patronising?'

They all laughed, if a little stiffly and the conversation continued as before, in short stop-start bursts. It was all so horribly stilted, not how Naomi wanted things to be. She had a sudden and inappropriate mental image of Colin being here and jollying things along with one of his lengthy shaggy-dog stories. He had prided himself on always being able to get the party mood going, even if it meant he dominated proceedings and ensured the spotlight remained on him

'How's your chicken, Willow?' asked Rick, 'it is cooked enough, isn't it?'

'It's absolutely delicious,' she replied, 'just as Lucas said. Top marks to you, Tom.'

Clearing her throat, and with no attempt to disguise her irritation, Martha said, 'Rick, I can assure you under no circumstances would Tom serve undercooked chicken.'

'Hey, I didn't mean to cause any offence,' Rick said. 'But what with the terrible news Willow had recently I just feel it only right we should take extra care.'

Her expression suddenly anxious, Martha looked at her sister. 'What terrible news? There's nothing wrong with the baby, is there?'

Willow shook her head. 'No, it's my friend Lucy, she had a miscarriage.'

'Oh, that's awful,' said Martha. 'What happened?'

'I don't know the details, only what Simon texted me on Lucy's behalf. I'm so sad for them both.'

'Perhaps now you can understand why I don't want Willow taking any unnecessary chances,' persisted Rick.

Sensing an undercurrent of discord between Martha and Rick, Naomi decided she'd had quite enough of his constant fussing. It was grating on her nerves, and what it must be doing to Willow was anybody's guess. 'Of course, we understand that, Rick, but Tom and Martha are in the same boat as you and Willow, so I don't think you need to worry unduly while here.' He looked far from happy at her admonishment, which she only meant as a mild rebuke, but really the last thing either Willow or Martha needed was a pessimist scaring them with predictions of doom and gloom. Pregnancy was scary enough without piling on any extra fear.

'So, Lucas,' said Tom, changing the subject, perhaps wanting to try and lift the mood, 'how long are you over here for?'

'I fly home tomorrow.'

'That's a shame,' said Willow. 'For Ellis, that is,' she added, turning to look at him. 'I expect you'd have liked him to stay for longer, wouldn't you?'

'You're right, Willow,' Ellis said, 'I would. Maybe you could talk him into visiting again and soon.'

She smiled. 'I'll do my best. But you'll be here for the wedding, won't you, Lucas?'

'Just as soon as I know the date, I'll be booking my flights. Oh, and just so as you know, Dad, I've decided I'm going to be your best man.'

'Is that so?' said Ellis.

'You're not going to turn me down, are you?'

'Are you kidding? I'm delighted!'

'Well, Mum, in that case, who's going to give you away?' asked Willow.

'I'm afraid I haven't given it any thought,' answered Naomi. 'But surely at my age it's completely unnecessary. I can walk up the aisle alone, can't I?'

'No, no, there are traditions to be upheld,' said Ellis. Sitting next to her, he placed his hand over hers. Naomi's instinctive reaction was to withdraw her hand from his, worried his gesture might embarrass her daughters, but she fought the urge to do so for fear of upsetting him. It was all such a minefield, this falling in love at their age; it was as if they couldn't help but offend somebody.

'I think Tom should give you away,' said Martha.

'Yes, that's perfect!' agreed Willow. 'Tom, you'll do it, won't you? Say you will!'

'Steady on, you girls,' he said, 'it's for your mother to decide something as important as that.' Then looking at Naomi, he said, 'It would be an honour to do it, if you'd like me to. There again, you might like to have Martha and Willow walk you up the aisle. Unless they are to be your bridesmaids.'

Martha let out a cry of protest. 'What a ghastly idea, a pair of pregnant bridesmaids waddling behind their mother!'

Naomi laughed. 'I'll take that as a no, then? Now please, can we stop all this wedding talk, you're making feel quite jittery about the whole thing. Any more of it and I'll suggest to Ellis that we simply elope.'

He gave her hand a small squeeze. 'I'm up for that if you fancy it. Vegas here we come! Or do you prefer Gretna Green?'

'So long as you still have a pre-nup organised first.'

Naomi levelled her gaze on her eldest daughter. 'Don't worry, Martha,' she said, 'we've taken steps in that direction already.'

Which was true. Next week she and Ellis had an appointment with a firm of solicitors in Chichester. She had decided against using the firm Colin had always used in London in the City; she wanted to do things her way and with somebody who didn't know her. Or more importantly, with someone who didn't know Colin. This was to be a new start for her.

But how she wished she didn't feel as though it had become such an uphill struggle. She missed those days when it had been just her and Ellis, when they had been seeing each other in secret and it had been a gloriously uncomplicated affair between the two of them. She had felt so blissfully liberated then; now that carefree happiness felt tarnished by the worry of trying to please everybody.

*

There was no avoiding the change in Rick's mood now they were on their way back to London.

For a start he was driving much faster than he usually did, and had barely opened his mouth to speak to Willow. His face was set like stone and he swore under his breath every time the driver in front of them hit the brakes, and for no apparent reason according to Rick. Other than, Willow suspected, to try and stop Rick from tailgating him so closely. Any nearer and they'd be in the boot of the poor driver's car.

Dad used to be the same. It would make Mum so anxious if he was angry when he was behind the wheel of the car. He'd mutter and grumble and swear like a trooper, and become angrier still whenever Mum told him to calm down.

'What's wrong, Rick?' Willow asked him. 'Has something upset you?'

'Do you really need to ask me that? Can't you work it out for yourself? Or do I have to do everything for you?'

Stung by his question and his acerbic tone, she said, 'Have *I* done something to upset you?' For the life of her she couldn't think what. Not a drop of wine had passed her lips during lunch, so at some point she must have said or done something that annoyed him. But what?

He grunted and flashed his lights at the car in front. Then with a burst of acceleration, he swerved the BMW out into the righthand lane to overtake. Admittedly he'd waited until the way was clear with no oncoming traffic, but even so, for a split second Willow was in fear of her life. Inside her, the baby reacted by suddenly moving in what felt like a very agitated manner. It caused Willow to put a hand to her stomach to calm the baby. *It's okay, little one*, she said silently, *there's nothing to worry about, go back to sleep.*

It was, she realised, the first time she had experienced a genuine connection to the baby. Was this what motherhood was all about; a selfless and unconscious desire to protect?

Now that Rick had pulled in and slowed his speed, she said, 'I thought you'd enjoyed yourself at Tom and Martha's. Didn't you like meeting Ellis's son?'

'Well,' he said with a snort, 'we all know you enjoyed meeting him.'

'What do you mean?'

'Come off it, Willow, you never stopped flirting with him from the moment he arrived.'

'What?'

'Don't try and deny it. I saw the way he looked at you and how you responded, all smiles and coy little remarks.'

'I did no such thing!' she remonstrated. 'Why would I flirt with him when he's going to be my stepbrother?'

'Shouldn't you say, why would you flirt with him when you're my girlfriend and carrying my child?'

'This is crazy talk, Rick. You must have misinterpreted my . . . my friendliness towards him. For Mum's sake, and Martha's, I just wanted everyone to get on. For us all to have a pleasant lunch. Can't you see that?'

'And what was all that talk about Tom being the one to walk your mother down the aisle? You know your sister deliberately suggested that, don't you? It was to freeze me out. Every time we get together, she always has to make some kind of pointed remark. She really couldn't make it any more obvious that she doesn't like me. What's more, I think she'd love nothing better than to split us up.'

'No! Why would she do that?'

'Maybe she's jealous.'

'She's never been jealous of me before. Far from it.'

'You didn't have me in your life before. And it wasn't just your sister having a go at me, your Mum did as well. I felt so humiliated and you did nothing to back me up.'

'She was only trying to reassure you that you don't need to worry so much.'

'Try telling your friends Simon and Lucy that!'

While he drove on, Willow tried to make sense of everything he'd said – had she really done or said anything that could be misconstrued as flirting with Lucas? Had she been too friendly?

'By the way,' he remarked, 'why aren't you wearing the necklace I gave you?'

Oh Lord, something else she'd got wrong. She'd hoped he wouldn't notice so she wouldn't have to admit that she'd lost it. *Mislaid it,* she corrected herself, it would turn up sooner or later. 'I forgot to put it on this morning,' she fibbed.

'You forget a lot of things, don't you, Willow?'

She laughed nervously to cover up her unease at lying to him. 'You know me, I'll forget my own name one day.' She reached out to put her hand on his leg. 'Don't be angry with me. You know I don't like it when you're cross. And it's not good for the baby,' she added, knowing that that would always be her trump card to win him round.

'You're right,' he said. 'But really you have to try harder not to upset me so much. You know how much I love you. I just can't bear the thought of another man stealing you away from me.'

'That's not going to happen,' she said, touched at his honesty and the depth of painful sadness in his face. She reminded herself that he just wasn't as confident and secure as he made out. Which wasn't surprising, given how he'd lost his parents.

Chapter Thirty-Five

'What a thoroughly unpleasant way to spend an hour of one's life,' said Naomi.

They were standing on the street after their appointment with the senior partner of Crambourne and Co Solicitors to discuss the drawing up of a prenuptial agreement.

'I couldn't agree more,' replied Ellis. 'Let's go straight to the wine bar for lunch. I need something to wash away the distastefulness of what we've just put ourselves through.'

'So it wasn't just me?'

'No,' he said with feeling, 'it was grim and has nothing whatsoever to do with how I feel about you and the life I imagine us sharing together.'

'It was like the very worst kind of business transaction,' said Naomi, when they were seated at the table Ellis had booked for them. 'It was horrible hearing it all distilled down into such matter-of-fact terms. There was no mention of love. Of our simply wanting to be together.'

'I suppose we should focus on why we're doing it,' he said.

She looked at him with an anxious frown. 'Remind me, why are we?'

He reached across the table and stroked her hand. 'To satisfy our offspring that we're marrying for all the right reasons. That we know what we're doing.'

'Back there in that office I kept asking myself exactly that, what on earth am I doing?'

'Second thoughts about marrying me?'

'No. Well . . . sort of.'

'Oh,' he said flatly. But he could add nothing else as their waiter appeared just then to take their order. He was an awkward young lad of about seventeen and stumbled over his words as he tried hard to remember the specials of the day. When his torment was over – they made it easy for him and each opted for the salmon en croute – he returned with two glasses of rosé. Alone now, Ellis risked the question he had to ask.

'Are those second thoughts serious? Do you want to call things off?'

Naomi looked away from him, across the busy wine bar and out of the window at the passers-by. 'Yes,' she said at length. 'I do.' Only then did her gaze return to meet his.

'Oh,' he said again, his heart grinding to what felt like a shuddering stop. 'Is it solely because of all that dry-as-bones legalese we've just sat through? Or something else?'

Lucas had warned Ellis that the process of organising a pre-nup could have unforeseen consequences. He'd told him this while Ellis was seeing him off at Heathrow earlier that week. Apparently, a woman Lucas worked with in LA who came from a well-off family had taken her parents' advice to have a pre-nup arranged, but by the time the document was drawn up and ready to be signed, her fiancé had decided he didn't much care for its terms. It emasculated him, so he claimed.

'It ruined everything,' said Naomi in answer to Ellis's

question. 'That hideous process stripped every ounce of joy out of my love for you. I felt sick to my stomach sitting there while our future was systematically taken apart by comparing the size of our so-called assets.'

'In that case, where does that leave us? Does it mean, and I hate to resort to clichés, that love isn't enough?' He hesitated before saying, 'You do still love me, don't you?'

'Of course I do! How could you think I don't?'

'For the rather obvious reason that you just said you wanted to call things off.'

'Oh Ellis, it's the fuss and bother of our marrying that fills me with dread. Don't you feel the same way, that it's not about us anymore, but how we please everyone else? I feel so harried by it all.'

After taking fortitude in several mouthfuls of wine, Ellis said, 'What are you saying you want to do, then?'

'Why don't we forget about getting married and just go ahead with our plan for you to move in with me?'

'Is that what you really want?' he asked. Out of consideration to Martha and Willow they had put off his moving in until after the weekend of the fête, and then Lucas's visit had further delayed things. Now he really wasn't at all sure where he stood.

'It most definitely is,' said Naomi. 'Then I'll wake in the morning without this depressingly dark cloud hanging over me.'

'My darling, I had no idea you felt so badly about it.'

'Each aspect of our relationship taken individually is fine, but put it all together and suddenly it feels like a tremendous ordeal to get through.'

'It's my fault, isn't it? I rushed you by proposing on my

245

birthday. I should never have done that. But it just felt so right. I hate the thought that I've made you unhappy.'

'You haven't. It's the situation that's done that, together with the weight of expectation that's been thrust upon us. I'm tired of tiptoeing around everyone's feelings, of pleasing everyone but myself. In a way I've done it all my married life. And,' she quickly added, 'that's nobody's fault but my own.'

'So it's time to assert yourself?' he suggested with a tentative smile.

'I'm afraid that makes me sound disagreeably self-absorbed.'

'Not at all. It makes perfect sense from what you've told me of your life with Colin.'

'But, Ellis, he's not entirely to blame. I can't ignore the fact that I allowed myself to be that person with Colin, the one who always tried to keep the ship on an even keel, no matter the price. For the most part, that's what mothers do, we perform an endless dance on the tips of our toes for fear of making a situation worse.'

'That sounds like you're blaming yourself for being abused by your husband.'

She cringed. 'Don't use the word *abuse*, it sounds so sordid.'

'If it wasn't abuse, what would you call it, then?'

She pursed her lips. 'I call it making allowances for the father of my children.'

'I'm sorry, Naomi, but that's not making allowances, that's making excuses for the man who struck you when he couldn't control his temper. You wouldn't countenance that behaviour from either Tom or Rick with your daughters, would you?'

She shook her head sadly. 'You're right, but please, let's not drag all that up from the past, not now. It's the future that

246

matters and your moving in with me. If you still want to. If I haven't spoilt everything between us.'

'Are you absolutely sure that's what you want?' he said. 'Won't you still feel you have to justify the situation to your daughters? Won't you still feel just as harried?'

'No, I don't believe I will because things will be less complicated between us.'

'And dare I say, less permanent?'

'Please don't think that. I genuinely want us to be together for ever.'

'But only on your own terms?'

He didn't mean to sound as sharp as he did, and he could see she was hurt by what she clearly felt was an accusation.

'I've upset you, haven't I?' she said.

'Yes,' he finally admitted. 'I'm disappointed. I like the idea of marriage with you. I don't even really know why. It just felt right when I asked you. Now I'm not sure what to feel. Perhaps I'm more committed to our relationship than you are.'

She sighed and slid her hands across the table to hold his. 'That's not true. I love you, Ellis, and I can't think of anything I'd like more than to wake up lying next to you every morning for the rest of my life.'

'Will you still allow me to buy you a ring? Or is that a complication too far?'

Before she could answer, their waiter approached with their lunch. With painful slowness, the lad set down the plates and various dishes of vegetables on the table, managing in his awkwardness to knock over the small vase containing a single pink carnation.

'It's fine,' said Ellis, picking the vase up, 'don't worry about it.'

Stammering an apology and looking as though his day couldn't get any worse, the lad escaped as fast as he could, only nearly to collide with a waitress carrying a tray of drinks for another table.

Poor devil, thought Ellis. *I know just how you feel.*

Chapter Thirty-Six

Jason's pen had been silent the whole time Martha had been speaking, which was actually more unnerving than when he was clicking it. As he was now doing while Steve, the creative director, took his turn to contribute to that morning's meeting.

Ever since Martha's pitch had secured them the account, Jason's manner towards her had changed. It wasn't the first time she had won over a client, yet for some reason in this instance she hadn't felt she had done enough to impress Topolino. But here they were, several months on it was now nearly the end of August and according to Charlotte Milner, Topolino's MD, they couldn't be happier.

To Martha's surprise, while coming in to work on the train this morning she had received an email from Charlotte saying that they had been so impressed with Martha's advice and level-headed input, they had decided they would like to have her services on a permanent basis at Topolino. There had been no time to reply to the email; besides, Martha needed time to think about it. There was also the small matter of her being eighteen weeks pregnant.

A conversation wouldn't hurt, would it? she imagined her father saying. Dad had always encouraged her to consider any opportunity that came her way, and while she was happy enough where she was, she was sufficiently intrigued, and flattered, to want to know more. She was jumping the gun, but she couldn't help but wonder what kind of generous staff discount would be available on all those gorgeous baby clothes.

When the meeting came to an end and everyone left to go back to their offices, and with more speed than usual – it was Friday and the Bank Holiday weekend beckoned – Jason approached Martha. She hoped he wasn't going to keep her long as she had a lot to do before leaving early that afternoon. At four o'clock she and Tom would be seeing their baby for the first time. She should have had this first scan last month, but she'd had to cancel on two different occasions because of work commitments, and then the hospital had had a problem and cancelled on her.

She had dreamt last night that the ultrasound scan she was booked to have today had identified a bundle of smiling and waving babies nestled inside her. So vivid had the dream been, she had woken with the strongest feeling that she might be expecting more than one baby, even though to her and Tom's certain knowledge there was no record of twins, let alone triplets, in either of their families.

'Doing anything interesting for the weekend?' asked Jason.

'We're going down to Sussex to see my mother,' she said. 'What about you? Off to your place in Southwold with . . . ' She hesitated as her baby brain grappled to recall the name of Jason's latest girlfriend. 'Georgia,' she settled on.

'No,' he said, 'I'm going alone. Georgia and I are no longer seeing each other.'

'Oh, I'm sorry.'

He shrugged. 'Don't be. Water under the bridge.' He gave his bearded chin a scratch. 'You know, I can't quite put my finger on it, but there's something different about you these days.'

She drew in her stomach muscles as discreetly as she could. 'It must be the yoga classes I've been doing online,' she said. 'You should give it a go sometime, it's very relaxing.'

He laughed. 'Somehow I can't see myself doing that. Anyway, I just wanted to say how much I appreciated your input earlier. And to say that Charlotte at Topolino can't sing your praises enough.'

'Well, that's good to know,' she said smoothly.

'I wouldn't be at all surprised if she tried to poach you,' he said with one of his knowing stares.

Martha spent the next hour dealing with emails and phone calls and after a hurried lunch, and yet another trip to the toilet, she encountered the new intern quietly sobbing over one of the basins. Jason, so the girl explained, had just yelled at her for spilling coffee over his desk. It was her first week at BND and she was terrified it would be her last.

'Don't give it another thought,' Martha assured her, 'he'll have forgotten all about it by the time we're back after the Bank Holiday weekend.'

This wasn't strictly true; Martha knew that Jason could harbour a grudge with the best of them. For that matter she was no slouch in that department, especially when it came to Rick. She still hadn't forgiven him for that dressing-down he'd given her on the telephone all those months ago. And as for his cloying overprotectiveness of Willow, that really irritated her. There was, she'd decided, something divisive about him. She hated admitting she could have been wrong, but she wholeheartedly regretted ever thinking he was the ideal boyfriend for her sister. Such was the strength of her dislike for Rick, she could almost feel nostalgic for some of the previous boyfriends Willow had brought home. The ones who were so laid-back and irresponsible it would never dawn on them to question Martha or put her in her place.

Thankfully she had been spared seeing too much of Rick in the last month or so. Tom had surprised her with a weekend away in the Cotswolds at a beautiful country hotel that had proved to be just what she'd needed to unwind. Until then she hadn't realised just how tightly wound she'd been. They'd also gone up to Yorkshire to see Tom's sister and father. Being with her husband's family had felt refreshingly uncomplicated compared to her own right now.

Tom was waiting for her at the hospital, and Martha, having drunk a half-litre of water on the way here, as instructed so that the scan would give them a clearer picture of the baby, was desperate for the loo.

Sitting in the waiting room, and to keep her mind off the need to relieve herself, she told Tom about the email she'd received from Topolino, offering her a job.

'If you weren't pregnant, would you be tempted?' he asked.

'Pregnant or not, I think it's worth finding out more,' she said, fidgeting in her seat to put less strain on her fit-to-burst bladder. 'I'll be perfectly straight with them and explain the situation. Not that I'll be able to hide things for much longer.'

She put a hand to her swelling abdomen, which was now straining against the waistband of her skirt. Another week or so and her wardrobe would have to be adjusted to accommodate her baby bump. She had already bought a few new clothes online in readiness, along with a bigger-sized bra, but she was hoping to go shopping over the weekend while down at Anchor House. It had actually been Mum's idea that, along with Willow, they go to Chichester, or perhaps Portsmouth so that she could treat her daughters to some maternity clothes and baby things. 'Let it be my treat to you,' Mum had said. 'We'll leave the boys at home and have some girl-time together.'

Martha had baulked at hearing Mum refer to Ellis, Tom and Rick as 'the boys' but she was slowly, if still a little reluctantly, coming to terms with Ellis being a part of the family. He had moved in to Anchor House some time ago, but all talk of marrying had gone on hold. According to Mum they had decided it wasn't necessary. Whether or not it was the first crack in their big romance remained to be seen, but for now, Martha was satisfied that a degree of common sense was being applied.

'Martha Adams?'

'That's us,' murmured Tom, taking her hand as they stood up and followed the nurse who'd called out her name.

It wasn't until she was actually lying on the couch and cold gel was being squirted onto her baby bump that Martha suddenly felt nervous. What if the scan revealed something wrong with their baby? Or what if her dream was a premonition of her expecting more than one? With Tom by her side, she gripped his hand tightly. He gave her a reassuring smile.

'Now then,' said the radiologist in a cheery voice. 'Do you want to know the sex of your little one?'

'Yes,' they answered in perfect unison.

The woman smiled back at them. 'Well then, let's see what we can see, shall we?'

Holding her breath, Martha turned her head to look at the screen. *Please, please, please, don't let there be anything wrong,* she silently hoped.

Chapter Thirty-Seven

In the weeks since he had moved in with her, Naomi and Ellis had been busy at Anchor House.

At her instigation, they had cleared out cupboards and wardrobes and jettisoned furniture which even Naomi, as an instinctive collector of things that might come in handy one day, had no trouble parting with. This was a fresh start for her, after all.

In an attempt to make Ellis feel properly at home, Naomi had also suggested they give her bedroom a long overdue makeover. Out with the old bed and in with a beautiful antique walnut frame bedstead with the addition of a fabulously comfortable mattress, which Ellis had sourced and paid for. She didn't know the exact cost of the mattress, but when he'd said it was top-notch hotel quality, she suspected she could have bought a new car for the same amount of money. All the old bedlinen had been replaced with new, and the sun-faded curtains that had hung at the window and French doors that opened onto the wooden balcony had also been replaced. Naomi had bought a roll of Colefax and Fowler fabric – cream linen patterned with blue hydrangeas – and made the curtains herself. She'd added drops of sheer voile too.

Before hanging the new curtains, she and Ellis had redecorated the bedroom with a wash of pale blue on the walls and then had a cream carpet laid. Something Colin would never have countenanced. 'Cream?' he would have said. 'That'll never take any wear!'

On a further shopping spree, and while browsing the antique shops in Petworth, they came across a new art gallery that had recently opened and they both fell in love with two beautiful watercolour seascapes. These were now hung either side of the new bed and softly illuminated at night by new bedside lamps.

It had been fun having a project to work on with Ellis and going by his enthusiasm for it, he'd enjoyed himself as much as she had. The next room she wanted to tackle was the smallest of the five bedrooms; she wanted Ellis to have it as his own dressing room. It currently housed what he had brought with him from next door. The bulk of his things was still in storage, Waterside Cottage being a partly furnished property. In the coming weeks, Ellis would decide what he wanted to keep and what he would sell or give away. The owners of Waterside Cottage, a couple Naomi had never met, but who lived in Kent, had yet to find new tenants for it. Or perhaps they had other plans for the property.

Now, as Naomi sat up in bed next to Ellis, the curtains pushed back and the voiles swaying gently on the sea breeze at the open French doors, she sipped her first cup of tea of the day while listening to the cry of the gulls, and thought how perfect life was with Ellis here. This time last year she would never have believed she would fall so happily in love again.

After that depressing hour spent in the solicitor's office in Chichester, Naomi had feared she might lose Ellis with her honesty about not being able to face the fuss of a wedding. The look of disappointment on his face had been unbearable, but he had brightened up when she had explained that she much preferred the idea of being officially engaged to him for the rest of her life. Two days later they had gone ring-shopping together. In one of her favourite antique shops in Arundel, she had spotted a stunning topaz ring. It had even fitted her without having to be altered.

'It's as if it was meant to be,' Ellis had said, taking the ring from her and paying for it. He had then kept hold of it until that evening, when they were strolling along the beach in the setting sun, and he had suddenly gone down on one knee. 'Corny as hell,' he'd later remarked, 'but it had to be done.'

Holding up her left hand now to admire the ring with its large topaz stone, Naomi said, 'Have I told you recently how much I love my ring?'

'Not since . . . hmm . . . let me think. It might be as long ago as yesterday,' he replied with a smile.

'I don't think I shall ever tire of looking at it,' she said.

'That's good, because I don't think I shall ever tire of you wearing it. Or tire of you,' he added, 'just in case you needed me to remind you of that.' He finished his tea and after putting his mug on the bedside table, he stretched his arms above his head. 'I'm reluctant to ask this, but do you suppose we ought to get up?'

'What's the hurry?'

'Your family will be here in approximately . . .' he glanced at his wristwatch, 'two hours and fifteen minutes, and here we are still in bed.'

Our family, she wanted to correct him, but she didn't. Some things couldn't be rushed. 'Are you anxious about seeing them again?'

'I'd like to say no, but that would be a lie. There always seems to be some kind of drama attached to our get-togethers.'

'Only because there's so much readjusting to do on all sides. The last time we saw them all was when Lucas was here, and then it was my turn to feel as though I was on trial. I was so anxious for him to like me. Martha and Willow had probably felt something similar.'

'You're right, and I know it's still early days, but it worries me that your daughters will never truly accept my presence. I don't know what more I can do to put their minds at rest.'

'We both know that's not strictly true. Willow is fine with you, it's only Martha who needs to accept that you're now a fundamental part of my life.'

'Can I ask you something very personal?'

'Of course.'

'Did you decide against marrying me because you thought it would placate Martha?'

She gave his question some thought. 'Maybe that was partly at the back of mind, but really it was a selfish need on my part to control things. Does that, and be honest, give you cause for concern?'

'Not at all. Perhaps it was selfishness on my part in my wanting to marry you. I wanted to seal the deal for fear of losing you.'

She put down her finished mug of tea and turned to face him. 'You're not going to lose me. I promise.' She kissed him, then raised her left hand to indicate her beautiful ring. 'Engaged for life,' she said with a happy smile. 'You're stuck with me for good.'

*

On their way down to Tilsham, and in the passenger seat of Rick's BMW, Willow ate the last piece of the Kit-Kat he had bought for her when he'd stopped to fill up with petrol.

'Better for that?' he asked as she screwed the foil and paper wrapper into a ball and dropped it in her bag at her feet. She knew better than to leave it littering Rick's car.

'Much better, thank you,' she said. 'Was I being very grumpy before?'

He smiled at her and, taking a hand off the steering wheel briefly, he patted her leg. 'You could never be grumpy, sweetheart. Maybe just a little tetchy because you were in need of some carbs. I said you should have eaten some breakfast, didn't I?'

'I know, but I just couldn't face it then.'

'You poor thing. You must see the doctor or the midwife next week, just in case there's a problem they should know about.'

'Oh, it's probably quite normal,' she said absently.

The morning sickness which had been such a pain for Willow had thankfully stopped some time ago, but now she suffered with awful indigestion. That's why she hadn't been able to eat any breakfast, despite Rick's encouragement. Bless him, he had tried so hard to tempt her to eat, but the acid rising up from her stomach to her throat was hideously vile and all she could manage was a cup of very weak tea. Her craving for salt and vinegar crisps had completely gone. In fact, she didn't think she could face another crisp ever again. Perhaps it was all that unhealthy fat and salt which had triggered the indigestion? Whatever the reason, it had made her lose a bit of weight, not that she'd shared that with Rick. He'd only fuss.

'Have you remembered the scan photo?' he asked.

'Yes, it's in my bag all nice and safe.'

Ten days ago they'd been for the second scan and unlike the first time, Rick had insisted they find out the sex of the baby. Willow had given in, knowing it meant so much to him. She also suspected that because Martha and Tom now knew they were expecting a girl, Rick felt he should know the sex of their child too.

'A girl!' he kept saying when he drove them home afterwards, as if no such thing had ever existed before. 'Just think, we're going to have a daughter!'

A daughter.

She, Willow Miller, was going to be the mother of a little girl. The thought both delighted and terrified her. Rick had already begun decorating the bedroom that would be for his Little Princess, as he now referred to the baby. Nothing, he claimed, would be too much trouble in creating the perfect home for his daughter.

Since the day of that scan, Willow had started to have the most vivid and disturbing dreams at night which had her waking in a panic that she'd mislaid the baby. 'I'm sure I put her in her cot,' she said in the dreams to Rick, 'but she's not there now.'

'Think, Willow!' he'd bellow. 'Think what you did with our daughter!'

But there were worse dreams than this that came to her now. Heart-thumping nightmares which she'd thought were a thing of the past.

Not wanting to dwell on that this morning, not when it was such a lovely day, she thought instead of how much she was looking forward to seeing her mother again.

'By the way,' she said, suddenly remembering what Mum had planned for them to do. 'Mum wants to take Martha and me shopping this afternoon. She thought you and Tom and Ellis could hang out together, maybe go for a walk and have a drink at the pub.'

'Are you sure that's what you want to do?' he replied.

'Yes. Why wouldn't I?'

'I couldn't imagine anything worse on a hot day like today. An August Bank Holiday weekend into the bargain. Wouldn't you rather relax in the garden or be on the beach with me? What with your shift work and me being away on a two-day conference this week, I feel like I've hardly seen anything of you lately. By the way, now that you're twenty-five weeks, you did tell them at work yesterday that you're pregnant and will be leaving?'

'I did,' she said, turning to look out of the window. Her work colleagues had congratulated her and marvelled at how well she'd kept her pregnancy secret, but Kyle had expressed his disappointment at the prospect of losing her. And that was because in the last month she had regularly hit her daily targets, far exceeding them on some days. In fact, she had done so well, Kyle had been talking about giving her a pay rise and promoting her.

No matter how hard she tried, Willow couldn't imagine being at home all day alone with a baby and being entirely responsible for that vulnerable life. What if the baby – *her daughter* – wouldn't feed? Or wouldn't sleep? Or was in pain and Willow couldn't stop the pain? Or what if Willow mislaid the baby, just like in her dreams.

The train of her thoughts led to a familiar sensation of panic uncoiling itself inside her. It caused her heart to beat faster and her mouth to go dry. For a ludicrous moment she wanted to push open the car door and fling herself out and roll away down the grassy verge.

To stop that from happening, she tightly clasped her hands together on her lap and closed her eyes. But that didn't help. It gave her mind the chance to roam freely, straight to the nagging belief that this was all a dreadful mistake, that she had somehow walked onto a stage and been given the wrong role to play. Nothing about her life now felt like the life she should have been living. It felt all wrong, being pregnant and being with Rick. But how could she think that when he was so good to her, when he spoilt her with so many gifts and cared so much for her? He was always telling her how much he loved her, even when she had done something carelessly stupid and upset him.

'Willow.'

She opened her eyes. 'Yes.'

'Sorry, were you asleep?'

'No, just thinking.'

'Well, if you open the glove compartment, you'll find something in there which I hope will give you something extremely nice to think about.'

Intrigued, she leant forwards and did as he said. 'Is it for me?' she asked when she saw a small but beautifully wrapped present in the glove compartment.

He laughed. 'Who else? Go on then, open it.'

Thinking it might be a replacement necklace for the one she had lost, she pulled at the pretty ribbon tied around the box. Then she removed the wrapping paper and lifted the lid on the box.

'Well,' he said. 'What do you think?'

She stared in stunned astonishment at the diamond ring. 'I think it looks awfully expensive, Rick,' she murmured.

He laughed again. 'It was. But so long as you give me the right answer, it will have been worth every penny. So what do you say? Will you marry me? Will you be, not just the mother of my child, but my wife?'

The idea of pushing open the car door and rolling away returned to her, and as though faced with the choice of that, or saying yes to Rick, she took a deep breath before answering.

Chapter Thirty-Eight

As always seemed to happen when Naomi's family gathered together, there was an undercurrent of conflicting emotions, of something being not quite right.

While Naomi and the girls were off on their shopping jaunt, Ellis, Tom and Rick had gone for a walk to Bosham and had lunch at the Anchor Bleu, followed by the walk back to Tilsham. For some reason though, what should have been an easy-going time was anything but. Perhaps the intense heat of the day had something to do with it; the temperature had soared to a sizzling 34°C. Bosham and Tilsham were packed with Bank Holiday weekend visitors and with the tide in, what few areas of beach there were, were crowded with day-trippers. The wily seagulls knew when they were on to a good thing and swooped down on the unwary, stealing whatever looked edible from unguarded hands.

It was always possible, Ellis thought, that actually he was the problem and not the hot sun, that Tom and Rick regarded him as an interloper. It made sense that if Martha and Willow didn't approve of him, there was every chance that Tom and Rick wouldn't either. But Ellis didn't really think that was the issue, and anyway, Willow had appeared to accept him as being part of the family now. There certainly hadn't been a problem the last time he had spent time alone with Tom and Rick, when they'd gone for a drink together the day of the fête.

Things had got off to an odd start when they'd all arrived and Rick, apparently bursting with the need to share his and Willow's news, announced that he had just proposed to Willow, and she'd said yes. Ellis considered it a strange way to propose, while driving, but then who was he to comment? He'd noticed that while everyone had admired the ring on Willow's finger, she hadn't seemed as happy as one might expect her to look. If anything, she looked vaguely embarrassed. Naomi must have decided it was an ideal opportunity to share their own news, a way of getting it over and done with, and had held up her own ring for inspection. A more muted round of congratulations followed, which was perfectly understandable.

Later, when Ellis, together with Tom and Rick, had returned to Anchor House from their walk, there had been a tricky moment when he had suggested that what they needed now was an ice-cold beer to cool them off after being out in the blisteringly hot sun for so long. He'd been about to open the fridge for the beers he'd put in there yesterday after shopping with Naomi, when Tom had beaten him to it. They both had hastily stepped back from the fridge as though each had inadvertently barged in on the other's territory. Ellis knew from Naomi that Tom had been a great support to her after Colin's death and could always be relied upon to act as her wingman, whether it was offering financial advice or pouring out drinks for people. Did Tom feel his newly acquired position – his promotion within the family – had been undermined by Ellis? If so, Ellis made a mental note to watch out for that in the future; he needed Tom as an ally if he was ever going to win Martha round.

The mood amongst the three of them had changed the second Naomi and the girls arrived back; it was as if they spontaneously relaxed. Breezing in with laughter and chatter and armfuls of shopping bags, it was obvious they had enjoyed a better day than their menfolk.

Now, in the sultry warmth of the evening as they sat around the table on the verandah, with dusk complete and the twinkling fairy lights hanging from the glass roof acting like stars above their heads, Ellis sipped his rosé wine thoughtfully.

For the last few minutes he'd been observing Rick through the flickering flames of the candles on the table. Seated next to Willow, he was leaning in particularly close to her with one of his hands absently twirling a lock of her hair. The gesture was so extraordinarily intimate, Ellis felt uncomfortable observing it, but found himself unable to look away. He had never seen a man openly do this to his partner before and while he wanted to believe it showed the depth of feeling Rick had for Willow, he couldn't help but wonder if it was actually an act of possession. The thought so perturbed him, Ellis glanced around the table to see if anyone else was looking at Rick with the same curious absorption as he was.

The only one who was, was Martha, and the expression on her face was one of undisguised disgust, as though she'd just caught Rick picking his nose. Then without warning, and maybe because she couldn't stand to watch any longer, she turned away and her gaze collided with Ellis's. For the briefest of moments, their eyes held, but whatever she was thinking, there was no pursuing it as just then there was the sound of a mobile ringing.

After some collective patting of pockets, the ringing mobile proved to be Willow's.

'Sorry,' she apologised, finding her phone hiding under her napkin on the table. 'Oh,' she said, when she checked the screen, 'it's Lucy.'

His fingers still playing with her hair, Rick frowned. 'Don't answer it,' he said, 'it can wait.'

'I think I should, you know, what with her miscarriage.'

With visible reluctance, Rick unwound the lock of hair from his fingers. 'Go on then,' he said with a shrug, 'if you must. But hey,' he added with a sudden smile, 'don't be long, you know how I miss you.'

They all watched Willow rise to her feet and walk away down the garden to talk to her friend in private. Turning back to look at them, Rick said, 'I know what you're thinking, that I'm just too romantic for my own good.' He raised a hand in the air and smiled. 'Guilty as charged, so shoot me now!'

'Somebody pass me a gun,' muttered Martha.

Tom laughed, but Naomi tutted. 'Really, Martha.'

'It's okay, Mum, he knows I'm only kidding. Isn't that right, Rick?'

The smile gone from his face, he was about to respond when they heard a cry from Willow.

'Of course I don't know anything about it!' her voice rang out in the stillness. 'There must be some kind of mistake. Are you really sure that it's . . . I mean . . . after all this time, could you really tell?'

Seconds passed and then they heard another cry from Willow. Then: 'Lucy, are you still there? Lucy?'

'What was that all about?' asked Rick when Willow rejoined them on the verandah and sat down again.

Even in the candlelight Ellis could see the paleness of her face. She looked like she had just received the worst of news.

When she didn't answer Rick, Naomi said, 'Willow, what is it? What's wrong? What did Lucy say to you?'

Willow fiddled with the mobile in her hands, then held it up and showed the screen to Rick. 'Look,' she said, a tremble to her voice. 'It's Cedric. Or what was Cedric.'

Whoever Cedric was, and whatever Willow was showing him, caused Rick to flinch. 'That's gross,' he said. 'Did Lucy send that photo to you?'

'Yes.'

'What, as some kind of sick joke?'

'It's hardly a joke,' Willow said. She was plainly upset and on the verge of tears. Ellis exchanged a look with Naomi. She appeared to be as puzzled and as concerned as he was.

'What's it a photo of, Willow?' she asked.

'You don't want to see, Mum, it's too awful.'

'If Rick can stomach it, I'm sure we can,' said Martha.

Willow shook her head. 'I'm not showing it to you.'

'Please,' said Naomi, 'just tell us what's upset you so much.'

Before Willow could reply, Rick said, 'I think you should put your phone away, sweetheart and calm down.'

'I'm perfectly calm,' she told him, sounding anything but calm as her voice rose. To the rest of them, and after taking a deep steadying breath, she said, 'Lucy and Simon decided to create a vegetable patch in their garden and after pulling down the old shed, they found the buried body of their cat, Cedric.'

'The one that disappeared while you were housesitting?' asked Martha.

Willow nodded.

'But how did it end up buried in the garden?' This was from Tom. 'And how do they know for sure that it is Cedric?'

'Because they took the body to the vet who'd put the identity chip in, and that confirmed it was Cedric,' answered Willow. 'And anyway, it's obviously him, you can see his collar around his poor little neck in the photo. It's decorated with diamanté, so there's no mistaking it.' She wiped away the tears that had now spilled over from her eyes. 'And his fur is still visible and—'

'Enough!' interrupted Rick, snapping forward in his seat. 'No more, Willow. This has gone on quite enough. You're working yourself up into an unnecessary state. Lucy was totally out of order sending you that picture. I've a good mind to ring her back and tell her so. Give me your phone.' He held out his hand, but the normally compliant Willow shook her head.

'Lucy sent the photo because she thinks we lied about Cedric wandering off,' Willow said. 'She thinks we killed him and buried him at the end of the garden behind the shed and then lied to her and Simon.'

Rick's chin took on a dogged tilt. 'And why the hell would we do that?' he demanded.

'I . . . I don't know,' faltered Willow. 'It doesn't make sense. Unless—'

'Unless what?'

She stared at him, his expression etched like stone in the candlelight. 'Unless you did it. Did you, Rick?' Her voice was no more than a whisper.

'Me?'

'Yes. I know I didn't do it, and nobody else could have had access in or out of the house or garden, because I always kept the doors shut. And the only time a door was left open was when you told me you'd accidentally forgotten to close the front door when you went out to the car. And that was the day Cedric went missing.'

When Willow went quiet, each and every one of them looked at Rick and waited for his response. If Ellis had felt awkward earlier watching Rick play with Willow's hair, he now felt excruciatingly uncomfortable. It was quite an allegation Willow had just made, and all the more potent because she didn't seem to be the sort of girl who went around accusing people of . . . well, frankly, of secretly burying cats.

'Well?' pressed Martha as the ominous silence lengthened.

Rick swivelled his head from Willow to Martha and looked at her with unnerving coolness before returning his attention to Willow.

'Look, sweetheart,' he said, reaching for her hand. 'It sounds worse than it really is. You have to believe me when I say I was only trying to protect you from any distress. I know what you're like, the slightest thing sets you off. All that happened was that the blasted cat slipped out through the open door and before I could do anything, a passing car ran over him. The driver of the car didn't even stop. He probably didn't know what he'd done. I knew you'd be beside yourself if you knew, so I dug a hole behind the shed and buried the cat. I thought I was doing the right thing in protecting you. You do believe that, don't you? I meant no harm.'

'But you let me search for poor Cedric for all those days. I was frantic with worry. You even helped. Or you pretended to look for him. When all the time you knew where he was, he was buried in the garden!'

Rick held on tightly to her hand as she tried to remove it from his grasp. 'I should have been honest with you, I know. I made a stupid mistake. I'm really sorry. Can you forgive me, please?'

He slowly cast his gaze around the table. 'Wouldn't you all have done the same to shield Willow from any needless pain? Wouldn't you?'

Chapter Thirty-Nine

Sunday morning and Tom was doing one of his favourite things; he was riding round the garden on his sit-on mower. With just a few more stripes to add to the lawn he thought how one day he'd be doing this with his daughter on his lap. Just as he and his sister had taken turns to do the same thing with their father when they'd been little.

It was now the second week of September and the air had a distinct hint of freshness to it that was reminiscent of so many back-to-school days from his childhood. It was funny how one never lost that feeling, or the memory of washing one's hair of a Sunday evening and hastily doing the homework that had been left to the last minute. With a wry smile, he thought that it wouldn't be long before he and Martha would be seeing their daughter off to school for her first day.

Having been firmly of the opinion that neither of them wanted to know the sex of their Little Beanie in advance, they had undergone an unexpected change of heart the night before going for the scan. Their original thinking had been that they didn't want to tempt fate by knowing too much, or become any more attached to their unborn child than they already were . . . just in case. To perform such an uncharacteristic U-turn for two staunchly rational people had taken them both by surprise. But then as Naomi had said when they spent the Bank Holiday weekend with her, they had better prepare themselves for plenty more surprises when it came to being parents.

'Parenthood makes fools of us all,' she had said with a laugh. 'What you believe makes perfect sense one day will seem quite ridiculous another.'

In the days since 'Catgate' – as Martha referred to that week-end a fortnight ago – Tom was surprised by yet another turna-round in thinking, that of his wife's opinion of Rick. Whenever his name came up in conversation, a glint would appear in her eye and she'd say, 'Who? Oh, you mean Rick-the-Cat-Killer?'

If Tom didn't know better, he would say that Martha was enjoying Rick's fall from grace, as she saw it. Which was odd, given how keen she had been on him when Willow first intro-duced Rick to the family. To say they were all taken aback by this new boyfriend, who turned up with Willow in a 5-series BMW and a Ralph Lauren shirt and Armani jeans, was a colos-sal understatement. Had he still been alive, Colin would have clapped Rick on the back and hailed him as the best thing to come his youngest daughter's way.

Tom had never been entirely convinced by Rick's ideal boy-friend credentials. But for the sake of family harmony, and because Willow did seem to be happy, he had not queried his suitability. But that day at Anchor House when Naomi had taken the girls shopping, Tom had found himself ill-disposed towards Rick. It was something about the churlish way he had waved Willow off as she'd happily climbed into the back seat of Naomi's car. It had been obvious that he hadn't wanted Willow to go, that he had wanted her to remain with him. For the rest of the day everything about Rick's manner had been grudging, as though he didn't want to be there. In turn, Tom's mood had been affected and, he was afraid to say, he probably hadn't been good company for Ellis, who had tried to make the best of a bad job.

Then in the evening during dinner, they'd had that extraordinary scene which had left them sitting in stunned silence. Since then, Tom had wondered what he would have done if he'd been in Rick's shoes. Would he have gone to similar lengths to protect Martha's feelings over something he knew would upset her? Probably, yes, he would. Husbands, wives, partners, they all did strange things at times. Nobody was immune from doing something out of character. Or doing something that was just plain bloody weird, like secretly burying a dead cat behind a garden shed and inventing a story that was nothing but a tissue of lies.

To have kept up the pretence must have taken some doing on Rick's part. Tom would have caved in and come clean with Martha. Maybe that was because his wife was not one to leave a stone unturned when it came to her rooting out the truth or getting to the bottom of something. Moreover, she was invariably right to do so. Was she right in this instance to regard Rick the way she did, with such apparent disdain?

The grass cut and the mower put away, Tom washed his hands in the small utility room before pushing open the kitchen door. Martha was sitting at the table working on her laptop. He had left her there more than an hour ago. She was determined not to be accused of slacking because she was pregnant, so was working harder than ever. Some of her colleagues had guessed she was pregnant and with the news out, she had officially informed HR of the situation.

'Much more to do?' he asked, going over to the fridge to help himself to a cold beer.

'Nearly done,' she replied. 'Can you put the kettle on for me, please? I'd love a cup of tea.'

'Herbal, decaf or proper builder's tea?'

'I've had my daily quota of proper tea, so it had better be decaf,' she said.

With the lid off his bottle of beer, Tom drank thirstily from it, then set about the business of making Martha a mug of tea. 'Chocolate mini roll with it?' he offered, knowing that she currently couldn't eat enough of them.

'Please,' she murmured absently.

When all was ready, he joined her at the table.

'There,' she declared, pushing the laptop away from her and stretching her back, then rubbing her baby bump, 'finished.'

'And here's your reward,' he said with a smile, passing her the mug of tea and mini roll.

'You're a saint,' she said.

'Aren't I just? What would you like for supper? I reckon it's warm enough for a barbecue, if you'd like it.'

'Sounds heavenly. And thank goodness we haven't got Rick-the-Cat-Killer here to nag you about cooking the meat properly.'

Tom took a long swig of his beer. 'You know you really should stop calling him that. One day you'll say it to his face by accident. And besides, he didn't intentionally kill the cat, did he?'

'Who says I'd say it to his face by accident,' she said, 'and not with deliberate intent?'

Tom looked at his wife thoughtfully. 'You've really taken against him, haven't you?'

'Yes,' she said simply.

'For lying to your sister the way he did?'

'If he could lie about something like that, who's to say what else he would deceive Willow about?'

'So now you have him nailed as a serial liar?'

'We don't know that he isn't, do we? I mean, what do we really know about him? He never speaks about his family, or any friends.'

'He's a condemned man in your book?'

Martha drank some of her tea then took a bite of the mini roll. When she'd swallowed the mouthful, she said, 'If you really want to know, I'd condemned him before Catgate.'

'Why?'

'Because of something he said to me. He as good as accused me of bullying Willow and of putting her down.'

'When did he say that?'

'It was during that phone call when he let slip that Willow was pregnant. And you know what, I've always had a suspicion that he did it deliberately. He just sounded so horribly smug.'

'Why would he do that?'

'Because he knew damned well it would upset me. That was his way of putting me in my place for what he perceived as my overbearing nature towards Willow.'

'That's a hell of a leap to make. And apart from anything else, why didn't you tell me this before now?'

After another sip of her tea, she said, 'I was embarrassed, and not to put too fine a point on it, humiliated. Let's face it, Tom, I don't always treat Willow as a responsible adult, do I?'

He smiled. 'That's what being a big sister is all about, isn't it? It's what mine does to me occasionally.'

'Well, it's given me cause to think that perhaps it's a habit of behaviour which I need to break. But the last thing I want is a self-righteous lecture from a pompous jerk who thinks he can just wade in and start dictating the terms of my relationship with Willow. And as for his sickening adoration of her, oh please, pass me the bucket!'

Tom could well imagine how annoyed Martha would have been by such a reprimand. He was disappointed that it was only now that he was hearing about the way Rick had spoken to her. 'Do you want me to speak to him?' he said.

'No! I don't want him to have the satisfaction of ever knowing that he rattled me. I have my pride.'

His beer finished, Tom fetched another bottle from the fridge. When he had it open, he said, 'You realise we're going to have to find a way to rub along with him, don't you, for Willow's sake, and that of our child's cousin?'

'Don't think I haven't thought that a hundred times already,' she said with a sigh. 'We're stuck with him.'

Unless Willow grows tired of Rick, thought Tom. *Or thinks twice about a boyfriend who could lie so convincingly to her.*

'And to think I was worried about Mum having a boyfriend,' Martha said. 'Ellis is practically perfect compared to Rick-the-Cat-Killer.'

Tom smiled. 'I never thought I'd hear you say that.'

'Me neither. But Ellis has gone up in my estimation. I'm sure he was having doubts about Rick that night around the table, before Lucy's telephone call. There was something in the way he looked at me when Rick was playing with Willow's hair. I honestly think he thought the same as I did, that it was a creepy act of possession.'

'Some might see the gesture as endearing. We've seen him do it before.'

277

'Yeah, and it doesn't get any more palatable each time we're subjected to it. Don't ever think of doing that to me.'

Tom laughed. 'I wouldn't dare. Not unless I was keen to have my hand bitten off.'

Chapter Forty

'Hello, Mrs Powell, I hope this isn't a bad time to call you. How are you?'

'Not very well, since you ask.'

'Oh,' said Willow, 'I'm sorry to hear that.'

'It's my hip; it's giving me merry hell. Although there's nothing merry about hell, or my wonky hip.'

'No, I don't suppose there is,' remarked Willow.

'I know it's just a saying – merry hell – but maybe the person who came up with it believed the devil really did have all the fun.'

'I'd never thought of it that way before.'

'Nor had I until now. Who did you say you were, dear?'

Grabbing her chance, Willow moved smoothly on to her well-oiled sales pitch. 'My name is Willow and I'm calling from AoK. I have a very special request to make of you this afternoon, Mrs Powell. You've been so very generous over the years in supporting the work your favourite charity carries out, but I wonder if you could possibly see your way to—'

'Willow's an odd sort of name,' the woman cut in. 'Is it one of those made-up ones? Between you and me, some of the names you hear nowadays are just plain silly and shouldn't be allowed.

I heard a young woman in the park the other day shouting out the name Magnolia. Have you ever heard of anything more stupid? Who in their right mind names a child after a tree, or the colour of paint? Is Willow your nickname? Are you tall and skinny with sticks for arms and legs?'

'Actually, it's my real name,' Willow answered pleasantly. 'It was my mother's choice. And I'm not that tall or thin. Quite average, really.' Determined to get the conversation back on track, Willow tried again. 'Now Mrs Powell, the reason I'm calling is—'

'Well, be quick about it, I can't stand here chatting all day, not with my hip and *Escape to the Country* about to start. Do you ever watch that? You know what drives me mad about that programme?'

'No,' Willow replied patiently.

'When those dozy people don't end up buying one of the houses they've been shown. I think it's rude of them. I always feel sorry for the poor owners having their hopes built up that they might get a sale out of having their house on telly. All that effort to tidy up and have everything shipshape, and then those idiots who couldn't make up their minds if their lives depended on it dither about and choose nothing. The plain truth of the matter is they only want to have their faces on the telly. See themselves as celebrities, I expect. Time-wasters, that's what they are.' She laughed abruptly. 'But I still watch it. Do you know why?'

'No.'

'Because I live in hope that one day I'll see the presenter turn on those couples and give them a piece of his or her mind. Now that would make good telly, don't you think?'

Willow was inclined to agree. 'So, Mrs Powell,' she tried once more. But she got no further.

'Well, it's been nice chatting to you, dear. That's the trouble with being old, you don't have the chance to chat that much; people are always in such a hurry. I can go for days without seeing or speaking to anybody. No time for the pleasantries in life, that's the trouble with folk. Like I say, it's been nice talking with you, but I really must get on now. Goodbye.'

Willow knew she'd lost her chance so reluctantly said goodbye too.

'Mind not on the job today, Willow?'

It was Kyle and he was standing right behind her. How did he do it? How did he creep up on her the way he did?

'It wasn't a convenient time for the woman to talk,' Willow lied, scrolling through the list of donors on her computer screen. Well, it wasn't that big a lie, Mrs Powell did have an appointment with *Escape to the Country* to keep, didn't she?

Seemingly satisfied with her answer, Kyle went to check on the latest recruit to AoK. He was yet another actor who needed an income between jobs and the flexibility to bunk off to go for auditions at short notice. Kyle didn't really like actors – too full of themselves, he believed – but he knew better than anyone that they could act up a storm when it came to pleading a good sob story to get a donor to increase their regular donations.

There was no answer from the telephone number Willow had just dialled, and seeing she was now eligible for a fifteen-minute break, she removed her headset and went to the office kitchen to make herself a drink.

While she waited for the kettle to boil, she felt her mobile vibrating in the breast pocket of her dungarees. Woe betide anyone who answered or made a personal call while they were supposed to be working.

As she thought it would be, it was Rick. When she was at work, he always liked to make sure she was all right, that she wasn't overdoing it.

'Hi there,' he said, 'what are you up to?'

'Just making myself a drink.'

'And you're okay? You're not feeling too tired or too stressed?'

'You know I don't work down a coalmine, don't you?' she joked.

'And you know what I'm like, I worry about you. How's our Little Princess?'

Willow put a hand to her bump, which the midwife had called a 'very small neat bump' during her last check-up. Rick worried that she should be bigger at this stage, but the midwife, who had recommended some antacid to sort out the indigestion problem Willow had previously suffered, didn't seem to think there was a problem.

'All bumps are different,' the woman told Rick firmly when he'd queried her size. He always took time off work to accompany Willow to her antenatal appointments. He asked far more questions than she did. Her mind just went blank when she was being examined or was talking to the midwife.

'She's fine,' Willow said in answer to Rick's question and just as the kettle clicked off.

'What are you drinking?' he asked. 'Not coffee?'

'Weak decaffeinated tea,' she lied, reaching for the jar of Gold Blend. It was only her second cup of the day – *and second lie of the day* – what harm could that do?

'What time will you be finishing this evening?' he asked.

'Six o'clock.'

'I'll swing by and pick you up in that case.'

'There's no need.'

'I know there isn't, but I like to look after you and this is my way of doing just that. I'll see you at six, and don't keep me waiting like you did last time, I don't want to risk getting a parking ticket.'

He ended the call and, her coffee made, Willow took it through to the small communal lounge. A couple of other co-workers were there, each on their mobile phone, deep in conversation with whoever was at the other end of the line. She opted for the table in the corner by the window which looked down onto a jumble of wheelie bins. *The glamour of it all*, she thought with a smile.

So why stay? She heard Rick's voice inside her head.

Because, when everything else felt wrong and out of her control, this at least felt normal. Here at AoK she could almost forget she was pregnant, and more importantly, forget that Rick had lied to her about poor Cedric. Everybody told little white lies, she did it all the time, she was even guilty of telling some enormous lies, but those were only to herself. What Rick had done was different. The untruth he'd told was just too awful.

She had sort of forgiven him, well, as best as she could, but Lucy and Simon refused point-blank to forgive Willow. She'd tried explaining to them what had happened, and why Rick had lied to her, but they refused to believe it. They were convinced that she had been in on it and had deliberately lied to them.

'If they can't accept your apology, or believe you, then they can't be genuine friends,' Rick had said to her. 'You're better off without them.'

But Willow didn't feel better off without Lucy and Simon's

friendship. She felt terrible about the whole thing, especially after they'd gone through the heartache of a miscarriage and then discovered Cedric's decomposing body the way they had.

Shuddering at the gruesome thought, and the memory of the photo Lucy had sent her, Willow played with the diamond ring on her left hand, turning it round and round. It still felt strange to her, wearing something so obviously expensive. She was terrified of losing it, goodness knows how much it was worth. It was certainly worth so much more than she deserved.

To stop the bubble of guilt that was pushing against the cork inside her and threatening to burst free, she told herself that while she didn't deserve to be given such a beautiful ring, her daughter was the reason she wore it. So surely that made it okay?

She was now twenty-eight weeks pregnant and Rick couldn't wait for the big day when she would give birth.

'I'll be right there with you every second of it,' he repeatedly assured her whenever she admitted to feeling nervous.

She knew it was something she had to face, but the thought of labour utterly terrified her. She wasn't good with pain. She was such a pathetic wimp.

Martha, on the other hand, wouldn't be scared. She'd probably yell and scream and boss everyone about and swear the roof off, but she wouldn't be frightened.

Wishing she could be more like her sister, Willow drank the rest of her illicit coffee and with a few more minutes to go before her breaktime was up, she checked her mobile for emails. For one in particular.

She and Ellis's stepson Lucas had recently struck up an email exchange. Curious about him, she had tracked Lucas down on Facebook and messaged him, not sure how he might react. Would he think she had been stalking him?

Thankfully he'd been only too pleased to hear from her and almost daily now they were in touch. His emails were refreshingly humorous and were a happy distraction for her. He was clearly very fond of his stepfather and had nothing but good things to say about Ellis. When Mum and Ellis had announced that they weren't marrying after all, that being permanently engaged suited them much better, Lucas had asked Willow if she knew why there had been a change of plan. She wrote back saying that from what her mother had told them, she just didn't fancy dealing with the palaver of organising a wedding and the difficulties it generated.

'I can relate to that,' Lucas replied to her. 'And who needs marriage these days anyway?'

Rick did. Ideally, he wanted them to marry before the baby was born, but realistically he knew that it would be better to wait until they had more time to plan the wedding. 'One thing at a time,' he'd said. 'Baby first, then we'll marry.'

He was so full of confidence and optimism about the future, something Willow didn't feel. She wished she did, she truly did. Increasingly she felt her old self, and her confidence, trickling away from her.

Disappointed that there wasn't an email from Lucas in her mailbox, she took her empty coffee mug through to the kitchen, washed it up, then returned to her desk. Where, surprise, surprise Kyle was hovering with a pointed look on his face. *Slave driver*, she thought. Even though she was still regularly hitting her targets, and even though he knew she was pregnant and would be leaving soon, he was hellbent on extracting his pound of flesh from her.

Yet for all that, as she slipped on her headset and dialled up the next telephone number on her list, she knew she would miss all this when the time came. She would even miss Kyle.

Chapter Forty-One

The call that Ellis had been dreading had come shortly after he and Naomi had been to see his mother.

There had been nothing out of the ordinary to indicate it would be the last time he would see Rose, although invariably when he drove away from the West View Care Home the thought would cross his mind that he might have just said goodbye for the final time. Yes, she had grown frailer as September drew to a close, and increasingly spent more time asleep, but then he had been observing those changes in her for a good while now.

The end when it came still shocked him. He was told that she had died peacefully in her sleep about the time he and Naomi arrived back at Anchor House after their visit. It was what he had feared would happen, that Rose would choose her moment to die when she was alone, as if she didn't want to burden him with her departure, that she could manage quite well without him, thank you very much. She had never been a sentimental woman, she'd been a pragmatist to her core, and right to the last she had done things her way. Her final words to them had actually been to Naomi.

'Take good care of my boy, won't you?' she'd said.

'Mum,' he'd protested, 'I'm sixty-five, I'm hardly a boy!'

With a slight nod of her head, she'd tutted. 'You'll always be my boy, Ellis. Always.'

'Of course I'll take good care of him,' Naomi had said. 'I promise.'

With hindsight, that exchange should have alerted Ellis to what lay ahead. He had often heard that in many instances those close to death choose their moment to die, and often they want to die alone. They've said all their farewells and want to slip away on their own terms.

In contrast, Ellis's wife had died in his arms. Diana hadn't wanted to be alone at the end and he had vowed it wouldn't happen. The minimal time he had not spent at her bedside, in the hospice while she was having palliative care for the remaining days of her life, had been a torture for him, filling him with the fear that he might break his promise to her. Death, when it came, was a welcome relief for Diana, for him too if he were honest. He had hated to see her beautiful body so utterly destroyed by cancer. She had fought so hard against it, but ultimately the disease had been the victor.

But thank God his mother had not had that type of battle to endure, just a slow but steady decline. Rose had frequently said that the last thing she wanted was a drawn-out deathbed scene. 'I don't want an audience,' she'd said. 'I want a quiet, dignified end.'

Now, as Ellis stood between Lucas and Naomi on a windless autumnal afternoon in the churchyard of St Saviour's and watched Rose's coffin being lowered into the ground, he hoped that she would have approved of the service, that it had been suitably dignified.

Rose had specified that she wanted a burial, not a cremation, but she had not made any stipulations as to where it should be. With Lucas's agreement, Ellis had opted for the church here in Tilsham. Maybe subconsciously he saw the church as cementing his future – this was where he intended to spend the rest of his days, with Naomi.

The Reverend Veronica Carlyle hadn't known Rose, but she had taken the information with which Ellis had provided her and made a decent job of celebrating his mother's well-lived life. Amongst those who had come today to pay their respects had been care workers from West View and most heart-warmingly of all, a fair number of the pupils Rose had taught, many of whom had travelled a long way to be here and were middle-aged and pensioner-age. Much like himself, he thought with a wry smile.

Where did the years go? One minute he was a child, then he was a grown man and married to Diana and with a young stepson, then he was a widower mourning the death of his wife, and now . . . now he had been given another chance. Another bite of the cherry. And he was determined to make the most of it, because not everyone was that lucky in life.

The light pressure of a hand on his arm broke into his thoughts. It was Naomi indicating that the burial service was over, and people were looking at him expectantly, as though for permission to move on to the next part of the proceedings. The final act before the curtain came down.

When he'd proposed that the mourners should gather for a drink at the pub in the harbour, Naomi had come up with a suggestion of her own. She'd said that she had nothing against the pub, but she felt Anchor House would be nicer. 'I'd like to do this small thing for Rose,' she'd said, 'it would be my gift to her.'

Once it was known in the village that his mother's funeral

was to take place at St Saviour's and the wake would be held at Anchor House, Jennifer Kingsbury and a couple of other stalwarts of the village WI had offered Naomi their assistance. Not long after breakfast that morning, trays of sandwiches, sausage rolls, mini quiches and cakes were dropped off, then Martha and Tom arrived with Willow and Rick shortly afterwards. It was good of them to come, despite never having met his mother. He took it as a good sign, another stepping-stone towards accepting him into their family.

Ellis was touched that people who hadn't known him for all that long had rushed to help; it made him feel even more a part of the community, and more importantly, a part of Naomi's circle of neighbourhood friends. He was, after all, taking Colin's place at Anchor House and there had to be some in Tilsham who would never truly accept him. Such as those at the sailing club where Colin spent so much of his time, and with whom Ellis had no real contact.

When they were back at the house, Rick advocated that he and Tom serve drinks, and Martha and Willow should help their mother to act as waitresses and pass round trays of food.

'Bit bloody sexist, Rick,' Ellis heard Martha say as he shook hands with a complete stranger who claimed to have been one of Rose's students. 'Why can't Tom and I serve drinks, or better still, Willow and I do it together?'

'It makes no odds to me,' Rick said with a shrug, 'I was only trying to be helpful.'

The death-stare Martha threw him should have stopped Rick in his tracks, but he merely smiled at her. Which probably infuriated Martha all the more. There was clearly some friction going on between the pair of them; Ellis had noticed it earlier when they'd all arrived. It wasn't anything he could specifically put his finger on, but there was definitely something. Naomi evidently thought so too because he'd noticed her frowning at something Martha said to Tom, as though they were having a joke at Rick's expense. Or maybe she just thought it was inappropriate on the day of Rose's funeral for someone to be making a joke.

Lucas had offered to help serve food as well, working alongside Willow, and the pair of them were weaving their way through the mourners standing around in small groups on the lawn. There was, it had to be said, nothing particularly mournful in the manner of the guests, not now they had a glass in their hands. But that was the way of these things, people always bucked up once the formality of the funeral service was behind them. It was, Ellis hoped, just as his mother would have wanted.

'How are you feeling?' asked Naomi, appearing at his side and with a glass of wine for him.

'Not so bad,' he said, taking it from her. 'Thanks for this,' he added, indicating the garden and everyone gathered there.

'There's no need to thank me, I wanted to do it for you.'

'Is it a painful reminder of Colin's funeral?' he asked.

She shook her head. 'Not really. His friends at the sailing club insisted they arrange the wake. I had very little to do with the organisation of it. They thought they were doing the right thing, but it actually made me feel surplus to requirements.'

He smiled. 'In many ways I feel the same right now.'

She looked at him, concerned. 'I'm sorry, would you have preferred to have done this at the pub, like you originally wanted?'

'No! What I mean is I know only a handful of people here today, it's as if I'm a guest myself.'

Leaning into him, Naomi kissed his cheek. 'It'll soon be over,' she said quietly. 'Another forty-five minutes or so and they'll start to drift away, especially when the food runs out.'

She was right. Within the hour, and with just one slightly curled-up smoked salmon sandwich and a scattering of cake crumbs left, the last of the mourners had taken their leave.

Loosening his tie and undoing the top button of his shirt, Ellis sank into a chair on the verandah. Lucas did the same, except he removed his tie and wound it around his left hand, just as he used to do as a boy when he came home from school.

'I don't know about the rest of you,' said Naomi, 'but I'm parched. Anyone else want a cup of tea?'

Everyone said yes and Ellis immediately made to stand up. 'I'll come and give you a hand.'

'No, you won't. You stay right where you are and relax. You look positively done in. Rick, would you like to help me, please?'

Rick hesitated, perhaps wondering why he had been singled out. Then: 'Of course,' he said.

When they'd gone, and wondering if by asking Rick for help, Naomi was trying to make him feel more a part of the family, Ellis said, 'What is it about funerals that make them so exhausting?'

'It's the pretence,' said Willow. 'Pretending to feel something when actually you don't.'

'Wow,' said Martha, 'that's a bit insensitive, isn't it?'

Willow flushed. 'Sorry,' she said, looking at Lucas and Ellis. 'I didn't mean it to sound quite so bad. What I meant was, that it's the effort you have to make to be polite to so many people you hardly know that is so wearing, when all you want to do is be alone and deal with your own feelings. I remember being like that at Dad's funeral.'

'Yes,' agreed Lucas. 'I felt the same way at my mother's funeral. I can remember listening to some woman going on and on about how she and Mum were at school together and how they did this, that and the other together, and I just kept wishing she'd shut the hell up so I didn't have to keep nodding my head as though I gave a damn. So yeah, when you say it's the pretence that's so tiring, you're spot on, Willow.'

Ellis had never heard Lucas speak this way before about Diana's funeral. But what struck him most, as Martha and Tom looked on, was the obvious connection between Lucas and Willow, the way they seemed so at ease with each other. It was as though they had known one another for years, and Ellis was strongly reminded of the close friendship he and Naomi had enjoyed when they'd been students at university. Reminded too of all the times they had missed their moment.

He might be leaping to conclusions, but he was glad Rick was inside with Naomi and not out here to witness the scene.

Chapter Forty-Two

The day shone bright and glittery in the way that an October morning so often did, and while Ellis was in the shower, Naomi, wrapped in her warmest dressing gown, was outside on the balcony drinking the tea he had made for her. After a lifetime of marriage, Colin had never made her tea the way she liked; he'd always been too heavy-handed with the milk. Ellis didn't make that mistake, he always got it just right.

The tide was out and down on the shore, the redshanks were busy poking about in the mudflats. In the distance, a soft breeze played across the surface of the water and shafts of early morning sunlight shone down through banks of clouds and glinted off the ripples. There wouldn't be many more mornings when Naomi would be able to enjoy her first cup of tea of the day this way. Not in her nightclothes at any rate. The forecast was for rain to push in from the west this evening and to linger for the next few days. She was glad for Ellis's sake that the weather had been as good as it had been yesterday. A funeral in the rain was just adding insult to injury.

Ellis had known that it was only a matter of time before his mother died, but it had still shaken him. Given the strong relationship he had with his mother, his reaction was only natural and had brought back memories for Naomi of losing her own parents, who had died when Martha and Willow were teenagers.

Her mother was first to die of a stroke and her father a few years later of sepsis, after stepping on a rusty nail and not bothering to go to the doctor. Not until it was too late. At the time, Naomi could accept that there had been nothing her mother could do to prevent the stroke that killed her, but her father's death had seemed so avoidable. If only he had been more careful . . . if only he had gone to the doctor . . . if only he hadn't been so reckless and pig-headed and made light of feeling 'a touch under the weather' on the telephone to her. 'Just some silly bug I'll soon shake off, I'm sure,' he'd said.

In many ways Colin had been quite like her father – both thoroughly headstrong and convinced they could make the world bend to their will. Kindred spirits, her father and Colin had got on famously together, and perhaps Colin had seen in Naomi's father not so much a replacement for his own, but someone he could respect and admire in a similar fashion.

Colin had lost his parents when he was at university; they'd died in a bomb explosion planted by the IRA at a restaurant in London. He never forgave those who were responsible for the murder of his parents, and years later he was still capable of exploding with a furious rage when *murdering terrorists*, as he saw them, appeared on the television masquerading as politicians.

Naomi had always believed that this was the source of his temper and internal anger, the death of his parents, to whom he had been devoted. Many times she had suggested he seek help, that talking through losing his mother and father in so violent a manner might help unlock what had the power to consume and overwhelm him at times. He refused, of course. Very likely he was scared to look too deeply inside himself, afraid at what he might find lurking there.

For a man like Colin, very much an alpha male, it was so much better to suppress the pain and anguish. Rightly or wrongly, it was why Naomi forgave him his outbursts. She didn't expect others to understand that. Or to understand that their secret – their dirty secret that he hit her – became a bond between them. He trusted her not to tell anyone, she even promised him that she wouldn't, but only because it was easy to keep a promise that was cloaked in shame and humiliation, that she, an intelligent woman, 'allowed' her husband to hit her.

She still felt that shame now and doubted she would ever really lose it. She knew that Ellis had been shocked by what she had shared with him, and that he would never understand how a man like Colin could behave so badly and get away with it.

But who were she and Ellis to judge when, the night of Geraldine's wedding, they had lain on the floor of that summerhouse and made love? She had been a married woman with her desire fuelled by the need to pay her husband back for his affair, and Ellis had been fully aware of that. So no, she would not judge Colin. The only person she had a right to judge was herself, and over the years she had done far too much of that. But not anymore. With Ellis, she was determined to live with a fresh clean slate.

A few weeks ago, he had taken her by surprise when he'd told her that not only had he renewed the rental agreement on Waterside Cottage for another couple of months but he had been in talks with the owners to buy it.

'But why?' she had asked, alarmed. 'Is it so you can have somewhere to escape if things go wrong between us?'

'I knew you'd think that,' he'd said, 'and it's absolutely not the reason I'm doing it. Apart from anything else, a beach-front property is a good investment.'

After that awful visit to the solicitor in Chichester, Naomi knew the value of Ellis's financial portfolio, just as he knew her worth, so she couldn't really see that he needed yet another investment.

'I'm thinking ahead,' he'd explained. 'It might be nice for Lucas to have somewhere to stay when he visits in the future. And also, Martha and Willow. Overspill accommodation, if you like.'

'But there's room here,' she'd countered.

'I'm told by friends,' he'd said with a smile, 'who already have grandchildren that the more space one can have, the better. Besides, I thought it would be a fun project for us to do the cottage up together.' He'd then produced some roughly sketched plans that showed how he wanted to open up the ground floor and install bi-fold doors so the beach and garden became a part of the cottage.

'You've put a lot of thought into this, haven't you?' she'd said.

'I have,' he'd admitted. 'I decided that I'd had enough of retirement, I need something to do. You have your garden, which I'm more than happy to help you with, but I suspect I might be trespassing on sacred ground in that respect.'

'Are you saying you're bored?'

'Not at all. But it's either doing up Waterside Cottage or buying a bike and wearing skin-tight Lycra.'

She'd laughed. 'Don't ever think of wearing Lycra. I shall kick you out without a moment's hesitation if you do that.'

'And rightly so. So, am I forgiven for wanting to buy next door?'

'Of course you are.'

With Rose's death, the idea that Lucas could use the cottage when he next visited was implemented far sooner than Ellis had imagined. As soon as a date for the funeral was fixed, Lucas booked his flights and flew over. He was given the option to stay with the rest of them at Anchor House, but he'd said he would be quite happy sleeping next door.

Her tea now finished, and to the left of her eyeline, Naomi caught a flicker of movement down in the garden. Leaning forwards, she saw Willow walking the length of lawn towards the gate and the beach. To the side of the gate, on the path that ran between Anchor House and the beach, Lucas appeared. After exchanging a few words and a smile, they set off along the shoreline.

There was nothing particularly furtive about the encounter, but watching them disappear from view, and seeing the natural synchronicity between the pair of them – the way they had so easily fallen in step with each other, their arms swinging at their sides and almost touching – Naomi felt a chill of foreboding.

Surely she was wrong? Willow and Lucas were merely two young people thrown together by their parents' relationship and were simply getting to know each other. It was all perfectly innocent.

But would Rick see it that way? Knowing the answer to her question would be no, Naomi wondered if she should say something to Ellis. But what? She could hardly ask him to tell his son to back off, could she? Not when he would quite rightly say that it took two to tango.

Oh Willow, she thought, *do take care*.

*

298

Martha's old bedroom, the one she now shared with Tom whenever they visited, had an unusual corner window with a built-in seat beneath it. As a child she had loved to sit there reading while listening to the sounds of the sea, especially if it was stormy.

The window gave a view of the garden and beach beyond, and standing in front of it while brushing her hair, she observed her sister and Lucas setting off for a walk together. Craning her neck, she observed them until they were out of sight.

'What's so interesting down there on the beach?' asked Tom.

'I didn't realise you were awake,' she said, turning to face her husband who was still in bed.

'I've been watching you for a few minutes. What were you straining to look at?'

Martha put the brush down and went and sat on the bed. 'Willow and Lucas going for a walk.'

'And?'

'Don't be obtuse, Tom.'

'Are you suggesting there's more to it than that?'

'Didn't you think last night they were awfully quick to agree with everything the other said? At one point they were practically finishing off each other's sentences.'

He sat up and rubbed his hands over his face, then ran them through his sleep-tousled hair. 'I just thought Willow was showing empathy. She's good like that.'

'Meaning I'm not?'

He smiled. 'I didn't say that. But you're always the practical one, whereas Willow is—'

'Is the big-hearted softie. Yeah, I get it. She's the good cop to my bad cop.'

'We all have our strengths.'

'Hmmm . . . '

He laughed. 'Don't you *hmm* me. Not when you look so gorgeous. If I'm not mistaken, you've reached the radiant stage of pregnancy now, haven't you?'

She pulled a face. 'Have I? I don't feel particularly radiant.'

'Trust me, you are. It's like you're glowing with good health. Pregnancy clearly suits you.'

Her hands placed around her swelling bump, she said, 'A shame it took so long for it to happen for us.'

'It didn't,' said Tom, 'not really. Some couples go through years of trying. We weren't even a full year.'

She smiled. 'It felt a lot longer.'

'That's because you're so wonderfully impatient to make things happen. That's another of your strengths.'

'Bloody hell, Tom, if you keep up with all these compliments, I'll think you're having an affair!'

Which made her think of Willow and Lucas strolling along the beach together. Turning towards the window, she wondered what on earth her fickle sister thought she was up to. And just what would Rick have to say about this?

The answer to that question was a sudden disturbing mental picture of Rick winding Willow's hair around his fingers.

Winding it tighter and tighter.

Chapter Forty-Three

'It's strange,' said Lucas as he walked alongside Willow, 'but it's only now that I really feel like my grandmother has gone. You'd think the whole church and burial thing would have made the point, but somehow it didn't. Does that sound weird?'

'Not really,' said Willow, 'and as far as I know, there aren't any hard and fast rules about these things. We all cope in our different ways. And yesterday you and Ellis had the distraction of all those people to deal with.'

He slowed his step and turned to stare out to sea. 'It brought back memories of my mother's death too.' A moment passed before he returned his gaze to Willow, his hands now pushed into his pockets. 'Did yesterday remind you of losing your dad?'

'Yes, I suppose it did,' she said absently.

'Were you close?'

'Not especially. Not like Martha was. She's what you'd call a proper chip off the block. I think I exasperated him mostly.'

'I find that hard to believe.'

'It's true. My sister has always had a great sense of purpose to her life, it was something Dad tried to encourage in us both. It worked perfectly with Martha, and not at all with me.'

'So what are you like, then?'

'Oh, I'm the cute fluffy black sheep of the family.'

Lucas laughed. 'The cute fluffy bit I can believe, but not the rest.'

'Well, every child ends up being labelled in their family, don't they? From an early age Martha was labelled the clever ambitious one and I was the silly one who didn't have a Scooby-Doo what she was going to do in life.'

'Is that how you see yourself?'

'Yes,' she said matter-of-factly. 'Sometimes I think I should be more like Martha, but then I think of the pressure she might be under, you know, having to live up to all those expectations, and I feel sorry for her.'

'She doesn't come across as being the sort to need sympathy.'

'Don't be fooled by that tough shell of hers. We all bleed if we're cut.'

He smiled. 'It strikes me that you have a very understanding and sympathetic nature. I hope your fiancé has too.'

'What do you mean?'

'That he won't mind me stealing you away for a walk.'

'Oh, he'll be fine.'

Willow wasn't entirely sure this was true, but what the heck, she was allowed to go for a stroll along the beach with someone who was, to all intents and purposes, her stepbrother, wasn't she? Perhaps if Rick hadn't been asleep, he might have come along too. As it was, when she woke up and looked at her mobile to see what time it was, she saw that Lucas had texted her.

Thanks for your support yesterday. You're a good listener. Sorry if I went on a bit.

Out of bed, and in the bathroom, she'd messaged him back.

You didn't go on at all.

Fancy a walk before breakfast?

Nice idea! See you at the beach gate in ten minutes.

Dressing as quietly as she could so as not to disturb Rick, and then conscious that nobody else was up, she silently padded downstairs in her stockinged feet to unlock the back door. It reminded her of being a teenager again, when she used to sneak out late at night to meet Finn from the village. He'd been her boyfriend at the time and she'd lost her virginity to him in the sand dunes and marram grass. It had been his first time as well and neither of them had been that impressed with the mechanics of it. Condoms and sand did not a good mix make. They'd laughed about it and the next time they'd chosen a better spot further round the promontory in the seclusion of the woods.

It had been funny seeing Finn again at the fête back in the summer; she wished now that she'd had more time to catch up with him properly. Another regret to add to the many, she thought sadly.

'Do you suppose we ought to be going back now?' asked Lucas when they'd reached the sand dunes and its myriad memories for Willow.

'Why don't we sit here for a while?' she said, in no hurry to return.

He looked at her with concern. 'You're not feeling unwell, are you?'

Willow looked back at him, confused. 'Why would you think that?'

His gaze dropped to her baby bump.

'Oh,' she said with a laugh. 'No, no, don't worry, I'm not about to go into premature labour, I'm a long way off from that.'

303

'Thank God for that,' he said as they sat down. 'I reckon I'd be pretty useless if that were to happen.'

'Between you and me,' she said, making herself as comfortable as she could, 'I reckon I'm going to be pretty useless too. I try reading the books and the stuff online, but it just scares me all the more.'

'From the way he was talking last night, Rick sounds like he has it all figured out, so you'll be in safe hands with him.'

'I can't help but think he'd make a better job of it than me.'

'I doubt that very much, and if I'm not mistaken, you have the distinct advantage over Rick in that your body is made for giving birth, and his most certainly isn't.'

She smiled. 'I'd willingly swap.'

'You know what, you might actually surprise yourself and breeze through it.'

'Only a man could say that.'

'Fair point,' he conceded. Leaning back, he tilted his head up towards the pale October sun, his hands resting on the sand behind him.

'Can I ask you something?' he said after a lengthy silence.

Willow scooped up a handful of sand and let it trickle slowly through her fingers. 'Yes.'

'Did you and Rick plan to have the baby you're expecting?'

'Are you asking that because you suspect you know the answer is no?'

'I guess so. You just don't seem to be as taken with the idea of motherhood as your sister is.'

She sighed and as she felt the baby move inside her, as though stretching out her legs, Willow scooped up another handful of sand. 'It's because I don't feel ready for it,' she said. 'Martha and

Tom were trying for a baby, they had it all planned out, whereas it happened by mistake for Rick and me.'

'Maybe that's the best way for something life-changing to happen. Just see how the cards fall and go along with it. Which would appear to be your forte.'

'It's yours as well, isn't it?'

'Yeah. I've never been a great planner. Things just seem to happen at the right time and in the right place for me. Born lucky, my gran used to say.'

Willow was about to say she wished she had met his grandmother, when the sound of crunching stones had her turning to look back the way they'd come. Walking towards them, his hand in the air waving to her, was Rick.

'Looks like your knight in shining armour has come to rescue you,' said Lucas.

There was a slight edge to his voice that made Willow feel protective of Rick.

She had felt the same thing yesterday when Martha had asked Rick if he'd buried any more cats recently. He'd smiled politely at her and said that since they were there for a funeral, maybe she ought to think twice about making a joke in such poor taste.

'Why would you say he's come to rescue me?' she said as Lucas helped her to her feet.

'He seems the sort to want to do that, that's all.'

'Is that a bad thing?' she asked with a frown.

'That's for you to decide.'

Chapter Forty-Four

Once they were in the car and on their way back to London, it was like waiting for a storm to break, and just as the sky turned ominously dark with rain clouds, Willow knew it was going to come; it was just a matter of when.

Many times as a child when she had done something that had annoyed her father, she had been in just this situation – waiting for the inevitable. Like the time she had accidentally scratched Dad's new car when her bike fell against it in the garage. Or the time she had been sick in his boat. On another occasion, Martha had wanted to take the blame for something Willow had done, knowing that Dad wouldn't be so cross with her. Martha so rarely did anything wrong, there was no way their father would be furious with her.

On that particular occasion Dad had been in a bad mood for several days and Willow had been messing about doing handstands in the dining room, while Martha timed her to see how long she could hold the position. But then disaster struck when one of Willow's legs knocked against the sideboard, sending a cut-glass decanter flying. It had been no ordinary decanter; it was old, and Dad treasured it because it had belonged to his father. Knowing that Dad would hit the roof with Willow,

Martha had offered to say that she had broken the decanter. But Willow couldn't let her sister do that: whatever punishment was due, it was hers.

From quite a young age she had trained herself not to be scared of Dad, not even when he was absolutely livid. While he raged and blustered, she could think of something completely different and disappear deep inside herself, even when he whacked the backs of her legs. If he did punish her with a smack, he always apologised afterwards and made her promise she would never tell Mum. He would often then be extra nice to her to make up for being so angry.

So yes, she knew all about storms blowing in and then blowing themselves out. That's how it would be with Rick during the journey home. While the syrupy tension between them thickened, she just had to wait patiently for the storm to break and let the thunder and lightning do its worst. Then the sun would burst through the clouds, the tension would be gone, and they'd both say sorry and carry on as though nothing had happened. These things never lasted. That was the nature of a storm; it was over as suddenly as it started.

And really, just as she had herself to blame for smashing Dad's special decanter all those years ago, it was her fault today she was sitting here waiting for Rick to take her to task. But how could she tell him that there was something about being in Lucas's company that made her feel like her old self again, the Willow who could drift along on the tide, taking each day as it came?

Irresponsible, that's what she was. Always had been. Always would be. In all truthfulness, and with her hand on her heart, she could say that she and Lucas had done nothing wrong, all they'd done was walk, talk and sit in the sand dunes. But it was why she had done that that would be playing on Rick's mind and causing him to be jealous.

Envy wasn't an emotion she ever suffered from and was, she'd once read, a trait of the insecure. It was probably a simplistic generalisation, but the more she got to know Rick, the more she could see that he really wasn't as secure and confident as he let on, so maybe that was why he was prone to jealousy. She supposed that's why she felt sorry for him at times and why she now felt guilty about upsetting him by what she'd done. As her father would have said, 'If only you thought things through, Willow!'

With her father's admonishment ringing in her ears, and wondering if she should broach the subject herself with Rick, just to get it over and done with, he let out a groan of exasperation at the driver in front of them. Despite him flashing his lights at the driver to move over, the car stayed resolutely – *stubbornly* – where it was and at the same speed. To make his point, Rick drove even closer to the rear bumper of the car.

'Any nearer and we'll be able to make small talk with the driver in front,' Willow said, in an echo of what Mum used to say to Dad.

Rick shot her a look. 'I know what I'm doing,' he said tersely. 'And I assume you did too when you went sneaking off behind my back to go to the beach with some bloke you hardly know.'

At last! she thought with a sense of relief, just as the first fat drops of rain began to splatter against the windscreen. 'I didn't *sneak* off,' she said, although that was precisely what she had done. 'You were sound asleep, and I didn't want to disturb you when Lucas invited me to join him for a walk.'

'Didn't you think I'd be worried sick about you when I woke

up and found your side of the bed empty? Anything could have happened to you.'

'Hardly.'

The driver in front still hadn't moved out of Rick's way and so he flashed his lights again and hit the horn. 'And why did Lucas have your mobile number in the first place?' he demanded.

'We swapped contact details after his last visit,' she lied. No way could she admit to Rick that she'd hunted Lucas down on Facebook. That would give him entirely the wrong idea. He'd never believe that she was simply curious to know more about the man who was going to be her stepbrother.

'Oh, and about time too!' Rick muttered as the car in front pulled over and allowed him to put his foot down and roar past.

Twisting her head to her left, Willow looked at the other driver as they sped by and tried to convey a smile of polite apology. The other driver was a young girl and gave Willow the finger. So much for trying to make amends, she thought.

'You're such an innocent,' Rick said, 'you never see people for what they really are.'

'What makes you say that?' she asked, watching the windscreen wipers swish to and fro, smearing dead insects across the glass.

'You can't see what Lucas is up to, can you? He clearly fancies you. I saw the way he kept looking at you last night; it was bloody obvious he wanted you all to himself.'

'Oh, that's nonsense!'

'Is it? Is it really? Because I think you might feel the same way about him. And what the hell were you talking about down on the beach this morning? Be honest, did he come on to you? Did you encourage him?'

'*No!* You've got it all wrong, Rick. He just wanted someone to talk to about his grandmother. I think he feels guilty that he didn't see more of her towards the end of her life.'

Rick grunted. 'Why didn't he talk to Ellis or your mother about his grandmother if he wanted to ease his conscience? Or even Martha? Why *you?*'

Willow let out a short laugh. 'Would you choose Martha to talk to if you were upset about something?' When he didn't respond, she said, 'Sometimes it's easier to talk to a stranger, or a relative stranger about something quite personal. And anyway, I'm known for being a good listener.' She thought of all those elderly donors who poured out their troubles to her when she was at work trying to extract an increase in donations from them.

He scoffed. 'You never listen to me.'

'I do.'

'You don't!' he shouted, thumping the steering wheel. 'You bloody well don't! You're like a child with your head up in the clouds singing la-la-la to yourself and blind to what's going on around you. But here's the thing, Willow, it's time now, as the mother of my child, for you to grow up and be the responsible adult you're meant to be. And that means you don't go off without me for cosy tête-à-têtes with other men!'

'*Our* child,' she said quietly, turning the diamond ring round on her finger.

His expression set like stone, he drove on in silence.

Then: 'I blame that family of yours. Your parents must have over-indulged you because you're the baby of the family. You're a classic example of last child syndrome. Take it from me, an outsider has a more focused perspective on these things. I can see the dynamics that go on in your family much better than you can. And as for your sister, I can read her like a book.'

'In what way?'

'In all ways. I told you before that I was convinced that she's jealous of you and this morning she proved it to me.'

'How?'

'It was Martha who told me where I'd find you, that you were on the beach with Lucas.'

'Surely she was just being helpful?'

'It was the way she said it and what she was implying. And why does she keep making bitchy remarks about that wretched cat I had to deal with? She does it deliberately to get a rise out of me. To make me feel even more of an outsider. She's nothing but a bully.'

'I think it's a sick joke she's taken too far,' said Willow. 'Not that there's anything remotely funny about what happened to poor Cedric.'

And poor Rick, she thought. He really didn't like being made fun of, and for some reason Martha seemed to enjoy reminding him of the lie he'd told. Willow would have to speak to her sister about that. It wasn't fair to Rick, especially if it made him feel an outsider to the family. She would tell Martha that he'd made a mistake and he'd said he was sorry, so that should be an end to it. She also needed to accept that, but with Lucy and Simon still not talking to her, it was hard for her to forgive Rick fully herself.

A mile or so further on, and in a change of tone, and reaching for her hand, Rick said, 'I'm sorry I shouted, but it's only because I love you so much and I'm frightened of losing you. I just want our life together to be perfect.'

She smiled at him, relieved that the storm had been so

short-lived. 'Life is seldom perfect,' she said. 'We just have to do the best we can.'

Instead of returning her smile, he frowned and snatched his hand away. 'You're supposed to say you love me back,' he said.

'Oh,' she said, 'well, of course I love you. You know that.'

For a moment he didn't respond and for that moment the silence between them was profound. It seemed to go on for ever as the wipers swished and the rain, heavier now, beat down on the roof of the car, making it sound tinny and insubstantial.

'Do you?' he asked finally. 'Because sometimes I'm not so sure.'

Keeping her smile firmly in place, Willow wondered if she did actually love him. But if it wasn't love, what was it, and was it enough?

'Bit late to be asking questions like that, isn't it?' she imagined the wriggling baby inside her saying with a wag of a finger.

Chapter Forty-Five

It was a blustery day in late October and with a wintry chill in the air, Naomi decided to light the fire in the sitting room.

For most of that morning she had been preparing for Geraldine's visit. The main guest bedroom, having undergone a makeover which Naomi and Ellis had done together in the weeks since Rose's funeral and after Lucas had flown home, was now ready. In the kitchen a ginger cake was out of the oven and cooling on the rack, along with some fruit scones and a pot of homemade raspberry jam.

Geraldine had at least given Naomi twenty-four hours' notice this time before arriving. She hadn't sounded her customary forthright self on the telephone, and afterwards Naomi had pondered the reason for her friend's visit. Not that there had to be a reason, other than two old friends spending time together, but the last time Geraldine had pitched up, she had most certainly had a reason.

'I expect she's coming for a progress report,' Ellis had said. 'Would you like me to make myself scarce so she can be thoroughly indiscreet with you?'

'Absolutely not,' Naomi told him. 'With Geraldine there'll be a total absence of discretion whether you're here or not. Having missed her chance last time she was here, she'll want to check you out for herself this time.'

'Will she prod and poke me like a show dog being judged at Crufts?'

'I wouldn't put it past her.'

'I can't wait,' he'd said with a grin. 'But I'll warn you now, if she makes any attempt to lift up my tail to inspect my nether regions I shall growl and bite her very hard.'

Naomi smiled now at the thought of Ellis biting Geraldine and struck a match before putting it to the kindling and screwed up balls of newspaper in the grate. She watched the flames take hold, thinking that as much as they'd joked about Geraldine's visit, they would both initially be slightly on edge.

Two people falling in love and wanting to be together should be the easiest thing in the world, but it wasn't. There was, it seemed, an endless obstacle course for them to negotiate, of having to prove themselves to friends and family. There had been one or two old friends of Ellis's at the funeral for his mother who Naomi had felt had been sizing her up, perhaps comparing her to Diana, and last week she and Ellis had gone to London to have lunch with some more of his friends. Bit by bit, they were chipping away at the building blocks of their old lives in order to create a new life together. Naomi just hoped that Geraldine wasn't on her way here to demolish what they had so far built.

One person with whom they hadn't experienced any difficulties with their relationship was Lucas. Ellis had frequently described him as having an easy-going nature and it was true, he did. In that respect he was very like Ellis. And Willow.

It had been obvious to Naomi and Ellis that there was an undeniable connection between Willow and Lucas. Undoubtedly Rick had noticed it too. At breakfast that morning, the day after Rose's funeral, Naomi had watched him closely. While the conversation had gone on around the table, there had been something of the coiled spring about him, as though he were trying very hard to contain his emotions. He hadn't joined in with the conversation in the way he normally did, but instead, when he'd finished eating, he'd put a hand to Willow's hair and played with a lock of it between his fingers. What had previously come across as a charming display of affection, if a little too overt for Naomi's taste, had felt at that moment a very different gesture, as if Rick was telling Lucas to back off, that Willow was his.

When they'd all left, and Lucas had gone next door to deal with some work he needed to do before returning to LA, and just as Naomi was wondering how best to raise the subject with Ellis, he had brought it up himself.

'Do you think I should say something to Lucas?' Ellis had asked.

'And say what exactly?'

It was a good question. In the end they decided that the problem, if indeed there was a problem, would simply fly home with Lucas. Once or twice since then Naomi had been tempted to say something to Willow, but she knew her youngest daughter of old; she wasn't a deliberately flirtatious girl, she was just naturally friendly, with an engaging personality. Naomi hoped that Rick saw things the same way.

After putting the fireguard in place, Naomi went to wash her hands. That done, she decided to make a start on peeling the vegetables for supper that evening. Then she remembered that Ellis had offered to cook.

She was still getting used to the idea of somebody else cooking for her. Colin had never cooked unless it was out in the garden with the barbecue. Even then Naomi would have to marinate the meat or fish and prepare the salads and desserts. But Ellis loved to cook and had added some of his own kitchenware to the cupboards in her kitchen.

Not *her* kitchen, she reminded herself, it was *their* kitchen. Just as Anchor House was *their* home now. But with her name on the deeds, she had to wonder if Ellis ever felt that he was no more than her guest here. Was that the real reason he had bought Waterside Cottage – the purchase of which had now gone through – to have some kind of ownership? Would it be better if she sold Anchor House and they bought somewhere else together?

No, she wasn't ready for that.

It seemed an age ago when Martha had suggested that Naomi should move to be nearer her and Tom. There had been no more talk of her selling up from either Martha or Willow. Had Naomi misjudged her eldest daughter's motives? Had Martha been genuinely concerned for Naomi's welfare, living alone as she had been, and did she now regard Ellis as a good thing in her life, somebody to take care of her? At the time when Martha had wanted her to move, Naomi had felt horribly patronised, as though she was being dismissed as a doddery old dear who couldn't be trusted to live alone, but who would be ideal for on-the-doorstep childcare.

Ironically, now that grandchildren were definitely on the way, Naomi could see the sense in living nearer to Martha and Willow. But then she would think of how much fun it would be having her grandchildren to stay here at Anchor House, playing with them in the garden and on the beach, and she couldn't imagine living anywhere else. How could she ever live without waking up to the sound of seagulls, of being deprived of a walk along the shoreline and bringing home an interesting piece of driftwood, of breathing in the salt-tanged air, or never having the joy of watching a redshank digging in the mudflats. And her garden – *her glorious garden* – she couldn't imagine giving that up. Although common sense told her that one day it would be too much for her, just as it had been for the previous owners. But for as long as she was in good health, and Ellis too, this was where she wanted to be.

Colin had often joked that the only way he would leave Anchor House was when he was carried out in a box; well, to all intents and purposes, he'd got his wish. Poor Colin, she suddenly thought, he would have enjoyed being a grandfather. He would have relished the role, especially in retirement and with more time to devote to little ones. A wave of sadness swept over her that he had been denied the pleasure of knowing his grandchildren.

The feeling was soon snatched away from her at the sound of two sharp rings of the doorbell. Geraldine had arrived.

Bracing herself, Naomi went to greet her friend.

Her overnight case dumped at the foot of the stairs, her coat flung over the newel post, and Naomi at the sink filling the kettle, Geraldine cleared her throat.

'You're going to need something stronger than tea,' she said.

Here we go, thought Naomi. 'If you're about to kick off with a lecture about Ellis, you can save your breath,' she said. 'Ellis is a permanent fixture in my life, and that's an end to it. So if you don't mind, tea is plenty strong enough for me.'

'Good Lord!' exclaimed Geraldine. 'What on earth makes you

think this is about you and Ellis. Although in some ways you are responsible.'

'Responsible for what?'

'For the decision I've made. I've left Brian and told him I want a divorce.'

Naomi was thunderstruck. 'You've done *what*?'

'I've left Brian. Now for heaven's sake, forget about boiling that kettle and pour me a glass of wine and I'll tell you all about it.'

In a state of shock, Naomi did as her friend said and took her through to the sitting room and the warmth of the fire. 'Now tell me what on earth has brought this on,' she said, when they were both seated.

'The truth is, after my last visit here and seeing the change in you, I went home and looked at Brian through fresh eyes. And do you know what I saw?'

'Whatever it was, I suspect it wasn't good.'

'It wasn't. I saw a boring man who bores the pants off me. He's bored me for years, it's just that I'd accepted that that was as good as it gets.'

'But Geraldine, when you were here you said that the two of you rubbed along quite happily.'

'Oh, forget what I said then. It was all window dressing. I was merely trying to make myself feel more positive about the unutterable dreariness of being with Brian. While there you were, fresh as a daisy, bursting with joyful rejuvenation.' She groaned. 'Dear God, I can't tell you how miserably jealous that made me feel when I drove home and found Brian stretched out on the sofa fast asleep and snoring like a warthog! Is it so wrong that I want some of what you now have?'

Naomi took a gulp of her wine. 'What does Brian have to say about all this?'

'Oh, you know, just what you'd expect, that you can't have bells and whistles your whole married life. That marriage is a marathon that settles into its own steady pace.'

'He has a point.'

'Says the woman who told me she's having the best sex of her life with Lover-Boy!'

'I never said that!'

'You didn't need to, not in so many words; it was written all over your smug little face.'

'Have I chosen a bad time to join you ladies?'

'Ellis!' exclaimed Naomi, alarmed at what he might have overhead. 'I didn't hear you come in.'

'Evidently,' he said with a raised eyebrow, coming into the room. 'Hello, Geraldine, long time no see. How the devil are you?'

She smiled back at him. 'I'm in fine fettle,' she said. 'And you look like you've fared well since I last saw you. What's with the scruffy jeans and daubs of paint on you?'

'I'm decorating next door. I'll leave Naomi to explain while I go up and change.'

When he'd gone, Geraldine held out her glass. 'Top-up, please, and then fill me in on your latest news. Has Lover-Boy moved in? Oh, and while you're fetching the wine, I wouldn't mind a slice of that cake I spied on the worktop in the kitchen.'

'Good plan,' said Naomi up on her feet, 'better we have something inside us to soak up the alcohol we're about to consume.'

Back in the sitting room, and despite wanting to hear more from Geraldine about her inexplicable decision to leave Brian, Naomi hurriedly explained about Ellis moving in with her and buying next door to do up. 'And before you ask, no he hasn't bought the cottage so he has somewhere to escape if it goes wrong between us.'

'I wasn't thinking any such thing.'

'Good, so let's get back to you and Brian.'

'What else is there to say?'

'Lots! Like where are you going to live? And what does Hilary have to say about it all?'

'She's furious with me and just as I knew she would, she's taken her father's side. I'm officially persona non grata. As for where I'll live, well, I was thinking there might be a temporary bed for me here, just until I've sorted out what I'm going to do. Or would I be playing too much of a gooseberry to you and Lover-Boy?'

Naomi's heart sank. Much as she loved her old friend, the thought of Geraldine being here at Anchor House for a prolonged length of time was a daunting prospect.

Chapter Forty-Six

With a decaf skinny latte in hand, and following a wafer-thin girl into the lift, Martha wondered, despite what Tom had said about her positively blooming, if there was anything less sexy than being pregnant.

This was a question she asked herself every time she saw her swelling body reflected back at her. At six months pregnant she was colossal, or that's how it felt to her, and she couldn't believe that she would grow bigger still. Tom described her as looking voluptuous, which she interpreted as voluminous and to make matters worse, her libido had hit the skids, and Tom's had gone up several gears. All she wanted to do every night when she collapsed into bed was sleep. Her energy levels had dropped again, and to an all-time low.

According to what she read online, the baby was currently about the size of a cauliflower and weighed approximately the same as a swede. Or was it a small marrow? Well, whatever it was, she didn't much care for her child being compared to a basket of vegetables. She preferred the certainty of clear-cut measurements, such as 34 cm in length and 760 grams in weight.

When the lift came to a stop on the fifth floor, the enviably slim girl gave Martha a friendly nod of goodbye and stepped out.

As the doors closed and the lift resumed its upward journey, Martha's thoughts turned to the day ahead. It was chock-a-block with meetings and, despite her baby brain's best efforts to derail anything she did, she was fully prepared for everything in the diary. Preparation was all, was the rule by which she lived. Her father had instilled that into her from a young age. It was why she'd never left her homework to the last minute or turned up at school on a games day without her kit.

The fear of not being prepared was a strong motivator and had always ensured that she never needed to fall back on some pathetic excuse to cover up for an oversight. Jason had teased her only yesterday during one of his head-round-the-door chats that she must have been a formidable head girl at school.

'Actually, I was described as an *exceptional* head girl,' she'd told him.

'Of course you were,' he'd said with a laugh. 'I must say, pregnancy suits you, Martha. You look particularly well.'

'Is this when I report you to HR for inappropriate behaviour?'

With yet another laugh from him, he said, 'I'm going to miss your acerbic humour while you're off on maternity leave.'

He might not have said that if he knew about the job offer she'd received. After speaking to Charlotte Milner, the MD at Topolino, and explaining her situation, she had expected that to be an end to the conversation, but she'd been wrong. A fresh-out-of-the-box mother on the team was just what they needed, Charlotte told Martha. She would bring a particularly apposite skill set and understanding of the marketplace.

So deep in thought had she been, Martha hadn't noticed that the lift had come to a stop on the eighth floor. She waited for the doors to open and admit someone, but they remained shut. With a tut of annoyance, she pressed the button for the tenth floor, but when nothing happened, she jabbed it again. And again.

But still nothing.

Hmmm . . . she thought with deepening annoyance.

She counted to five, then pressed the button once more. Her initial relief when the lift gave a judder and began to move upwards was soon gone when it jerked to an abrupt stop, and then dropped sharply before making a loud creaking noise and coming to another sudden stop. Imagining the lift plummeting all the way to the ground floor, Martha gripped the handrail with her free hand. Standing very still, scared to move in case it caused the lift to drop again, she held her breath and slowly stretched out a hand towards the control panel. She pressed the button to open the door, but nothing happened. There was only one thing left to do, and that was to summon help by pressing the emergency alarm button.

After what seemed an age, a man's reassuringly calm voice filled the small space and introduced himself as Andy. He informed her that he was a maintenance contractor and needed a few important details from her, such as her name, the exact location of the building and the lift ID, which was on a panel above the doors.

'And how many of you are in the lift?' he then asked.

'Just me,' she said. *And my precious unborn baby*, she wanted to add.

'And you're not hurt in any way?'

'No. But I'm pregnant and—' Panicky fear unexpectedly had the better of her and her throat constricted – *What if she and her baby were about to die?*

'And?' prompted the reassuring voice.

She fought hard to loosen the tension in her throat. 'What if there's a cable that's about to snap and the lift crashes to the ground floor?' she said.

'That's not going to happen. There's always more than one cable attached to a lift, and what you're imagining only happens in the movies.'

'You're not lying to me, are you, just to make me feel better?'

'No Martha, I'm not lying. Is it all right if I call you Martha?'

She wanted to scream *NO! Just get me out of here!* 'Yes,' she said.

'So Martha, do you suffer from claustrophobia?'

'No.'

'That's good,' he said, as if ticking off a list of questions.

'And when's your baby due?'

She had to think. When? When was her due date? Come on brain, you can do this. 'In three months,' she said finally.

'Is it your first?'

She knew what he was doing; he was keeping her occupied in an attempt to keep her calm. 'Yes,' she said. 'But if you don't mind, can we keep the small talk to a minimum and you just get me out of here?'

'Absolutely. Help will shortly be on its way.'

'Really?'

'Yes. Do you have your mobile with you?'

'Yes.'

'Do you want call someone to inform them of your whereabouts?'

Her *whereabouts?* She was trapped in a bloody lift, not lost on the North Circular!

'Your husband perhaps?' he said. 'Or your wife?' he added, as though remembering the rule book when it came to inclusivity and avoiding any offence.

'I'll try my husband,' she said, knowing that the signal was never very good inside in the lift. That was when she realised she was still holding the paper cup of coffee she'd picked up in the foyer. She placed it on the floor of the lift and took out her mobile.

Amazingly, luck was on her side and with a couple of bars of signal, she rang Tom. But it went straight to his voicemail. With nothing else for it, and not wanting to alarm him too much, she left a message for him to ring her.

Next Andy asked for her office number so he could alert them.

'Does that mean I'm going to be stuck here for hours and hours?' she asked, once she'd given him the necessary details.

'I doubt that. But for now, why don't you make yourself comfortable. Do you have anything to eat or drink?'

'I have some coffee,' she said, gingerly lowering herself to the floor. She was still scared that the slightest movement might cause the lift to plummet and send her crashing to her death.

'That's good. Now I'm going to go a bit quiet for a while, is that okay with you?'

'Yes,' she said.

Her legs sticking out in front of her, Martha took a sip of her coffee. At the same time she rested a hand on her baby bump. 'There's nothing to worry about,' she told the baby.

As if in response, the baby seemed to stretch out a leg to give her a swift kick that landed in her lower ribs.

'Okay,' said Martha, 'so you don't agree, but there's no need to get all antsy with me. I mean, it's not my fault I'm stuck here in this lift. Do you think I planned it?'

She kept up a steady monologue of nonsense while she drank

her coffee. Martha knew that at this stage of the pregnancy, her baby could hear her voice and could react to it. The baby's eyelids were open at twenty-five weeks too, and her brain and lungs and digestive system were formed as well, although not fully developed. She was a truly wondrous little being who regularly hiccupped inside Martha and could keep her awake with her constant fidgeting as if she were bored and looking for something to do. 'Just like her mother,' Tom said, 'always on the go, always needing to be busy.'

Family lore had it that Martha had been a fractiously fidgety baby. 'You came out of the womb, kicking and screaming and ready to pick a fight,' Dad had always joked. 'There you were, your little fists tightly clenched, ready to fight your corner.'

Mum was a little more generous with her version of Martha's baby years, explaining that she was a typical first child and that they, as parents, were learning on the job and didn't always get it right. 'You probably picked up on our lack of confidence,' Mum said, 'and by the time Willow came along, we felt we knew what we were doing and didn't worry so much, so that made her less anxious too.'

Out of the two of them, Martha was happy to concede that Tom would be the more patient parent. She would always be impatient for the next phase, just as she had been impatient to conceive. Now she was impatient for the day when she would go into labour.

Just not today, she thought. Giving birth in a lift with only Andy's disembodied voice to help was not what she wanted. Not when her baby was too small to be born now . . . not when her daughter's chances of survival were so slim.

No sooner had she pushed this panicky thought from her

mind, than her stomach tightened, and with such force, she gasped.

'There's nothing to worry about,' she murmured, putting down her coffee cup and massaging her bump that was now as tight as a drum. 'This is all perfectly normal.'

She breathed in deeply, then exhaled slowly.

In.

Out.

Braxton Hicks contractions.

It was when the womb tightened and then relaxed, she reminded herself. A sort of trial run for the real thing and could be triggered by all sorts of things, including dehydration or a full bladder. Hmmm . . . best not to think of her bladder, she thought, not when she routinely spent an insane amount of time going to the loo. At work it was embarrassing how often she had to go. Several times she had to ask the intern to cover for her when she'd been caught short.

She winced again as the tightening intensity of her stomach muscles increased.

Another breath in.

Another breath out.

She had experienced them twice before, so she knew the score and she'd read extensively about the phenomenon online. Just as she'd read up on everything else to do with being pregnant. Preparation was all.

So she knew that she was not about to go into labour. Absolutely not. She wasn't going to be one of those panicky women who set off for the maternity unit with a false alarm every time she experienced a twinge. Willow had admitted the other day to Martha that she'd had a moment when she thought she might be in labour. 'If Rick had been with me,' she'd said, 'I'm sure he would have insisted we went straight to the hospital.'

'What made you so sure you weren't in labour, given how far along you are?' Martha had asked.

'Complete denial,' she'd said with a careless laugh. 'I'm going to keep on denying I'm having a baby until the day she arrives.'

As another mini contraction took hold of her, Martha started at the loud ring of her mobile. Assuming it was Tom, she didn't bother looking at the screen.

But it wasn't Tom. It was Willow.

'Hi Martha,' her sister said, 'you might think I'm being silly, but I had this weird feeling that I should ring you.' She laughed in Martha's ear. 'I know, it sounds bonkers, doesn't it, but I couldn't stop thinking about you? Is everything okay?'

'Funny you should say that,' said Martha.

'And help is definitely on the way?' asked Willow when Martha had explained that she was stuck in a lift.

'I certainly hope so.'

'Hey, it's a bit spooky-woo-woo of me thinking I should ring then, isn't it? It's not like we've ever been telepathic or anything like that before. Had I better ring off if you're waiting for Tom to call?'

Martha hesitated. It was good having the distraction of her sister chatting with her, and who knew when Tom might check his voicemail and call her back? 'No, don't ring off,' she said. 'You're keeping me from worrying that I'll never get out of here.'

It was then that she realised the Braxton Hicks contractions had stopped. The only movement inside her now was her hic-cupping baby.

'So, what are you up to?' she asked Willow. 'Are you at work?'

'No, I go in this afternoon. Actually, this is my last day.'

'How do you feel about that?'

'Sad, if I'm honest. I think motherhood is going to be a lot harder than begging people for more money.'

'You are looking forward to being a mother, aren't you?' Martha asked.

'I would if I thought I'd be any good at it. When you think about it, what have I ever been good at?'

'You'll be fine.'

'That's what Lucas says.'

Does he, thought Martha. 'And how is Lucas; have you heard from him recently?'

'Yeah, he's in touch every now and then.'

'Does Rick know?'

'Umm . . . not really.'

'What does that mean?'

'It means I don't tell him. It's better that way.'

There was so much Martha wanted to say in answer to this, but should she? Even as a bossy older sister, it really wasn't her job to police Willow's relationship with Rick. It wasn't as if she would be that upset if things did go wrong between Willow and Rick, would she? And wasn't being attracted to somebody else a symptom of a relationship that wasn't working?

As much as her common sense told her to leave well alone, Martha couldn't resist asking the one question she wanted to ask.

'Willow,' she said, 'do you love Rick?'

'Umm . . . I think so.'

'You don't sound very sure.'

'I want to love him. I really do. But it's all happened so fast between us.'

'Too fast?'

'Yes.'

'Has Lucas muddied the waters?'

'No!'

'I'll take that as a yes.'

She waited for her sister to respond, but she didn't. 'Willow?' Still nothing.

Oh dear, Martha thought, perhaps she'd gone too far with her questioning. She then looked at the screen of her mobile and saw that the signal had gone. She sighed with frustration.

While she waited for the signal to return, in the hope that it would, there came a reassuring voice.

'Hi Martha, how's it going?'

It was Andy, back from whatever he'd been doing.

'I'm fine,' she said. 'Do you have any good news for me?'

'I most certainly do.'

Seconds later and she could hear voices the other side of the lift doors. Then, as she hauled herself up on her feet, the doors magically opened, and she was greeted by two men in hi-vis jackets and a small contingent of co-workers.

Jason was there too. 'Bloody hell, Martha,' he said, 'if you wanted a later start to the day, you only had to ask.'

She didn't know whether to laugh or cry with happy relief.

Chapter Forty-Seven

After trying to ring her sister back and getting no answer, Willow then tried Tom's mobile, but it went straight to voicemail. She left a message for him to ring her, then rang Anchor House. To her surprise it wasn't her mother or Ellis who answered; it was Auntie Geraldine.

'I've left your Uncle Brian and am staying here until I've made further plans,' Geraldine barked out before Willow could explain why she was ringing.

'Oh,' she said, completely flummoxed. 'But why?'

'Why not?'

'Because . . . because you've always been Auntie Geraldine and Uncle Brian. I can't picture the two of you any other way.'

Geraldine tutted. 'That's the feeblest reason to stay married I've ever heard.'

A terrible thought occurred to Willow. 'He hasn't been having an affair, has he?'

'Good Lord *no!* Mind you, I might have more respect for him if he had. It would at least show he has some get-up-and-go in him.'

Willow couldn't help but feel sorry for Uncle Brian. 'Is he very upset?' she asked.

'I wouldn't know. He's hopeless at expressing himself.'

About to ask if he had been given the chance to express himself, Willow remembered why she'd rung. 'Is Mum there?' she asked.

'No, she's next door with Lover-Boy.'

'With who?'

'With *whom?*' Geraldine corrected her. 'And she's with Ellis, of course. That's what I called him back in the day when they—' Geraldine broke off abruptly. 'Well, that's all water under the bridge. Nothing we need discuss now. Would you like me to ask your mother to ring you?'

'No. Well yes, if she wants to. But the important thing is to tell her Martha is stuck in the lift at her office building, but there's nothing to worry about, help is on the way.'

'If there's nothing to worry about, why have you telephoned with a message which will only cause your mother to do just that?'

Once again Willow was flummoxed. 'Well . . . I just thought it was the kind of thing Mum would want to be told. You know, what with Martha being pregnant.'

'Knowing Martha, she'll have herself out of that lift unaided and back at her desk before the cavalry has so much as put its boots on.'

Another time and Willow might have agreed with this senti-ment, but recalling how anxious her sister had been for Willow to stay on the line chatting to her – *'You're keeping me from worrying that I'll never get out of here.'* – she wanted to say that Martha wasn't as invincible as Geraldine, and many others, made out. But instead she said, 'Just pass on the message and I'll be in touch if I hear any more.'

Seconds after she'd ended the call, her mobile rang. It was Tom.

332

'It's okay,' he said, when Willow began to explain why she'd left him a message to call her, 'I've just spoken to Martha and she's out of the lift now.'

'That's a relief.'

'Yes. I think she's a bit embarrassed about the whole thing. You know how she hates to be made a fuss of. Anyway, she's insisting that she's perfectly all right and is carrying on with the day as normal.'

'That's good.'

'By the way, thanks for trying to contact me. I was with a new client so couldn't take any calls. Anyway, how are you?'

'Oh, I'm fine, muddling along as usual.'

'How many more weeks do you have to go now, I've lost track.'

'Eight.'

'So if all goes to plan, you'll have your baby easily in time for Christmas?'

'Yes,' she murmured, thinking there would be nothing easy about it.

After she and Tom had said goodbye, her mobile rang again. This time it was Mum, and hearing how worried she sounded, just as Auntie Geraldine had predicted, Willow rushed to tell her that she'd heard from Tom and Martha was okay.

'Thank goodness for that,' Mum said. 'Were there others in the lift with her?'

Willow told her mother all that she knew and then asked about her old friend being at Anchor House. 'Has she really left Uncle Brian?'

'It would appear so.'

'But why after all these years and when they've always seemed okay together as a couple?'

333

'She wants more than "okay". She wants excitement. More specifically, she wants what I have with Ellis.'

Willow thought about this for a moment. 'What about what you had with Dad?' she then asked.

There was a silence down the line. 'I suppose that was different,' her mother said eventually.

'Can I ask you something personal, Mum?'

'Yes.'

'If Ellis had moved in next door while Dad was still alive, would you have . . . would you have been attracted to him? Would he have been a temptation?'

'Heavens, what a question! What makes you ask such a thing?'

'It was something Auntie Geraldine said. She referred to Ellis as your Lover-Boy and something to do with him being water under the bridge. Was he more than just an old friend when you were students together?' Willow was thinking of Martha and how adamant she had been earlier in the year, and when they were first getting to know Ellis, that he and Mum weren't telling the full story about how well they used to know each other.

'As students we were just friends,' her mother said in answer to her question, 'it was . . . later, a few years later, that he came to mean more to me.'

'Did you regret not marrying him, then? Was he what you might call a lost opportunity?'

'Willow, are you asking me these questions because you're worried you've made a choice you regret, or think you might come to regret?'

Taken aback by her mother's question, how intuitive it was, she tried to think how best to answer it. She badly wanted to be honest, to tell the truth and admit that she had got everything

334

wrong and it was all her fault, just as it always was. But she was terrified that if she did say the words out loud, everything would come tumbling down around her and then what?

'It's perfectly natural to have doubts about all sorts of things when you're pregnant,' Mum said, saving her from having to respond.

'Yes,' Willow said quietly, 'you're probably right.'

'But on the other hand, it doesn't do to dwell on things when you're pregnant. Would you like me to come and see you?'

'What about Auntie Geraldine?'

'Don't give her another thought. She'll be quite happy here bossing Ellis around. Shall I come today? I could be there in time to take you for afternoon tea, if you like. Somewhere decadently smart as a treat for us both. What do you say?'

The fact that her mother was suggesting she dash up to London straight away made Willow realise that she must be worried about her. 'That's a lovely idea, Mum, but it's my last day at work. I'm going in at two o'clock and then when the shift is over, a group of us is going for farewell drinks.'

'Shall I come tomorrow then? Seeing as you won't have work to go to? Or better still, why don't you come down here for a few days? Have a mini-break with us.'

'Without Rick?'

'Why not? It would be lovely for me to have some special time with you. It's ages since we've been able to do that, just the two of us. Ellis will happily amuse himself. What do you think?'

The thought of spending time down at Anchor House, and before motherhood swallowed her up whole, was wonderfully tempting. To lie in bed in her old bedroom listening to the seagulls and the waves lapping at the shore would be just perfect.

To go for a long walk and feel the autumn wind in her hair. To shelter in the sand dunes, and just have space to think. But what would Rick think about her spending time away from him? He'd hate it.

'I'll check with Rick and get back to you,' she said, already accepting she wouldn't be going anywhere, that it wouldn't be worth upsetting Rick. He'd been so touchy lately, the slightest thing setting him off. He said it was because he was under a lot of pressure at work and that she didn't understand the first thing about how tough it was for businesses to survive, that the effects of the pandemic on the global economy were still with them and would be for a long time yet, blah, blah, and then some more blah, blah. It wasn't her fault any of that happened, but the way he banged on anyone would think it was. He had kicked off again last night because he'd insisted that she needed to make a will. She'd made the mistake of laughing and saying there was no hurry, she'd get around to it one day.

'That's so typically irresponsible of you, isn't it?' he'd said, 'always putting something important off.'

'I'll do it,' she'd said.

'You should do it soon.'

'Yes,' she'd said, only half listening.

'After all,' he'd gone on, 'you have that trust your father left you, and those shares.'

Rarely did she think about the shares Dad had left her, and Martha as well, probably because she was determined to follow Tom's advice and keep them until the stock market picked up. But because she wasn't paying attention to Rick when he was badgering her about making a will, he had suddenly grown

336

angry and gone off on one and shouted at her and thrown the TV remote so hard against the wall it had smashed.

'If it's a problem, Willow,' Mum said, bringing her back to their conversation, 'and really it shouldn't be, because why on earth would Rick mind you spending time with your mother, I'll come and see you for the day? He couldn't object to that, surely?'

'Of course not, it's just that he worries about me.'

'Yes, darling, and I worry about you too, which is why I think it would be good for you to have a short break down here for a few days.'

'It would be nice,' Willow conceded. 'But don't you have your hands full with Auntie Geraldine?'

'I can send her packing back to Brian. I'm convinced she's just making a point to him.'

'Maybe Uncle Brian might not want to have her back so soon, perhaps he's glad of the peace and quiet.'

Her mother laughed. 'And who would blame him for that? Now meanwhile, whatever it is on your mind that's troubling you, don't fret unnecessarily. Do you promise?'

'I promise.'

When she'd said goodbye to her mother and had plugged in her mobile to recharge the battery, she wandered through to the room that Rick had had redecorated in readiness for the baby. Willow had wanted to paint it herself and stencil something cute around the walls, like a line of fluffy ducklings. Mum had taught her how to do stencilling years ago and it would have been fun for Willow to make more of a personal contribution to their daughter's room, even if it hadn't been perfect. But Rick wouldn't hear of it. 'I'm not having you clambering up stepladders only to topple off and hurt yourself,' he'd said.

The room now was fresh and bright with pale lemon walls finished off with white woodwork. Beneath her bare feet was a new ivory-coloured carpet that had only been put down a few days ago and still had that new woolly smell. Where there had once been a large bookcase, there was now a cot and above it was a mobile with dangling stars and moons in silver and gold. Willow went over to it and set it off playing 'Twinkle, Twinkle Little Star'. While it tinkled away, she opened the top drawer of the chest of drawers and ran her hands over the neatly folded baby clothes she and Rick had bought together. They were all so impossibly tiny. She picked out a white body suit and tried to imagine a baby inside it. She couldn't.

She put it back in the drawer, closed it, then went and sat in the low chair next to the cot. She tried to picture herself sitting here at night while feeding the baby. She planned to breastfeed, just as she'd been encouraged at the antenatal classes she and Rick had attended, but knowing her luck she'd be rubbish at it. Rick had said she wasn't to worry about that, that he wanted to do his share of feeding their daughter, so it might actually be better to bottle feed anyway. It would save her any needless stress.

She knew that she was lucky to have a partner who was so looking forward to being a father. At the antenatal classes they'd attended together, some of the other fathers-to-be had admitted they were scared of the responsibility that lay ahead. Willow had wanted to put her hand up and say she knew just what they meant.

So maybe it was just as well Rick was so confident about parenthood; he would make up for any deficiency on her part. His certainty should reassure her, as should his desire for everything to be perfect for their baby's arrival, and his need to protect her, but it only made her feel even more inadequate.

The intensity of his love sometimes made her feel as though she were being slowly suffocated. It was just all too much. She understood why he was like he was: it was because he was so scared of losing her. He'd lost too much before and couldn't bear the thought of it happening all over again to him. But if only he didn't love her so much.

And if only she could love him more.

Listening to the mobile as it came to a tinkling stop, she thought of all the times she'd regretted something she had done or something she had said. But what was the point in wishing she had lived her life differently? This was where she was now and for the sake of her daughter, she had to forget about how life might have been for her.

Her mother had been right to leap to the conclusion that she regretted a choice she had made. But then she had regretted so many choices over the years. She knew what Mum had also assumed was the problem, just as Martha had; that Lucas was at the bottom of it all. To a degree they were right, but not in the way they thought. What Lucas had done was to open her eyes to the truth, that she would rather be with someone like him than Rick.

With Lucas, even when they were just chatting on FaceTime she could be her true self, or as near to her true self as she could allow herself to be with anyone. With Rick she was always trying to be someone she wasn't. It was the same with the gifts he bought for her: none of them was her taste, they were all Rick's taste. Everything was a reflection on how he wanted her to be. Which only added to her sense of failure because she could never be that person. Just as she could never be the daughter her father had wanted her to be.

From nowhere she heard his voice. *'So you're going to mess this up as well, are you, Willow? Well, well, there's a surprise!'*

No, she thought defiantly, this was her chance to change and prove her father wrong.

She placed her hands around the large solid ball of her stomach. 'It's a lot to ask of you,' she said softly to her daughter, 'but will you change me for the better? Will you be the making of me? Because something needs to be.'

Chapter Forty-Eight

'There was really no need for you to do this.'

Jason tutted. 'No need whatsoever, Martha, but I'm doing it all the same.'

'You were just terrified I might go into premature labour and make a mess on the office carpets, weren't you?'

'If I was worried about that, do you think I'd have you in my car, running the risk of ruining the leather seats?'

Martha smiled. 'It's a nice car.'

'So it bloody well should be for the price.'

'Not much room in the back though,' she said, twisting her head round to look at the minuscule space where there was just enough room to put a small overnight bag; that's if you only needed a toothbrush.

'One doesn't buy an Audi R8 for space,' said Jason. 'It's all about the performance.'

'Obviously.'

In spite of her determination to remain at the office after being rescued from the lift, Martha was now reluctantly grateful that Jason had effectively taken her hostage and bundled her off the premises. She'd made it through the first meeting of the day, but when it was over and she'd risen to her feet to return to her desk, she'd suddenly felt dizzy and had felt herself falling.

When she came to, and in her befuddled light-headed state, she was vaguely aware that she was on the floor and Jason was barking out orders to give her space and for someone to fetch a glass of water. Within a few minutes her head had cleared, and she was being helped to her feet. Feeling acutely embarrassed at the commotion she had caused, she'd apologised, but Jason told her to be quiet, and what was more, he was taking her straight home. In vain she'd protested that she was perfectly all right, but he was having none of it.

'We'll call your husband from my car and explain that you're on your way home,' he'd told her.

The worst of it had been when she'd stepped into the lift and had experienced what she could only think was a mild form of a panic attack. The baby must have picked up on her reaction and had started jumping about inside her like a gymnast performing backflips.

'Yeah, I know, a scary prospect getting stuck a second time in the lift, and with me for company,' Jason had quipped, taking her arm. 'But let's work on the theory that rarely does lightning strike twice in the same place. Especially on the same day.' He'd kept his hand on her arm all the way down to the underground car park.

Now, as she sat in the passenger seat of his car as he drove at speed out of London, she said, 'You realise you're going to have to shoehorn me out of this seat, don't you?'

'Don't worry about that; if needs be, I'll use a crowbar, then sling you over my shoulder.'

'With the extra weight I'm carrying on board, you'll give yourself a hernia.'

He shot her a glance. 'It would be worth it though, just to see the look of horror on your face.'

'I think I've given you enough entertainment for one day,' she said.

'You do that every day in the office, Martha. You amuse me endlessly.'

'I'm glad I'm such good value.'

'Talking of value. Will you accept the job offer from Topolino? Did they tempt you with an appropriately juicy carrot?'

She made an attempt at insouciance. 'I don't know what you're talking about.'

He laughed. 'I knew they'd want to poach you.'

'On what basis?'

'That you came up with exactly the right campaign for them. What did Charlotte offer you to jump ship?'

Martha could see there was no point in denying what Jason clearly already had a good handle on. 'It's a generous package,' she said, 'and worth considering.'

'I should hope it is. You'd be a valuable asset to them. For what it's worth, I wouldn't want to lose you. I value you enormously and the team is going to miss you while you're on maternity leave. Just so you know, if I need to compete with Topolino, I will.'

Martha had to wonder if this whole day was one big surreal dream – getting stuck in the lift, fainting in the office, being driven home by her boss who was now negotiating an increase in her salary if she stayed.

She was still trying to come up with a suitable response when he said, 'You don't have to give me an answer now, not after the day you've had, but I do want you to know that I'd personally

343

be very sorry to lose you. There, now that we have that out of the way, you can relax. How about some music?'

'Sure,' she said, thinking that relaxing was the last thing she was capable of doing. But after he'd tapped at a couple of buttons on the steering wheel, gentle piano music filled the car.

'Nothing like a bit of Satie, particularly the Gymnopédies, to unwind the mind and body,' he said.

'I had you down as more of a thrash metal fan,' she teased.

'That's what I play on my way into work of a morning, it pumps me up ready to kick ass.'

She could well believe it. 'I think you should have "Eye of the Tiger" playing at full blast in the foyer to herald your arrival,' she said.

He laughed. 'Now why didn't I think of that?'

They were only a short distance from home and where Tom would be waiting for them, when Martha knew it was now or never for her to ask the one question she had always wanted to ask her boss.

'Jason . . .'

'Yes?'

'Why do you click your pen during any meeting we have?'

'Do I?'

'You know you do. You give it three clicks in quick succession every time you do it.'

'How interesting. And why do you think I do that?'

'To put people on edge.'

'And does it?'

'I can't speak for the others, but it drives me crazy. It's like Chinese water torture waiting for the next click.'

He shot her another sideways glance. 'Who knew that within

that tough outer shell of yours, Martha, you were such a sensitive little soul.'

'So why do you do it?'

'It helps me think. Anything else you want to ask?'

'No, nothing else.'

'Good, because I have something else to say to you, and I don't want any arguments. You're to take the rest of the week off; show your face in the office and I'll have security escort you from the building. No, don't even think about disagreeing with me. You've had a helluva day and I want you fully rested before you come back on Monday. Maybe you should see your doctor, just to be on the safe side. Yes?'

'You're quite the mother hen when you want to be, aren't you?'

'If caring for my employees makes me a mother hen, I'll take it. Now, according to the satnav, we're five minutes from our destination.'

Five more minutes, thought Martha, and then she'd be home with Tom and this bizarre day would be over.

Chapter Forty-Nine

Late that night, and back from the pub and farewell drinks with a crowd from work, Willow was more than ready for the day to be over. But first she needed something to eat and, more importantly, for Rick to calm down.

She had just put two slices of bread into the toaster and was patiently, and rather self-consciously as Rick watched her, waiting for it to pop up. She was starving, having only eaten a packet of pork scratchings all evening. Her friends from work had surprised her with a beautiful boxed set of Beatrix Potter books for the baby, and earlier, before she'd arrived for work, they'd decorated the office with pink balloons and Jeanie had made cupcakes with pink icing. They'd all made such a fuss of her, and when their shift was over, they had taken the balloons with them to the pub and tied them to the back of their chairs. Kyle had joined them for a drink but hadn't stayed for long, which meant they could relax and enjoy themselves all the more once he'd gone.

She'd told Rick that she'd be home at nine o'clock, but she hadn't rolled in until nearly eleven. It wasn't until she was on her way home in a cab that she'd checked her mobile and seen all the messages he'd left her and how many times he'd tried to ring her. *Uh-oh*, she'd thought. Letting herself in at the flat, juggling the present and cards she'd been given, along with a couple of pink balloons, she'd been greeted by a furious Rick demanding to know why the hell she hadn't answered any of his calls. Didn't she care that he'd spent the entire evening frantic with worry, he'd yelled. She'd apologised and explained quite truthfully that there had been so much noise at the pub she hadn't heard her phone ringing, but it didn't wash with him. He'd checked her breath too, to make sure she hadn't been drinking any alcohol. Thank goodness she hadn't, or that would have only made things worse.

He was still watching as she opened the fridge to find the butter, and then the cupboard where the jar of peanut butter was kept.

'I don't know how you can eat that disgusting stuff,' he said. 'It can't be good for you, all that fatty oil.'

'It's good fat,' she said, 'I'm sure I read somewhere that it's good for me and the baby.'

'Says the girl who's been out partying all night,' he said disdainfully. 'Is that good for you and our baby too?'

'It was my leaving do, Rick, I'm allowed that, aren't I?' The toast now ready, she began spreading the butter onto it. Except it was so cold from being in the fridge, she had practically to hack chunks off to put on the toast.

'But you should have checked your mobile,' he insisted. 'Just once would have been enough to put my mind at rest. But oh no, you were having far too good a time without me to think about that. Which is just another example of your selfishness. You never think about anyone but yourself, do you?'

'That's so not true, Rick. I'm always thinking of you. That's why I told Mum today that I'd have to check with you first about going to stay with her for a few days.'

He stared at her. 'I can't possibly take any time off work at the moment to go traipsing down to Sussex.'

Dolloping a generous amount of peanut butter onto the first of the two slices of toast, she chose her next words with care. 'Mum thought that would be the case, so she's suggested I go on my own. It's my last chance before the baby comes to do something like this. It'll only be for a few days. A sort of mini-break.'

He shook his head. 'Absolutely not. At this stage of your pregnancy I don't want you going anywhere without me.'

'But you'll be at work all day and I'll be stuck here alone with nothing to do.'

'*Stuck?*' he repeated. 'What's that supposed to mean?'

'It means I'll be here twiddling my thumbs just waiting. It'll be so boring for me.'

'You'll be doing what you should be doing and that's resting.'

'But I'd be resting down at Mum's.'

He shook his head as though she had just said something incredibly stupid. 'Oh, Willow, is this how it's always going to be?'

'What do you mean?'

'You disagreeing with me and doing as you please and not giving a damn about my feelings or what I want. Just as you did tonight. Just as you always do.'

There was a marked change to the tone of his voice. Thankfully the anger had drained away; now he just sounded exasperated with her. Or perhaps disappointed in her. Yes, that was it. He felt she had let him down. And let herself down too. Dad had said that about her when she'd gone home to tell her parents that she was giving up on university, that it simply wasn't for her. 'Oh, Willow,' he'd said, 'you've let yourself down again, haven't you?'

She swallowed back the painful memory and tried to concentrate on spreading the peanut butter evenly over the second slice of toast, thinking as she did so that tonight was all too reminiscent of those times as a teenager when she'd stayed out late and found her father waiting up for her. Mum would be there as well, but really her role was to stop Dad from losing his temper too much. That was how it was in every relationship, she supposed, there was the strict parent and the not so strict parent. A good cop and a bad cop. With their own child, Rick, in his love for his daughter, would doubtless be overly strict and protective of her and would prevent her doing what she wanted to do. Whereas Willow would be the one to let their daughter have her freedom. Probably too much freedom.

Thinking of her mother and how she had frequently had to find a way to get round Dad, Willow tried another tack with Rick. 'It's okay,' she said, turning to look at him with a smile. 'If you don't want me to go down to see Mum, I won't go. It's not that big a deal. I just wondered whether you might enjoy a bit of peace and quiet without me. I do seem to keep upsetting you at the moment. Maybe we're both a little uptight right now, what with the baby and everything. Wouldn't you like to spend more time at the gym, or with your friends, without worrying about me?' Seeing friends was something Rick rarely did, in fact she couldn't remember the last time he had, but it was a worth a try.

'You're my priority,' he said, moving closer and putting a hand to her cheek, 'not my friends. Can't you see that I'd worry the whole time you were away from me?'

'But I'd be perfectly safe and well with Mum. I'd be back before you'd even missed me.'

'No,' he said with steely finality, the palm of his hand pressed more firmly to her cheek. 'You're not going alone.' He kissed her forehead, then removed his hand from her cheek. 'Tell your mother that we'll both come at the weekend. Or better still, tell her the weekend after would be more convenient.'

'But Rick—'

'No!' he said, thumping his fist down on the worktop. He so startled her, the knife in her hand slipped from her grasp and dropped to the floor, but not before knocking against Rick's trouser leg and one of his suede shoes and leaving a trail of greasy stains.

'For God's sake!' he shouted, 'do you have to be so bloody clumsy? Look at the mess you've made!'

'Sorry,' she said, bending awkwardly to retrieve the knife, but at the same time catching the sleeve of her cardigan on a slice of toast and that too then dropped to the floor, peanut butter side down. She sighed and, on her knees, she was about to scrape up the buttery mess when she felt herself being yanked upright by her hair and Rick was staring furiously into her face, his eyes blazing.

'Why do you keep ruining everything?' he yelled. 'God knows I've done my best to be patient with you and to tolerate your stupid sloppiness, but you just don't give a toss, do you?'

'You're hurting me, Rick,' she gasped, 'please let go.'

He brought his face nearer to hers. 'Why, so you can wreck something else? So you can annoy me some more?'

'I didn't do it deliberately, and I said I was sorry.' She tried to wriggle out of his grasp, but he yanked her hair even tighter, pulling her closer to him.

'Sorry, sorry, sorry, that's all I ever hear from you. Nothing but excuses and pathetic whingeing. Have you any idea how aggravating that is?'

Before she could stop herself, the word *sorry* slipped out from her again and, slamming her hard against the worktop, his free hand struck her across her face. The second blow caught her even harder across her cheekbone. Her ears ringing and tasting blood, she tried to back away from Rick, but she was jammed so hard against the worktop, there was no escape. 'I don't mean to annoy you,' she said, fear making her tremble.

'But you do. All the time! All the sodding time!' He grabbed her shoulders and began to shake her so violently her head flew backwards and forwards. The room spinning around her, a terrifying memory came flooding back and she started to scream. To scream and scream just as she should have screamed all those years ago.

Then suddenly the room went completely still and the powerful hands that had been shaking her so forcefully fell away from her shoulders. The stillness brought an end to her screaming and her body went slack. She felt winded, dazed and sick with the horror of what had just happened. And with the memory she had tried so hard to forget.

Backing away from her, his hands now hanging limply at his sides, Rick stared at her. 'Oh God,' he murmured, 'what have I done? Willow, I'm so sorry.'

'It's okay,' she said more calmly than she felt. 'It's okay.' But it wasn't. And it never would be.

He shook his head then raised his hands, palms up, and scrutinised them as though not quite believing they were his. 'I didn't mean it,' he said, returning his gaze to her. 'You know that, don't you? Deep down you know I'd never want to hurt you. But you keep pushing me by trying my patience.'

She nodded dumbly.

He took a step towards her and closing the gap between them, he put his arms around her, making her flinch. 'Please,' he begged, 'say you forgive me. Whatever I did, whatever I said, I didn't mean it. None of it.'

He was hugging her so tightly, she could scarcely breathe and, worried that he was pressing too hard against the baby, and desperately wanting him to let go of her, she said, 'I forgive you.' The words nearly choked her.

When she managed to push him gently away, she saw that he was crying. 'I didn't mean it,' he repeated. 'It's just that all evening I was so worried about you. All I could think was that you weren't coming back to me. I love you so much, Willow. You do believe that, don't you?'

'Yes,' she said. She put a hand to her throbbing cheek, and her mouth which felt swollen and tender. When she looked at her hand, she saw that her fingertips had blood on them.

'You must have bitten your lip,' he said with a frown.

Afraid to disagree with him, she nodded. 'Rick,' she then said, 'you won't ever do this again, will you? Do you promise?'

'Yes,' he said in a low voice. 'But Willow, you must promise that you won't hurt me anymore.'

'When have I ever hurt you?' she asked.

'Every time you go against me, you hurt me. Every time you want to spend time with your friends and family and not me, you hurt me. All I want is for you to love me. You do love me, don't you?'

She knew the answer he wanted to hear, so she forced herself to say the words, knowing with all her heart that she didn't and never would. 'Of course I love you, Rick.' Again the words nearly choked her.

Chapter Fifty

Naomi had tried several times to ring Willow, but each attempt had resulted in her having to leave a message on her daughter's voicemail.

It was now midday and Ellis would be back soon with Martha. After being stuck in the lift at work yesterday and then fainting, Martha had sensibly followed her boss's advice and was taking the rest of the week off from work. She had managed to see her midwife at the local surgery and had been told that other than a slight rise in her blood pressure, there was nothing to worry about. Naomi had suggested Martha join Willow and come and stay for a few days, half expecting her eldest daughter to say no, that she'd spend the time doing something useful at home, but Martha had readily accepted the invitation and said she'd drive down in the morning. This had been overruled by both Naomi and Tom; and saving Tom the job, Ellis had volunteered to fetch her, Willow as well. But there had been no word from Willow as to whether she was coming or not.

Picking up her mobile, Naomi checked it again.

'Like a watched pot that never boils, your mobile is not going to spring into life because you've looked at it,' remarked Geraldine, glancing up from that morning's copy of the *Telegraph*.

'How many times is it now that you've checked to see if the silly girl has replied to you?'

'I don't know,' said Naomi with a frown. 'And please don't call her a silly girl. She's far from silly.'

'I stand corrected. Would scatterbrained be more acceptable to you?'

'Not really,' muttered Naomi crossly. She returned her attention to tidying up the pelargoniums which she'd brought inside to overwinter in the conservatory. Which was where she and Geraldine had been since having their morning coffee, a ritual her friend stuck to no matter where she was or what was going on around her. It was the kind of intransigence that she despised emphatically in Brian but, to Naomi's amusement, didn't recognise in herself.

'What's worrying you most?' asked Geraldine some minutes later.

'I would have thought that was obvious,' answered Naomi. 'Willow said she'd ring me, and she hasn't. She's thirty-two weeks pregnant and—'

'Have you thought that she's simply forgotten all about it, or even that she's gone into an early labour and there just hasn't been time for either her or Rick to contact you?'

'Well, of course I've thought of that, I've thought of every conceivable reason for her not ringing me!'

'Hey, don't get all snappy with me. Why don't you try Rick's mobile?'

'I have and there was no reply.'

'In that case there's not a lot else you can do, is there?'

*

Ellis took it as a good sign that Martha had agreed to let him drive her down to Anchor House and an even better sign that she seemed quite relaxed with him. On the A3 now and making good time, he decided to sound her out about something he had wanted to discuss with her for a few weeks now.

'There's something I'd like your opinion about,' he said.

'If it's about you and Mum, then really I'd sooner you didn't go any further.'

Ellis admired her forthrightness, a character trait he strongly suspected she'd inherited from her father. 'No,' he said, 'it's nothing to do with Naomi and me. It's about Rick.'

There was an imperceptible turn of her head towards Ellis, almost as though she wanted to face him, but was reluctant to do so. 'What about Rick?' she said.

'Do you like him?'

There was a small beat before she replied. 'What makes you ask that?'

'I think you share the same view as me, that he's unhealthily possessive of your sister.'

'That infers there's a healthy way to be possessive?' she said.

'Okay, it was a bad choice of words on my part. But semantics aside, do you feel he's too possessive of Willow?'

'Yes. And seeing as we're being honest with each other, I think there's something creepy about him.'

'I agree.'

'You do?' Now she did turn her head to look at him properly. 'What does Mum think?'

'I'm not sure. It isn't something I felt I should raise with her. I'm not family, after all.'

'True. But you're raising it with me?'

'That's because I believe you feel as repelled as I do by the way he plays with Willow's hair.'

She grimaced. 'You're right, it sets my teeth on edge every time he does it; it's as if he's staking out his ownership of her. Mum must have mentioned something about that to you, surely?'

'Not in so many words, but I suspect she doesn't want to criticise Rick, even in private, seeing as he's the father of her grandchild-to-be.'

'That's Mum all over; she never wants to rock the boat. Willow's the same. They both have a natural tendency to think well of people and give them the benefit of the doubt. As you know by now, I tend to think the worst of people until proved wrong.'

'There's an obvious question I could ask after a statement like that, but I shan't go there.'

'Which is to your credit,' Martha said. 'Also to your credit is that you do seem to make Mum happy. But I'll warn you now, should that change, you will be my first port of call.'

'I'd expect nothing less. And I hereby solemnly swear that if I am the cause of a moment's unhappiness for your mother, you will have every right to take me to task.'

'Hmmm . . . You talk a good talk, Ellis, I'll give you that.'

He couldn't help but smile. 'They're not empty words, Martha. I wouldn't insult you by saying something I didn't mean.'

'Good. Now it's my turn to ask you a question. What's going on between Lucas and Willow?'

This was shakier ground for Ellis and he thought hard before answering. 'Nothing as far as I know,' he said evenly.

Martha tutted. 'Oh, come on, Ellis, we both know full well there's *something* going on between the pair of them. Question is: what?'

356

'You're right,' he admitted. 'But I don't think—' he broke off, unsure how to phrase what he wanted to say. With Martha he could see that every word counted. 'I don't think any lines have been crossed,' he said finally.

'Meanwhile, they're naively kidding themselves it's all perfectly innocent between them?' she said, sounding unconvinced.

'But we've all done something similar, haven't we?' remarked Ellis. 'I know I have. What about you?'

'What? Flirted with somebody when I know perfectly well I shouldn't?'

He smiled to himself at how literally she took his words. 'It doesn't have to be as blatant as flirting,' he said, 'often it's just a feeling one has when around a person. A shifting of equilibrium, you might say.'

'If I felt that and knew it was inappropriate, I'd be quick to shut that feeling down.'

How very noble, he thought, and how very black and white the world must be to Martha. He could almost envy her that degree of certainty, but experience had taught him that certainty in life was a fool's game. He for one couldn't condemn Lucas for feeling attracted to Willow when he himself had had an affair with Naomi all those years ago.

With Haslemere behind them and heading towards Petersfield, Ellis was taken aback by Martha's next question.

'Have you ever wondered about the lies Rick told Willow regarding that cat he buried?' she said.

'In what way?'

'That maybe he's lying to cover up something far worse.' Martha hesitated. 'What if Rick killed the cat?'

'Indirectly he did, by leaving the door open.'

357

She shook her head. 'What if he deliberately killed the wretched thing? He could have broken the cat's neck, and no one would be the wiser.'

'But why would he do that? For what purpose?'

'To teach Willow a lesson.'

'Sorry, you've lost me now.'

Repositioning the seat belt that lay across her abdomen, she said, 'Look, this might sound a bit far-fetched, but hear me out. The day the cat went missing, I'd asked Willow to come and see me. I wanted to talk to her about you and Mum.'

Ellis smiled. 'To discuss how to get rid of me?'

She had the grace to smile back at him. 'Not exactly, but the thing is, I distinctly remember Willow saying that Rick hadn't wanted her to come. He'd wanted her to go to the gym with him.'

'What, so you think he killed the cat because he couldn't get his own way? You're right, it is far-fetched.'

'But you agreed with me that there's definitely something creepy about him.'

'Yes, but what you're describing sounds more like a psychopath and I'd hate to think that the father of Willow's child is as dangerous as that; it doesn't bear thinking about.'

'Hear me out some more. You know about gaslighting, don't you?'

'Sorry? What's Victorian gas lamps got to do with anything?'

'It's when your partner makes you doubt yourself in order to control you. It makes you feel you're going crazy.'

As though a light had been switched on, Ellis saw exactly where Martha was going with this. 'That's a hell of a leap you're making.'

'I was reading up on the subject this morning while I was waiting for you. Rick fits the profile to a T. He's possessive, he spoils Willow with expensive presents and bit by bit he's distancing her from her family.'

'I haven't seen any sign of the latter.'

'I have. He's accused me of bullying Willow, of patronising her and basically of not being a very nice sister. It's a classic case of divide and conquer.'

'When did he accuse you of all that?'

'A few months ago.'

'Have you spoken to Willow about it? Or your mother?'

'No. I was embarrassed by the accusations because I know at times I do come across as the bossy big sister. I only recently told Tom what Rick had said.'

'What did he say?'

'He wanted to have a word with Rick to tell him he was out of order, but I asked him not to. I didn't want there to be any more trouble than I felt there already was.'

'And too often words said in the heat of a moment are not the wisest,' Ellis said.

'I know what you're probably thinking,' Martha then said. 'That I'm determined to think the worst about Rick because of what he said to me.'

'That would be petty, and I don't believe you would waste any thought or energy on something so trivial. But if you're right about Rick and what he's doing to Willow, where does that leave us? What's his ultimate aim?'

'To control her. To make her entirely his possession.'

'Wouldn't she realise what's going on?'

'Apparently the process is like slowly boiling a frog alive in a pan of water; the victim doesn't notice the gradual changes going on in their life.'

Ellis cringed. After checking his mirrors, he pulled out to overtake a minibus of schoolchildren, and said, 'Has your sister given you any indication that she feels uneasy about Rick and her relationship with him?'

'She doesn't love him, that much I know.'

'Really?'

'She admitted it when she was talking to me while I was stuck in the lift at work. Her actual words were that she *wanted* to love him, which means she doesn't. I'm convinced she's dug herself an almighty hole and thinks there's no way out of it.'

'I hate to say it, Martha, but everything you've put forward amounts to nothing but supposition.'

'But you know it's true, don't you? And I tell you what else I suspect might be true.'

'Go on,' said Ellis.

'When we first knew that Willow was pregnant, Tom wondered if Willow might have deliberately got herself pregnant to trap Rick, him being her first boyfriend who ticked all the right boxes in that he was financially secure, had his own home, could afford to give her nice things, etcetera. I disagreed with Tom on that, and still do, for the simple reason my sister isn't the mercenary type, it's just not her style.'

'I don't think it is either.'

'Anyway, I tried looking at it another way. What if Rick trapped Willow by deliberately getting her pregnant? When you look at it that way round, it all fits. On the face of it she is the classic ditzy people-pleaser and would be an ideal victim for being manipulated.'

'For what reason though?'

'Power. It's always about power and being in control, to cover up some underlying inadequacy.'

It was on the tip of Ellis's tongue to say that she could be describing her own father, but he managed to keep his mouth shut. Instead he tried to decide if even half of what Martha had said about Rick could be true. And if it was, what could any of them do?

Chapter Fifty-One

Willow had spent most of the morning hunting for her mobile as well as the charging cable for her laptop, the battery of which was dead. In the end, she gave up looking and packed a small suitcase. Then she wrote a note for Rick, which she left propped up on the worktop by the coffee machine. Along with the diamond ring he'd given her.

Now, looking out of the train window as it swept through the countryside that was gilded with autumnal shades of gold and russet in the October sunshine, she wondered about the note she had written. It had taken her several attempts to get it right, or as right as it could ever be. She just hoped that once he'd calmed down, Rick would see things the way she did, that it had been a mistake between them. They were oil and water, sliding around each other, but never truly becoming one.

Not that she'd put anything about oil and water in the note, there had been no point using metaphors when she had to be straight with Rick.

I'm very sorry, she had written, *but I seem to do nothing but annoy you these days and so I'm going to Mum's. I know you won't like it, but I think it's for the best.*

I know also that you care about me and that you were upset at losing your temper the way you did last night, and that it was only because you'd been worried about me being out so late, but you scared me. You probably didn't mean to, but you need to know that you did, and that can't be good for our baby. It would be better for us both if you didn't contact me for a few days. I need time to think, and I believe you do as well.

Take care and please don't be too cross with me.

Willow

She knew the manner in which she'd signed the note would hurt Rick. He would have wanted to read the words, *With all my love, Willow.* Or something similar. But she didn't love him. Oh, she'd tried. She'd tried so very hard to give him what he wanted from her. For a while she had almost believed that she did love him, but that was because she'd needed to believe everything would work out. Love conquered all, that was the theory, wasn't it?

It was possible that she was incapable of truly loving anyone, that she was damaged goods destined always to chase the dream of somebody to love and to be loved in return, but failing miserably. Was it her unlovability that provoked Rick and brought out the worst in him?

A vigorous movement inside her made her aware of the life she and Rick had created together. The baby had been restless for most of last night, twisting and turning, shoving and poking, and had kept Willow awake while she lay rigidly on her side with her back to Rick. Not that she had expected to sleep. Reluctant to get in bed with him – she had only done so because she'd been afraid what he might say or do if she didn't – she had been too on edge to sleep, too shocked at what he had done to her and what the future now held.

Her greatest fear, greater than how cross Rick was going to be with her when he discovered she'd gone, was whether she would be capable of loving their child in the way any child deserved to be loved. She hoped with all her heart that she could.

At Havant station, and aware that she should have found a payphone to call home to let Mum know she was on her way, Willow found a taxi to take her to Tilsham.

'You look like you've been in the wars,' the man said.

Puzzled, Willow stared at him as he put her case in the boot of his car. Then she remembered that her sunglasses only partially covered her painfully bruised eye and cheek, and the scarf she'd put on to hide her swollen mouth had slid down and her split lip was fully exposed. 'My own stupid fault,' she said with a trilling little laugh. 'I clumsily missed my footing while out shopping yesterday. I'm one of those hopeless people who can trip over her own shadow.'

He cocked his head and held the car door open for her to climb in, saying, 'In your condition you need to take more care. When's the baby due?'

'I have another eight weeks to go, so don't worry, I'm not about to ask you to take me to the nearest hospital.' She gave another trilling laugh which even to her ears sounding annoying and unconvincing.

'Not long, then,' he said, settling himself behind the wheel of the car. 'Where to?'

She gave him the address and wondered how many more lies she would tell in the coming days.

'Promise me you won't tell anyone,' Rick had said last night while tearing off a square of kitchen roll and dabbing gently at her bleeding mouth. He'd said again how sorry he was and repeated that she must have bitten her lip when his hand made contact. How reasonable he'd made it sound, as though it had been her fault that he'd hurt her.

Maybe it was. Maybe, as the taxi driver had said, she needed to take more care of herself. None of this would have happened if she'd had the sense not to stay out so late and give Rick cause to worry about her.

This morning when he was showered, shaved and dressed and had made her a cup of tea before he'd left for work, he'd helpfully suggested she put a cold compress against her eye and cheek. He'd then made her promise she would stay in for the day and reminded her of the promise she'd made the night before, that she wasn't ever to tell anyone what he'd done. He'd said he wouldn't be able to take the shame of anyone knowing. Well, that made two of them.

Of those two promises she'd made, she'd already broken one by leaving the flat. But then she suspected the promise Rick had made to her last night wouldn't be one he would be able to keep. The blazing anger she'd seen in his eyes just before the first blow had struck convinced her that he had been itching to slap her for some time, and that until then he'd somehow managed to control himself. In that split second when he'd raised his hand, had it felt like an enormous and welcome relief to him? Had he momentarily relished the sensation of complete release, of letting go of the frustration and tension within him that had been building?

As confused as she felt by the mix of her own emotions, there was one that refused to quieten in her mind. Had she driven Rick to lose his temper? Had she pushed him too far with her carelessness and lack of thought? Had she, as she'd done before, brought this on herself?

Was this how Mum had felt? Had she blamed herself for those times when Dad had lost control and hit her? Willow had only witnessed it happen on a couple of occasions, both of them when she was very young. The first time had been when she'd woken from a bad dream and, unable to get back to sleep, and hearing a strange noise coming from downstairs, she had crept out onto the landing to see what was going on. Peering between the banisters, she had seen through the open door of the sitting room to where her father stood with his fist raised and where Mum was backing away from him, her hands covering her face. Frightened, Willow had fled to her bedroom and in the morning, she had convinced herself that she must have dreamt what she'd seen, because Mum and Dad were acting just as they always did at the breakfast table, smiling and chatting quite normally. If Dad had hit Mum, surely she'd be upset? And anyway, Dad wouldn't do something like that, would he?

When it happened again, another time when she'd been unable to sleep and had crept out onto the landing, Willow knew instinctively that what she'd just witnessed was something she should never mention, not even to Martha; it was a secret that grown-ups kept to themselves. But had Mum ever told anyone about it? Auntie Geraldine perhaps? Or had she kept quiet because she was too ashamed to tell anyone, just in the same way that Willow felt too embarrassed to admit this terrible thing Rick had done to her?

Not that guilty shame was anything new to Willow. She was well acquainted with it.

'Here we are then,' said the taxi driver, turning into the driveway of Anchor House.

Home, thought Willow with relief. She paid the man and was about to carry her case the short distance to the front door when he insisted on doing it for her. It was a kindly gesture on his part, but it reminded her of Rick, of him always rushing to help her, of him suffocating her with his overly protective care.

They had only taken a few steps when the front opened and there was Mum. All the way here Willow had been determined to keep it together, but the sight of her mother and the obvious concern on her face stripped away that resolve, and suddenly overcome with fear and helplessness, she began to cry.

Chapter Fifty-Two

Naomi's relief at seeing her youngest daughter instantly vanished when she saw her distress and the shocking state of her face.

'Willow, whatever has happened to you?' she cried in alarm as the taxi driver acknowledged her and returned to his car.

Willow's reply was all but drowned out by her gulping sobs. The only words Naomi caught were 'It's my fault . . . I shouldn't have . . . I'm so sorry.'

Shutting the door, Naomi guided her daughter through the house to the kitchen. Her loud sobs attracted the attention of everybody else and they all appeared at once, with Martha leading the way.

'Bloody hell, Willow!' she exclaimed, 'what have you done to your face?'

'It's . . . it's nothing,' Willow mumbled, a hand raised to cover her mouth.

'It doesn't look nothing to me. How did you do it? Oh my God, don't tell me Rick did this to you!'

With sickening dread seeping through her, Naomi said, 'Don't hound the poor girl, Martha, at least give her a chance to take off her coat before subjecting her to a cross-examination.

Come on, Willow, let me help you out of your coat and get you comfortable. How about a cup of tea? And have you eaten? Martha, put the kettle on, and Geraldine, don't just stand there gaping like a fish, make yourself useful and find the cake tin in the pantry.'

'What shall I do?' asked Ellis.

Naomi caught her breath and scratched her head distractedly. She'd run out of things with which to divert attention away from Willow, who had now shrugged off her coat and was sitting at the table, in the place where she had always sat ever since she was a toddler and old enough to sit in a proper chair. 'Tissues,' she said to Ellis as Willow sniffed and let out another sob. 'There's a box over on the dresser.'

In a flash Ellis had fetched it and with the kettle now filled and plugged in, Martha turned around and joined Naomi and Willow at the table. Geraldine reappeared and once again Willow was the focus of everybody's attention.

'I'm sorry for causing such a fuss,' she said, plucking a tissue from the box.

'Don't be ridiculous,' said Geraldine, banging the cake tin down on the table with about as much delicacy as a pile-driver. 'You turn up here in tears looking like you've been in a fight, a fuss is the last thing I would call it. I just hope you're not going to claim you walked into a door.'

'Geraldine!' remonstrated Naomi. 'For goodness sake, show some sensitivity, will you?'

'Don't look at me like that, Naomi. Not when it's obvious that this is history repeating itself.'

There was a highly charged pause as Naomi exhaled deeply and took in the enormity of her friend's words.

'What do you mean, history repeating itself?' demanded Martha.

'Not now, Geraldine,' Naomi warned her in a stern voice. Ellis caught her eye and she knew what he would be thinking: that Geraldine was right, and the awful thing was, she knew it too. She knew what had happened to her daughter with every fibre of her body, which was vibrating with a seething anger she had never before experienced. She had to make her darling Willow tell her the truth, and make her understand that no excuses could be made for Rick and what he'd done. Naomi had made that mistake with Colin and nothing on earth would allow her to let her daughter to do the same. No man was ever going to knock her daughters about and get away with it. *Never!*

'Would you rather I made myself scarce?' asked Geraldine.

Naomi was about to say that perhaps that would be best when Willow said, 'No, don't go, please stay.'

With the kettle now boiling, Naomi asked Ellis to do the honours. 'There's a box of decaffeinated in the cupboard,' she said gratefully to him as he nodded and set about the task.

Then gently taking her daughter's hands in hers, and swallowing back the anger she felt at the sight of her horribly battered face, Naomi said, 'Did Rick do this to you? You mustn't be embarrassed or ashamed to tell the truth if he did.'

Willow's bruised and swollen lips trembled, and tears sprang to her eyes. 'It wasn't his fault . . . not really . . . I annoyed and upset him last night because I came home late.'

'No, Willow,' Naomi said softly, her throat constricted with the injustice of it. 'Whatever you said or did, that did not give Rick the right to hurt you.'

Her expression as fierce as Naomi had ever seen it,

370

Martha pulled out a chair and sat opposite her sister. 'How many times has he done this to you?'

Willow raised her tearful gaze from the tissue she had screwed up into a tight ball and looked at Martha. 'This was the first time, but he's been very angry with me before. I just always seem to annoy him, and it makes him lose his temper.'

'Oh, so that makes it perfectly all right then, does it?'

'Geraldine, please, you're not helping.'

'Mum, it's okay,' said Willow. 'Auntie Geraldine is only saying what you're probably all thinking.'

'Does he know where you are?' This was from Ellis as he placed a mug of tea and a small jug of milk on the table in front of Willow.

'I left him a note saying I was going to spend a few days here and that I thought it was a good idea to have some time apart.'

'So he left for work this morning just like it was a normal day for him?' said Naomi, a fresh wave of fury flaring in her.

'Yes, he made me promise I wouldn't go out. Or tell anyone what he'd done.'

'I bet he did!' muttered Martha.

'Why didn't you call me?' asked Naomi. 'I would have come for you straight away.'

With shaking hands, Willow added some milk to her tea. 'I wanted to, but I couldn't find my mobile. Or the cable charger for my laptop.'

'I guarantee Rick took them so you wouldn't have any way of contacting us,' said Martha grimly.

'Would he do that?'

Martha made an exasperated sound. 'How can you ask that, Willow, after what he's done to you? The man's a control freak!

371

Everything he does is about him wanting to control you. And if you factor that in when you think about all the little things he says or does, you'll see them in a completely new light. It has nothing to do with caring for you, or even loving you, it's about controlling you.'

'He says that about you, that you boss me about and bully me.'

'I know. He told me that himself on the phone.'

Willow looked surprised. 'Why didn't you tell me?'

Martha sighed. 'Because it wouldn't have done any good, and you might not have believed me, not if Rick denied ever having that conversation with me. He was out to come between us, and really that was his big mistake.'

'What do you mean?' asked Willow.

'I was no longer taken in by him. Oh, he was very convincing to begin with, he had me thoroughly fooled, but then the cracks started to open up. Especially over that business with Lucy and Simon's cat. If he could lie about that, I couldn't help but wonder what else he would cover up.'

'You sound like you've put a lot of thought into this,' said Willow.

To Naomi's surprise, Martha then turned to look at Ellis. He nodded back at her.

'We both have,' Ellis said. 'I just had an uncomfortable feeling about him, but Martha felt concerned enough to do some online research and tell me about it earlier this morning.'

'But you never said anything to me?' said Naomi, reeling from this revelation from Ellis.

'I didn't want you to think I was interfering in family matters,' he said.

'If I'm permitted to speak,' said Geraldine, throwing a look

372

at Naomi, 'is what we're discussing known as coercive and controlling behaviour?'

'Yes,' answered Martha. 'Eventually Rick would have driven a wedge between Willow and the rest of us so he'd have her completely to himself and would then be free to do exactly what he wanted.'

Willow frowned. 'That sounds a bit over the top.'

'And it's not over the top that the father of the child you're expecting has hit you so hard you have a blackened eye and a split lip?'

When Willow didn't answer her sister, but reached for another tissue and blew her nose, Ellis said, 'We need to accept that in all likelihood Rick will come down here begging forgiveness and swearing he'll never do it again.'

'That's precisely what he'll do,' said Naomi with a steely tone. 'But Willow, I'm afraid it will be over my dead body if that man crosses the threshold of Anchor House ever again. I simply will not allow it, even if he is the father of your child. Trust me when I say he will never change.'

'Your mother's right,' said Geraldine. 'You must believe her. She knows what she's talking about.'

Not wanting her friend to elaborate any further, Naomi cleared her throat warningly and Geraldine fell silent.

'As usual, I haven't really thought things through,' said Willow miserably. 'I have no idea what I'm going to do next.'

'For now, you don't have to think about that,' said Naomi. 'All that matters is that you're safe here with us. So drink your tea and let me cut you a slice of cake.'

'Thanks, Mum.'

Trying to conceal the absolute fury she felt towards Rick, that he could harm her precious daughter, Naomi took the knife and plate that Ellis had produced. She had to grip the knife hard to stop her hands from shaking. If Rick were in the room now it would take every scrap of her willpower not to plunge it deep into his chest, to avenge the wanton violence he had carried out on poor Willow, a defenceless young woman carrying his child.

The more she thought of what Willow had gone through, the more Naomi felt as though a lifetime of suppressed anger was about to unleash itself. All those years of self-deception she'd put herself through and which, in so many ways, had caused more harm to her than the actual physical blows. She was reminded of that day in the garden following Geraldine's last visit, when she had learned that Colin had not been held in the high regard she'd always believed, that maybe her oldest friends were not the only ones to have seen through the flimsy artifice of their marriage. Seated on the wooden bench overlooking the beach that day she had been consumed with regret and a sense of worthlessness, and the belief that everything she had done for the sake of her family had been for no real reason. But then Ellis had appeared and suddenly none of that had mattered. The past was the past, it was the future that counted.

But today once again she was forced to confront the harm she may have unwittingly caused. In striving to create the illusion of a perfect marriage, which now seemed no more than a tawdry trompe l'oeil, had her actions led to where they were now, with history having repeated itself, just as Geraldine claimed?

Chapter Fifty-Three

Later that afternoon, and while Geraldine and Ellis offered to prepare an early supper together, Naomi suggested to Martha and Willow that the three of them go for a walk while the weather held.

As they trudged along the beach in a strong buffeting wind, shafts of milky light pierced through banks of darkening clouds, and the sea, grey and roiling, resembled Naomi's churning emotions. But as apprehensive as she felt, she was determined to do what she knew she had to. They'd reached the sand dunes when she decided that this would be where she finally told her daughters the truth.

'Let's sit here for a while,' she said, 'if it's not too cold or too uncomfortable for you?'

'It's fine by me,' said Martha, 'my thermostat seems to be switched to a permanently high setting these days.'

'Mine too,' said Willow.

They sat either side of Naomi and she suddenly wanted to put her arms around them both and hold them tight, just as she had when they were little. She felt as though she were about to jump off a cliff and, selfishly, she needed her daughters to stop her from feeling so terrified.

Watching a lone sailing boat in the distance heading around the promontory, perhaps on its way to Bosham harbour, Naomi summoned up her courage. 'There's something I have to tell you,' she began nervously, 'and I'm very much afraid it's going to upset you. You might not even want to believe me, but—'

'Is this about you and Ellis deciding to marry after all?' interrupted Martha.

'No,' she said, 'it has nothing to do with Ellis. It's about your father. And Martha, I know how much you loved him, so this will be particularly hard for you to hear.' She swallowed and once more steeled herself. After a small pause, she carried on in a rush. 'Earlier today, Geraldine, in her inimitable way, referred to history repeating itself. By that, she meant that your father had a violent streak and when things became too much for him, he lost his temper and his self-control and would sometimes take out his angry frustration on me.'

In the seconds that followed, the sound of the foaming tide dragging at the sand and pebbles, and the cry of a seagull swooping low over the turbulent water, seemed unbearably loud.

'I don't believe you,' said Martha. 'Not Dad. Why would you say something so awful about him?'

'Because it's true.'

'No! It can't be. Not Dad.'

'Martha, it is true,' said Willow in a voice so faint it was made almost inaudible by a sudden gust of wind. 'I know it is.'

Naomi turned her head to look at her youngest daughter. 'How do you know?' she asked.

'I saw him. I saw him hit you.'

'No!' cried Martha angrily before Naomi could speak. 'Stop it, the pair of you!'

'I'm not lying,' said Willow, 'and nor is Mum. I saw him do it.'

'Oh Willow, why did you never say anything?' asked Naomi.

'Because I was only a child and I thought it was one of those things that happened between grown-ups that was never spoken about. Like catching your parents having sex. You know they do it, but you don't ever want to think about it or admit to anybody else that they do it.'

'But why?' said Martha. 'I don't understand. Yes, Dad had a temper, but he wasn't a violent man. He just wasn't like that.'

'What kind of a man do you think hits a defenceless woman?' asked Naomi.

Martha covered her face with her hands in distress. 'I don't know, I don't know!' she cried. 'Just not somebody like Dad. He wasn't a monster.'

'No,' agreed Naomi. 'He wasn't. But he was someone who couldn't always control himself.' She reached for her eldest daughter's hand to try and comfort her, but Martha snatched her hand away and pushed it into her coat pocket.

'When did this all go on?' she demanded.

'Throughout most of our marriage,' Naomi answered matter-of-factly. 'The first time he hit me, I made him swear he would never do it again, and despite his protestations of remorse and shame, and his promise that he would never repeat what he'd done, he did, time and time again. It was always stress-induced, brought on by some problem at work. I think it had a lot to do with the way he lost his parents when he was so young, suppressed grief perhaps. Whatever the cause, it was beyond his control.'

'Only recently I remembered you once telling me that,' said Willow. 'It was after Rick told me how exactly he'd lost both his parents when he was younger. His father was an alcoholic and was knocked down by a car and then his mother committed suicide. Rick actually found her body.'

Calling to mind how evasive Rick had been about his parents, Naomi said, 'I did wonder why he was so reluctant to talk about them. But why didn't you say anything to us?'

'He didn't want people to know. He made me promise I'd never tell you.'

Martha frowned. 'Look, I don't care about Rick and his parents, but if Dad had a problem, Mum, why didn't you get help for him?'

There was an undeniable tone of accusation to her question, as if Naomi was at fault. Rather than point out that Martha was falling into the classic trap of blaming the victim, she said, 'I tried on many occasions to persuade him that counselling might help, but he refused point-blank to consider it. I think he was scared of what inner demons he might be forced to confront.'

'But how come we never saw any bruises on you?' Again, Martha sounded as though she doubted the veracity of what Naomi had shared with them.

'He was either clever with where or how he struck me, or I had to resort to using make-up to conceal the marks.'

When Martha didn't respond, Naomi turned to face Willow. 'I'm so sorry you witnessed any of it, truly I am. I wish you'd told me.'

'I just didn't know how to,' Willow said sadly.

'But you've carried this for so long, and when you didn't deserve to.'

'Presumably Auntie Geraldine knew this . . . this awful secret of yours?' interjected Martha.

'I never once mentioned it to Geraldine,' Naomi replied, 'I can only imagine that something gave me away. In fact, such was my shame at what I was hiding from everybody, I couldn't bring myself to tell anyone. Not until I told Ellis a short while ago.'

Martha groaned. 'Oh Mum, how could you?'

'Because I wanted him to know the whole of me, the good bits and the bad. Especially the bad. And I didn't want there to be any secrets between us; I wanted a fresh start that was built on truth and honesty. After so many years of lies and pretence, it was a relief to say the words out loud. But it was also terrifying. I felt completely vulnerable and laid bare and horribly disloyal to your father. To you two as well.'

'If it was so bad being with Dad, why did you stay with him?'

'Why do you think, Martha? For the sake of you girls. I couldn't bring myself to destroy the life we had as a family. Or ruin the love you had for your father. It would have broken your heart, and his too.'

Martha picked up a stone and threw it angrily at the retreating sea. 'But it's okay to do that now?' she said, 'for me now to know that my father wasn't the man I thought he was, that he was an abusive wife-beater?'

In the painful silence that followed, Willow said, 'What did you mean by Ellis knowing the bad bits about you, Mum?'

'I mean the shame, Willow. The shame that has been like a second skin to me all these years.' More firmly, she said, 'And I won't let that happen to you. If you forgive Rick what he's done and go back to him, you'll live in constant fear of him losing his temper again. You'll also end up living a lie and you'll hate yourself for pretending to the world that you're fine, when, deep down, you're not.'

'I think it's too late for that,' Willow murmured. 'I've already been living a lie.'

Chapter Fifty-Four

It had happened during the first term of her second year at Warwick University and was, of course, her own fault; she shouldn't have drunk so much. Although that wasn't her first mistake: that had been to go to the party in the first place. She hadn't planned to, but at the last minute she had abandoned the essay she'd been part-way through writing and gone. The other two girls with whom she shared the house were away in London for the weekend, so with no company for a few days, a party had seemed like a great idea. She could not have been more wrong.

She'd lost count of how many tequila shots she'd downed by the time he approached her. She'd noticed him watching while she'd been laughing and joking with a group of friends and had liked the look of him. Tall and powerfully built, his hair was thick and dark and from beneath his brows, a pair of sultry dark eyes had stared at her with obvious interest. Even when he raised the bottle of beer in his hand and tipped his head back to drink from it, his eyes never left hers.

Making his way over to her, he said, 'It's time we said hello, don't you think?'

'I thought you were one of those shy types,' she'd said, playing along, 'and didn't have the nerve.'

He smiled at her with amusement. 'So, the tricky part over, tell me your name. Mine's John.'

They danced and chatted and drank some more for the next hour. He told her that he played rugby. 'You do like rugby players, don't you?' he asked. By now the volume of the party had increased and he had to shout in her ear.

'I do as of tonight,' she shouted back with a drunken giggle. He was just leaning in to kiss her, when a couple of his mates appeared behind him.

'Can't you see I'm perfectly happy right here working my charm on this gorgeous girl,' he told them with a wink when they suggested they move on to a new club that had opened in town.

She'd been drunk enough to think how sexy he was to claim her like that.

She was still thinking the same when she found herself upstairs with him and he was kissing her, his hands finding their way under her top. He took her into one of the bedrooms and just as he closed the door and turned the key, something clicked inside of her and she knew that she didn't want to be there. It didn't feel right.

The only light in the untidy room came from the harsh glare of the street lamp directly outside, and it revealed all too clearly the look of eager expectation on his face.

'Let's not hang about then,' he said, unbuttoning his jeans, 'there'll be others who'll want to use the room.'

Suddenly he didn't seem so attractive to her, or so sexy. He was just a big sweaty man towering over her. She stepped away from him and moved towards the door. 'I don't think this is a good idea,' she said, offering up an apologetic smile. 'Let's go back downstairs.'

He stared at her. 'It doesn't work that way.'

'Yes it does,' she said with more confidence than she felt.

A vein ticked at his neck, a thick neck that now she was seeing him through different eyes, gave him the look of a bulldog. He continued to stare at her and just as she had her hand on the key to unlock the door, he grabbed her and swung her round so he had her in his grasp.

'I know your type,' he said, 'you're all the same, you lead a guy on and then say you've changed your mind. But like I just told you, it doesn't work that way. Not with me at any rate.' He pressed his mouth hard against hers and shoved her onto the bed.

'Please don't,' she said as she struggled to push him off. But she was no match for his strength, or his intent as he ripped at her clothes. She tried calling for help, but that only made him clamp one of his large hands over her mouth. Barely able to breathe, and with the volume of music downstairs turned up even louder, as though to disguise the awful grunting sound he was making as he rammed against her, she had no choice but to let him get on with it. All the while in her head she was screaming for him to stop.

Thankfully it didn't take him long and afterwards, when he was buttoning his jeans, he said, 'Try telling anyone that was against your wishes and nobody will believe you. Everyone saw you come up with me quite willingly. You knew exactly what you were doing.'

She left the party straight away and back at the empty house, she ran herself a bath and cried and cried. But no matter how thoroughly she scrubbed herself, she could not wash away the stain of her stupidity. Why had she drunk so much? Why had she been so easily flattered by somebody who had proved himself to be no better than a savage thug?

In the days and weeks that followed, she withdrew from student life and rarely left her room other than to go to the nearby shop for food. Her housemates worried about her, but she wouldn't tell them what was wrong. Who would believe her anyway? She had gone up those stairs with John quite willingly. People would remember her dancing with him and kissing him beforehand. They would say she had wanted him as much as he had wanted her. That's how it would appear to anyone who had seen them together. So no, she kept quiet rather than be called a liar out to cause trouble.

But trouble lay in store for her when she realised she had missed her period. She wanted to believe it was caused by anxiety and not eating properly, but a trip to the chemist followed by a pregnancy test soon put paid to that hope.

She didn't hesitate. Not for a moment. She would not let guilt stop her from doing what she had to do. No one was going to persuade her to give birth to the child of a man who was no better than a rapist. So she found the information she needed – there was plenty of it about on the university campus – and two weeks later she swallowed the first of the two tablets she had to take. The next day she took a couple of painkillers as advised, and then the second tablet the clinic had given her. She then waited for the medication to rid her body of the unwanted thing inside her.

Yet just as she had not been able to wash away the stain of her stupidity, nor could she rid herself of the worthlessness that consumed her from then on. It made her abandon her degree course, and whatever sense of direction or ambition she'd previously possessed was now gone. It all seemed so pointless. And confirming what her father had always said about her, that she could never stick at anything and see it through, she drifted aimlessly through a series of dead-end jobs and boyfriends.

Then twelve years later, she met Rick, who everybody believed was the perfect boyfriend for her. A boyfriend who would provide some much-needed stability in her life.

Chapter Fifty-Five

'It's all my fault, Ellis,' Naomi had sobbed. 'Everything that's happened to Willow is down to me. I failed to do the single most important thing a mother should do, and that was to keep her safe.'

Ellis had listened in horror to what Naomi had reluctantly shared with him when they'd come up to bed. She hadn't meant to tell him, but the burden of it had been too much and she'd broken down and told him everything. Afterwards, and out of respect to Willow, she'd begged him not to breathe a word of it to anyone. A man of his word, he'd promised her faithfully that he wouldn't.

To his great sorrow there was nothing he could say that would shake Naomi out of the erroneous belief that she was to blame for what had happened to her daughter. All he could do was hold her and let her cry out her distress. For Willow's sake she had held her emotions in check throughout the day and evening, but alone in bed with Ellis, her strength had given way to tears of self-recrimination and anguish. Her heart, she'd said, was shattered into a thousand pieces by what Willow had shared on the beach with her and Martha, and she would never forgive herself for what her youngest daughter had gone through.

Eventually she had succumbed to emotional exhaustion and fallen asleep, but next to her, Ellis lay wide awake in the darkness, his mind too restless to switch off and call it a day. He kept thinking how wrong it was that victims frequently ended up blaming themselves, while the likes of Colin and Rick – the perpetrators of the abuse – never did. Did their declarations of remorse and pleas for forgiveness ever have an ounce of genuine sincerity to them? Ellis didn't think they had, for how else could they do what they did?

Naomi's justification for blaming herself was on the grounds that she had put Willow, at a young and impressionable age, in a position whereby she had witnessed acts of violence which she had then absorbed as being normal, simply part and parcel of being in a relationship. Ellis had tried to reason with Naomi that if anyone was to blame it was Colin.

'If Colin were still alive,' Ellis had asserted, 'wouldn't you hold him accountable for what Willow saw as a child? Does he not have a part to play when it comes to apportioning blame?'

'Of course he does,' she'd said, 'but there's no one to blame but me for my cowardice in not leaving Colin. And because I stayed, I ensured that Willow's view of what constitutes a healthy relationship was skewed.'

'It wasn't cowardice,' he'd said gently. 'It took courage for you to stay, to put your children first. If anyone was a coward, it was Colin for refusing to seek help, for being too afraid to face his demons.'

'But look where my decision to stay got Willow,' she'd replied. 'I gave her the example that if you were treated badly, you just took it on the chin. Quite literally.'

'Willow may have subconsciously thought that was true,'

387

Ellis had countered, 'but she came here today because she knew what Rick had done to her wasn't right.'

'But she ended up in a potentially lethal relationship because of me.'

'No,' Ellis disagreed. 'The bastard who raped her did that. He destroyed her self-esteem and that's the real reason she valued herself so poorly and allowed Rick to manipulate her. And maybe, to a lesser extent, it happened with other boyfriends in the past.'

'Please don't say that,' Naomi had said. 'I can't bear the thought of her thinking she deserved so little in life.'

But wasn't that what Naomi had done? Ellis thought now while staring into the darkness.

The more he thought of what had happened to Willow, the more he could feel his body fill with some primordial urge for revenge on the poor girl's behalf, to track down the man who had raped her and after he'd dealt with him, he'd then deal with Rick.

The idea of them all being taken in by Rick's act of civilised behaviour sickened Ellis. Although he hadn't been taken in entirely; aspects of Rick's behaviour had set tiny alarm bells ringing, but really no more than that. Not until Martha opened up to him in the car earlier that day. At the time, some of what she'd said had seemed highly improbable, like her suggestion that Rick might have deliberately killed that cat, but now Ellis could well believe it. A sadist in full sight, he thought with a shudder of disgust.

Knowing that sleep would continue to elude him in his present frame of mind, and doing his best not to disturb Naomi, he quietly eased himself out of bed. Just as quietly, he crept downstairs, taking his mobile with him on the off-chance he might be able to chat with Lucas. He suddenly needed to know that Lucas was all right. He'd move heaven and earth if he thought his stepson needed his help but didn't feel able to ask for it. Sometimes it was too easy to accept a person was the way they were and never question it. Just as everyone had with Willow.

Potentially Lucas had a ton of issues that could affect his mental wellbeing – the death of his father when he was a child, his mother remarrying, and then, much later, his mother's death – but just because he appeared to be okay with it all, that didn't mean he was. Remembering the day of Rose's funeral, when Lucas had spoken to Willow so candidly about his mother's funeral, and in a way that Ellis had never before heard him speak, he promised himself that he should explore those feelings further with his stepson.

Amazingly, Lucas answered his phone after only two rings and explained he was in his car on the way to the airport for a flight to New York, where he was due to give a talk at a symposium of digital media types. It was hard for Ellis to imagine Lucas doing such a thing, as he'd always hated to be the centre of attention, preferring, in his own words, to 'lurk' unobtrusively in the background.

'Are you nervous?' Ellis asked him.

'Not really. I know my stuff, and the company wouldn't send me unless I did. I'm fully prepped, so it's just a matter of conveying my knowledge as clearly and as succinctly as I would if I were in the office.'

With a feeling of pride, Ellis said, 'Good for you.'

'So what's with the middle-of-the-night call, it must be about two in the morning there?'

Ellis told him what Rick had done to Willow, and of Naomi's

abusive relationship with Colin and how she had admitted for the first time today to her daughters what had gone on in secret, but that Willow, as a young child, had witnessed some of what had taken place. Keeping his promise to Naomi, not a word did he say about Willow being raped as a student. When he'd finished, the line was so deathly quiet, he wondered if he'd lost the connection. 'Are you still there, Lucas?' he asked.

'Yes. I was just figuring out how best to respond.'

'I know the feeling.'

'This'll sound like I'm being wise after the event, but I didn't take to Willow's fiancé. He struck me as a bit weird with the way he was always touching her, it gave me an uncomfortable feeling.'

'I know what you mean.'

'And I certainly didn't think he was her type. What's going to happen next?'

'I keep wondering that myself,' said Ellis.

'What's the answer then? Because she mustn't go back to Rick. Willow must see that it would be the same situation as you've just told me about Naomi putting up with her abusive husband for all those years. I still can't believe she stayed with a man like that. Why the hell do women do it?'

'That's a whole other debate and not something we, as men, generally can easily understand. Not unless we've been in a similar situation.'

'On a practical note, I hope somebody has had the sense to put together some photographic evidence of what Rick has done to Willow. She might need to produce it to prove he's been violent towards her.'

'Martha already thought of that and, much against her wishes, Willow did in the end allow her sister to take some pictures.'

In the background, all those miles away, Ellis could hear the sound of a siren. When it had passed, Lucas said, 'Look, Dad, I'm almost at the airport, so I'll have to end the call, but I have one more question. Do you think I had anything to do with what Rick did to Willow? I'd never forgive myself if that was true.'

'There's enough self-blame going on right now,' Ellis said firmly, 'so please don't start reproaching yourself.'

'You haven't answered my question.'

'Your name hasn't come up in anything Willow has said, but I would say that it was obvious to us all that the two of you took an instant liking to each other, which means Rick would have seen it too. It seems to me like he didn't need much of an excuse to show his true colours.'

'But I probably didn't help matters, did I?'

'Maybe you did. Maybe this needed to happen sooner rather than later.'

'Do you think she'd be okay if I contacted her?'

'I don't see why not. Before today you wouldn't have asked me that question, would you? She's no different to the person she was when you last spoke.'

Was that an overly simplistic thing of him to say? Ellis pondered a few minutes later when he'd wished Lucas good luck with his talk and rung off.

Was there now a danger they would treat Willow differently, that she would now forever be cast in the role of victim? He hoped not. Otherwise she would never be able to move on and put this behind her.

But as Naomi had said, being raped and then terminating the unwanted pregnancy had shaped her from then on. It perhaps explained why she found it so hard to commit to anything, possibly believing she didn't deserve anything good and lasting in her life.

How could the poor girl ever unpick all that? And what would she feel every time she looked at the baby and was reminded of Rick?

Worse still, what if Rick convinced her that he could change, that for the sake of his child he would do it? Knowing Willow with her naturally kind heart, she would probably give him a second chance. Just as Naomi had with Colin.

All evening they had been on tenterhooks wondering whether, after going home and discovering the note Willow had left him, Rick would show up at Anchor House. But there had been neither sight nor sound from him.

Ellis had been ninety-nine per cent sure that Rick would try calling, that he would be confident enough in his ability to persuade them that everything Willow had told them had been a lie. Of course he hadn't hit her! How could anyone think he had when he loved her so much? He might even say that yes, they had argued, but she had fallen over and for some unaccountable reason had come up with a terrible story to make him look bad. Pregnancy, he might say, had made her behave irrationally, which he had done his best to cover up to save her any embarrassment. They already knew that he was a credible liar, so why wouldn't he try to convince them that black was white and white was black? He was smooth enough to think he could get away with it.

This and a hell of a lot more had passed through Ellis's mind when it came to second-guessing Rick's reaction to Willow being here with them. It reminded him of somebody he had once worked with who had made a series of catastrophic errors of judgement over a client's portfolio. When Ellis had challenged him, he had refused to acknowledge any fault on his part, but had justified his position even more tenaciously, all the while digging himself a deeper and deeper hole by insisting he was right. The only thing he'd been concerned about was managing his image, rather than resolving the problem he had created, or accepting he was responsible for it.

Odds-on, Rick would do exactly the same. He would lay whatever blame he could on Willow. But whatever excuse or reason he gave in the hope it would exonerate him would be a waste of his breath. There was nothing he could say or do that would make any of them think well of him. He was, if it didn't sound too much of an exaggeration, a dead man walking as far as this family was concerned. Though how things would work out when Willow gave birth was anybody's guess. As the child's father he would have rights, and that was what worried Ellis most.

Chapter Fifty-Six

The combination of yesterday's revelations and the baby inside her lying at an awkward angle, seemingly pummelling her ribs with both feet, had resulted in a restless night's sleep for Martha. When she checked to see what time it was and she saw it was almost seven o'clock, it was with a sense of relief that she dispensed with the futility of trying to sleep.

Myriad emotions had spun her thoughts into a tangled and sticky web for most of the night, wrapping her in guilt. She had treated her sister far from fairly over the years, but if she had known the horror of what Willow had gone through, she would have acted very differently. Less exasperation and a lot more compassion. And she would have made sure that vile monster who had raped her would have paid for what he'd done. The injustice of what had happened to Willow made her angrier than she could articulate.

On top of all that was what Mum had revealed about Dad. Martha's first reaction had been to call her mother a liar, to deny every word of what she said. But there had been such a calmness to Mum's confession that Martha knew she had to accept that, as shocking as it was, Mum was telling the truth. There was also Willow's corroboration to factor in, that she had actually witnessed the violence, as well as Auntie Geraldine's suspicions. It was, she was forced to acknowledge, an open-and-shut case.

But just as Mum must have made excuses for Dad, so too did Martha want to invent some plausible and acceptable reason for his behaviour. But the truth was, in her condemnation of Rick for what he'd done to Willow, she had to condemn her father too. She could not make any allowances for him. Which left her feeling betrayed, as though she had loved and admired a fraud of a man, and consequently, everything she had built her life on was crumbling beneath her feet. None of it was real. She had been conned.

Tom had been predictably shocked by what she told him about Willow on the phone last night, but when she tried to tell him about her father her voice had cracked, and she'd begun to cry. She knew that if she alarmed Tom too much, he would grab his car keys and drive down to be with her, so she pulled herself together and forced the words out.

'How could I have not known?' she'd said to Tom. 'How blind could I have been? All this time I've complained about Willow having her head in the clouds and not having a clue what was going on around her, while I was the one unable to see what was going on right under my nose!'

'But it wasn't going on under your nose, Martha. That's the thing about abuse, it's kept hidden.' He'd then offered to drive down to be with her, just as she thought he would.

'No,' she'd said. 'I'm perfectly all right.'

'What if Rick shows up?' he'd asked.

'Don't worry; Mum, Ellis and I can handle Rick. And don't forget,' she'd added lightly to reassure Tom that she really was okay, 'Mum's friend, Geraldine is here, so she'll act as our first line of defence.'

He'd made a small attempt at laughter, but she could tell he was humouring her. 'If you change your mind,' he'd said, 'or if you just want to talk, call me.'

'I will, I promise,' she'd said gratefully.

Now, as she pushed back the duvet and got out of bed, Martha thought how lucky she was to be married to such a kind and considerate man who would no more raise his hand to her than grow a second head.

Thank God she hadn't been attracted to and married a carbon copy of her father. As difficult as it was to confront, the love she had felt for the man who meant so much to her was now irrevocably tainted with shame. She was unspeakably ashamed of him. He'd been a perpetrator of domestic violence who had got away with it for years and she didn't think she would ever think well of him again.

Hearing the sound of the loo being flushed in the Jack and Jill bathroom that she shared with her sister, Martha put on her dressing gown, the one Mum always kept there for her. She then went out onto the landing and after knocking lightly on Willow's door, she let herself in.

Willow was back in bed, sitting up and clutching her old rag doll which Mum had made for her when she was little. With the duvet pulled up almost to her chin, she looked poignantly childlike, her hair in messy plaits which she hadn't brushed out before going to bed. The cut to her lip had formed an ugly scab now and the bruising to her cheek and eye had fanned out to spoil yet more of her face.

'How're you feeling?' asked Martha, closing the door behind her and going over to sit on the edge of her sister's bed.

'Not so bad.'

'Did you manage to sleep?'

'Off and on.'

'Me too.'

Still clutching the doll, Willow looked at Martha. 'I'm sorry . . . you know . . . about Dad. That must have been a terrible shock for you. You were always so much closer to him than me.'

'If I'd known the truth, then I wouldn't have been.' She was about to say more, that she wished Willow had confided in her all those years ago, but changed her mind. They both knew that if her sister had told her what she'd witnessed, Martha would never have believed her. She would have called her a liar and probably a lot worse. 'I'd rather not talk about Dad, if you don't mind,' she said. 'I'm more concerned about you.'

'Oh, don't you worry about me, I'm sure I'll survive.'

Her voice was maddeningly light, an echo of how Willow had always underplayed things. Now it didn't ring true to Martha's ears. Now she understood it for what it was, a veil drawn over whatever real emotion Willow was experiencing. It was one of the things about her sister that had annoyed Martha, her apparent refusal to face up to the important decisions in life and take responsibility for herself. With painful acceptance, she now knew that Willow had been forced to make some far tougher decisions than any Martha had had to. She had more than taken responsibility for herself. Too much so.

'But the question is, Willow,' she said gently, 'how will you cope?'

Willow gave a small shrug of her thin shoulders. 'You know how hopeless I am at planning things. The baby will arrive and somehow I'll just have to find a way to cope.'

Martha smiled. 'Then it's just as well you have a sister who's the bee's knees when it comes to putting together a plan of action. And Mum's no slouch in that department either, so I'm sure between us we'll come up with something to support you. More immediately, I think you should see a doctor today, if only to have the bruising to your face officially recorded in your medical notes. I'll get Mum to ring the local surgery. Okay?'

Willow nodded.

'Then I would recommend that one of us should speak to Rick. He needs to know that as a family we are now shielding you from him.' Hearing how bossy and dictatorial she was sounding, Martha softened her tone. 'That's if you think that's a good idea?' she added.

'I suppose I should be the one to speak to him,' Willow said, hugging the rag doll more tightly to her. 'I'm going to have to at some point, aren't I? He is the father of the baby, after all.'

More's the pity, thought Martha.

'But at least he's respecting my wishes and giving me time to think. I was so worried he might come hurtling down here after reading my note, or ring the house.'

Martha didn't think respect came into it; cowardice was probably much more the mark. She decided to raise the matter which she'd discussed with Ellis in the car yesterday. 'Do you think Rick deliberately got you pregnant?' she asked.

Willow frowned. 'Why would he do that?'

'To trap you. To make you his. Was he in the least bit shocked or even annoyed when you told him you were pregnant?'

Willow seemed to think about this. 'No,' she said eventually. 'I'd dreaded telling him but when I did, he couldn't have been nicer or more delighted.'

'And you told me, didn't you, that because you were taking

a rest from the pill, Rick had taken care of matters? What if he fixed things so that an accident would happen?'

'But I would have known, surely? And really, what does it matter how or why I've ended up pregnant? I am and that's all there is to it.'

It mattered to Martha though. She knew in her bones that Rick had orchestrated this whole thing and she hated the thought that he had used her sister the way he had.

'Willow,' she said, 'there's something I have to say to you. Something which is long overdue. I haven't always been a good sister to you, and I'm really sorry for that. Rick accused me of bullying and patronising you and I hate to admit it, but in many ways he was right. Actually, I'd go further and say that there have been times when I've been nothing but a cold-hearted bitch towards you.'

'Oh, that's nonsense!' said Willow. 'You've never bullied me. You're just naturally bossy, you're the big sister, that's all.'

Martha shook her head. 'No, Willow, I can't go along with that. And I can't help but think that had I been a better sister you might have told me what happened to you that night at the party. I would have been able to help you. Was I really so unapproachable that you couldn't tell me?'

'I couldn't tell you, in case you let on to Dad. I couldn't face him ever knowing. He would have said I had only myself to blame, and maybe I did. I shouldn't have drunk so much. I shouldn't have gone out that night, I should have been sensible and stayed in to finish that essay. That's what you would have done. And Dad did always compare us. I could never live up to the high standard you'd set so effortlessly, and this would have been the final straw when it came to his already low opinion of me. I could never please him in the way you did. I was a continual disappointment to him. I suppose I was always a bit scared of him, and his disapproval.'

'That's hardly surprising, given what you'd witnessed as a child. You might not have fully understood what you'd seen, but some kind of self-preservation instinct would have kicked in and made you wary of him. It might even have been that he sensed that in you, and that could explain why he gave you a hard time.'

'I'd never thought of that. But please don't think I ever minded that he favoured you over me. I didn't. I was immensely proud of you, but I never envied you. In fact, I felt sorry for you at times, that Dad expected so much of you and that you expected so much of yourself.'

Martha could have wept at her sister's generosity and at the injustice of their father having defined them from so young an age. 'Oh Willow,' she said, 'you have such a sweet and forgiving nature, and perhaps deep down, I've always been envious of that. I'm headstrong and opinionated and sometimes that gets in the way of my judgement, and my ability to be nice. Just ask Tom! But you could surely have confided in Mum about the assault on you and then being pregnant? She has always been your greatest cheerleader. There's nothing she wouldn't have done for you.'

Willow's face suddenly looked sad. 'No,' she said softly. 'Mum would have told Dad, she wouldn't have kept something like that from him. And anyway, I saw it as my mistake which I had to deal with myself. I wanted to carry on with my life as though that awful thing had never happened. By never telling anyone, not even Mum, I hoped I could almost kid myself into believing it was nothing but a bad dream. Which sounds pathetic, doesn't it? But I also didn't want people to know about it, because then I'd forever be labelled as a victim, and I didn't want that. I didn't want their pity or my shame to be known.'

'You had no reason to feel any shame. You did nothing wrong. You weren't to blame. You might not have believed it before, but you must now. You really must.'

'I know,' Willow said, 'that's what Mum kept saying to me last night. She was so upset, wasn't she?' added Willow after a pause. 'I hate knowing that I've done that to her. I heard her crying in bed with Ellis. I don't think I've ever heard her sound so distraught.'

'It's because she loves you.'

'I suppose that's how we're going to be as mothers, aren't we?' said Willow, casting aside the rag doll and placing her hands over her stomach beneath the duvet. 'It's a scary thought, isn't it, feeling that depth of responsibility and love? Or perhaps it doesn't feel so scary to you?'

Martha smiled. 'I assure you it does. There's so much to learn while on the job, and potentially so much to get wrong. But you know what, we'll muddle through just like millions of other new mothers have done.'

'Well, muddling is what I do best,' said Willow.

'Don't put yourself down. You'll be great.' Then, conscious that she was venturing into an area that her sister might not feel able to discuss, that it was just too personal for her, Martha chose her next words with great care. 'Do you ever think of the baby you . . . ' she hesitated, 'didn't have?'

'You mean the baby I got rid of?' Willow said bluntly.

Martha nodded. 'Yes.'

'I never saw it as a real baby at the time. How could it be when I terminated it when it was no more than a tiny blob of cells? But if you're asking if I ever wondered what the child would have been like as the years went by, then yes, just occasionally it would creep up on me.' She turned her head to look away, to the window where the curtains were pushed back, and the weak early morning light was breaking through clouds of indigo and violet. She stared at the sky for the longest moment, as though momentarily distracted. Then returning her gaze to Martha, she said, 'This might sound selfish, but what I thought much more about was what my life might have been like if I'd never gone to that party.'

Her sister's words brought a lump to Martha's throat. 'That's not selfish at all,' she said, 'it's perfectly understandable.'

Having always seen herself as the stronger and more capable sister, that certainty was now gone for Martha. To have survived what she had all on her own, Willow had proved herself to have the kind of strength Martha doubted she herself possessed. Humbled to her core, she leant forward, and as much as their baby bumps would allow, she hugged Willow with a tender love she hadn't felt before.

Chapter Fifty-Seven

Later that afternoon, and when they hadn't long since been back from the doctor's surgery, Mum having insisted that Willow be seen by both a doctor and a midwife, there was a ring at the front door. Being as jittery as she was, the sound of the bell made Willow jump. It startled the baby inside her too, setting her off performing what felt like a series of cartwheels.

It had to be Rick. Finally, he'd driven down here to have it out with Willow. The storm, like so many before, was about to break. In a way she welcomed it; it would be a relief for the waiting to be over. Maybe then her blood pressure would sort itself out.

The midwife Willow had just seen had said that her blood pressure was higher than it should be and had warned her that she needed to be careful. Willow had wanted to say that after the last twenty-four hours, it was a miracle her blood pressure hadn't skyrocketed off the chart. The midwife had also noted that her ankles were showing signs of swelling and while that was relatively normal for an expectant mother at thirty-three weeks, she advised Willow to rest as much as she could, and with her feet up. Which was what she had been doing in the kitchen when the doorbell had rung. Now, and with a rush of adrenaline, she was on her feet, as though ready to meet the storm head on.

'I'll go,' said Ellis, already moving towards the door.

The lightning-fast way he reacted made Willow think he was expecting it to be Rick as well. Everyone else must have thought the same because while he was out of the kitchen, Mum, Martha and Auntie Geraldine gathered around Willow as though creating a human shield. She knew that after what she'd told them yesterday, and on top of what Rick had done to her, they couldn't stop themselves from being ultra-protective of her, or treating her with kid gloves. They meant well, she knew that, but somehow it only made her feel worse.

She'd had no intention of ever telling anyone what had happened to her, but after listening to her mother's painful confession on the beach yesterday, it had suddenly felt right to do the same, to shed the coat of lies she'd worn all these years. If Mum could do it, why not her?

But it hadn't been easy reliving that brief time in her life and with each word she'd wrenched from that dark place deep inside her, she had felt a part of her disappearing. She was no longer the person everyone had thought her to be. Now they could see her as she really was, someone who had tried so hard to shut out the world so she could live in her own safe little bubble.

She might have expected to feel better after breaking her vow of silence, to feel the relief of a great weight lifted from her shoulders, but she hadn't. If anything, she felt worse, even more weighed down with the burden of now carrying everyone else's shock and anger.

As the murmur of voices in the hall grew louder and Ellis reappeared in the kitchen doorway, Willow saw that it wasn't

Rick with him, but a short-haired woman in a black leather jacket with a red scarf tied around her neck. A few paces behind her was a gangly uniformed policeman. The woman flashed what appeared to be some sort of official ID and introduced herself as Detective Constable Fowler, adding that she was part of a major crime investigation team.

It was when she asked Willow and Martha which one of them was Rick Falconer's fiancée – a Miss Willow Miller – and then suggested that perhaps they might all like to sit down, that a feeling of dread swept over Willow.

Whatever storm she had feared was about to break, it wasn't this and even now, after Mum and Ellis had driven her to London, and she was being shown through to the ICU at the hospital where Rick had been admitted the previous night, she couldn't believe what had happened to him.

According to what witnesses had told the police and paramedics when they'd arrived on the scene, Rick had been about to get into his car which was parked outside his flat when he'd seen an elderly woman on the other side of the road being mugged by two youths in hoodies. Without a thought for his own safety, so the witnesses said, he'd gone to the woman's assistance and then one of the attackers had knocked him to the ground and the other had stabbed him several times. He'd lost a lot of blood before the ambulance arrived and had undergone emergency surgery when brought in, Willow was told.

It had taken the investigating police officers last night and all of this morning to track her down. Using Rick's mobile phone records, and going to his place of work, they had discovered that he had given Willow as his next of kin with the HR department, but only after they had found out where she worked and they'd approached AoK had they then found a way to contact her. Willow still had Mum listed as her next of kin; it had never crossed her mind to change it to Rick. That simple oversight on her part said so much about their relationship and she suspected it would prick at her conscience for a long time to come.

The doctor who had greeted her explained with cool efficiency, but not unkindly – perhaps taking into consideration that she was obviously pregnant – that Rick's condition was critical. He had been stabbed in the chest and the neck. Now as Willow stood at the end of the bed Rick lay in, she felt an enormous shift in her emotions. Her eyes blurring with tears, she listened to the beeping of the equipment to which Rick was attached and to the doctor as he described Rick as a hero for going to a stranger's aid the way he had. 'He acted selflessly and with such courage,' the doctor said. 'There are not many who would do what he did.'

'No,' Willow managed to say. 'It was very brave of him.'

Giving her a long hard look, the doctor said, 'May I ask how you came by the bruises to your face?'

'It's nothing,' she said self-consciously.

The intensity of the man's gaze increased. 'Would you like to talk to someone about it? We have people here in the hospital you could chat to quite informally.'

'No,' she said firmly.

Frowning, the doctor then said he would leave her to have some time on her own with Rick. 'Talk to him as normally as you can,' he said before going. 'Hopefully your voice will help bring him back to us.'

'Is he unconscious?'

'Yes. He sustained a severe head injury when he was knocked

406

to the ground. But there's every chance he can hear what's going on around him.'

Alone, Willow took a cautious step nearer to the bed, irrationally scared that she might wake Rick and that he'd be furious with her for not coming to see him sooner.

Looking down at him, she tried to make sense of what had happened, based on the information she'd been given. Had he found her note and engagement ring and been so angry – or so upset – that he'd rushed outside to his car to drive down to Tilsham to see her? If that was true, then it was her fault that he was lying here with life-threatening injuries. What if he died? What if she had to live with that on her conscience?

The steady rise and fall of his breathing was being maintained by a ventilator via a tube inserted into his mouth. Several large dressings had been applied to his neck and chest, and at various strategic points on his upper body, pads had been placed from which wires led to various monitoring devices. He was also attached to an intravenous drip.

Her own chest tightening as though she too needed help to breathe in the stifling warmth, and her legs shaky with the shock of seeing Rick like this, she thought that only a few hours ago she had been determined to tell him it was over between them. She had planned to stand up to him and say that he was nothing but an abusive bully, a wolf in sheep's clothing, a monster even.

But that couldn't be who he really was, she thought, taking in his helpless body. Not when he'd tried to do the right thing by helping an elderly woman who was being mugged. There had to be good in him to have done that, surely?

Just as her father, she supposed, hadn't been entirely bad.

Talk to him as normally as you can, the doctor had said. But what was normal now? What could she possibly say to Rick?

Did you deliberately mark me out as a willing victim, as Martha believes, somebody whom you could manipulate for your own sick pleasure?

Did you deliberately get me pregnant?

Did you ever really love me?

Do you even know what love is?

And was it you who killed Lucy and Simon's cat?

None of which she actually said aloud. Instead she bent down closer to Rick so that her lips were almost touching his ear.

'Rick,' she said, 'it's me, Willow. I don't know if you can hear me, but if you can, I just want you to know that I forgive you. And I'm so sorry that this has happened to you because of me.'

The medical staff assured Willow that she would be better off going home and having a proper night's sleep, for her baby's sake as much as hers. They promised her that if Rick's condition changed in any way, they would ring her. She still didn't have her mobile phone, so Mum provided her contact details.

They were nearly back in Tilsham – Willow couldn't bear the thought of staying in Rick's flat, even though it would have been so much more convenient – when she felt a strange tightening in her stomach, followed by a dull ache in her lower back. It happened again when Mum let them in at Anchor House, and once more when she was brushing her teeth before going to bed. But she pushed it from her mind. It was too soon for the baby to arrive. She was still telling herself this when she padded downstairs at three in the morning to make a drink to help her sleep. She was exhausted, physically and mentally, but worrying about Rick meant she just couldn't relax enough to fall asleep.

Waiting for the kettle to boil, she was suddenly gripped with the severest of pains that made her double up and cry out. When the pain had passed, and catching her breath, she switched off the kettle and decided she had better go back upstairs and break the news to her mother. She felt unnaturally calm. Not at all how she imagined she would feel when she went into labour. Even labour that was seven weeks earlier than it should be. Was this normal? Or should she be panicking?

No, she told herself firmly. Panic was the last thing she or the baby needed. She could do this.

Chapter Fifty-Eight

It was ungenerous of her, she knew, but after what Rick had done to Willow, and might have continued to do if given the chance, Naomi struggled to accept the way he had been hailed a hero.

The attack on Rick, and his subsequent death eight days later, made the national news, and once again there were demands made of the Mayor of London and the Government to put an end to knife crime once and for all. The elderly woman whom Rick had tried to help had been interviewed by the media and with a trembly voice she had said that, had it not been for a stranger's bravery, for which she would always be grateful, it might well have been she who had died. In every interview she made a point of extending her sincere condolences to Rick's devastated fiancée and family.

In fleshing out the story of a stranger's act of heroic courage, newspaper reporters had done their homework and found out that Rick had a pregnant fiancée. It had all the ingredients of a perfectly newsworthy story with a perfectly tragic ending, exactly what would appeal to their readers.

On the pavement where the attack had happened, a shrine of flowers had appeared with mawkish RIP messages for a man nobody in the area had actually known. A man whom nobody, not even those with whom he'd worked, ever really knew.

But then that was true of them all, thought Naomi as she stood at the kitchen window drinking the last of her coffee and watching Willow walk to the end of the garden with Ellis.

It was now the first week of December and four weeks had passed since Rick's death and only in the last few days did Willow seem more like her usual self. During those difficult weeks, and despite them all saying she mustn't, Willow had blamed herself for his death. For such a tender-hearted girl, it was a heavy load to carry on top of everything else.

Her coffee finished and putting her mug in the dishwasher, Naomi heard her mobile ping with a text message. Picking up the device, she saw it was a message from Geraldine. After a barrage of communications from Brian begging her to return home, Geraldine had come to her senses and done just that. Once home, she discovered that Brian had arranged for them to go on a cruise to the Galapagos Islands.

'I call it very high-handed of him to book the trip without checking with me first,' Geraldine had grumbled to Naomi. To which Naomi had told her friend to stop complaining and just be pleased that Brian was finally doing what she had wanted him to do, and that was to act with more spontaneity.

Any news on when the inquest will take place? Geraldine had texted.

Still no word, Naomi replied.

They'd been told it could take a while for Rick's post-mortem to be done and for the coroner's inquest to reach a verdict – probably death by unlawful killing – and only then would Rick's body be released for burial. With no family of his own to arrange

411

his funeral, that task would fall to Willow as his next of kin. When the time came, Naomi and Ellis would help as much as she would allow them to. She seemed so very determined that things should be done right for Rick, that she owed him that much.

Detective Constable Fowler, who had been dealing with the case – which was now classed as murder, having previously been referred to as offensive wounding with intent – didn't inspire confidence that the culprits would be found. CCTV had yielded nothing more than a few seconds of blurred footage.

There had been an awkward moment that day when the detective and her sidekick had turned up here to tell Willow that Rick had been involved in a serious assault. Giving Willow a scrutinising look, the woman had enquired about her cut lip and black eye. She made the question sound as though it was in some way connected to the attack on Rick, especially when she then asked Willow where she had been at the time of the assault. Naomi had quickly nipped that line of questioning in the bud and made it very clear that Willow had been with them. Geraldine had then blurted out how Willow had come by her injuries, which Naomi wished she hadn't. The detective seized on this nugget of information and, granted she was only doing her job, it was galling for them all suddenly then to be considered suspects, as though they had planned the attack to exact revenge on the man who had hurt a member of their family. It was a ludicrous suspicion that thankfully gained no traction.

Interestingly, this aspect of Rick's character, that he had been physically abusive to his pregnant fiancée the night before he was attacked, was never mentioned in any of the newspaper reports.

After all, it would have ruined the heroic image they had created of him. Willow had said the omission didn't bother her, that in fact she preferred that nobody ever knew about that darker side to Rick's personality. What purpose did it serve to make it known? she'd asked them all. More importantly, there was the baby to consider. She was adamant that under no circumstances did she want her daughter ever to know something so awful about her father. It was to remain a secret between them.

As if there hadn't been enough of those in the family, Naomi thought now with a heartfelt sigh.

But perhaps it was simply a fact of life, that every family had its secrets. Her own last remaining secret, that she had cheated on Colin with Ellis in the early years of her marriage, had played on her mind, given that she had vowed to start her life afresh with a thoroughly clean slate. Ellis was firmly of the opinion that it was an unnecessary confession. 'If you tell your daughters about that,' he'd said, 'then by rights you would have to tell them about Colin's adultery as well. Haven't they had enough to contend with?'

She could see the sense in what he said, so she had kept quiet, deciding that burdening Martha and Willow with yet another layer of shock and betrayal was best avoided. More than ever, it was essential that they looked to the future, not the past. And that future now contained Naomi's first grandchild, a precious baby girl who'd had to fight for her survival in the days following her unexpectedly early arrival into the world.

She was a darling little girl who looked just like Willow when she'd been a baby. The resemblance was uncanny and when Naomi had at last been allowed to hold her, it had been like being transported back in time to when she first held Martha and

Willow and had experienced that exquisite sensation of falling in love.

She had been with Willow throughout the birth at the hospital, holding her hand and helping her as much as she could, veering from abject terror that something might go horribly wrong, to utter joy when it was all over and they saw the baby for the first time, if only briefly before she'd been whisked off to the Special Care Baby Unit.

Born at thirty-three weeks and classed as a moderate to late preterm baby had meant an initial period of specialised care was needed in the neonatal ward, but Willow's daughter proved to be a tough little fighter, and after ten days was able to breathe and feed without assistance. That had been a truly momentous moment.

During the weeks of special care, Willow could barely be parted from her baby and did as much as she could to look after her daughter. The rest of them were allowed to visit, taking it in turns to be with Willow and offer support. The nursing staff at St Richard's Hospital in Chichester could not have been more helpful or understanding and went a long way towards building Willow's confidence as a new mother.

Happily, three days ago the baby, who was still unnamed, was deemed well enough to be allowed home, and for now, home was here at Anchor House. So far the transition had had a positive effect on both Willow and the baby, both of whom seemed to be thriving.

Naomi was so very proud of her youngest daughter. With everything she had gone through, including the horror of what had happened to her as a student, she had shown extraordinary strength and resilience. Even Martha had admitted that she didn't think she would have coped half so well as her sister had.

What really touched Naomi's heart was seeing the strong bond of love that Willow so clearly felt for her baby. It reminded her of the conversation she'd once had with Colin when he'd said that what their youngest daughter would need in life was for somebody to take care of her and Naomi had disagreed, saying that the making of Willow would be having someone she could take care of. How true that now seemed.

As if agreeing with Naomi, there came a snuffling sound from the baby monitor on the dresser. Having promised Willow faithfully that she would listen out for the baby and call her if there was a problem, she went and stood next to the monitor to make sure she didn't miss anything. After a few more snuffling sounds, all went quiet. Which of course meant she was compelled to go upstairs to double-check all was well. Smiling to herself, she remembered doing exactly the same when Martha and Willow were babies.

As she climbed the stairs as stealthily as a cat-burglar, she wondered how things were going next door.

*

Watching Willow take in the improvements he'd made to the ground floor of the cottage, Ellis asked her what she thought of it all.

'You've done so much in such a short space of time,' she said, shrugging off her coat and putting it on the back of a chair. 'I love the way the kitchen and sitting area now opens out straight onto the garden, it's like the beach is even nearer.'

'That was what I hoped I'd achieve by installing the bi-fold doors,' he said, standing next to her so that they were both facing the garden and sea beyond. 'Do you want to see upstairs? I finished painting the landing last night, so you'll have to excuse the smell of paint.' He indicated that she should go up the narrow flight of stairs first.

At the top, he led the way into the smaller of the three bedrooms. All it contained was one piece of furniture and when Willow saw it, she looked puzzled. 'Why is there a cot in here?' she asked.

'Because I wondered if you might like to make this your home with the baby.'

The puzzled expression deepened. 'But it's yours. You've been doing the cottage up as an investment. Something for Lucas to enjoy, perhaps.'

'That's true,' he said, 'but you need somewhere to live, and this seems perfect to me.'

She went over to the cot and rested a hand on the rail. 'Did Mum ask you to do this?'

He smiled, having expected this question from Willow. When he'd first raised the idea with Naomi, she had been overwhelmed that he would do this for Willow, but then she worried that Willow would regard it as an act of charity too far and say no. Everyone had their pride, and maybe this would be the moment when Willow would feel she had to make a stand for going it alone.

'Your mother knew you'd say that,' Ellis said, 'and the honest answer is no, she didn't. She was as surprised by my suggestion as you are. And please don't think your mother and I don't want you with us next door, but wouldn't you like your own independent space? Your own little nest for you and the baby?'

She shook her head with a wan smile. 'It's a nice idea, but I can't pay you any rent.'

416

'Have I asked for any?'

She moved from the cot to the window which looked down onto the small garden and beach. 'It's extremely sweet of you, Ellis, but I couldn't possibly accept. I really couldn't.'

Ellis wasn't to be beaten. 'Yes you can. Just view it as a temporary measure, if only to keep your mother from worrying about you. Having you close by, for however long you're comfortable with, will give her peace of mind. Otherwise, if you go back to London, she'll worry constantly about you. And you needn't worry that there would be any annoying interference from us; we'd help as much or as little as you wanted.'

She turned around from the window and smiled so sadly at him he thought she was going to turn him down flat.

'Do you truly mean it, Ellis, that you'd let me live here?'

'I wouldn't have suggested it if I didn't mean it.'

'What about Lucas? Won't he have something to say on the matter?'

'Such as?'

'Perhaps he sees it as his inheritance?'

'He doesn't, I can assure you of that. I've discussed it with him, and he can't think of a better use of the cottage.'

'Did he really say that?'

'He did, and a lot more besides. He said that if you didn't accept the offer, he'd never speak to me again. Which means by hook or by crook, I have to employ all my persuasive charm to convince you to say yes.'

'But what if I'm still here in a year's time?'

'Then we'll have celebrated your baby's first birthday together and be looking forward to Christmas again. Now why don't

417

I leave you on your own for a while so you can picture yourself living here? How does that sound?'

*

Still in the bedroom where Ellis had left her, Willow stood at the window and looked out at the pale sky and milky sea which was as smooth as glass.

In the days after bringing her daughter home from the hospital, the weather had turned stormy, whipping up the sea into a roiling cauldron of crashing waves. Wind and rain had lashed at the windows and only the very hardy had braved the elements to go for a walk along the beach. Now, on this calmest of days, the sweep of curving seashore was garlanded with ribbons of seaweed and pieces of driftwood.

Willow had joked with Martha that maybe the bad weather was a sign that she should call her baby Storm, but they'd both agreed that actually there was nothing about her that was the least bit stormy. She was such a quietly contented baby and wonderfully easy to settle after a feed. When she did cry, it was never for long.

At the hospital the nurses had encouraged Willow to touch her baby as much as possible, and to talk to her. Initially she had been terrified of holding such a fragile little thing, but very quickly any fear she felt was eclipsed by a strong need to hold her precious baby, and to tell her that she was going to be the most loved child in all the world. Sometimes those blue-grey eyes would stare back at her with such an intensity, Willow's heart would swell so much it felt as though it was pressing against her rib cage. That was the power of love, she thought as she pictured her beautiful little daughter sleeping next door in Willow's old bedroom, her face a sublime picture of angelic serenity.

Her mind lingered over the mental image of her sleeping baby and a thought came to her.

Serenity, she repeated inside her head.

She said it again, this time out loud.

Serenity.

Serenity Miller.

A happy smile crept over Willow's face. Finally, and with only a few days to go before she had to register her daughter's birth, she had come up with a name for her, a name that was perfect in every way. It made her want to rush next door and run upstairs to wake her daughter and give her the good news.

But putting her happy excitement on hold, she had something important to do.

Back downstairs, she took out her mobile from her coat pocket. It was the mobile she hadn't been able to find the morning after Rick had been so violent with her. It had been found, along with her laptop cable, by his work colleagues when they'd been clearing out his office desk. He must have deliberately taken the phone and cable with him that morning when he'd gone to work, hoping that it would prevent her from contacting her mother and sister. That he could have been so calculating still hurt Willow, but she refused to dwell on just how far he might have gone in controlling her, or how badly he might have ended up hurting her. If she did let her thoughts wander in that direction, it never did her any good. For her baby's sake – *for Serenity's sake* – she had to lock that part of Rick's personality away and never let it affect her relationship with her daughter.

When she thought of Rick, she felt no real depth of grief. How could she when she hadn't loved him? She had cared for him and tried so very hard to love him, but it just hadn't been there. She doubted that he had loved her either, not in the proper sense of loving another person. What she felt for him was profound shock at the manner of his death. And guilt that maybe she had been the reason for him dying. The guilt was fading, but it still had the power to creep up on her now and then. But she was determined not to let it get the better of her.

Without a doubt her relationship with Rick had changed the course of her life, just as being raped all those years ago had done, but this time it was different. Whereas previously, as a result of a bad decision on her part, she had been set adrift not knowing what to do with her life, now, with a child to take care of, she had a sense of purpose. The way ahead was unclear, but she knew she would do whatever it took to give her daughter the best life she could.

She was running the risk of waking Lucas in LA, but she rang him anyway. He had frequently said that she could call him any time she wanted and while she was mindful of his work hours, they had spoken quite often. If she ever found herself worrying about the future, he could always say something that made her laugh or helped her to see things with a fresh perspective. She had come to value the closeness of their friendship and saw him as the brother she would have always liked to have. Such was their closeness, she had even told him about being raped as a student.

He answered after only a few rings.

'Is everything all right?' he asked groggily.

She apologised for waking him and launched herself into the reason for her call.

'Willow,' he said, 'just let my dad help you. It would mean a lot to him. His offer is completely genuine and I for one think it's a great idea. I can just picture you there and, speaking as her uncle, I think it would be great for my niece.'

Smiling at the way he regarded himself as an uncle to her baby, she could picture herself here as well, and being happy.

'What don't you like about the idea?' Lucas asked her.

'I feel guilty about saying yes,' she said. 'I don't feel I deserve it.'

'What do any of us really deserve? But you certainly didn't deserve what Rick did to you, or what happened to you as a student. So accept Ellis's offer and see how it pans out. It'll give you time to decide what you're going to do next.'

'Next is what worries me. I currently have no real means of supporting myself.'

'We've discussed this before. Rick made his daughter the sole beneficiary in his will, so once the legal side of things has been resolved, and his flat sold, that should give you some sort of financial security.'

'For *her*, not me,' she said.

Of all the things that Rick had done, what had surprised Willow the most was that he had been so organised as to have arranged an online will leaving everything to his child who was yet to be born. Who did that? *Other than a complete control freak*, was what Martha had said; what's more, a control freak who didn't want to leave anything to the mother of his child. When Willow had been informed of the existence of the will, it had reminded her how cross Rick had been when she had laughed about making a will herself.

'Technically you're right,' said Lucas. 'But as the child's

mother you will have access to funds to enable you to provide for her, so that's something. And don't forget those shares you have which you told me your father left you and the trust fund you'll have access to before too long. If needs be you can cash those in. Now promise me you'll accept Ellis's offer so that I can go back to sleep.'

Willow knew that she would be mad to turn down the offer and really, what alternative did she have?

'Okay,' she said, 'I will. Oh, and before I leave you to sleep, I've come up with a name for your niece.'

'About bloody time,' he said good-humouredly. 'What is it?'

'It's Serenity. What do you think?'

'I think it's great, and very you. Now go and give Ellis the good news.'

'I will,' she said.

After she'd rung off, she looked around what was going to be her new home and began to visualise herself living here. It would, she had to admit, be perfect.

Chapter Fifty-Nine

Rick's funeral service was held at the crematorium in Chichester four days before Christmas. The funeral directors had suggested that it might be better to put it off until January, but Willow wouldn't be swayed; she didn't want to start the new year with it hanging over her. It was a decision Martha and the rest of the family had fully supported, agreeing that it would be better to get it over and done with, and with as little fuss and bother as possible. Something else Willow had insisted on was that the service was held conveniently near Tilsham rather than in London. She'd said she had wanted to save them the bother of a depressing journey into town. Had the decision been down to Martha, she would have chucked Rick's body into the Thames and left it at that!

It had been a perfunctory and austere service. The only mourners present, if you could call them that, were Mum, Ellis, Martha and Willow – with Serenity fast asleep in her pram. Tom couldn't make it as he'd driven up to Yorkshire first thing this morning to stay at his sister's before bringing his father back to spend Christmas with them. Tom's sister and her husband were taking off to Antigua for the festive period.

There had been no hymns sung during the service, and the

eulogy had been mercifully short. Martha had held her sister's hand the whole time, not because she was worried Willow might cry, but to show her solidarity. It was something Martha regretted not doing in the past; she had always been too quick to criticise or judge Willow, and she had vowed never to do that again. She owed it to Willow to be a better sister, certainly a more loyal one.

But was it blind unquestioning loyalty on Martha's part that had caused her to be so blinkered and biased when it came to their father? And loyalty too that had made Mum endure the periodic bouts of abuse to keep the family she loved together? Was there a case for there being too much loyalty within a family, that sometimes it was misplaced and not deserved? Perhaps so.

It upset her to think that because of her devoted loyalty to her father, she had lapped up the attention he had given her. That he had so obviously favoured her over Willow was something she had simply accepted. Not once had she challenged it. Why would she when she had thought that it was Willow's fault for always annoying Dad? But now she felt sickened by the memory and she was adamant that if she and Tom were lucky enough to have more than one child, she would never favour one child over the other.

All her hostility towards Ellis had been caused by her constantly comparing him to the man who had meant the world to her. At the time it had been inconceivable to her that her mother could be so disloyal to Dad. Yet gradually she had begun to warm to Ellis, and that was before Mum's awful revelations. In recent weeks he had been an enormous support to them all, especially Willow, giving her the keys to Waterside Cottage for as long as she wanted to live there. She planned to move in with the baby at the start of the new year, another sign that she was putting the past behind her and making a fresh start. Martha had nothing but admiration for Willow, something she'd never thought she would say. And far from being unable to cope as a new mother as she had feared, Willow took it in her stride. But then Serenity was such a sweet, placid little thing. Martha just hoped her own daughter would have the same easy-going temperament.

Her official due date was six weeks away, but both Martha and Tom were convinced, based purely on how gigantic she was, that the baby would come sooner than that, if only by a week or so. Everyone said the final weeks of pregnancy dragged, that each day felt like a week in itself, and they were right. Being on maternity leave didn't help in that respect, but Martha had taken the decision to finish work before Christmas rather than go back for just a few weeks.

On her last day in the office they had thrown a surprise baby shower party for her, complete with cake and Champagne. Except she had to make do with fizzy water while everybody else guzzled their way through several bottles of Moet. Ironically, her farewell gift was a very generous Topolino voucher, which Jason took great pleasure in presenting to her.

'Nice touch,' she said to him.

'Well, now I know you've turned down their offer to go and work for them, I can afford to be magnanimous.'

In the end it hadn't been a difficult decision to say 'thanks, but no thanks' to Charlotte at Topolino. Martha's loyalty, as she'd discovered after that day of being stuck in the lift at work, lay with BND and when her maternity leave was over, she would happily return. In a bid to encourage her to stay, Jason, as he'd previously hinted at, had promised her a special bonus package to welcome her back.

With Rick's coffin now disappearing behind the curtains, and clearly in no hurry to drag things out any longer than was necessary, both Mum and Ellis rose from their seats to indicate that they had done their duty, they could all go home now. The ashes, according to Willow's instructions, would be scattered in the crematorium garden at a later date.

Ellis was helping Mum with her coat, when Martha noticed a woman on her own at the back of the chapel. Had she attended the wrong service by mistake? If so, she must have thought it a very lacklustre affair.

Pushing the pram, with Serenity still sleeping peacefully in it, Willow led the way along the aisle of empty seats, but just as she neared the last row, the solitary woman hitched a handbag over her shoulder and stood up. She had a timid, worn-down appearance, as though life had not treated her well. Martha put her in her late sixties, possibly older. Her short, wiry grey hair was unflatteringly cut and from her washed-out face, a pair of watery grey eyes stared at them nervously.

'I'm sorry to intrude,' she said in a breathy voice, her gaze darting towards the inside of the pram, 'but is that Rich . . . I mean, Rick's child?'

Martha took a step forwards, ready to shield Willow from any unwarranted questions, but Mum was ahead of her.

'Why do you want to know?' she asked. Her tone wasn't exactly rude, but it certainly wasn't overly friendly.

Fiddling with the gloves in her hands, the woman said, 'I'm Rick's mother.'

426

Once they had recovered from their shock, they found a quiet sheltered area outside where they could sit down, and the obvious questions flowed.

How could she be Rick's mother when he'd told Willow that she had committed suicide?

Why had Rick lied?

And what else was there that might now come to light?

In essence it was an unremarkable tale of a boy growing up with a father who drank too much. A father who, after leaving his wife, was replaced by a stepfather who had little interest in Rick, other than making him toe the line.

'I tried my best with him,' the woman said, whose name they now knew was Eileen, 'but he was always so difficult. He was ashamed of me. He said I was weak because I wasn't a better mother, that I didn't put him first. And then the trouble started.'

'What kind of trouble?' asked Martha. She couldn't help but feel suspicious of this woman who had shown up out of nowhere. Why was she here? Was she going to start demanding grandparent rights? Or was she here to challenge the will Rick had made, leaving everything to his child? Did she think she was entitled to a share?

'A neighbour's cat disappeared and a week later it was found hanging from a tree.'

Willow let out a small gasp. She was on her feet now, rocking the pram to keep Serenity asleep, even though she didn't appear to be stirring.

'And when it happened twice more and he said how funny it was that cats kept disappearing and then showing up dead,

427

I just knew in my bones that he had something to do with it. He hated cats, he said they were sly and you could never trust them.'

An uneasy hush fell on the group as they all looked at each other. It was broken by Eileen blithely continuing.

'Which was ironic because he lied and cheated as easily as breathing. In the end, and after he turned eighteen and finished his A-levels, my husband insisted that he move out. It sounds terrible, but it was a relief when he did leave us; the arguments were escalating, and he frightened me when he lost his temper. He seemed so angry with life.'

'Did he go to university?' asked Willow. 'He told me he did.'

The woman shook her head. 'I doubt it. Unless he talked his way in somehow.'

'So where did he go?' This was from Mum.

'I know what you're thinking, that as his mother I let him down, but he was so difficult. It really was better for him to go. I never knew for sure where he went, but I assumed it was London. The last words he said to me were to swear he would never speak to me again, that he was going to change his name and reinvent himself.' She paused as if to catch her breath. 'He would often say that, that he was going to be *someone*, not a pathetic nobody like me or his stepfather. I suppose by telling you his parents were dead, that was how he felt about us. It was his way of cutting all ties with his past.'

'Was Rick Falconer actually his name?' probed Martha. 'You called him Rich when you first approached us.'

'Rich was what I always called him; it was short for Richard. His surname was Watson, which was his dad's surname. And mine until I remarried.'

'So how did you know he was dead?' queried Ellis.

'I saw it on the TV and in the newspapers. To begin with I couldn't believe it was him, but then I knew that it was. A mother would always know her own child, even as a grown man.'

'But how did you know about the funeral today?' Martha persisted. The family had been careful not to let the date or whereabouts of the cremation become general knowledge and, to Martha, this weak, ineffectual woman didn't come across as being the resourceful sort who would know her way round Google to find out something like that.

'One of the newspaper articles I read said that his fiancée and her family lived in West Sussex, so I took a chance and rang the crematorium here. I said I wanted to send flowers.'

She suddenly turned to look at Willow, her expression pleading. 'He was good in the end, wasn't he, by trying to help that old lady?' Her tone was pitiful, as though seeking some kind of assurance that, as his mother, she hadn't failed her son entirely.

'Yes,' Willow said, without hesitation, and avoiding Martha's questioning gaze. 'He acted with selfless courage. That's something to be proud of, isn't it?'

Itching to contradict her sister, to tell this pathetic woman what a monster she had helped create, Martha forced herself to keep quiet.

'I always knew there had to be some good in him somewhere,' said Eileen. 'And I suppose he proved himself right, in that he not only made a success of his life, but he made a real name for himself. The papers called him a hero, didn't they?'

'Yes,' murmured Willow.

Martha felt for her sister. This might be helping Rick's mother come to terms with her son's death, and her abject failure in caring for him, but it was the last thing Willow needed. The last thing any of them needed on today of all days.

Mum plainly thought the same. 'Well,' she said briskly, 'it's been a long and difficult day and I really think we should be—'

'Why weren't there more people here for his funeral?' the woman interrupted. 'I'd have thought more of his friends and work colleagues would turn out for him.'

'This is what he would have wanted,' Willow answered her. 'He didn't like a lot of fuss.'

'I see,' she said. Then pushing back the sleeve of her coat to look at her watch, she said, 'I'll have to go soon to catch my train. I mustn't miss it. I need to be home before my husband gets back tonight from his fishing trip. That's how I was able to come today.'

'What do you mean, *able* to come?' asked Martha.

'He wouldn't have been happy at the idea of me coming here. So it's better he never knows that I did.'

'Do you have far to go?' asked Mum. Perhaps, like Martha, she was concerned that if the woman lived nearby, she might want to start making regular visits to see her granddaughter.

'I live in Gravesend,' she replied, 'and . . . well . . . because I don't get out much, I found the journey coming here a bit daunting. I had to change trains in London and very nearly didn't make my connection.' She looked again at her watch and this time she suddenly seemed agitated, as if the thought of her return journey was making her anxious. She rose clumsily to her feet, dropping her handbag in the process. 'Before I go,' she said in a flustered voice, the bag now hitched over her shoulder, 'may I take a peek at the baby?'

Her request had them all standing guard around the pram,

ready to protect Serenity from the unwanted stranger amongst them.

All except for Willow who, in her typically generous fashion, lowered the hood of the pram so the woman could have a better look.

'Boy or girl?' she asked.

'A girl,' Willow replied.

'She doesn't look anything like Rick, does she?' the woman said with a sniff. 'Is she a good baby?'

'Yes,' said Willow. 'She's a perfect angel.'

Watching the woman peering into the pram, Martha bristled with latent hostility. *Don't even think about it*, she wanted to say, *you're not coming within an inch of that child ever again.*

'What's her name?'

'Serenity.'

'That's a strange name,' the woman said, straightening up. 'But then you young folk think of such odd names these days, don't you?'

When nobody responded she seemed to remember the train she was so worried about catching. 'I must go,' she said. 'I've done what I came to do and please don't worry that I'll make a nuisance of myself. You won't hear from me again. My son wouldn't have wanted me to know his child, and so I intend to respect that wish. Goodbye.'

They watched her go and when she was out of sight, they looked at each other as if they couldn't quite believe what had just happened.

'What a very sad woman,' murmured Willow.

The old critical and judgemental Martha would have tutted and rolled her eyes and said, *Trust you to be so soft, Willow!* But she didn't. She put her arm around her sister and said, 'I agree. Now come on, let's go home.'

Ellis drove them back to Anchor House, the mood in the car subdued. Until the last few miles of the journey when Serenity decided she'd had quite enough of being so good, and livened things up by voicing her eagerness to be fed. Her cries, as insistent as they were, were a welcome antidote to the utter dismalness of the day.

That evening Tom rang from Yorkshire to ask how the funeral had gone.

'I almost feel sorry for Rick now,' he said when Martha had filled him in. 'The poor sod didn't exactly have the best start in life, did he? And it raises the eternal nature versus nurture question, was he born bad or made bad?'

'We'll never know for sure, but I'm afraid it doesn't mean I can forgive him. Or that ghastly mother of his. I know it's perverse of me, because I don't want her anywhere near Serenity, I really don't, but I can't stop asking myself what kind of a woman would throw away the chance to play an active role in the life of a grandchild she's just discovered she has? She literally just walked away without a backward glance.'

'But you don't know how difficult that might have been for her to do. From what you've said it sounds like she didn't want her husband to know that she'd attended her son's funeral, which probably means her loyalty to him overrides anything else.'

There was that word again, thought Martha with a small jolt. Loyalty. It was yet another example of it being wholly misplaced.

For all the questions and suspicions the day had raised, there was one certainty Martha was glad of. That she and Willow had been lucky enough to have such a wonderfully loving mother.

Chapter Sixty

It was a glorious afternoon in early March. The sky was the colour of bluebells and bright sunlight spangled the swelling surface of the water. In the distance a motorboat could be heard chugging into the harbour and as always, there was the ever-present call of seagulls and the rhythmic push and pull of waves on sand and pebbles. The fresh spring air was fused with salt and seaweed.

Naomi and Ellis had been sitting on the beach in companionable silence for some minutes, each lost in their thoughts while relishing the simple pleasure of being together. After a hectic few days, it was lovely for it to be just the two of them. Not that Naomi hadn't enjoyed having a house full of family and friends staying with them. But relaxing here in the sun-warmed sand dunes with Ellis and sharing a picnic of leftover party food, including two slices of Christening cake and a bottle of wine, was just heavenly.

The double baptism two days ago at St Saviour's for Serenity and six-week-old baby Eliza had been a wonderfully joyous occasion. Tom had asked his sister and brother-in-law to be Eliza's godparents and, much to Willow's delight, when she'd asked her friends Lucy and Simon to be godparents to Serenity, along with Lucas, they had readily accepted. A couple of months away from the birth of their own baby, they had put the unpleasant incident with their cat behind them now. It was possible that because of the way Rick died they felt it inappropriate to hold a grudge against Willow any longer.

Just as he'd flown over to spend Christmas at Anchor House, Lucas had taken another flight to be with them for the weekend, timing a work commitment in London to coincide with his visit. He had stayed at Waterside Cottage with Willow and Serenity, and whether he stayed in the spare bedroom or not was absolutely no one's business but their own. Whatever the relationship was between the two of them, Naomi and Ellis were determined not to enquire. On the face of it, Willow and Lucas behaved like a pair of close friends, or brother and sister, but both Naomi and Ellis knew from personal experience how friendship could so easily tip into something quite different.

Brian and Geraldine had also been with them for the weekend and it had been good to see them happily bickering amongst themselves. Some things should never change, Naomi had told them, and their marriage was one of those things.

Both grandchildren had risen splendidly to the occasion and behaved extraordinarily well during the baptism service, although Eliza had appeared to frown and raise a tiny fist as if in protest when the Reverend Veronica Carlyle had splashed water onto her forehead. A sign of things to come, Naomi had thought with a smile. Later, while watching her daughters taking selfies of themselves with their adorable babies, she was overcome with love for them. With all that had happened in recent months, combined with motherhood, they were now closer to each other than they'd ever been.

Convinced that she wouldn't go all the way to her due date, Martha had proved herself right and, after a textbook labour with Tom at his wife's side, Eliza had arrived exactly a week early. So far, she had been a model baby and was already occasionally sleeping through the night. Everyone had said that they would expect nothing less. Yet for all Martha's capable efficiency, there was a new and more gentle side to her these days, an acceptance that perhaps there were things she couldn't control and that actually it didn't matter. Being a mother had softened the spikiest of her edges and that, in Naomi's opinion, was a good thing.

There were fleeting moments when Naomi caught herself thinking of Colin and what he was missing out on. *Another generation of my Miller Girls!* he would have proudly boasted. Except they weren't his Miller Girls any longer. They had all, including Naomi, moved on to be their own person in their own right.

Suddenly putting his arm around her, and breaking into her thoughts, Ellis said, 'I've just realised that it's exactly a year and two weeks since I moved here.'

Naomi turned her head and smiled at him. 'It's been a tumultuous year, and hardly what you expected when you moved into the village. You probably thought you'd found some quiet little backwater where you could conveniently set up temporary camp before moving on to something more permanent and exciting.'

He pulled her closer to him. 'What I found here far exceeded anything I could have imagined. And based on this first year with you, I'm curious to see what this one will bring.'

'Well, my guess is that you're going to want another house project to keep you busy, and I have a suggestion in mind for Willow when she feels she's ready.'

'What's that, then?'

'I've been thinking it might be fun to start up my gardenalia business again, maybe focusing more on online sales rather than renting a shop. I'm hoping Willow might like to help, and who knows, if she takes to it, I could step back and spend more time looking after Serenity while she does the lion's share of the work. What do you think?'

'I think you know perfectly well that it's a great idea. But what if Willow wants to leave Tilsham and go back to London? Or move somewhere else?'

'Then I'll have to rethink things. What will be, will be.'

'A sentiment I fully endorse,' he said. 'And one we should drink to.'

He delved into the picnic basket for the bottle of wine and after refilling their glasses, he was about to raise his glass to touch hers when he hesitated.

'But if there was one thing you could make happen, rather than leave it to chance, what would it be?' he asked.

'Oh, that's easy,' she said. 'I'd like us to be married.'

Surprise flickered across his face. 'But I thought you didn't want that? I thought—'

'I've changed my mind. So how about it, will you marry me?'

The surprise was gone from his face now and replaced with a wide smile.

'Is that a proposal?'

'I do believe it is,' she said.

'In that case, my answer is a resounding yes.'

She leaned in to kiss him, then leaning back, she tapped her glass against his. 'Now that really is something to drink to, don't you think?'

'Without a doubt,' he said, putting his arm around her once more and pulling her against him.

They stayed there in the sand dunes happily making plans until the tide came in and the warmth of the day had passed. Then hand in hand, they walked home to Anchor House.

Acknowledgements

Firstly, thank you to everyone at HQ Stories for helping to settle me into my new home, especially those two shining stars of the publishing world – Kate Mills and Lisa Milton – who made it all possible.

Anna McSweeney was kind enough to help me with some all-important information, as was Andrew Jackson, and I'm most grateful to you both.

Once again, I must thank Sally Partington for her keen copyediting eye. You fair put me to shame, Sally!

Lastly, a very big thank you to the amazing booksellers who have kept the plates spinning during unimaginably challenging times. Thanks to you and all your hard work, and when they most needed to, readers were able to lose themselves in the pages of a good book. Three cheers to you all!